Tramping Through Mexico and Other Adventures

Tramping Through Mexico and Other Adventures

Bill McLaughlin

Copyright © 2002 by Bill McLaughlin.

ISBN: Softcover   1-4010-7938-5

Text and photographs Copyright © 1996, 1997, 1998, 1999, 2000, 2001, 2002 by Bill McLaughlin

North to Labrador! was originally published under a different title and in serial format in the Halifax Chronicle-Herald during the summer of 2001.

Escape to the Everglades, Against the Wind, and *A Delaware Journey* were originally published in serial format in the New Jersey Sunday Herald from June 1996 to February 1999.

All rights reserved. No part of this book may be reproduced or transmitted in any form or by any means, electronic or mechanical, including photocopying, recording, or by any information storage and retrieval system, without permission in writing from the copyright owner.

This book was printed in the United States of America.

To order additional copies of this book, contact:
Xlibris Corporation
1-888-795-4274
www.Xlibris.com
Orders@Xlibris.com
16846

Contents

TRAMPING THROUGH MEXICO

13

NORTH TO LABRADOR!

157

ESCAPE TO THE EVERGLADES

189

AGAINST THE WIND

243

A DELAWARE JOURNEY

329

FOR JESSICA

"A venturesome minority will always be eager to set off on their own, and no obstacles should be placed in their path; let them take risks, for God's sake, let them get lost, sunburnt, stranded, drowned, eaten by bears, buried alive under avalanches—that is the right and privilege of any free American."

—Edward Abbey from *Desert Solitaire*

"Always the general show of things
Floats in review before my mind,
And such true love and reverence brings,
That sometimes I forget that I am blind."

—From the poem *Inspiration* by Henry David Thoreau

"Allons! whoever you are come travel with me!
Traveling with me you find what never tires.
The earth never tires,
The earth is rude, silent, incomprehensible at first,
Nature is rude and incomprehensible at first,
Be not discouraged, keep on, there are divine things well envelop'd,
I swear to you there are divine things more beautiful than words can tell."

—Walt Whitman from *Song of the Open Road*

Acknowledgments

I owe a great debt of thanks to the hundreds of people I have met and interviewed in the course of writing these adventures. This collection would not have been possible without their contributions. They are the true authors.

Many people also contributed invaluable assistance by providing contacts, suggesting story ideas, and places to visit. I regret that I will never be able to properly thank them all.

Special thanks to my family for their support and understanding. Thanks also to my extended families at the many hostels where I have stayed and worked. I am especially grateful to Edwin and Owhnn at the Everglades International Hostel where I completed *Escape to the Everglades* and where I put the finishing touches on this compilation. My thanks also to Sue and Marlene at the Bay of Fundy hostel, the folks at Margarita's in Mexico, the downtown San Diego hostel, the Hostel in the Forest in Georgia, the Mabou River hostel on Cape Breton, and the Heritage House hostel in Halifax. Thanks also to Jack at the Goodland Country Club in Hackettstown for providing not only the bare essentials but also a peaceful place in which to work.

I would also like to thank my trusted friends who volunteered to read this manuscript in its various stages of completion. Special thanks to my friends and editors Annie, Beth, Deborah, and Joe who helped improve these stories despite my stubborn and cranky arguments.

Perhaps my largest debt of gratitude goes to a man who has been dead for 140 years. Often quoted in these pages, his admonishments to "simplify, simplify," and to live life "close to the bone," have nurtured my life's philosophy. Without his sturdy confirmation of my own inclinations, I'm not sure I would have been able to march as confidently to the beat of my own particular drummer. Thanks Henry.

And finally, none of these stories would have been possible without the interest of readers. To those who have shared these stories with me, and those who are about to, I can only say thank you for the opportunity. Writers without readers is a sad thing indeed.

I hope that this collection will please the reader. Despite all the help I have received, any shortcomings are entirely mine.

Bill McLaughlin

Hackettstown, NJ
17 September 2002

TRAMPING THROUGH MEXICO

"The essential thing is to become again the light vagabonds of the Earth."

—Jean Giono from *Joy of Man's Desiring*

Prologue

*"If we meet no gods, it is because we harbor none.
If there is grandeur in you, you will find grandeur in
porters and sweeps."*

—Ralph Waldo Emerson

What journey ever begins on the first day of travel? Rather, it starts from somewhere within the deepest folds of ourselves. So it was with this trip to Mexico.

My first trip to Mexico was five years earlier when, writing about the prevalence of pollution in the Río Grande, I followed that river hundreds of miles along its border with Texas. Except for the small village of Boquillas del Carmen nestled in the foothills of the Sierra del Carmen, I visited only the large border cities of Juarez and Matamoras.

But the sounds and smells of even those *Texican* cities tantalized me. The open air markets and street vendors, the soft brown eyes of children hawking sweets and novelties, all entreated me to stay, to linger. But the poverty and the squalor, the desperate look in the eyes of street children and my own disturbing reflection found there, etched these images into my mind and Mexico rose to the top of my list of places to explore.

I wanted to find small villages and large landscapes; beaches and mountains, canyons and rivers. I wanted to sit on a bench in a village square and pass the time with the old men. I wanted to play with the children and listen to the young girls and learn their notion of the world and their place in it. I wanted to camp alone in the Copper Canyon among the reclusive Tarahumara of the Sierra Madre. I wanted to discover what Baja's most endangered residents could reveal about the fate of men and whales and oceans.

I chose Mexico not simply because it is at once a foreign country and a close neighbor, but because Mexico, the land itself, is part of North America, my homeground: my native soil. I am not interested in Mexico's flags and anthems, but its flowers and animals, its skies and rocks.

The following is the result of those longings, a personal account of three months of traveling by foot, bus, thumb, and train through Baja California and the Sierra Madre.

Hopefully these pages retain some of the wonder of that landscape and the warmth of the remarkable people who inhabit it.

Chapter 1

> "*My heart is warm with the friends I make,
> and better friends I'll not be knowing;
> Yet there isn't a train I wouldn't take,
> no matter where it's going.*"
>
> —Edna St. Vincent Millay

My fellow passengers and I moved slowly out of the Amtrak station, rattling past empty coaches filled with the ghosts of yesterday's excursions. Heading west across a continent, in three days I would arrive in San Diego and begin the journey south through Mexico. What meager materials, this pen and paper, to record such a beginning: crowded bus and railway stations; bustling, bristling people; blurry echoes of urgent, incomprehensible announcements. We sat politely side by side in that glass and steel projectile, propelled along a knife's edge between light and dark, past and present; strangers thrust together, speeding toward the unknown.

I rode the dog (the Greyhound bus) out of Wilkes-Barre, Pennsylvania. From my journal: "Feels good to be back on the road. A gray day, warm for January in northeast, Pa. Slag heaps the size of houses border the towns of Sugar Notch and Ashley. Black mounds tower against a coal-smoking sky. Sheets of highway slice through limestone hills while naked trees stand in waiting, snoozing till Spring. But I am hurling toward that season; rushing toward summer as well, defying both time and Nature."

The bus followed Route 11 winding beside the muddy Susquehanna River on its way to the Chesapeake Bay and bringing with it crisp mountain spring waters, autumn leaves, old tires, silt, pesticides, fertilizers, and other souvenirs of its journey through the farm country of New York and Pennsylvania.

I arrived at the Amtrak station in Harrisburg, checked my backpack but learned I must pick it up in Fullerton, California for the change of trains to San Diego. "Hope all goes well," I wrote in my journal. How interesting to think where my pack really ended up.

From my journal, "Starting to slip into a more relaxed state of mind now. Waiting by the stairs that lead to my train. The woman at the ticket counter had said, 'Oh, you're going all the way.' If she only knew how far I'm going!"

The inside of the Harrisburg station is remarkable. Immense vaulted ceilings reminded me of the days when the railroad was king. The wooden benches have high, over-your-head backs and a waxy dull finish. What a treat to sit on real wood instead of plastic or pressed board furniture.

How many people have sat in this station? I can't help but imagine all those faces, hurrying to their destinations. How many have departed from this very bench for adventures, weddings—wars? How many mourning travelers have made the long journey home to bury a parent or sibling? How many have simply wandered aimlessly from station to station, adrift in a sea of anonymity, envying even those who travel in grief; jealous of their sad but purposeful trips.

The bus was slow and confining but on the train I could stroll from car to car, loaf in the observation coach which has large windows and swiveling seats. It is the observation car in which people congregate and pass the time. There is a guy here telling stories—mostly about himself. It seems he's got the ear of a young girl. She is very generous with her laughs. I think he's a bore. He is the second one I've met today. The other was a man who talked to the bus driver for three hours all the way from Wilkes-Barre to Harrisburg. Then he cut in front of me at the baggage window.

He interrupted my turn with the clerk to get his own business done. While on the bus from Wilkes-Barre, he told the driver, loud enough so everyone could hear, that he didn't like people from New Jersey. "They only think of themselves," he said. I was reminded of that as he edged himself in front of me and stole the clerk's attention. I like to think that it was his fault, for interrupting the baggage clerk, that when I got off the train at Fullerton, my backpack continued all the way to Los Angeles.

The current bore is talking very loudly about getting high: . . . blah . . . blah . . . blah. "The first thing I did when I got to Balboa Park was drop some acid . . ." What an exciting experience! And such a story! I have nothing against anyone who wants to recreationally medicate themselves but I find it laborious to have to listen to the account. The cowboy hat, tattoos, and those boots (made from some sensitive, less boastful creature), all added to my instant dislike of this fellow. But that is the wrong attitude for the beginning of a long journey, or maybe it is just a reaction to a little tension, a bit of apprehension. And maybe not.

Back in my seat I try to sleep but it is impossible, there are people everywhere, coughing, snoring, sneezing, and talking. Ahead of me and to the left is a blind man with a golden retriever tucked neatly underneath his legs. The man is wearing ear plugs and listening to a tiny radio. We are clicking and clacking our way to Chicago. During the night, I find two empty seats together and I am able to stretch out a bit and close my eyes.

Somewhere around Pittsburgh, in the weak morning light, we pass an Amoco refinery. Acres and acres of tank farms mingle with rusted, hulking skeletons of buildings and abandoned rail yards while plumes of toxic white smoke chug into the sky. What a mess we have made of this Earth! Perhaps H. L. Mencken said it best in his 1927 essay, *The Libido for the Ugly*. Mencken writes about the shabby buildings and homes in this area, as seen from the train.

> Here was the very heart of industrial America, the center of its most lucrative and characteristic activity, the boast and pride of the richest and grandest nation ever seen

on earth—and here was a scene so dreadfully hideous, so intolerably bleak and forlorn that it reduced the whole aspiration of man to a macabre and depressing joke. Here was wealth beyond computation, almost beyond imagination—and here were human habitations so abominable that they would have disgraced a race of alley cats . . . One cannot imagine mere human beings concocting such dreadful things, and one can scarcely imagine human beings bearing life in them.

As the sun peeks over the edge of the world, I hear singing on the train's loudspeaker: "Though you may be sleeping, the coffee is brewing, come to the cafe car and start chewing!" It is 6 a.m. The cafe car is open—coffee! Paul, the singing cafe car man is a hero to all of us caffeine junkies and insomniacs.

The train ride improved on the second day when I realized that sleeping in the observation car was tolerated by the conductors. No more scrunching up trying to sleep in a seat. Entering the car after dark, it had an eerie, post-tragedy look. Bodies were everywhere, stretched and sprawled on the natty, grimy carpet. Experienced train travelers came prepared with sleeping bags, or pillows and blankets. Others, like me, simply laid down, stuffed a sweater under our heads and were thankful for the luxury of stretching out full-length and nabbing a few hours of pseudo-sleep.

Directly under my head, just past the sweater and filthy carpet, the train wheels rumbled in my ears. We stopped often through the night at stations where sometimes only a solitary figure stood, finishing a cigarette, clutching a steaming cup of coffee under the ghostly glow of a yellow street lamp; a lonely light spilling over rows of empty benches. At every station it is the same: mysterious strangers moving toward secret destinations in the black of night.

From my journal: "Out of Chicago: great walls of flickering lights, a dark gray city, impervious to the lightly falling snow, Nature's gallant but futile effort at purity. The blind man pushes his tiny radio along the window's dark glass. Like all of us, he is trying to improve his reception."

The next day I met Kristen. She was smart, funny, and loved to laugh. We spent the remaining day and a half talking, laughing, and laughing some more. She was returning from a holiday visit with her boyfriend to her parents' home in Connecticut. Because she doesn't like to fly, she hopped the train while her boyfriend flew home. I admired her instantly for this. She worked as a freelance photo-journalist in LA. She was a thoughtful, cheerful traveling companion and I missed her greatly the moment I stepped off the train. We hugged and kissed, promised to write as we hurriedly scribbled our email addresses. We had left this ritual for the last possible moment. A melancholy mix of denial and resignation settled over our silly sounding words: "Goodbye. Yes, of course I'll write. You too. I will. Have fun. Good luck!" Did we really say good luck? I can't remember but it's possible. Ridiculous. It was over.

My backpack had decided to visit LA but train officials assured me that my luggage and I would reunite in San Diego. During the train ride, I kept my small daypack with me. The daypack contained books, maps, tickets—all the stuff I really needed. The backpack held my tent, sleeping bag, cooking supplies, and clothes; nothing I needed right away, but everything I needed to continue my trip into Mexico.

The train from Fullerton to San Diego was bright and clean and moved quickly down the coast offering occasional views of the Pacific. I had not seen this ocean for five years. How different it is from the Atlantic. The Pacific exudes a forbidding wildness, its rocky shorelines and even the shape of its waves make it seem less inviting than the Atlantic. I think vaguely of Kerouac's *Big Sur*. There is an indelible sense of foreboding in those pages. Dark, moist leaves of salty words throbbing in *simpatico* with the black moods of both the sea and the man; each unable to resist the draw of the other. But there it is, and despite its name, an ocean to be reckoned with. I will be following this coast south for more than 1,000 miles through two countries. Languages will change, currencies and customs will change, the land itself will change. But the ocean will not. It will pulse and pound this shoreline every inch of the way.

And I am not the only one heading south along the coast this time of year. Offshore, maybe only a mile, are the migrating California gray whales. I can't see them through the tinted Amtrak windows or past the gaudy ocean-front developments, but I know they are there, completing the longest migration (more than 12,000 miles) of any mammal. Each winter they leave the Arctic for the warm waters off the coast of Mexico. There, in sheltered lagoons, the females give birth to their calves and prepare them for the arduous ocean voyage north. These whales, recently threatened with extinction, have rebounded. But the threats continue, not from brutal whalers, but from industrial development in their remaining nursery lagoons. I didn't know it then, but those whales and I would soon meet where the warm Pacific waters lap the arid edges of the Vizcaíno desert. And my view of that ocean, and its citizens, would be forever changed.

My first moods of apprehension have vanished. Raw excitement has taken its place. Stepping off the train in San Diego, I was alive! This sense of aliveness is the narcotic that makes traveling so addictive. There you are in a strange city: the buildings, the faces, the shops, all absolutely new and undiscovered. The streets have their own rhythms and rules. Step into the middle of this chaotic energy and find your necessities: a bed, a meal, and if you are lucky, an interesting and honest conversation.

I rented a bed in a four-person dorm at a downtown hostel. After nearly four days on the train, a hot shower was the first order of the day, a nap the next, and dinner in a local Indian restaurant completed my first day in San Diego. What a luxury to sleep fully stretched out! The next day I fetched my delinquent backpack from the Amtrak depot. My backpack, just in from LA, has been through some hard traveling in its time. It has that worn, experienced look in which I secretly take pride. Though I often lustily gawk at those new internal frame packs in bold colors, loaded with doodads, hidden pockets, thick padding, and buckles on buckles, my old navy blue pack is reassuring simply because I know how to fix it. The pack bag attaches with common rings and pins to an external aluminum frame and not that much can really go wrong. But it does look as if it was kicked from the East Coast to the West. The baggage man at Amtrak handed me the pack and in an apologetic tone, reaching for a claim slip, said, "It wasn't like this when you got on the train was it?" Yes, I proudly told him. It's been around I guess. Anyway, no one is likely to steal it, eh? His solemn "No, I guess not," seemed to me a disapproval of my tattered pack. But the choice is simple: I could, like him, be working today. And perhaps, after I paid all the expenses that result from having a regular job—like rent, phone bill, car payment, insurance, clothes, etc., I could in a few years have enough extra money to buy a very nice pack and travel with abandon for a week on my vacation. Or, screw work and go with what I have—today.

In the afternoon, I wandered down to the waterfront where a boat show was in progress. I nabbed some food from a hoity-toity table set up for yachties and sat on a bench eating, watching pelicans and tourists lumbering by. I thought again about Kristen and wished she were here making me laugh. I tried to sneak into the boat show but found too many guards posted at the gates and I wasn't about to blow $7 on a ticket. I was thinking in pesos now. That $7 US meant nearly 70 pesos: a night in a flea bag hotel or a whole day of restaurant meals.

The balance of my last day in the United States of America was spent gathering information on crossing the border and obtaining some last minute supplies. Another luxurious night of sleep at the hostel and then finally: Southbound!

Chapter 2

*"No man should travel until he has learned the
language of the country he visits.
Otherwise he voluntarily makes himself a great baby,
so helpless and ridiculous."*

—Ralph Waldo Emerson, Journals, 1833

From my journal: "Leaving for Mexico in the morning. Need to be at the school by 4 p.m. to register. Getting excited now. Starting to feel like a traveler again, not just someone away from home."

The next morning, after spending 20 minutes figuring out how to get a damn ticket from the machine, I hopped the San Diego trolley to the Mexican border, walked over the bridge, said good morning to the Río Grande, passed through the high-gated turnstile—and I was in Mexico.

Tijuana is a chaotic melee of cabs, vendors, tourists, and hustlers. At first glance it is like all the border cities: grimy and predictable. I wondered, what a different view of this town you could get by living here for a year, becoming part of that energy, the border culture (the music!), the mingling of language and custom. But I had no time to linger. I was starting school today. I had enrolled in Spanish language immersion school in Ensenada. I would study six hours a day while living for a week with a Mexican family. My Spanish vocabulary at the moment hovers at about 5 words. I wanted to make an effort to speak the language of the country I was visiting. It was a matter of respect and also understanding. If I wanted to understand the people of Mexico I had to attempt to speak with them in their language. Of course, one week would not make me fluent, but I had hoped that intensive study combined with constant conversing would at least foster a decent start. And slyly, creeping from the back of my mind to the front, it occurred to me that I also wanted to correct an injustice from long ago. I found the bus terminal, somehow managed to buy a ticket for the right bus, and began the two-hour ride south to Ensenada.

The bus was modern and air-conditioned. Like most Baja busses, it ran on time, was comfortable, and even had movies. It seemed to take an hour just to wrench ourselves from the grip of Tijuana. Slowly the congestion of the city changed to scattered shacks and settlements on barren hillsides. Houses were constructed of anything at hand: sheet metal, pallet wood, even cardboard. Gradually the desert stretched before us under a wide, glaring azure horizon and we sped southward through the otherworldly *desierto* landscape of Baja California. I was reminded of a passage from Joseph Wood Krutch's lyrical book, *The Desert Year*, in which he muses on the stark Sonoron desert, contrasted with the spectacular red rock monoliths of the Colorado plateau to the north:

> It has discovered its modes and it sticks to them; indifferent to your attention or lack of it. Love me or hate me, the desert seems to say, this is what I am and this is what I shall remain. Go north for astonishment if you must have it. What I offer is different.

I could barely stay in my seat. One side of the bus was the desert and on the other was the Pacific. I bounced back and forth across the aisle, looking at one, then the other. My fellow passengers were asleep or vaguely watching the movie. It was a western, in English, with Spanish subtitles. All I remember was a buxom barkeep and a few bad hombres alternately chasing her and each other.

Ensenada was a sprawling, bustling city. I got exited the bus accidentally in the midst of a residential neighborhood and had some trouble finding a cab. Once I found the cab, the driver had some trouble finding the school. We eventually made it and in the confusion I had a good look at the city. There are more than half a million people in this desert outpost. They are squeezed onto a dry wedge of land between the mountains and the sea. The influence of the *Estados Unidos* was everywhere. It was in the cars, the hotels, the touristy *cantinas* and curio shops. In the center of town is the *malecón*, or waterfront, where a massive Mexican flag marks the harbor. Ships and yachts come and go; it is a favorite stroll for young couples and tourists; a prosperous location for the *churro* and *burrito* vendors. From the waterfront you can clearly see the tiny houses that fill the mountains surrounding the city. They seem to have been erected on the most unlikely patches of land, sprouting up regardless of how steep the hillside or how skinny the ledge. Many have stilts which support the overhanging, yawning edge of these mountain goat homes. Residents walk or drive to their little houses on narrow zigzagging roads that weave up and down the mountainsides. Soon I would know just how high the mountain and just how narrow the roads.

At the school I signed up for a week of classes. The school was housed in a three-story pleasant aqua color building sporting a large banner that read: "Learn Spanish by the Sea." The classrooms, offices, and a small kitchen were on the ground floor with apartments above for long-term students. I met some of my teachers and learned that arrangements were being made with my *familia*. After a flurry of phone calls and some last minute negotiations, I was zipping through the back streets of Ensenada, my backpack stuffed into the trunk of a small car. We drove about 10 blocks from the school, passed through the gates of a Spanish-style villa in a modest, middle class neighborhood— and I was home.

Chelo and Fausto welcomed me like a lost son returning from a long journey. Suddenly, I was at once returning and beginning my adventure. After a few brief hellos and how are you's-we were speechless, not because we didn't have anything to say, but we each had exhausted our vocabulary in the other's language. I was shown my room, given some directions I could not understand, and found myself sitting on a lumpy bed in a nicely furnished bedroom, with a private bath, wondering, what the hell am I doing here? I figured out through about 20 minutes of interrogation and interpretation that dinner, or *almuerzo*, would be served in about an hour or two. I went for a walk in the neighborhood and somewhere during that hour wandering streets and alleys, peering into front yards and shops, my mood changed from that of alienation to admiration to a vague but palpable sense of belonging. I *lived* here now. I was not just some afternoon interloper. Not just some *feo Americano* out for an overdose of hedonism at the expense of a developing nation and its people. Or at least I'd like to think so. Exploitation takes many forms and is unusually clever at the art of disguise, hiding easily behind the thinnest of rationalizations. During my travels, I would cite my week at school and my attempt to understand the language as a form of respect for the country and the people I was visiting. I myself, would meet far too many ugly Americans in my three months here.

Chelo and Fausto were in their late 50s, and had two grown sons, one who lived with them and one who lived close by in Ensenada. Chelo was a kind, plump woman with a warm smile and overflowed with empathy for her house guests. She had a dresser drawer filled with cards and letters from travelers who had stayed here while attending school. Her cooking was a point of pride and I quickly learned that a flurry of compliments would soon bring back platters of warm tortillas and well-stuffed burritos. Chelo, after dinner, would sit at the kitchen table and help with the *tarea* or homework. Her English was better than she thought, but we spent a lot time with our noses in dictionaries and phrase books. She was always ready to laugh at my failed attempts at telling jokes in Spanish. Most of the time, the joke was on me. Fausto worked on the shrimp boats. He would work for weeks at a time away from home. He was a stout, solidly-built man who had few words to say, in Spanish or English. His English was not as good as Chelo's but he managed to communicate. He seemed perpetually tired. While it was Chelo's job to wake me up ridiculously early, it was Fausto's job to wake up Chelo. Every morning he could be found in the kitchen making breakfast for Chelo, quietly exploding the stereotypical macho Latino husband myths. Every few days Chelo's mother would visit. She was a frail old woman who could barely maneuver around the house by herself. Yet nothing in Chelo or Fausto's attitude suggested to me that she was ever considered a burden.

That afternoon, after a dinner of steamed vegetables, rice, and tortillas, a dark cloud settled over the house: Harold came home.

"Ah, Señor Harold," Chelo piped. She was slightly excited on introducing the two gringos who now inhabited her house. Harold owned a car and had been out riding around. He was in his 60s and from Southern California. He had come to Ensenada to learn Spanish and, it turns out, to look for land on which to build houses of ticky-tacky along the coast of the Baja. My house mate, a developer. He was arrogant and considered Mexico and Mexicans inferior; existing solely for his self-enrichment. You know Harold. You have probably met him far too many times; a perpetual lemon sucker; sour, dour, announcing his dissatisfaction at the top of every hour. He complained about Mexico. He complained about Ensenada. He complained about the house in which we lived. He complained about the price to stay in the house in which we lived. (Harold and I each received a private room and bath, three meals a day, a host family that helped us with our homework in the evening, and most importantly, made us feel welcome in a strange country. We paid $25 a day.) Harold was finishing up two weeks of Spanish school when I arrived. He had decided to stick around and investigate land opportunities after school concluded. Oh yes, he complained about the school also. But now he was going to take his newly minted Spanish *palabras* and interact with real Mexicans—and hopefully, steal their land, build some cheap houses, and start collecting rent; the same scheme he was operating in southern California. He even spoke disdainfully of his most loyal tenant. "He could have bought a house himself with all the money he's paid me over the years." The thought nearly forced the lemons out of his mouth. He insisted on telling me the monetary value of everything he owned, and damn it he had a right to have the best. The worst story he told concerned his summer house at Lake Tahoe. He complained that he would have to start a very expensive remodeling job in the spring. Poor Harold, he had bought a 30-foot sailboat to use on the lake, but the boat was too big for his garage! Why not get a smaller boat, I naively asked. "Oh no, I *want* a big boat!" The words echoed through my head. I heard them in English and I heard them in Spanish. I pictured Señor Harold alone, on a tiny lake in a boat so big that the bow touched one shore and the stern the other. Bigger! Bigger! I could hear him shouting, standing on the deck, hands on hips, his snappy white Captain's cap with the gold emblazoned emblem in the center (a dollar sign?), his crisp white linen suit flailing in the breeze.

 Here we sat in a modest home in a poor country where life was measured not in the quantity of material possessions but in the quality of the time you spent with your family, eating and preparing meals, and enjoying the company of your friends. I Want A Big Boat! Barring an epiphany (and I do hope he has one) Harold will leave Mexico as he arrived: clue-less. What is worse is that he will most likely go back, take his usual seat at the yacht club bar in Tahoe, and declare to all his acquaintances that Mexicans have no appreciation of civilization. His arrogant, superior tone will rise a notch as he describes his land-grabbing exploits. Saliva will peek out from the corners of his mouth as he forgets himself and triumphantly squeezes a little envy from the other greedy landlord/speculator/developers with whom he casts his lot.

 My campaign of ruthless, merciless revenge began the next morning. Chelo woke me early so that I could be at school by 8 a.m. A ridiculous hour of the day for any activity. Normally I can barely make a cup of coffee at that hour. Now I was expected to be showered, dressed, down for breakfast and making chit-chat (in a foreign language no less!) before merrily going off to school. At the risk of sounding Harold-*esque* I must express a disappointment: Mexican coffee. I had hoped to find rich, dark espressos and robust brews. My friend from Mexico, *El Capitan*, who I had met in the Everglades two years before, taught me how to make espresso using Cuban coffee and lots of sugar. His friend Mauricio, a painter, would invite us to his home and carefully prepare fine coffee, served in delicate demitasse cups with whipped and caramelized sugar. Mexico, I thought, would be coffee heaven. It would be good, it would be cheap, and it would be everywhere. It was nowhere. The coffee on Chelo and Fausto's table every morning, afternoon, and evening was instant Néscafe. Not just here, but all through Mexico, Néscafe had a coffee monopoly. Néscafe was a joke among gringos. We were certain that translated, Néscafe meant: *No es cafe*! And it wasn't.

I had to walk about 10 blocks to school each day. The mornings in Ensenada were chilly. This was their winter. By afternoon, temperatures would rise into the mid 70's or low 80's and I don't remember one cloudy day here. The first day of school was the worst because I needed directions. Two precise words in English are "left" and "right," simple and straightforward. In Spanish, the word for left is *izquerda*; the word for the right is *derecho*. I stood outside the iron gates of my adopted home on that first day of school while Chelo, with wildly flaring arms, and a string of *izquerdas* and *derechos* (and me still not sure which was which) spilling rapid-fire from her mouth, launched me down the street amid a chorus of barking dogs and amused onlookers. I promised myself that if nothing else, I would master the words for left and right. How could I contemplate a three month trip through this country and not nail down these two simple but crucial words? Compounding the problem is that I am one of those people who continually confuses left and right. There are quite a few of us out there. Driving in a car you'll say "Okay, turn left here" and we automatically make a right. I'm not sure if being left-handed has anything to do with it but it's an awfully good excuse (I also find being left-handed a handy excuse for not putting up curtains, installing storm windows, or fixing cars). I soon learned that I could reliably confuse the concept of left and right as easily in Spanish as I could in English. This was progress!

I did find my way to school that first day. I was introduced to my teacher, Jose, and my classmates. Jose was in his early 20s and gave the impression this was his first time teaching. He was thorough and patient. Miguel was in his late 20s and had recently met a young (15 or 16?) Ensenada girl and had fallen in love. He was from somewhere up north, like Detroit, and had driven his pickup truck down here on a lark. Now this roaming midwesterner was talking about buying a taco wagon and getting married. School was the first step, his new girlfriend knew little English. I hope their relationship remains as good once they begin actually speaking to each other. My other school buddy was Padre. Padre was a Catholic priest from the Philippines. He had been reassigned to an Hispanic parish in LA and so the Church had sent him here for about three months of classes. Miguel, Padre, and I made up our beginners Spanish class. Jose did a great job, answered our questions and had a good sense of humor. He also possessed a sick and twisted idea of the proper amount of homework to assign. But I think it was school policy to pile on the *tarea*; it was the first thing Chelo would ask when I came home each day, "*Mucho tarea, Guillermo?*" We studied verbs and nouns, conjugations and conversations. Six hours a day of this soon transformed my stumbling, insecure attempts at Spanish into something else. Not quite real Spanish, but something I could use to communicate. Just having Jose help with pronunciation bolstered my confidence to try to speak. A good sense of humor is perhaps the most important element; a willingness to laugh at yourself and let others join in the fun. Which brings me to my campaign for complete and merciless revenge.

Carlos Pizzaro. The fact that I can remember his name is proof enough that he did irreparable damage to me. I was a freshman in high school. Carlos Pizzaro was my Spanish teacher. The first day of class he made fun of my attempts at speaking Spanish and hit me over the head with a rolled-up newspaper. The class went hysterical and I was so deeply embarrassed that I don't think I ever voluntarily spoke again in his class. From that day on, I was his foil. If he wanted to illustrate the wrong way to do anything, he called on me. This experience had been well-buried in my sub conscience until I started planning this trip. Making the arrangements for school brought it all back. I resolved to remake this bit of adolescent history. I would, 30 years later, prove to Carlos Pizzaro that yes, I could learn Spanish and that he was the stupid one, not me. The first day of class was a success. No one ridiculed me. No one even hit me over the head with a rolled-up newspaper. And when we made mistakes, we laughed with each other, not at each other. Ha! Take that, Carlos Pizzaro!

My morning walk each day to school that week included a stop at the local *farmacia*. This was my first lesson each morning as I attempted to buy a pack of gum or other small item. Once the cashier realized I was inept, she patiently counted out the change for me. On Monday I was a toddler, by Friday I was functioning at the level of 10-year-old. Another success! In the evenings, I would sit at the kitchen table and do my three hours of homework. Spread out in front of me were my dictionaries, phrase book, and stacks of lesson sheets. I conjugated until my eyes were bleary. Chelo hovered around, making herself available for questions. As the week progressed, our discussions became longer, more interesting. But I soon realized that while my Spanish was improving, I could not say what I wanted. Yes, I could tell you I was hungry, ask if you were chilly, and inquire what time the bus arrives. But I was speaking Tarzan Spanish: Me hungry. You cold? What time bus? Functional but frustrating. This would plague me throughout my trip. I may have vanquished the terror of Carlos Pizzaro, but I could not discuss ideas. I could not really have a meaningful conversation with these people whom I found so warm and so interesting. It eventually improved but that week of school merely whetted my appetite for more.

Harold invited me for a drive around Ensenada after dinner the next day. He wanted to find his way to the outskirts of town and up into the mountains to investigate the homes that were perched there overlooking the city, the same ones I had seen from the waterfront. Immediately after setting out, I realized that Walter's social skills were matched only by his driving skills. We weaved, we jerked and lunged through the congested streets of Ensenada. I tried but could not suppress the image of Harold and I in a tiny bumper car, sparks flying from overhead while pedestrians gawked from the sidewalk like idle carnival goers. Gradually we left behind the narrow streets of Ensenada for the impossibly narrow roads that climbed into the mountains. We edged around blind curves. The road turned to a dusty dirt track. We passed scrub brush and cactus. And up we went. We passed tiny houses in various stages of completion. And up we went. We passed dogs and children and more dogs all milling in the road, hanging off steps and miniature porches. And up we went. The road gradually narrowed until there was barely room for one car. Of course there were no gringos up here. There was no reason to be here. This was a neighborhood. People, mostly poor, some very poor, lived here. Our presence set them on edge. Just by being there I had the sense that we made them feel even poorer. I was uncomfortable. Harold was amused. And up we went. Now a car came the other way. Harold waited. I suggested, as visitors, we were the ones who should back up and let the other car pass. Harold disagreed. His car was too big he said. The other car was smaller, it should let us go. Finally, both drivers gave in and began a complicated series of maneuvers—first moving forward—then backing up—okay—now you get over there—watch out for the cliff! We inched back and forth along the indistinct edge of that crumbly dirt road high above the city. I could see the waterfront and the big Mexican flag from here. My position had been exactly reversed from the previous day. Instead of looking up, now I was looking down, way down. Thankfully, our rumba with the other car convinced Señor Harold to call it a day. And down we went. On the way back to the house we stopped at a waterfront *cantina* for a nice hot cup of Néscafe.

I had started that week with Chelo and Fausto dreading the early morning revelry, the notion of speaking before noon, and the idea of returning to a formal school room. By the end of the week, I knew each and every dog along my daily route. I was conversing in Tarzan Spanish (up yours Pizzaro!), thinking in pesos, and becoming unbearably itchy to get moving. Exactly one week after saying hello to Fausto and Chelo I was saying good bye. My departure was as sad as my arrival had been awkward. They had provided me much more than a place to stay and a few meals. They were my introduction to an entire country and my view of Mexico would be forever colored by that week. I was now truly a guest in this land.

After saying our good byes, (Harold even came down from his room to wish me luck! He was leaving the next day.) Fausto gave me a lift to the bus station. I stood outside the busy terminal, my beat up *mochilla* hanging heavy from my shoulders and felt the elation that comes only from the wrenching away, from casting your *self* on the outgoing tide. My journey south through Baja California was about to continue. Yipppeee!

Chapter 3

"Whoever starts out toward the unknown must consent to venture alone."

—André Gide

At the bus terminal I bought a ticket for the 11-hour ride to the town of San Ignacio. I had about an hour to kill before boarding the bus. I was standing in front of the terminal, watching Ensenada go by when I noticed three young guys staring at me. One of the guys said, "Hi," in English. He said it in a way that was not friendly. As Whitman might put it, these were the local "roughs." Naturally, they were taking the same bus. Naturally, they sat right behind me. I could sense they wanted to make fun of me. What better way to kill time on a long bus ride than torment a gringo? And they tried. I responded the only way I could think of. I ignored whatever nonsense they were currently saying and simply blurted out, in nearly perfect Tarzan Spanish, that I had just come from Spanish language school. Yes! They are impressed. Then I have to tell them that I only studied for a week. Everyone laughs, including me. Yes, I say (in Spanish), it is not much, but something is better than nothing, no? Unanimous! Once they are back on my side, I deliver the knock-out punch: not only did I study six hours a day—plus *mucho tarea* at night—but I lived with a *familia Mexicano* for a week! (Okay, I might have said two weeks.) Aha! I had 'em! They were mine! Transformed. No, my little *bandidos*, I am not some *feo Americano* out to trample your culture and ridicule your customs. No, I am a guest! I am *your* guest! In time, I would learn to embellish this spiel to a well-honed speech.

Afterwards, we talked about where we lived and the differences in our lives. We gave each other language lessons. My willingness to embarrass myself with Spanish permitted them to embarrass themselves with English. And we did. I learned they were on their way to the cape and Cabo San Lucas to find construction work. They would spend about 24 hours on this bus in their quest for work—with no guarantees. Cabo San Lucas is the victim of foreign investment and unbridled development. It is being overrun with garish hotels and resorts. Yes, it is creating jobs for these young people, but jobs only for today, not tomorrow. When the building boom is over they will have lost their most valuable resources. They will have lost their beaches, their quality of life, and their passage to the future. They will instead inherit a land of hotels at which they cannot afford to stay (upscale hotels get about $260 a night in winter). Once they have traded their land and their future for day work, they will be schlepping luggage and fetching $7 drinks for the likes of Señor Harold—for less-than-a-living wage—while enriching transnational corporations whose only purpose is to exploit.

Here's another take on Cabo San Lucas from the Lonely Planet guidebook for Mexico:

> ... its quintessential experience might be to stagger out of a bar at 3 a.m., pass out on the beach, and be crushed or smothered at daybreak by a rampaging developer's bulldozer. Cabo's most sinister bottom-feeders are avaricious, unscrupulous developers and time-share sellers who have metamorphosed a placid fishing village into a depressing jumble of exorbitantly priced hotels, pretentious restaurants, rowdy bars and tacky souvenir stands...

From my journal: "We are in the desert now! The mountains are growing larger and more dense, like giant ripples rising from the surface of a pond. They are a dusty, tired green beneath a hazy blue curtain fringed with whipped and wispy clouds; a desolate country of rollicking boulders and thorn brush. Towering cardóns march *en masse* toward the disappearing sun, leaving only their lengthening shadows behind."

Late that evening, as our bus sliced through the dark desert and we slept that half-sleep so common on buses and trains, the "Hi" guy shook me by the shoulder, waking me up. "San Ignacio," he said. "Tell the driver you want to get off—he's not stopping."

Gracias, amigo.

San Ignacio is a palm-lined oasis on the inland edge of the Vizcaíno desert. There is a town square stolen from the imagination of weary desert travelers. Everywhere are bougainvillea vines and flowers; cool shaded benches on which old men sit across from a stone mission built when their grandfathers were suckling babies. There are few cars; the roads are unpaved. Scattered chunks of sidewalk tumble haphazardly around the square. There is a cafe and small grocery store. Pastel-colored houses border the square separated by skinny alleys running crookedly between buildings. Stately trees stand guard, their trunks painted white and adorned with big colorful dots and the happy drawings of children. The mission church was built from blocks of volcanic rock four feet thick and assembled without mortar. Ancient wooden doors hung above the stone steps looking out over the square and the peaceful people of San Ignacio. Idyllic. The oasis itself was near the road leading to the center of town. Date palms, planted by missionaries hundreds of years before, encircled the water providing habitat for dozens of different species of birds. The source of the water in this desert is a mysterious underground stream. Locals say it comes from deep within the mountains and mesas that surround little San Ignacio. And while I would spend many an idle hour loafing on the shores of that palm-fringed lagoon, it was a wider water that had brought me to San Ignacio.

I stepped off the bus into the chilly night air at about 11 p.m. A single car with its engine running waited on the side of the road in front of the town's Pemex station (Mexico's exclusive, government-owned gasoline company). I threw my pack in the trunk of the cab and settled in for the one and a half minute ride into town. I goofed and mispronounced the name of the hotel I wanted and instead of spending the night in a $7 dump, I stayed in a $20 dump. Ouch! Early next morning, I had my first look at San Ignacio. At the cafe on the square, I found actual brewed coffee (an oversight for which I am sure some marketing executive at Néscafe has already lost his/her job). I took my oversized, steaming cup to the nearest sunny bench and waited patiently for San Ignacio to wake up.

An old man, warming himself in the morning sun, ambled over to my bench. His leathery, cinnamon skin was deeply wrinkled from a life spent outdoors. I learned he was a retired clammer. He had lived in San Ignacio all his life and had been clamming for more than 30 years. It had been a good life, he said, sometimes hard, but good. Unlike the younger people I had spoken with so far on my trip, he was less interested in life "up north." I had the sense that he wanted to make sure I understood that though he was not wealthy, he was rich in the things that mattered. Finally, I asked him about the whales. He beamed. San Ignacio was the portal to the Vizcaíno desert and eventually to the sea. Two and half hours on a washboard dirt road from San Ignacio, at the other end of the Vizcaíno desert, lies Laguna San Ignacio, where female California gray whales have birthed and raised their calves since miracles like oceans and whales have first existed. This is one of the best places in the world to see whales up close. The whales at San Ignacio have a reputation for being "friendly" because they seem to be as curious about you and will sometimes even allow you to scratch their barnacled backs! Tragically, Mitsubishi and the Mexican government were planning a giant industrial salt extraction complex on the shores of the pristine *laguna*. The old fisherman winced when I mentioned it. He told me no one wanted it. It would mean the end of the whales. While tourism and whale-watching weren't exactly bustling enterprises here, the whales have put San Ignacio on the map. They are a source of pride.

The old man knew that visitors, like me, who come for the whales, tend to linger, enchanted by the charms of San Ignacio.

The morning sun gradually brought the town to life like an ancient reptile twitching and blinking in the warm light after a winter's sleep. I left the old fisherman at the square and began my search for a campground. On the road back toward the lagoon, I saw a wooden sign with scrawled writing: "Camping $3." I undid the wire loop holding the floppy wooden gate and squeezed in. The campground was a date palm grove. Grass, growing between the trees, had been recently cut; there was a water spigot and an old shanty outhouse. Perfect. I was camped there for two days before anyone even came by to collect the money. I pitched my tent in the grove between two 100 foot trees, pulled off my boots and took a delicious nap, lulled to sleep by the mid-day heat and the soft breezes swooshing through the palms. It was good to be back in my tent again. Since the start of this trip I had slept on trains and buses, in houses, motels, and hostels. But no sleep is as sweet as when I am snug in my sleeping bag, close to the Earth, inside my sheer nylon womb.

That afternoon, I explored one of the other campgrounds in town. It had tent sites and little cabins, a bar and small cafe. I ordered a cold beer and sat at a table in the grass contemplating my next move. A sense of something exactly the opposite of urgency overcame me. I met a few campers who also wanted to cross the desert and see the whales. There was a van and driver for hire in town but we needed to get 8 to 12 people together to make it economical. We would each pay about $20 for the round-trip ride and then another $30 for the *panga* and whale guide. As I sipped my beer people came and went, and within a few hours we had a small group willing to go early the next day. We needed only one more person to round out the group—and here he comes. Down the road on a bicycle loaded with touring gear and decked out in a Captain America suit, came Paul. He was a tall weedy guy from California in his early 30s who was bicycling the entire length of the Baja. His riding shorts and shirt were covered in blazing red, white, and blue stars and stripes. He had a star-spangled bandanna and bright flashy wrap-around sunglasses.

If the US flag could get up and walk this is what it would look like. Fortunately, he was no patriot, or at least he kept his nationalism to himself. I suspect, but never confirmed, that the purpose of the outfit was to proclaim his presence to drivers and not get struck by a car, a likely outcome given the Baja's twisting roads, blind curves, lack of guard rails, and plunging roadside chasms. The degree of danger at every turn can be measured simply by counting the heap of smashed cars at the bottom of the breach.

He joined me for a beer, signed up for the whale trip, and pitched his camp with me down the road. We spent that night exchanging bicycle touring stories, road recipes, and equipment reviews. Paul was also an amateur historian of Baja and Mexico. He told me the story of William Walker, a US general who in 1853 violated the Treaty of Guadeloupe Hildago and retook La Paz (US troops had occupied La Paz during the Mexican-American war, 1846-48) with hopes of establishing a new slave state to counter the abolitionist movement back home. Walker proclaimed himself the "President of Lower California" but was prosecuted by the US and pursued by the Mexican army. The rascal was soon forced to flee Mexico. Two years later he led a successful coup in Nicaragua and declared himself President. He was rousted shortly after. Before his career as a soldier of fortune, Walker had earned a medical degree while still in his teens. He studied law and was admitted to the bar in New Orleans where he worked as a lawyer before moving on to journalism. The British captured Walker in Honduras in 1860 where he had attempted yet another takeover—his last. He was executed by the Honduran authorities shortly after.

Paul had a telling respect for history and his stories were a testament not only to his thorough research but to his regard for the colorful characters whose lives he knew so well. Sitting there under the palms and the stars on that balmy January night, I felt as if I was hearing a first-hand account. I would not have been surprised if old William Walker had wandered into our camp. The roguish filibuster, decked out in camo, biting the end of a fat Cuban cigar, would perhaps draw up on the grass with us. Sitting rapt as Paul carefully recounted his life, I could hear him gently correcting a few minor points, then kindly (death having relieved him of his ambition) encouraging Paul to continue. It did not seem to matter whether the subject was a scoundrel or a saint (the two usually being indistinguishable anyway). Paul treated them with equal respect and care. For him, they had only to be interesting.

During the night something kept intermittently hitting my tent and waking me; in the morning I discovered it was my breakfast. Dates! Like manna from the heavenly skies. What a sweet addition to my morning oats. They practically fell into the pot! Those barbarian missionaries were good for something after all. The campground owner had gathered hundreds of dates and left them on a large piece of plywood to dry in the sun. These, plus what fell from the heavens, supplied a good deal of my food during my stay in San Ignacio. When I think of San Ignacio I think of Paradise. I think of brilliant blue skies with beauty marks made from clouds, warm breezes, towering palms, and nourishment free for the taking (or catching) and, oh yes, whales. Whales!

The next day we were off. About 10 of us piled into a van and headed for the sheltered waters of Laguna San Ignacio. During the three hour ride through the desert we stopped for plenty of pee and picture breaks. The desert floor was littered with tiny shells, reminding me that this desert was once at the bottom of the Pacific. The farther into the desert we went, the higher and thicker the cardóns became. These are cacti similar in shape and size to the saguaro of the US southwest. The main difference seems to be the angle at which the arms of the plant extend from the trunk. Cardóns are exquisitely suited for life in the desert. From the *Audubon Society Nature Guide* on the Sonoran Desert:

> The Vizcaíno subdivision extends from 26° to 30° N, occupying the western two-thirds of the peninsula. Here eerie landscapes, dominated by a variety of large agaves—especially Maguey—many yuccas, Boojum, and a columnar cactus, the cardón, form architecturally

complex scenes. Probably the largest world's largest cactus, cardón replaces saguaro here; they resemble one another, but cardón has more, and longer arms.

Naturalist Ann Zwinger, in her wonderful book on Baja, *A Desert Country Near the Sea*, offers us a bit more:

> During a rain shower a cardón may absorb up to a ton of water, or 95 percent of its weight. Once the water is inside, the stem's thick waxy cuticle prevents it from evaporating. Barco, that excellent observer, wrote that if a piece of cardón were mashed and wrung out, 'the liquor is obtained in great abundance. When this liquor is boiled and the foam is skimmed away, it becomes like a balsam, and it is surprisingly good to cure wounds and sores.' However, Ducrue reported its use for toothache, and commented that 'it does cause the teeth to fall out. Providing support for all these trunks and stems, which average thirty feet in height, is a hardwood framework of vertical rods, which stiffen the ribs, a marvel of engineering, perforated with small holes placed vertically an inch or less apart, lightweight, yet extremely strong. With the lack of large trees for building material, the dead wood of the cardón is well utilized for a great many building functions—walls, rafters, and fence rails—as well as fish spears and bedsprings!
>
> If the cardón is helpful to man, it is all things to smaller creatures and provides services to the who's who of peninsula birds. Early in the morning the resident vultures, dozens at a time, perch on the tips of the cardóns with their wings outstretched to warm; they look like northwest totem figures, brooding and symbolic.

When cardóns are clustered together, they are referred to as *cardónales*: a cardón forest. Zwinger suggests the likely reason:

Without a deep anchoring tap root, cardóns are vulnerable to wind throw. Although the root system provides such efficient water uptake that few other plants grow within the perimeter of the root's reach, they are seldom seen growing in solitary splendor. It has been suggested that the protection from upsetting winds achieved by growing closer together overrides the competition for water.

The desert through which we were traveling was named for Sebastián Vizcaíno, a Spaniard who explored the Baja as far north as San Francisco from 1596 to 1603. Many of the place names on the peninsular originated from his voyages. Baja California was thought to be an island and referred to by the Spanish as *Isla de Cardón*. The cardón remains a symbol of this desert country, imparting its unlikely but refreshing shade of green to this otherwise ferruginous landscape. Like a sly wink to those that know, a 30-foot cardón is Nature's billboard for the abundance of life and resources in a place many thoughtlessly dismiss as barren.

I sat in the front seat with Carlos, our driver. After I asked him about a few of the plants we were passing, he cheerfully pointed out each one commonly used by locals. Many cacti, like the ubiquitous nopal, or prickly pear, bear fruit; a delicacy known to even non-desert dwellers. Carlos explained the particular uses for each plant and the seasons in which it was available. A desert traveler would need to know which plants contained moisture or indicated where it lay below the desiccated surface. About midway to Laguna San Ignacio we passed a truck which had broken down. The driver, who had been sitting patiently in the front seat, came out to speak with Carlos. I couldn't follow the conversation, but it appeared that the driver was waiting for help and had declined a ride with us. I wondered how long he would have to wait on this vacuous desert road. We had not encountered another car nor did it seem likely that we would. I asked Carlos if he was going to call someone when we reached the bay. No phones where we're going, he said. I hoped that this stranded man knew his plants as well as Carlos.

As we made our way west, sentinel mountains, including an active volcano, huddled to the northwest. The desert flooded the horizon as San Ignacio faded into a quivering green mirage directly behind us. I peeked at my Moon *Baja Handbook* as we bounced over the remaining few miles of washboard:

> Many mothers and calves at Laguna San Ignacio actively seek out tactile encounters, i.e., petting and scratching. They also like to play hide-and-seek with the boats, sometimes blowing bursts of bubbles into the bow, then spy-hopping (extending the head vertically above the sea surface) to see the effect their shenanigans may have had on the passengers.

I'm ready for whales! We pull up at a lonely fish camp where we meet our guide, Felipe. Felipe explains, with the help of a "rule board," what we can and cannot do. I'm relieved to find out that our little *panga* will not be chasing whales; we must wait for the whales to find us. We can however, position ourselves in the most likely spots in the laguna. Felipe is an earnest kid about 17 years old. He has been studying English and asks us more than a few times how he is doing with the instructions. I instantly recognize a kindred spirit: his spiel about learning English was remarkably similar to my well-honed soliloquy on learning Spanish. We achieved the same result: a tender empathy. We put on our life jackets and boarded the little boat as Felipe continued to endear himself to us. We chugged along for about 30 minutes. The water was as flat as the desert we had just crossed. In the crisp morning light, we could see clearly across the lagoon to the shoreline of Isla de Pelicanos, an officially-protected nesting grounds for pelicans, osprey, and a variety of other birds. Laguna San Ignacio is a pristine place. Yes, there were a few fish camps. Yes, we were in a fossil fuel-powered boat, and yes we had an impact. But just 100 years ago, whalers, unable to bring their large ships into the shallow lagoon, came in small boats like ours to hunt the female whales and their calves. The whales would have no part of this brutal slaughter. They capsized the boats so methodically that the whalers eventually considered the endeavor too dangerous. Here's a brief description from Captain Charles Melville Scammon, a notoriously efficient 19th century whaler, writing about the hazards of slaughtering nursing females further south in Magdalena Bay:

> The casualties from coast and kelp whaling are nothing compared with the accidents that have been experienced by those engaged in taking the females in the lagoons. Hardly a day passes but there is upsetting or staving of boats, the crews receiving bruises, cuts, and, in many instances, having limbs broken; and repeated accidents have happened in which men have been instantly killed, or received mortal injury. The testimony of many whaling-masters furnishes abundant proof that these whales are possessed of unusual sagacity. Numerous contests with them have proven that, after the loss of their cherished offspring, the enraged animals have given chase to the boats, which only found security by escaping to shoal water or to shore.

Had the whales not staked out and defended their nurseries, I would instead be standing at the corner of 79th Street and Central Park West at the American Museum of Natural History—clutching a ticket instead of gunwale. Still, massive damage had been done to the population and the California gray whale teetered on the brink of extinction. Scientists now estimate that population at about 26,000. But while gray whales here are recovering, the gray whale population that migrates along a corridor from Russia to the South China Sea is now almost extinct. Oil and commercial development around Russia's Sakhalin Islands, plus uncontrolled hunting and conflicts with commercial fishermen have all contributed to their rapid decline. There may be less than 100 gray whales left in those western North Pacific seas.

We came to a stop not far from where the Pacific enters the bay; where Mitsubishi wanted to build a 1.2 mile-long concrete pier near the whales' entrance to the lagoon. There! A spout! Another one! Soon we see a mother and calf close by. They have come to take a closer look. They don't come too close at first and Felipe says that's because we are here in the early part of the season and the whales may not be as friendly. They finally come within a few yards of the boat, but they don't seem interested in back scratches or belly rubs. Felipe says it could also be because the calves are still too young and the mother is cautious. And maybe, he adds with a charming sincerity, they just don't feel like it. To sit in that little boat and watch a mother and her calf swim deliberately near, is enough. Once, the calf left its mother's side, came close by and swam with its head completely out of the water, his glossy black eyeball checking us out! It is difficult to get a sense of their size, even though we can see their undulating outline through the water. They are massive, reaching 40 tons and up to 50 feet long. The whales we see are dark, nearly black, and heavily mottled white with barnacles and parasites. The babies' skin is still smooth; crustaceans have not yet had time to colonize. The defining moment came when the mother and calf swam directly under our boat. Forty feet of whale seemed to take an hour to pass underneath. Instantly, we understood the ease with which she could have sent us tumbling overboard. We were speechless. They emerged on the other side, the mother surfaced and blew, mimicked immediately by her calf. Side by side they swam off, apparently satisfied with their initial foray into eco-tourism.

Back at the fish camp, we had lunch with Felipe's family. We sat around a large table in the kitchen. Plates of fresh fish, beans, tortillas, and salad filled every available space around our plates. After lunch, Felipe and I stood outside, gazing across the bay to the jagged spires of Isla de Ballenas. I asked him about Mitsubishi's proposed salt plant. He said that the results of the government's environmental impact study had just been announced. Sadly, he added, they had decided to proceed with the complex. Felipe predicted that San Ignacio would turn into another Guerrero Negro, a dirty, industrial town to the north. "It will threaten the whales and our way of life," Felipe said. Felipe's gut reaction has been backed with facts from many of the world's most prestigious conservation groups. The proposed 116 square-mile salt plant would pump 6,000 gallons of water *per second* out of the lagoon. That water would then lie in shallow clay beds evaporating under the tropical sun, leaving only the sea salt behind. Bulldozers would scrape it up and giant dump trucks would lug it to waiting cargo ships and trucks. Six million tons of it a year. Additionally, all the hazardous chemicals associated with this type of industrial activity such as diesel oil, gasoline, acetylene, copper slag, hypochloric and sulfuric acids, grease and oil, vinyl and epoxy paints, antifreeze and solvents would leach into the bay and accumulate in the water, the fish, the turtles, the sea lions, and finally, in San Ignacio's most endangered citizens. According to the International Fund for Animal Welfare, Mitsubishi's plant at Guerrero Negro has had three recent toxic brine spills which threatened not only whales but killed 94 endangered sea turtles and thousands of fish.

Nothing anyone said or wrote had prepared me for the sanctity of this place. A few weeks after my visit, the project was aborted due, at least in part, to a world-wide outcry. While the immediate threat to the whales is over, we must remain on guard. There is too much money at stake here to dismiss the threat of exploitation. The Mexican government can't be trusted. Their would-be partner in crime, Mitsubishi, is the world's largest corporate destroyer of rainforest and one of the most insidious and destructive transnational corporations in existence. If Laguna San Ignacio can't be saved, nothing can. The whales have put their trust in us. I hope that we have earned it. From Henry Beston's sage book, *The Outermost House*:

> We need another and a wiser and perhaps a more mystical concept of animals. Remote from universal nature, and living by complicated artifice, man in civilization surveys

the creatures through the glass of his knowledge and sees thereby a feather magnified and the whole image in distortion. We patronize them for their incompleteness, for their tragic fate of having taken form so far below ourselves. And therein we err, and greatly err. For the animal shall not be measured by man. In a world older and more complete, gifted with extensions of the senses we have lost or never attained, living by voices we shall never hear. They are not brethren, they are not underlings; they are other nations, caught with ourselves in the net of life and time.

On our return to San Ignacio, we once again passed the stranded truck driver. Now, six hours later, he was napping in the shade under the truck. He and Carlos spoke briefly. There was no sign of help (dust clouds could be seen miles away indicating if a car was approaching); he was surprisingly calm. It was, I was learning, the Mexican way: *No problema!* I passed my remaining *gallotas*, over to Carlos for him. If he didn't know which cacti to eat, at least he could have a few cookies while he was waiting, and waiting, and . . .

Back in San Ignacio, we regrouped at the campground and discussed our experience over a few cold beers. Paul left the following morning. He was heading back north, he said, though there was a sense of hesitation in his voice. He didn't really want to leave Mexico. I waved as he and his overloaded bicycle rolled down the only road in town.

I said good-bye to San Ignacio the next day. I lugged my backpack to the highway and waited for the bus. At the Pemex station across the street from the bus stop, workers were readying the concrete building for new paint. About five men, scrambling over the structure like ants, were hand-scraping the old paint. The late morning sun beat down on their already brown skin. Some wore large wide-brimmed hats and neckerchiefs, some wore no hat at all. This was their mild winter sun; by midday it burned as hot as any summer in New Jersey. We waved at each other. At the rate they were going this was probably a three-week job just for scraping; painting would be another few weeks. I thought about how different it would be in the US First, a building that required maintenance would be demolished. It would be replaced with plastic, covered with aluminum siding. It would change owners and have to be demolished again long before it ever needed a paint job. If, by some chance, they did decide to keep an old concrete building, a sophisticated, computer-controlled machine would be dispatched. The machine, accompanied by one laconic employee (part-time, minimum wage, no benefits) would finish in an hour.

The morning warmth turned to afternoon heat as I waited for the southbound bus. Dust rose from the road and mingled in the dry air with car exhaust and gasoline fumes. I found a spot in the shade, closed my eyes and listened to the slow, steady sound of scraping, scraping.

My next stop was the town of Santa Rosalía. I needed cash. San Ignacio didn't have an ATM or even a bank. The whale excursion had emptied my wallet. Santa Rosalía, which had a bank, was located about two hours southeast across the peninsula on the Sea of Cortez. This would be my first encounter with that brilliant sea. But I would have another encounter in Santa Rosalía, one that would eventually get me drunk, detained by the Mexican army, and pierce my heart with the arrow of loneliness. Bless you Santa Rosalía.

Chapter 4

*"Any extraordinary degree of beauty in man or woman
involves a moral charm"*

—Ralph Waldo Emerson

I was in Santa Rosalía less than one hour. My real destination that day was Mulegé, farther south, and like San Ignacio, another small town without a bank. My plan was to hit the ATM in Santa Rosalía between buses and then continue on to Mulegé for a few days of camping by the sea. Across the street from the bus terminal was the Sea of Cortez. The bus ride had afforded only a few seductive views. The inner harbor, where I now stood, failed to reveal its charms.

In his book detailing his voyage around Baja California, *The Log From the Sea of Cortez*, author John Steinbeck's reason for not stopping at Santa Rosalía seemed as good today as when he sailed by in 1940:

> We did not plan to stop at Santa Rosalía. It is a fairly large town which has long been supported by copper mines in the neighborhood, under the control of a French company . . . And it looked, from the sea at least, to be less Mexican than other towns. Perhaps that was because we knew it was run by a French company. A Mexican town grows out of the ground. You cannot conceive its never having been there. But Santa Rosalía looked 'built.'

> There were industrial works of large size visible, loading trestles, and piles of broken rock.

Ironically, the few travelers I spoke with that had stayed in Santa Rosalía said they found it one of the most genuine of Mexican towns due to its lack of tourists. Santa Rosalía's claim to fame is a pre-fabricated church, designed by Alexandre Gustave Eiffel, and erected here in 1897. But I had no time for churches, especially French ones. I was more interested in banks, regardless of the fame or ethnicity of their designers. Again from *The Log*:

> A little feeling of hurry was creeping upon us, for by now we had begun to see the magnitude of the job we had undertaken . . .

After a harrowing, high-speed cab ride, I made it back from the bank with about 10 minutes to spare. I was standing outside the depot when she stepped off the bus I was about to board. She lit a cigarette and exhaled her question, blowing smoke up and over the Sea of Cortez: "Where are we?" So simple. But I could find no breath to answer. She was probably the most beautiful woman I had ever seen. Not beautiful glamorous, gorgeous, Hollywood, or Cosmo. Not society beautiful, dripping with makeup or jewelry. But translucent, pure and true, innocent and knowing with just a hint of tragedy, as all true beauty must possess. She was lighted from within and I bathed, if briefly, in her luminescence. She had . . . Down boy, down! All right, she was cute, really cute. Natalie was in her mid-twenties, tall, blond with freckles, eyes as blue and clear as the sea across the street from where we stood. Her European accent and insouciant traveler's attitude conspired against me. I was doomed. She wore a floral-patterned bandanna tied in the usual way with little blond curls poking out. It was as if I had never seen a bandanna before, though I was, at the moment, wearing one.

I found my breath and we made a little chit-chat. She and her friend Ellen were heading south to La Paz. Natalie and Ellen were from Sweden. Ellen had been traveling for about three years; Natalie had recently joined her for a month of slumming through Mexico. The rest of the story would come later.

We boarded the bus together, I said hello to Ellen who seemed a bit cool behind her black-out sunglasses, and the three of us hardly said another word until I got off in Mulegé, about an hour later.

From my journal: "Now heading south once again, parallel to the Sea of Cortez. Out my window, a sliver of blue peeks through the siennas and umbers of the desert and pools seductively at the end of a dusty track just out of reach. Am I already in love with this blond from Sweden?"

At Mulegé I grabbed my pack and stepped off the bus. There were those words again: "Good-bye. Good Luck!" And though I registered a slight twinge of loss, the arrow of loneliness had not yet even been drawn.

Mulegé had the unfortunate disadvantage of not measuring up to my expectations. When this happens, the place in question can either redeem itself through actual experience or the traveler must simply move on. The one course of action guaranteed to achieve unsatisfactory results is to prolong your visit seeking restitution of your expectations. I had envisioned a small village oasis like San Ignacio but Mulegé was bigger, busier, and full of tourists. It was overflowing with RVs and their little white-haired kamikaze drivers. There is nothing worse than traveling through a poor country and witnessing a cavalcade of 50-foot RVs. These rolling mansions are better equipped and more luxurious than any home they speed past. Indeed, they are worth more than the towns through which they roar. They stop at the only gas station for 100 miles and suck up every available drop. They descend on the local *groceria* and clear the shelves of fresh bread and pastries, fruits and vegetables, leaving only sacks of rice and beans and a few unidentified animal parts behind the butcher's glass. But at night, even they must rest their guzzling diesels and capacious appetites. They must snake their way to an AAA-approved, gringo-safe RV park; an exotic, tropical port-of-call complete with manicured lawns, vending machines, and bottled water. A place where there is nary a chance of encountering any actual Mexicans except the obsequious English-speaking trailer park employees (full-time, below living-wage, no benefits) whose only purpose is to serve. The best part is that they already know the people in the next paved, full hook-up, pull-through site: Mr. & Mrs. Snowbird, retirees from the great *white* north who can, in the cool of the early evening, be overheard among their lawn chairs and portable plastic cocktail tables inquiring, "Say buddy, do you know anywhere I can get some good shrimp—cheap?"

On my walk through town, local resentment was palpable. The warmth which I had felt in other towns was missing here. It was replaced by a familiar capitalistic phoniness. I had the sense that if the locals could suddenly do without the income they had now become accustomed to, they would not hesitate. But, in a shared desperation, they found themselves in bed with the very people they had grown to despise. This was not the Mexico of my initial acquaintance.

I followed the map in my guide book to a campground on the outskirts of town. I pitched my tent in the shade on a grassy spot among some stunted date palms. There was another tent here and beside it a yellow sea kayak. No one was home at the moment, so I made a pot of coffee (not Néscafe, but ground coffee, boiled in a pot of water and strained through my bandanna, otherwise known as "cowboy coffee"), aired out my sleeping bag, and settled in to my new neighborhood. The campground was loaded with RVers. Fortunately, this island of grass was set aside for tent campers. We could hardly hear the incessant droning of the RV generators. A few steps away from my tent was the Río Mulegé, a small river that flowed from its headwaters at the oasis into the Sea of Cortez. The riverbanks were lined with date palms and thick, tropical undergrowth. Sitting with my coffee on the river, far from town, Mulegé began its campaign of persuasion. Later that afternoon, the owner of the kayak came by. James told me he was kayaking nearly the entire length of the Baja. He stopped in Mulegé to resupply and meet up with his friend Mickey who was joining him for the remainder of the trip. I was reminded once again of Steinbeck's comments, this time about Mulegé:

> We passed Mulegé, that malaria-ridden town, that town of high port fees—so far as we know—and it looked gay against the mountains, red-roofed and white-walled.

Another well-known writer, Erle Stanley Gardner, best known as the creator of the Perry Mason mystery series, had also come this way. Gardner was an avid enthusiast of central Baja prehistoric rock art. He spent many years exploring and writing about archeological sites between here and San Ignacio. I had originally considered an expedition to some of these sites, but decided for the whales, having to choose because of my limited budget. The whales, it seemed, were a better investment, more ancient than cave paintings yet members of my own moment in time.

South of Mulegé is a 30-mile long bay of turquoise water, desert headlands, and sandy beaches known as Bahía Conceptión. Much of the traffic I saw in Mulegé was either coming from or going to Bahía Conceptión. Mulegé was the closest supply point for snow birds living in RVs on the beach. I decided to stay away from Bahía Conceptión. I heard the beaches were lousy with RVs and that many of them directed their sewer hose down into the sand, creating dangerous health conditions. If I had wanted to sit on a beach with sewage, I could have stayed in New Jersey.

The next day I followed a dirt track from the campground along the river to the sea. I was ready to meet the Sea of Cortez. At the inner harbor in Santa Rosalia, I was a spectator, high above the water with my feet firmly on concrete. Now, I pulled off my boots and greeted this great water properly. Suddenly, I was standing in one of the richest bodies of water in the world; one of the most productive marine nurseries on Earth. More than a 100 miles east across the water lay the Mexican mainland. In two months I would be standing on the other side of this sea, deep within the Earth's lush maternal folds: the Sierra Madre.

At one end of the beach I climbed a lighthouse and was treated to a panoramic view of the sea and Mulegé's winding green river. Magnificent frigate birds hovered above me like unfastened weather vanes pointing into the wind. Few creatures have superlatives in their official names like the *fregata magnificens* does. Locals call them *tijeras*, or scissors, because of their V-shaped split-tails. Their grace and beauty came close to unseating my favorite sea bird: the pelican. But after careful consideration, I am remaining loyal to that ungainly fisher, for it seems it may need all the admirers it can enlist. Small fishing *pangas* puttered in and out of the channel. A huge shrimper loomed offshore, anchored just off the point to the north. Shrimpers, and by extension, the people who buy and eat shrimp, are killing this sea. Steinbeck, writing in the *Log*, warned us more than 50 years ago,

> In about an hour we came to the Japanese fishing fleet. There were six ships doing the actual dredging while a large mother ship of at least 10,000 tons stood farther offshore at anchor. The dredge boats themselves were large, 150 to 175 feet, probably about 600 tons. There were twelve boats in the combined fleet including the mother ship, and they were doing a very systematic job, not only of taking every shrimp from the bottom, but every other living thing as well. They cruised slowly along in echelon with overlapping dredges, literally scraping the bottom clean . . . they were committing a true crime against nature and against the immediate welfare of Mexico and the eventual welfare of the whole human species.

And from Moon's *Baja Handbook*:

> In 1996 the Sacramento Bee published a . . . report by Pulitzer-winning writer Tom Knudson, exposing corruption among fishing interests and the state governments . . . The evidence presented in the report is

clear: over-fishing by greedy commercial interests is devastating the natural balance in the Sea of Cortez. Reading the report is virtually guaranteed to put you off eating seafood . . . primary culprits include gillnetters, purse seiners, spear-fishermen, and shrimp trawlers.

For every pound of shrimp, 10 pounds of other creatures are thrown back; dead and wasted. James told me that the squid, once a lucrative source of income for local fishermen and an important indicator species, was practically gone, the victims of commercial over-fishing. If the squid weren't doing well, it was a bad omen for the less conspicuous species. James was an activist and specialized in marine ecosystems. We mused about how easy it would be with a kayak to cut the anchor line on a shrimper as the crew slept. Bye bye!

An old camper van was parked on the beach near the lighthouse. Strewn close by was a beat-up lawn chair, dog food bowls, and a small river kayak. On my way back down the beach, the occupant of this encampment shuffled out of the van. Bill was from California. He was 77 years old and was camping with his two dogs. He told me his family worries about him down here but that hasn't stopped him. He walks the beach, kayaks every morning, and enjoys meeting the locals. I thought about all the people his age (and considerably younger) back at the campground huddled together like frightened pups around their mother's teat. They were paying at least $25 US a night to camp on a lawn that could have been in Iowa but for the palms and here was this adventurer living for free on the rim of a sparkling sea with absolutely nothing between him and the next moment.

That evening, after yet another bland dinner of packaged macaroni and cheese, I wandered down by the river. Somewhere near the boat ramp two old fishermen, concealed by darkness, stood over a concrete table cutting up their day's catch. Their soft, languid voices intertwined and floated off with the river toward the sea. They tossed scraps to a pair of waiting seagulls whose appetite was hardly diminished by the coming of night. At that same moment, the shrimper's crew were busy lowering the dredges to the bottom of the Sea of Cortez while Mr. & Mrs. Snowbird sat inside their plastic palace dipping shrimps into cocktail sauce.

The following night, the kayakers and I sprawled on the lawn in front of our tents. We each possessed a *ballena* of Tecate, or in other words: one big ass bottle of cheap beer. Our eyes were on the skies. There, on the grass, we talked and laughed as the Earth's shadow slowly but completely obscured our gleaming moon. The full lunar eclipse turned that familiar body an eerie, rusty orange. It cast its new light on the river and on the sea; on aged beachcombers and surly shopkeepers; on retired machinists and farmers and their well-coifed lap dogs; on scissor-tails and pelicans; on a pair of seagulls waiting silently for the murmuring of an old fisherman. And finally, on the very least of us.

Chapter 5

> "... But he also said that to be stood up against a
> Mexican stone wall and shot to rags was a pretty good
> way to depart this life. He used to smile and say:
> 'It beats old age, disease,
> or falling down the cellar stairs.'"
>
> —from *The Old Gringo*, by Carlos Fuentes

The bus ride from Mulegé to La Paz took about seven hours. Our route hugged the coast as far as Loreto. We passed Bahía Concepción and I saw that I may have made a mistake in not going there. There were many RVs on some of the beaches, but on others there were few if any cars or people. I realized that because I was traveling on foot, I could have easily found plenty of hidden nooks and secluded beaches. The bay's water was travel-brochure turquoise and clear as air. In the foreground, the green desert dissolved into white sandy beaches that looked out toward gold and purple mountains looming across the sea. I resolved at that moment to return here with a kayak and spend a winter season exploring the shores and sanctuary islands of Bahía Concepción. These islands are important nesting sites for birds and marine animals. Permits are needed to step ashore and only low-impact camping is allowed. As I settled in for the long bus ride, I dreamed of kayaking and snorkeling in those seductive waters. I imagined a little camp on a silver beach unreachable by car, miles from any town. Alone in nature, separated by distances not measurable by the usual increments. From Joseph Wood Krutch's Baja classic, *The Forgotten Peninsula*, on the bay:

> ... it is also perfectly proportioned and in every other respect designed as if for maximum beauty and impressiveness. The water could not be bluer, the great sandy beaches could not be whiter, and their curves could not be more exquisitely right.

Beyond Loreto, the Transpeninsular highway turns inland and passes through the intensively farmed flatlands of Ciudad Constitución. From there, the road continues south, bending eastward again to meet La Paz where it juts into the Sea of Cortez, forming Bahía de la Paz. As the bus rolled down from the highlands to the sea, I had my first look at La Paz. I was enchanted. This was the magic city. The waterfront, the narrow streets and food vendors, the ancient buildings, the parks and statues, even the tourists here were different—two-thirds were Mexican! La Paz cast its spell on me so thoroughly that I would, time after time, delay my final departure. "One more day" would become my mantra. Steinbeck's comments from the *Log* are memorable:

> ... a cloud of delight hangs over the distant city from the time when it was the great pearl center of the world. The robes of the Spanish kings and the stoles of bishops in Rome were stiff with the pearls from La Paz. There's a magic-carpet sound to the name, anyway. And it is an old city, as cities in the West are old, and very venerable in the eyes of Indians of the Gulf. Guaymas is busier, they say, and Mazatlán gayer, perhaps, but La Paz is *antigua*.

Steinbeck would later use La Paz, and a folk tale he heard here, as the basis for his novel, *The Pearl*. I felt at home in La Paz even before the bus came to a stop. It would be my jumping off point for the 10-hour ferry ride to the mainland. I would also leave from La Paz for explorations south to Pacific beaches and the mountains of La Laguna. I would return to the city of peace seeking refuge, as well. Again, from the *Log*:

> La Paz, the great city, was only a little way from us now, we could almost see its towers and smell its perfume. And it was right that it should be so hidden here out of the world, inaccessible except to the galleons of a small boy's imagination.

I left the bus at the terminal in the center of the city. With guidebook in hand, I decided to walk to my destination, a youth hostel located about a dozen blocks from the bus terminal. This was a test of my direction-finding ability. By now, I had mastered left and right and even straight ahead. Or so I thought. After wandering for nearly two hours, with a lot of backtracking, I stopped a young girl of about 17 and pleaded with her for directions. After about 30 minutes of hand signals, body language, and much silliness, we finally figured out that we were standing in front of the very building I was seeking! The hostel was housed in an athletic center and primarily served student athletes visiting from other parts of Mexico and the Baja. I said good-bye to my new friend. She gave me her phone number and asked me to call her the next day, but I never did. I didn't want to end up like Miguel, pushing a taco wagon around La Paz to feed my growing *familia* of *niños*. And she was just charming and funny enough to make that happen.

As I entered the doorway, a young American guy about 24, with dreads and a backpack bigger than mine, came loping out. He told me he was being evicted because a new sports team was arriving this evening and they had first dibs on rooms. Dave was heading downtown to a cheap hotel and invited me along. He was winding up his trip through Baja and heading home in a day or two. Dave knew the city bus routes so we hopped on a local for the 15-minute ride downtown. Surrounding us in the back of the bus were the real people of La Paz on their way home from school and work. Teenagers giggled at the two gringos with our giant backpacks and scruffy beards and long hair. They were too embarrassed to talk to us but I could feel their eyes absorbing every detail. Dave, with his dreads and hemp necklaces and earrings, drew most of their attention. We were both grubby looking from the road, in stark contrast to the neat and clean people on the bus. Gringos were supposed to be down at the waterfront, eating overpriced meals in fancy restaurants. They were supposed to be in the hotels and milling around the marina. We weren't supposed to be riding the local. As usual, we all had a good laugh at ourselves while savoring the dissolution of our most cherished prejudices.

Dave had reserved a room at the Pensión California, which was more like a hostel than a hotel. The building was originally constructed as a convent and is one of the oldest structures in the city. The rooms had thick concrete walls painted yellow with dull red trim. Each room had a dumpy bed and a rickety set of drawers. A naked, buzzing florescent light hung precariously close to the unenthusiastic ceiling fan. The lock for the door was simply a latch and ring through which you slipped the shank of a padlock while you were inside. The bathroom sported a toilet, sink, and a shower all in the same concrete closet. You could (if you wanted) take a shower while you sat on the toilet. The best part of the Pensión California was not the swanky rooms, it was the open air courtyard. There were tables and chairs for reading, sunning, and kvetching. An Amazon parrot swung in his cage, tormenting the staff. Date palms grew right out of the floor; green potted plants were perched on every ledge. In the middle of the courtyard, there was a large sink and stove on which to cook meals. The floor and walls were covered in red clay Spanish tiles. Hanging from the walls were funky paintings: bizarre mixtures of Aztec, Mayan, and Greek mythology including three-headed creatures, human sacrifices, and pudgy naked women sprawled on antique velvet couches. There were also picture frames filled with faded snapshots of adventurers who have stayed here. Glancing at these eager faces I realized I was just another atom in the universe of eccentrics revolving around the sun that was the Pensión California. But what really distinguished the joint was the array of *vagabundos*, drifters, families, and tourists that found their way to this dump. A typical morning at the Pensión California would find an artist at her easel attempting to capture the red and white brick stairway with the potted cactus and elegant iron railing; a German motorcyclist on a 12-month run from Alaska to Tierra del Fuego; a Mexican family of five between apartments; a pair of cheery Australian backpackers; and of course a few American and Canadian kids freshly arrived and determined like only 19-year-olds can be, to drink as much tequila and beer as physiologically possible without dying. What united us all? What brought this temporal universal harmony to our disparate collection of wandering souls? The price, 10 bucks a night. For that measly sum you received a private room with bath, the ability to cook your own meals, and, if you were lucky enough to have a room next to the water heater: warm showers. All this in the heart of downtown just steps from the famed *malecón*, or waterfront. Clearly, Pensión California is the low-bagger's place to stay in La Paz. There is also a sister hotel down the street, Hostería del Convento, another old convent which charges only $9 a night but the courtyard there is not as airy, not as rich in eccentrics.

Our room had two beds so Dave invited me to split the room with him; a decision he may have later regretted. Dave was my guide to La Paz that day (though he kept getting lost). He had been there about a week, trying to tear himself away, repeating the mantra, "Just one more day, Just one more day," until the money ran out. He took me to what was to become my favorite restaurant, the Café Revolución. We sat on a balcony gazing down past the fancy iron work at the crowded street below. Like me, Dave was a vegetarian and a low-budget traveler. The challenge was to find the largest quantity of fresh food for the least amount of money. After eating more packaged macaroni and cheese and ramen noodles than any human being should ingest, I was ready for some good restaurant fare, though my wallet wasn't. Dave to the rescue again! At the Café Revolución, they served whacks of really good free chips and salsa. We each ordered a plate of rice and beans which came with a generous side of fresh salad and a pile of steaming corn tortillas—all for about $1.50. We both threw in at least as much for a tip and from then on whenever I went to the Café Revolución I was treated like Frank Sinatra walking into the Sands Hotel in Vegas (whatever that means). After dinner, we headed down to the waterfront. As darkness overtook La Paz, anchor lights on the sailboats moored in the inner bay began twinkling against the black sea beyond. Young couples, speaking in whispers, strolled along the harbor-side, stopping now and then to kiss and dream out loud. Families shuffled under the palms with groups of children clutching ice creams, running, giggling, and crying.

On the way back to the hotel, we passed a small internet cafe where people, mostly travelers, drank coffee, checked their emails, and surfed the web. I glanced in and saw a familiar floral-patterned bandanna. Natalie! She and Ellen were staying around the corner from us at the Hostería del Convento. Natalie said maybe they'd stop by later to hang out. Dave and I went back to our room. We waited about an hour; Dave said he didn't think they were coming. It was already about 10 p.m. He went out for a walk while I stayed behind. "They're not coming dude," he told me. From my journal: "Sitting on the bed. The buzz from the fluorescent light is making me sleepy. Someone down the hall is singing softly, a Mexican ballad I think."

Disappointed, I went to bed. Later, as I was drifting off: Knock! Knock! I opened the door to find Ellen and Natalie and another guy named Dave, standing there hysterical, clutching a gallon of cheap gin. When the other Dave returned (the rightful occupant of this room) he found four people, barely visible through a thick cloud of cigarette smoke, sprawled over the beds laughing way too loud at nothing in particular. What's worse than walking into your own room and finding silly people drinking, especially when you haven't had a drop? Dave, realizing that he could never catch up, passed a joint around, stayed a few minutes and then went out to the courtyard to read. Later, we changed places so he could sleep. I don't remember exactly what happened that night but I do know that we stayed up nearly till dawn, laughing, drinking gin and hatching a plan for the next day. The other Dave was a surfer from California. He was on his way south to the beaches around Todos Santos before being waylaid by these Swedish she-devils. I mentioned that I was heading there also, to camp on the beach. Natalie and Ellen liked the idea of camping for a while and the next thing I knew, we were flying down the Transpeninsular, a wee bit hung over, crammed into a psychedelic 1968 Volkswagen bus stuffed with four people, three backpacks, a guitar, coolers, camping equipment, and a wide assortment of surfing paraphernalia—including a long board on the roof. We looked like a scene out of some second-rate, spaghetti beach movie: *Gidget Goes to Hell*. The other Dave had declined to come along. He helped us pack and sent us off with hugs and good wishes.

About an hour later, with Swedish pop songs pumping from the oversized speakers, we came to an abrupt stop at a rude reality: a military roadblock. Checkpoints and roadblocks are not uncommon along the Transpeninsular. Regardless of their frequency, they are unsettling. Armed soldiers board buses, search cars, and can detain you for hours or even days if they want. Once, at Guerrero Negro, an armed soldier walked through the bus and simply pointed at five or six passengers, including me. I intuitively followed the others off the bus to wait on the side of the road. I will never forget the chill at the end of that soldier's finger. I still don't understand the purpose of isolating us. Someone told me they were searching around our seats for hidden contraband while we waited outside. But ridiculously, I was standing there holding my daypack which could have contained plenty of *drugas y armas*. No one ever looked in it. As the soldiers walked down the bus aisle they pounded the ceiling with their palms, searching for drugs, guns, and perhaps even stowaways. Maybe they were looking for illegal American CEOs, sneaking into Mexico to establish thieving and destructive transnational corporations and thereby stealing that opportunity from some poor Mexican CEO (like President Fox, a former Coca-Cola executive). Road blocks and searches were something to avoid if possible. The tales among travelers in Mexico about people being harassed, framed, and fined are too numerous to ever not take a Mexican soldier and his gun seriously.

"Don't worry," said Dave. "I never have a problem. I just tell them I'm going surfing. They always wave me through." The next minute, we were standing on the side of the road emptying our pockets while three soldiers industriously ripped apart everything in the van. They looked in every nook and corner, in every compartment, and in every box. While handing them his wallet, one soldier noticed Dave's hands were shaking. The suspicion grew thick around us. They made us all hold out our hands at arm's length as they inspected them for tremors. They made the girls roll up their sleeves, checking for track and needle marks. A higher ranking soldier was called in. They huddled and conferred, turning occasionally to stare back at us. Meanwhile, I couldn't help glancing up at the soldier stationed behind the machine gun in the turret perched atop the military truck just 100 feet away. The soldiers went away and for a moment we thought we would soon be leaving. They returned with a drug-sniffing dog. This was not some hulking, intimidating German shepherd, but a small, cream-colored mutt who you would never suspect had a career in the military. He was conscripted, no doubt, for his olfactory talents as opposed to his imposing physical attributes. They closed all the windows in the van and put the dog to work. It was at this precise moment that the four of us looked at each other, suddenly realizing we were strangers. What did I really know about these people? Ellen and Natalie knew each other of course, but none of us knew Dave or if, like he said, his hands do sometimes shake. Was Dave carrying a kilo of pot under a wheel well? Was he transporting drugs to his surfer friends on the beach in Todos Santos? Dave was now also complaining of a stomach ache. What were Ellen and Natalie carrying in their backpacks? Sweden is a liberal country, drugs are no big deal there. I took out my dictionary and looked up the word for hitchhiker. Sergeant Muttface came up empty, much to the dismay of his comrades. They took him out, walked him around a bit, then put him back into the van. We tried to make a little conversation but our eyes were glued on that dog. We watched him sniff every corner of the van. We watched as they paraded him around the outside, pointing and encouraging him to poke his whiskered sniffer in certain likely quarters. Still, the littlest soldier could find nothing. Then, just as we were feeling confident that we would soon be on our way, the head soldier, leading the dog away, politely said, "One moment, please." He returned by himself, carrying a small package the size of a hard cover novel, thoroughly wrapped in many layers of plastic and taped securely. He walked past us without any attempt to conceal his parcel. He opened the back door of the van and carefully hid the mystery bundle underneath a pile of clothes and blankets. We looked at each other in disbelief. Were we being framed? He didn't even try to hide it! He waved to his lackeys and they brought back Sgt. Muttface. They opened the passenger-side door, Muttface hopped in and made a beeline for the contraband. He merrily plowed through everything in his way. He commenced barking as if this "bust" had guaranteed him a three-day furlough to Miss Kitty's House of Pleasure for Four-Legged Soldiers. Good boy! They told him. Good boy! We were stunned. This was it. Because they had searched our wallets, they knew how much money we each had. Like *The Old Gringo*, I wasn't worried about getting shot to rags; my fear was extortion. I could feel "the bite" coming—and it wasn't from the dog. I imagined phoning my friends and family from a dank prison cell, pleading with them to send money. The head soldier now retrieved the package, heaping praise upon the dog and walking toward us, his hand extended, holding the loot as if in evidence. I turned to my dictionary in haste and blurted out the word for "test." Was that a test? I asked. "Yes," he said pleasantly, "A test for the dog. You can go now."

One mile down the road, just out of sight of the checkpoint, four scared-shit gringos let out a chorus of howling laughter that could have straightened the hair on Pancho Villa's chin and turned his blood to milk.

We four happy people arrived in Todos Santos ready for anything. I had been warned about this Pacific coast village. The word on the traveler's circuit is that too many gringos had taken up permanent residence here. It was, I was told in somber tones more fitting of a fatal medical prognosis—a tourist town. But what I found was so remarkable that any objection to the tourists or the artsy Southern California influence was quickly overruled simply by walking one mile in any direction from the center of town. And the center of town was not so easily dismissed. Like San Ignacio, it had a lovely square, filled with bougainvillea and alive with people. Instead of a looming, ancient church, it had a community *teatro*, or theater. I was pleasantly amused to later read the following description of Todos Santos by Joseph Wood Krutch in *The Forgotten Peninsula*, written 40 years earlier:

> It is also, I think, the most attractive of all the southern towns. Because it lies practically at sea level and precisely under the Tropic of Cancer, it is fully tropical and, so it strikes me, would be the most attractive community in all Baja had I not already given San Ignacio that distinction. Its adobe buildings are more substantial and more spruce than those of any of the other southern towns; even in February its neat little public square is blazing with bougainvillea, *Tecoma*, and other tropical flowers . . .

We arrived at the beginning of the annual arts festival. Every day for almost a week, the square was host to outdoor concerts, art shows, food vendors, and plays in the *teatro*.

Dave found his friends, Stephan and Joanna, who were also surfers from California. Natalie, Ellen, and I decided to head to the surfer's beach with them. Four miles of bad road brought us to the edge of the Pacific. This beach, whose name, if it had one, I never learned, was miles long. I had pictured a crowded, noisy strip full of blond people drinking beer and reciting bad Kerouac poetry amid a forest of fiberglass surf boards. Happily, the beach was nearly deserted. Dave and his friends went north, we went a little south. We threw our packs down and ran to the water. A high dune ridge ran along the length of the beach so that you could not see the waves break until you were on top of the rise. I ran to the ridge, stopped and stared in disbelief. Whales! Only 100 feet from where I stood were at least six gray whales swimming past. Some were blowing, others were in closer, nearly in the surf.

    This was a magical time. All I had to do was live completely in the moment. What I could not grasp with my hands, I had to hold in my heart. Each morning I would take my coffee to that high, sandy ridge and watch the whales swim past. Sitting there, my toes dug into the warm sand, sipping cowboy coffee, with absolutely nothing to do, was about as perfect a way to start a day as I have ever found.

> *"The waves uprear their spume of pearly spray,*
> *arching above the sand and grainy gold*
> *whereon they break and washing glide away."*
>
> —Bernardo de Balbuena (1562-1627)
> from the poem, *Immortal Springtime and Its Tokens*

    Later, Ellen, then Natalie would wake up, and I would make them each coffee and breakfast on my little camp stove. We would take our morning bath together in the surf and then lie in the sun to dry. At night we would make a fire on the beach, watch the stars, and talk and laugh. Occasionally, they would break into Swedish and I would listen to the music of their speech, rising and falling inflections: crescendos, andantes, pianissimos—they were all there.

    During the week, we made several forays into town for supplies and fresh water. At night, during the arts festival, we listened to musicians playing in the square, drank beer, and ate tacos. We wandered through a frenetic maze of large canvases of desert colors and bronze faces, past umber potteries and green hand-woven baskets.

From my journal: "Went into town last night. Saw a guitar and harp duo play on the little stage. They played traditional Mexican folk songs and ballads. The harp player, like his instrument, was huge. Incredibly, this ham-handed man was plucking the most delicate and ethereal notes from that harp. His meaty paws moved blithely over the strings releasing strains of liquid silver among the crowd. My eyes battled with my ears trying to reconcile this seeming contradiction."

As the days unraveled, I learned more about my tent mates. We had the luxury of spending lots of time with each other. Natalie and I would walk the beach and talk. Mostly we laughed. We could barely look at each other sometimes without laughing. We sat and watched the whales, went swimming, drank beer, and made avocado sandwiches. Most of the time we did nothing. Just being together on that deserted beach was enough. She was an artist at heart. She loved to sing, and play, and paint. She told me about her life in Sweden and her plans for the future. Back home, she sang in a blues band, played a bunch of instruments, and wanted to earn her livelihood singing.

I learned that Ellen was married. She and her husband had just sailed their 30 foot boat from Hawaii to Baja, a 35-day ocean crossing. Natalie flew in from Sweden to visit Ellen and cruise the coast for a month with her and her husband. They had been best friends and had not seen each other in many years. Apparently, shortly after Emilie's arrival, Ellen and her husband had a fight. She and Natalie left him and the boat up north in Ensenada and started south through Baja by bus. They had a vague plan to meet up with the husband and the boat at the Cape and so would have to leave in a few days. I asked her if he would be safe sailing the boat to Cabo by himself. She insisted he was an excellent sailor but that didn't stop her from worrying. Natalie and I would find her sitting on the dunes, sadly staring out at the ocean. "I miss my boat," is all she would say. Ellen described her husband as a rough and ready type complete with a few bullet holes here and there from his wayward youth. More to the point, she said of him, "He can shoot the balls off a mouse at 100 yards with a 45." And I believed her.

Beyond our camp on the beach, 10 miles south and west of Todos Santos, the mountains of Sierra de La Laguna rose 7,000 feet behind us. In the evenings as the sun set, those mountains glowed with golds and blues and purples, finally morphing into black silhouettes looming against the star-speckled sky. Because of its relation to the Pacific, this mountain range receives more rainfall than any other spot on Baja. The rains, combined with moisture from low moving clouds, nourishes plants and animals found together nowhere else on Earth. The jewel and namesake of these mountains, La Laguna, is a mountain meadow, a dry lake bed nestled between two 7,500 foot peaks. It is far from the beaten path and offers those willing to visit a rare sub-alpine environment—in the middle of the desert. I decided to climb La Laguna.

Our last night on the beach we made a roaring fire and drank warm beer. Natalie sang Swedish folk songs while I laid in the sand listening, my head in my hands, looking up at her with the golden fire glow on her face. Suddenly, I realized how much I was going to miss her.

The next day we all piled back into Dave's van and headed to town. We had tacos and beer, took some pictures, and said good bye. Ellen and Natalie were heading south to the cape with Dave, Stephan, and Joanna to look for the missing boat and husband. I was going to get a cheap room in town, clean up a bit, and provision for my excursion to La Laguna. I don't think it would have been as sad if everyone had gone their separate ways. But only I was leaving our little group. Natalie and I took a long time to finish, but finally, she climbed into Dave's van and they were gone. And that arrow of loneliness went clean through.

Chapter 6

"The mountain remains unmoved at its seeming defeat by the mist."

—Rabindranoth Tagore

I took a dingy room at the Hotel Guluarte. I repacked my pack, separating and sorting the items I would need for my hike. Seeing the contents of my pack strewn over the bed reminded me why it was so heavy. Though I had been recently living in shorts and a T-shirt, I was carrying clothes for the colder temperatures I would encounter on the mainland, high in the Sierra Madre. I was also told that La Laguna could be cold—even freezing at night. In addition to long johns, fleece pants and sweater, three pairs of wool socks and a wool hat, I also had two fat guidebooks, one for Baja and one for the mainland. I still had my big dictionary and phrase book, a full-size SLR camera and two lenses, plus my tent, stove, fuel, pots, flashlight, etc. Adding five days and 10 pounds of food (mostly oats, coffee, rice, beans, salsa, fruit, peanut butter, candy bars, and tortillas) still left another eight pounds to be added for four liters of water. According to my guidebook, there would be no available water until I reached the top. This meant that I must hike the seven miles in one day. Normally, that's not a problem. But the Sierra de La Laguna tilt eastward, creating steep slopes on the western side. Seven miles of rugged trail would bring me more than six thousand feet up. You can measure the difficulty of a hike by the altitude gain over distance. I don't have the exact formula handy, but I can now say with complete assurance that this particular hike achieves an unofficial rating of: crazy hard! Of course, without the complete four-season wardrobe on my back and the international library I felt compelled to carry, it would have certainly been a more pleasant experience.

My plan was to be at the grocery store as early as possible, obtain a ride, and arrive at the trailhead and begin hiking in the coolest part of the day. Nice plan. The guidebook advised milling around the grocery store in the late morning to find a rancher who might be willing to give me a ride to the trailhead. The grocery clerk agreed but suggested I come early in the morning. On the way back to my room, I picked a piece of cardboard out of a garbage can with which to make a sign. Back at the hotel, I packed my 5-day food supply, showered off the crust of salt and sand that had accumulated on me, and was asleep by 8 p.m.

The next morning, I lugged my pack to the store, borrowed a black marker and wrote a sign asking for a ride and offering to pay for gasoline. I sat on the steps sipping Néscafe, watching sleepy Todos Santos come alive. About an hour later an old man in a battered pick-up truck stopped to look at my sign. Yes, he said, I could give you a ride. How much can you pay? Since a cab driver in town wanted to charge me $30, I offered him $20. I thought a dollar a mile would be a fair price and he agreed. Off we went. First we had to drop off his friend. Then we had to go back to his house. I started to get concerned when I watched him load the supplies. This was supposed to be a 10-mile ride. First came the spare tire. Then the two five-gallon jugs of water. What was that heavy thing wrapped in an old blanket—a battery? Back and forth he went, politely refusing my offers to help. Meanwhile, the sun was rising ever higher; it was getting warm and I knew my plan to begin hiking early had evaporated with the morning dew. Finally, he loaded the last item: his wife. Where the hell were we going? Had my Tarzan Spanish failed me? Did I just unwittingly arrange a ride to Mexico City? I took out my map and pointed to the road and trailhead. Here, no? *"Si!"* Ten miles, no? *"Sí!"* Okay, let's go! His wife was a plump, cheery woman who emitted a distinctive earthy bouquet. The three of us bumped and bounced along until finally we entered the desert and I immediately understood the reason for the back-up provisions. After seeing the road we were about to take, I was now under the impression that he traveled a bit on the light side. The road narrowed and the ruts deepened. In some spots, we barely inched along; where the road was smooth, he recklessly tried to make up for lost time. At one point we passed the crumbling remains of an old chapel. The old couple quickly crossed themselves in perfect unison; a simple, pious gesture performed in silence amid this desolate landscape. Farther on, steam began escaping from underneath the hood. We stopped. There was no need to pull over—there wasn't anywhere to pull over to. We were on a narrow dirt track in the thick of a *cardónales*. The cardóns grew right to the road, like sentinel soldiers on a parade route; tighter than security at a Bush coronation. The old man got out, opened the hood, and emptied a gallon or two of water into the radiator. And off we went. Soon we arrived at the trailhead. It was here I realized I had made a big mistake (again!). I thought perhaps there would be a few cars and trucks going to town and back. But now I saw that there was absolutely no practical reason for anyone to come here. I had only arranged for a ride here—not back. He wanted to know what day he should pick me up. I wasn't sure if I would have to pay him or not. The twenty bucks I spent to get here was all I could spare for this adventure. Rather than have him come back and me having to shell out again (and he surely would have deserved it), I told him not to bother. He couldn't believe it and asked me another two or three times. Finally he gave up, convinced I was out of my mind to be willingly stranded here. He and his wife sped away, disappearing into the maze of cardóns and leaving me literally, in the dust.

    I shouldered my pack and headed around the gate and down the dusty road that led to the trailhead. There was an old van parked here that I assumed belonged to a local rancher. The village where I had planned to top off my water supply was gone, vanished. I learned later that their spring had dried up about 10 years before.

Here were those mountains I had viewed all week from the edge of the Pacific. They had seemed so distant, so remote. Now all I had to do was follow this dusty path to the clouds.

> "... we turn our eyes to the mountains,
> and to-morrow we go climbing toward cloudland."
>
> —John Muir
> *My First Summer in the Sierra*

At the base of the mountains the local flora had changed dramatically. There were still cardóns and prickly pear, but now small pines and oaks were recharging the palette of colors, providing patches of faint shade. My guidebook estimates the hike to the top at anywhere from five to eight hours. I gulped half a liter of water (the most efficient place to carry water is in your belly) and started the ascent. The trail itself was well-worn from cows and burros. At times it followed dry washes and crossed slides, other times, it was a deep narrow trench, its walls extending over my head. But always, it climbed upward. The only relief I received from trudging higher is unwanted; every time the trail leads briefly down, I must struggle harder to regain what I lost. Clearly, there is no way to climb 6,500 feet in seven squiggly miles without a lot of sweating and panting. At some points I could go only 25 feet without stopping to catch my breath. I estimated the angle of ascent at about 30° and often worse. I lost my sense of time on the mountain. After climbing for more than an hour, I reached a clearing where I was certain I could measure my hard-won progress but found only that I was still among the foothills. Meanwhile, the sun intensified its efforts to draw every salty drop of moisture from my reserves.

Here is a guaranteed three-step program for successfully climbing the Sierra de La Laguna: Trudge, pant, and rest. A strict adherence to this formula will mercifully deliver you, eventually, to the top. I came at last to a clearing where, to my astonishment, I turned and saw the Pacific ocean stretching for miles north and south along the coast; reaching endlessly west to the horizon. Wispy streaks of white traced the outline where the land meets the sea. This was no sharp delineation, but a mingling of matter, a torn and jagged edge like a sheet of thick paper ripped in two and hastily restored. Now I was standing among thick stands of piñon pines and cactus together. I threw off my pack, crossed over a ridge, and climbed atop a granite boulder. I stood there, my arms outstretched absorbing this miracle of which I, but a mote, was part.

I was also heartened by the fact that my guidebook said that after achieving this splendid view of the Pacific, La Laguna was only 20 minutes farther. This wasn't so bad, I thought. Yes, it was hard, but after all, this view! It can't be had without a little work, I reasoned. Thirty minutes later, then sixty minutes later, I began to think that La Laguna was more elusive than I first suspected. I stopped for a drink of water and emptied the second of my four liter containers. Now I was half way through my supply. Views of the Pacific became more spectacular the higher I climbed but it was becoming clear that I had no idea of how far I had gone or how long I had hiked. As I prepared to continue, I stood up and nearly fainted. My head spun and my face felt flushed. My knees buckled under the weight of the pack and I slumped back down against a tree. I quickly drank half of the third liter of water and ate some peanut butter. Now there was no going back. I didn't have enough water to make it back down and through the 10 miles of desert to the main road. I had to reach the top. The sun, the exertion, the excessive weight of my pack were all pressing down upon me as my destination kept slipping farther away.

After a 30-minute rest in the shade, I resumed the trudge. Now the trail seemed to lead away from the Pacific and behind the mountain. It turned suddenly cooler here and the pines, shielded from the harsh Pacific winds, seemed to flourish, providing more shade and foiling the penetration of the sun's oppressive rays. I descended into a green valley, cursing the loss in altitude yet relieved by the shade and easy pace. Suddenly, through the trees I thought I saw a glint of water. Instead of joy, a brief panic rolled over me. Oh no, I thought, now I'm hallucinating. I must be in trouble. As I came closer, I realized it was water—a stream! I had stumbled upon a grotto. There were cottonwood trees and tall oaks, a lively creek with wide pools of glimmering water. And green—so many shades of green! In just a few steps I had moved from the parched arid mountainside to a cool, lush ravine. I drew nearer and noticed a blue tent on a bluff above the headwaters of the stream. I was not alone.

The hikers, a couple from Canada, emerged to greet me. I asked them how much farther to La Laguna. Their answer nearly knocked me over. I was still at least three, maybe four hours away! Incredible. Could it be that it took me nearly all day to go four miles? I quickly came to a decision. This pleasant hollow, verdant and moist, was to be my base camp. I would stay here tonight. Tomorrow, rested and well-watered, I would hike to the summit with just my day pack. The hikers showed me where they were getting their drinking water. There were signs of cattle all around the stream banks. This meant that the water was unsafe for drinking without treatment. The hikers used small containers to catch the water as it flowed directly from the rock. They drank this without treating it which I thought was a bad idea. "We've been drinking it for two days and we're okay," he told me. I replied that if you were to get giardiasis (a common intestinal parasite), you wouldn't know it for at least a week, probably two. Suddenly, miles from this little spring on a crowded bus on a very hot day, I joked, you may find yourself doing the Aztec two-step. How those words would come back to me! I gathered my water from the same rivulet but used a filter to purify it. They began packing for their return trip that afternoon. They had been lounging, waiting for the day to cool. It was their van that I saw parked near the trailhead. I related my predicament about getting back out of the desert and they kindly volunteered to leave me some of the water they had stashed in the van on their way out. They soon left me alone in this splendid place. I pitched my tent where theirs had been, on a slab of level ground surrounded by yuccas and thorn bush, overlooking the sparkling rill.

I made a wonderful supper of rice and salsa. I had dates for desert and even made a pot of fresh coffee. My spirits, which had been trampled under the weight of my pack and the heat of the sun, now rebounded and I knew I would reach the mountain meadows of La Laguna the next day. My only disappointment would be that I could not sleep there; I would have to return to base camp. Still, I was ready to compromise if it meant not lugging that pack another four miles up. As I sat there, the most amazing thing occurred. As the sun slipped to the other side of the mountain, darkening the ravine, a chorus of frogs began a boisterous celebration. Frogs! Here I was in the middle of a desert surrounded by such unlikely pairings: oak trees and yucca; prickly pear and frogs! I went to bed exhausted, laughing at my own good luck, gently lulled to sleep by the most enchanting of water music.

Wind, the Earth is sick from silence.
Though we possess light and color and fruit,
Yet we have no music,
We must bestow music upon all creation.

To the awakening dawn,
To the dreaming man,
To the waiting mother,
To the passing water and the flying bird
¡Life should be all music!

—from a 16th century *cantares Mexicanos*

I awoke early the next day refreshed and eager to begin. I threw my camera and lenses, two liters of water, lunch and snacks into my daypack and headed out. Even with this lightened load, it was a tough three hours of climbing. What I had previously thought a sweeping view of the Pacific and the coast, now, by comparison, was cramped and narrow. From this higher elevation it seemed as though I could see the entire peninsular. Those foothills and lower mountains on which I had struggled now appeared like bumps on a relief map; a heat rash on the land. At my feet were russet grasses waving golden seed heads, thorny bushes with leathery leaves, and isolated clumps of green oaks scattered on the hillsides. I could plainly see the trail below, a thin brown track, as if some giant, in an idle moment, had run its index finger crookedly around the mountain. And there was silence. No planes, no cars; nothing but the wind and a few birds. Only 10 miles of desert, followed by a seven mile climb, could accomplish this degree of isolation. And yet, I was puzzled. Yesterday and today I had noticed what looked like fresh burro droppings along the trail. While I am not an expert in burro scat (my expertise lies in the excrement of a much larger animal, also associated with Mexico) I had no doubt that someone was ahead of me. Also, every now and then I could hear the tinkling a of bell. Mostly I could hear nothing but my own heavy breathing, but every so often, it came faintly on the wind and then disappeared. These mysteries did not diminish the sense of isolation but instead amplified it.

    The trail soon turned away from the Pacific and descended through a pine forest, cascading down a series of rocky ledges, spilling me out onto more than 100 acres of sub-alpine meadow. The summer grass had turned to gold. A stream meandered from one end of the meadow to the other, pausing occasionally to pool and bear witness to a patch of sky, then continue its journey to the edge and down to the sea. This meadow was once at the bottom of an ancient spring-fed lake. The water eventually escaped through an eroded arroyo and Nature began its transformation. I wandered around, gawking at the surrounding peaks. I walked the stream to its canyon get-a-way route and ate my lunch under the pines. I could have easily believed I was in the Black Hills of South Dakota or those wild lands between Yellowstone and the Tetons. What I could not comprehend was that I was in Baja! If I had any sense I would have come here with a botanist. Many of the plants here are found nowhere else in the world. The plants I did recognize continued their bizarre behaviors. The cardóns now sported beards; clumps of Spanish moss hung from their spiny arms. The surprising array of mosses, ferns, and other bromeliads was due to the higher than average rainfall and the moist Pacific clouds that envelope these mountains. Simply stated, I was eating a peanut butter sandwich at the bottom of an ancient lake, in the grass of a sub-alpine meadow, watered by the clouds, in the middle of a desert. Not so simple.

As I was exploring the other end of the meadow a small dog appeared followed by two men on burros. The men wore informal uniforms with official looking patches on their shoulders. They were the rangers of La Laguna. La Laguna is now protected by the government because of its diversity of flora and fauna. The rangers and I had a brief chat. They were friendly but reserved. They patrolled the trails and were supposed to be keeping the cows from eating the rare plants and preventing the destruction of streamside habitat. A job that, judging by the hoof prints along the entire length of the stream, they didn't take all that seriously. They were probably ranchers themselves.

Near the trail I stumbled upon a life-sized mural of Our Lady of Guadalupe, Mexico's ubiquitous patron, painted on a large boulder. On the ground in front of the image was a small altar with candles and prayer cards. Her popularity stems from a reported sighting in 1531 in Tepeyac, near Mexico City. Octavio Paz, in his book, *The Labyrinth of Solitude,* gives a detailed history of this important symbol:

> It is no secret to anyone that Mexican Catholicism is centered about the cult of the Virgin of Guadalupe. In the first place, she is an Indian Virgin; in the second place, the scene of her appearance to the Indian Juan Diego was a hill that formerly contained a sanctuary dedicated to Tonantzin, "Our Mother," the Aztec goddess of fertility. The Virgin is the consolation of the poor, the

shield of the weak, the help of the oppressed. In sum, she is the Mother of orphans. All men are born disinherited and their true condition is orphanhood, but this is particularly true among the Indians and the poor in Mexico . . . In addition, The Virgin—the universal Mother—is also the intermediary, the messenger, between disinherited man and the unknown, inscrutable power: the Strange.

Though its location here, twenty miles from the nearest village, was jolting, these impromptu manifestations of faith, though usually not this elaborate, are a common sight in rural Mexico. Wherever I went, even the most remote places, there were small altars, statues, candles, and crosses along the roads and nestled in groves and grottos throughout the countryside. Some were markers for loved ones who had died and rough wooden crosses bore their names in scrawled letters; others, in the most isolated locations, seemed to serve as satellite chapels, complete with fresh flowers and lanterns. I'd like to think they were constructed and tended for the wanderers and the lost among us. Many even had bottles or cups for the passerby in which to drop a coin or two. Steinbeck has a lovely passage in the *Log* about such roadside reverence:

In the brush beside the track there was a little heap of light, and as we came closer to it we saw a rough wooden cross lighted indirectly. The cross-arm was bound to the staff with a thong, and the whole cross seemed to glow, alone in the darkness. When we came close we saw that a kerosene can stood on the ground and that in it was a candle which threw its feeble light upward on the cross. And our companion told us how a man had come from a fishing boat, sick and weak and tired. He tried to get home, but at this spot he fell down and died. And his family put the little cross and the candle there to mark the place. And eventually they would put up a stronger cross. It seems good to mark and to remember for a little while the place where a man died. This is his one whole lonely act in all his life. In every other thing, even in his birth, he is bound close to others, but the moment of his dying is his own.

One last gaze across the meadow and down I went. Now this was hiking! The vast Pacific spread before me as I loped along for two hours until once again I was sitting comfortably back at base camp, my head swathed in a cold wet bandanna and my naked feet cooling in the breeze.

I still had three days supply of food left and all the water I could filter. I decided to save one day's food in case I had to walk out. That left two days for exploring in the mountains. From my base camp I hiked in all directions. I hiked back to the Pacific side and spent a long day making photographs and taking notes. I hiked up beyond the little stream and followed its elusive trickle deep within the mountain. I followed winding side trails that led nowhere in particular before abruptly ending. I discovered a ratty shelter made of wood and cardboard. I found small fire pits filled with bottles and cans. One day, I found cows; the next day, they found me. Zwinger gives a nice description of Baja cows in *A Desert Country Near the Sea*:

> Peninsula cattle are long-legged and rangy, with medium-long horns, high square rumps, and a hurried prancing gait that is almost horselike. The variety of colors is encyclopedic: Dalmatian-spotted black and white; black with brown; liver and white; cinnamon brown; tan and cream; speckled gray—one of every persuasion.

I was sitting in camp when the bovine parade came to town. These cows were big! There must have been at least a dozen. They ambled past me single-file and down to the stream. They walked right in and started drinking. From the front of the herd came a familiar, ghostly sound: the tinkling of a cow bell. The cows ignored me and I was satisfied with the arrangement. But one cow, a youngster, the color of buttermilk with huge dark brown eyes, developed an interest in me. I confess I do not know what to do upon meeting a cow. A bear, yes. A mountain lion, certainly. Even snakes, I know what is called for. Horses, dogs, cats, and children, for each there is an appropriate response. But a cow? Do you pet them? Do you offer a little snack? Her skin looked so smooth and creamy; I wanted to reach out and scratch her head. But her imposing size and protruding horns discouraged me from extending my hand. I spoke to her in a friendly voice, offered encouragement and shared my astonishment at her bulk, which was now inching alarmingly close. Before we became too intimate, I decided to draw a line, so to speak. I raised my voice, waved my hands, and indicated it was time for her to rejoin her own kind. No good. I informed her that I was a staunch vegetarian, and respected the rights of all creatures to live freely and with dignity. Nothing. I yelled "get lost" in English and in Spanish. Now she was really curious. I looked around for an escape route but I was on a bluff, surrounded by rock ledges and a steep hillside filled with cactus. There was not enough room on this patch of land for both of us and her girth was blocking the only exit. I decided to get tough. I picked up a pot and started banging it. Oh, she thought, look at this little man, jumping around making noise, how interesting, let's get a closer look. Now she was only about two feet away, nearly trampling my tent and knocking over my cooking gear. What I did next sounds so *udderly* ridiculous I should be ashamed to relate it. It was nothing less than the last resort of a desperate man. I put my head down, made little horns with my fingers (I'm not kidding!) grunted and growled, and scraped my feet like a bull ready to charge! Laugh, go ahead, but guess what? That's right! She took one look at this apparition, backed away (there was no room to even turn around!) and galloped down the trail! Hah! I put the *cow* back in coward!

There were other, less intrusive visitors to the grotto. Each afternoon, as dusk settled over the mountains, hummingbirds appeared, buzzing among the blossoms. A flock of cat birds came after each of my meals and dutifully performed their scrupulous housekeeping. Toward evening of the last night I noticed large wet spots on the walls of my tent. A sage-like scent filled the air and I realized, though the sky above me was clear, that I was becoming enveloped in moist Pacific clouds. Later, the sky disappeared and I found myself in a fog as thick as on any seacoast.

I began the hike down the next morning. I went slowly, exercising caution on the steep slides. Going down is easier but more treacherous than going up. This was not the place to sprain an ankle—or worse. I stopped often to absorb the view, make photos, and contemplate the landscape. By midday I was back at the gate. The Canadians had left me a gallon of water with a note taped to the plastic jug. I put the note in my back pocket and forgot about it. I divided the water among my four liter bottles. By then, the heat of the day was bearing down full blast. I pitched the tent to provide some shade, laid down, and decided to throw myself at the mercy of the fates. This was after all, the Mexican way. ¡No problema! If I didn't get a ride today, tomorrow, with plenty of water, I could walk back (or at least wander hopelessly until I lost consciousness).

A few hours later, a van rumbled along the dirt road packed with a family from La Paz. They were on their way to the beaches but had decided to stop here first. The man told me that he used to hike in the mountains when he was younger. "Three hours," he told me. "I hiked to the top in three hours." I told him it took me two days. We laughed. He caught me staring at his big belly while I was contemplating his three hour feat. These days, he added with a bit of humility, he liked to drink beer more than hike. He sat in the shade of his truck and made good on his word. As they prepared to leave, he offered me a ride. I struck my tent in record time, squeezed in with grandma and the kids, and away we went. They dropped me off at the highway, I stuck out my thumb, jumped in the back of a pick-up truck, and was instantly transported from the magical landscapes of deserts and mountains, meadows and grottos, to my favorite taco stand in

Todos Santos, where I sat munching a *quesadilla* and savoring an icy cold beer. *¡No problema!*

On the beach, I had longed for the mountain; on the mountain, I missed the sea. I followed a winding dirt road on the outskirts of town for two miles until I found myself once again at land's end. I threw off my boots and ran to the surf, gleefully announcing my return to a pod of whales and a few stoic pelicans. With my feet in the cool Pacific waters, I turned and watched the sun cast its last amber light on the distant peaks of the Sierra de La Laguna. And I tried, in vain, to comprehend the true distance between two points.

> *"Sometimes your glassy sheen is struck to foam*
> *on every side by your dark wantoning nymphs;*
> *you fondle them with many a secret clasp*
> *and languidly receive their loving kisses."*

—Ignacio Manuel Altamirano

From my journal: "So many whales! At least a dozen today. Some were spy-hopping. Can hear them breathing and blowing from my tent! A father and his three boys are fishing. We are the only ones around for miles. Mac and cheese with onions and peppers for dinner. A beautiful sunset now—waves are pounding, lots of spray. Starting to get chilly."

I spent an idyllic week camped on the beach. I found a small *tienda* about 20 minutes away where I could replenish my water supply and buy groceries. Todos Santos was only a 30-minute walk. The road to town zig-zagged past fancy adobe *haciendas* with elaborate gardens and trellises filled with bougainvillea and exotic orchids and flowers. There were orchards and small farms along the route growing chilies and beans and lemons, watered by the abundant springs that had first brought the Pericú and later, Spanish missionaries and *mestizo* settlers to Todos Santos. Though close to town, few people ever visited this beach. One morning as I climbed out of my tent, a *charro* on horseback cantered by and waved. A few people would come at the end of the day to watch the sun slip beneath the horizon and blast the sky with color. Some would come with their cameras aimed at the whales, especially in the late afternoon when they were closest to the shore.

I would sometimes wake in the middle of the night and wander down the beach. Often my thoughts would turn to Ellen and Natalie; the camp fires and long talks, our laughing and playing. But solitude has its own rewards. And it wasn't until I was alone here that I really came to know this place. Walking by myself at night, the surf sounded louder, the sea smelled saltier, and the distance between men and whales nearly vanished in the dark. As Rachel Carson wrote in *The Edge of the Sea*:

> The shore at night is a different world, in which the very darkness that hides the distractions of daylight brings into sharper focus the elemental realities.

I learned that the reason for the lack of people here was that swimming was dangerous. The violent surf was known for its infamous "leaper" waves that would suddenly vault far onshore and drag unsuspecting tourists into the water where the strong undertow and rip tides would send them back to California the hard way. After a week, I decided to hitchhike about 10 miles south to a beach near the town of Pescadero, where I had heard the swimming was excellent.

What a difference! Dozens of motor homes were clustered in an abandoned RV park. Surfers and their vans filled every nook along the approach to the beach. A long row of tents was pitched on a high dune ridge. Compared with the Jersey shore, it was empty; compared with where I had just been, it was Coney Island. I found a spot on the ridge for my tent and discovered why there was so many people here. The beach was situated behind a protruding rocky headland which protected it from the prevailing northerly winds. The water deepened so gradually and the waves broke so gently that you could walk for a thousand feet and still be only up to your waist. I spent long, lazy days swimming, reading, and exploring the cactus-covered headlands.

My neighbor in the next tent, about 50 yards away, was an ex-pat, Luddite, anarchist inventor who had retreated here from the US, bracing for Y2K havoc. While he was not alone in his prediction, he arrived on this beach a year early to prepare himself. He cooked on a stove fashioned from three discarded #10 tin cans. I add that specific because, as he explained, the diameter combined with the length of the chimney was of crucial importance to maximize fuel efficiency and optimize the draft/heat relationship. And I thought they were just a bunch of rusty cans. He made candles from old tuna tins and sewed his own clothing from local muslin. He was in his late 30s, grizzled, sunburnt, surprisingly overweight, and dressed for a toga party. He was camped in a dark green beat-up army pup tent at the end of this row of brightly colored nylon dome wonders. His disheveled camp clearly proclaimed that here lived an individual. You would find no trendy beachwear, no Italian sunglasses, no $30 bottles of imported sun screen or corporate logo'd beach umbrellas. His tin can stove, chugging a steady stream of wood smoke, announced this was the wrong side of the tracks; the squat and squalor of Paradise. I went over to say hello and we talked as he labored over a black crusty pot bubbling with a goopey liquid he claimed was oatmeal. He demonstrated the floppy cardboard wind scoop at the end of his tent and explained the physics of cool air displacing warmer air and how with the addition of this device his tent was always comfortable, even at midday. A 40-foot wire wound its way out of the tent, along the ridge pole and down the beach. Inside, the wire was attached to a small short-wave radio receiver which connected him to the outside world and a static-filled chorus of evangelical/conspiracy broadcasters. His camp held the choice remains of many a local garbage dump. He made the necessities of life from the things others threw away—no small accomplishment in Mexico.

His camp was situated at the end of the ridge, closest to the neat and orderly RV settlement—the border zone between surfers and retirees. The mere sight of this primitive, loin-clothed man sent many a well-coifed lap dog into a hysterical yipping fit. The RVers made it clear that he had ruined their view of this picturesque bay. Life under the awning of a 50-foot Winnebago would never be the same. He was a source of local consternation and arguments erupted almost daily. I liked him immediately.

His most interesting invention was his kite. Every afternoon he would stumble from the dark enclosure of his tent into the bright sunlight, place his little plastic bag kite in the sand, step back 20 or 30 paces, and coax it high into the Pacific breeze. I can't remember the scientific theories (though I heard them often enough) which explained why this particular kite was superior. His aerodynamic formulae, sadly, were lost on me. It was enough for me to sit and watch this toga-clad wild man flying a little yellow kite, rudely yelling at all the children who inevitably came by to ask for a turn.

My other immediate neighbors were a couple from Switzerland. He had recently quit the Swiss army and had decided to see Mexico and Central America. He sported fresh stitches and a bandage across the bridge of his nose. He was learning how to surf and had just covered the part about keeping the board from hitting you in the head. In the army, he was training to be a commando instructor. He had taken part in an interactive virtual reality training program. The program took place inside a house, supposedly occupied by the "enemy." As you, the commando, moved through the rooms, the program followed you. The point of course was to kill them before they killed you. Because of the level of reality it conveyed, he found himself "hyped up and fearful." He entered a room and in his panic, shot and killed a small child. The experience, though only a program, changed his life. Three days later he was out of the army and headed for Morocco. "I wasn't going to train people how to kill children," he told me. Now he wanted to get his scuba instructor's license so he could make a little money and travel. Though Switzerland is known as a neutral country, nearly 40 percent of its population, he estimated, are involved with some aspect of the military.

Because of the high quality and constant upgrading of their arsenal, they have become one of the world's largest suppliers of arms.

The main disadvantage to this beach was the long trip to town for supplies. I had to walk two miles down the dirt road to the highway. Once on the highway, I could walk another two miles or, if I was lucky, hitch a ride. Pescadero was a dusty place with a few *tiendas*, some houses, and two schools. Though it lacked the visual charms of Todos Santos or San Ignacio, it emitted a strong sense of the genuine. There was nothing here that was not necessary. The old men had plenty of benches to sit on. There were enough trees for shade, the stores were well-stocked, and the pace of life was mercifully slow.

I was re-supplying at a dingy *tienda* when a large woman abruptly confronted me. She was an imposing figure, wore a dirty house dress and her short natty hair stuck out in all directions. She had a full moon face and was inexplicably interested in me. I told her how much I liked Pescadero. We both agreed that Todos Santos had too many gringos living there. How is the water here?, I naively asked. Water in the desert is always a serious matter. The quality and quantity is a point of pride in each town. Is it as good as the water in Todos Santos?, I persisted. To answer this question, she invited me back to her house which turned out to be right behind the store. From the sidewalk, we entered a small courtyard. Above us was a web of trellises and beams from which plants hung so thickly that I could not see the sky. It was a cool and pleasant space. On either end of the courtyard, were two compact adobe rooms. They each contained a mattress on the floor and a few sticks of furniture. Her 94-year-old father was shuffling between the rooms. In the center of the courtyard was a picnic table at which the family took their meals. Spread over the entire length of the table were the crusty remains of breakfast. Lustily attached to those remains were more flies than I have ever seen in one place. She scattered them with a wave of her flabby arm and started to clear a space for us to sit. She explained that there is a mountain-fed spring here in Pescadero. It is cold and clear and far superior to the water in Todos Santos. She moved to a large barrel, swished away a thick carpet of flies, took a rusty cup from its nail and scooped out a big sample of Pescadero water. "Here," she said beaming at me, as if I were about to share a delicious secret. It was then that the little voice in the back of my head started screaming: *Don't do it! Don't do it!* I looked at her proud and eager face. The voice was pleading now, nearly in tears: *Run away! Run away!* I glanced over to the barrel where the flies had once again resumed their copulating, egg-laying, and defecating. I looked back at her, took the cup and downed it. "More?" she asked.

One morning, a few days after my visit to Pescadero, I awoke with a rumbling in my belly. I dashed from my tent and into the cactus field. I discovered that my usually reliable plumbing was in disrepair. I spent the rest of the day lying in my tent feeling nauseous. Two days later, weak and feverish, I left the beach and boarded a bus to La Paz.

Chapter 7

"I enjoy convalescence. It is the part that makes the illness worth while."

—George Bernard Shaw

I have a theory. To know a place you must get sick in it. Not deathly sick, but severely incapacitated at least. I now believe that to gain the pulse of a foreign city, it is necessary to downshift from the usual traveler's pace and perspective. Imagine, lying on your back in a cheap hotel, alone, without the usual comforts of friends and family, far from your favorite doctor, herbalist, or pharmacy; surrounded only by the unfamiliar as your internal organs wretch and writhe, spewing their vile, putrefied contents out of every orifice. Now that's traveling!

The Pensión California was full so I stumbled around the corner to the Hostería del Convento and took a $9 room. I bought and drank a half-gallon of water. I turned off the light, put on the ceiling fan, and laid naked on the bed wondering how high my fever was. Within a few hours, I was feeling better. My intestinal problem, I guessed, had been compounded by too much sun. Two weeks of living on the beach perhaps had dehydrated me and stressed my system. Because water was always a chore to fetch, I tried to conserve it. Lying there supine on that lumpy mattress I realized my folly. I dozed occasionally only to have my dreams invaded by gigantic women proffering rusty cups brimming with crawling flies. My plan was to rest for a day and then strike out for the mainland. I would take the 10-hour ferry from La Paz to Los Mochis then board the Chihuahua al Pacífico railroad to the Copper Canyon and the Sierra Madre. Nice plan.

Lying in that cool dark room, well-hydrated and out of the sun, my condition quickly improved. Within a few hours I felt stronger, even hungry. Convinced I was well again, I headed to the Cafe Revolución for a hearty plate of rice and beans, just what I needed, I thought. I made sure to drink plenty of extra water with my meal and resisted the temptation to have a beer. Feeling good, I took a different way back to the Convento, wanting to explore a little. Then, suddenly in the middle of downtown La Paz, that old familiar rumble began in my belly. The difference between living on a beach and in the middle of a city became apparent. Here, there were no cactus fields, no long, lonesome stretches of thick thorn brush to hide behind. The rumbling worsened and I could feel beads of sweat forming on my forehead—and it wasn't from the salsa. My pace quickened. I headed in the general direction of my hotel, or more accurately, my toilet. Oh what a thrill, to be lost on the streets of a strange city guided only by a vague sense of direction and a precise sense of urgency. By the time I found the Convento, I was doing that little walk we all know so well. I scooted past the cute girl at the desk and gave her, no doubt, the most strangely contorted smile she has ever collected at that station. I was now using obscure muscles discussed only in medical books. There was an incredible pressure building in my nether regions that was demanding relief; like a festering volcano, like a million tons of water seeking the single weakest point in a dike. Yet, I was going to make it. Here I was, already in the hallway, just steps away. I pulled the key from my pocket as I approached the door, congratulating myself on such quick thinking. The sweat was increasing and I felt as if, by will alone, I was containing the whole of Lake Mead behind the most fickle and unreliable of damns. I hastily thrust the key into the padlock but to my dismay discovered that it was upside-down. The eternal second in which it took for me to correct my mistake was the very same second I needed to scurry across the room. As if on cue, at this interminable delay, the Hoover damn of my flimsy being exploded. As I fumbled with the lock, it burst forth with a vigor seemingly greater than the mere biological matter of which it was composed. It continued to erupt with great force even as I opened the door and galloped to the pearly white object of my desire. But it was too late. Too late.

I spent the next hour cleaning; cleaning my clothes, cleaning the floor, cleaning the bathroom. I was standing in the shower rinsing out my pants when I came across the note in my back pocket from the Canadian couple I had met in the Sierra de La Laguna. The irony of my comment to them regarding buses and bowels did not escape me. Unfortunately, the note was now illegible.

The next morning, feeling slightly nauseous, I packed up and headed out to catch a bus for the ferry terminal. Waiting for the bus, I realized I wasn't going anywhere. I was still weak, still feverish. The thought of taking my queasy stomach and cranky orifices on the high seas for a 10-hour ferry ride was not very appealing. If I was going to be sick for a while, I could think of no better place than La Paz. Rooms were cheap, supplies were plentiful, and there were doctors and clinics should my condition become worse.

I went to the *farmicia* and obtained a thermometer, some anti-biotics (available over the counter), Pepto-*dismal*, vitamins, and aspirin. I checked into the Pensión California and began a slow but determined recovery.

Like Mr. Shaw, I too tried to enjoy this period of convalescence. After a few days of rest, I started wandering around La Paz in increasingly larger radii (though never immediately after meals). My previous visit here had been brief. I had spent all my time with Ellen, Natalie, the two Daves, and a gallon of gin. Now I was operating at a more relaxed pace.

I had time to investigate. I visited museums, went to the movies, and strolled the *malecón* in the mornings and at sunset. At the harbor, I wondered where the English corsair Woodes

Rogers might have landed in 1709. With him that day in La Paz was Alexander Selkirk, a man he rescued from nearly five years of self-imposed isolation on a deserted island near Chile. Selkirk's story of life on that island would become immortalized by Daniel Defoe in his book, *Robinson Crusoe*.

I sat in the courtyard, read newspapers, and practiced my Spanish with (on) the staff. My favorite time of day was early morning. The crisp air and soft light illuminated La Paz to its best advantage. Standing in front of the Pensión California with a mug of cowboy coffee in hand, I watched the streets come to life.

The sweepers were the first indication that La Paz would rise once again to meet the day. Crooked old men and the sound of their sweeping gradually filled the streets. They drizzled water from hoses over the sidewalks to immobilize the elusive dust. They diligently swept away the previous day's grime and offered La Paz a clean start. Taxi cab drivers began lining up their cars at popular corners. To save gasoline, they pushed their cabs ahead in line as the lead car departed with its fare. While they were waiting, drivers polished the chrome, cleaned the windshields, and brushed the floor mats. Next to appear were the vendors. Great blocks of ice were skillfully chopped into gleaming slivers and packed around fish and meat, fruits and vegetables. The taco wagons brought the sounds and smells of sizzling meats and herbs. A bent man with a long stack of wooden bird cages strapped to his back made his way up the street each morning. The cages were filled with brightly colored finches and parakeets, parrots and canaries. He slogged along solemnly in sharp contrast to the merry chirping and peeping of his cargo. Statuesque young women, in navy blue blazers and skirts, walked together three or four abreast, down the middle of the street to their jobs in the fancy department stores. School girls and boys in neat uniforms hurried past, engrossed, like children everywhere, in their own private, urgent world. Small crowds of people gathered on street corners, waiting for the local *collectivos*, the small school buses and vans that shuttled people to and from their jobs each morning and afternoon. The *norteña* music—

guitar, bass, and accordion—began crackling from the tinny speakers above the doorway at the local record shop. The morning optimism of La Paz grew steadily each minute, inspired by the rustling palms, the presence of the sea—white sails on cobalt water—briefly glimpsed between buildings. Perhaps if enough sweeping is done, if enough good mornings are said, if only the cabs can retain their luster and the buses run on time; and if the children can continue to walk unescorted, free from the epidemic of violence of their northern neighbors, if perhaps all these things can occur anew each morning, then maybe, this city of peace, will for one more day, earn its hopeful name.

There was another smell in the mornings: *la panaderia*, the bakery! When I arrived here the first time with Dave, I noticed he went out early and returned with goodies from the bakery. I asked him how to get there. "Go out the door, turn left, and follow your nose," was his answer. The bakery near the Pensión California was the best I found in Mexico. In the morning and again in the afternoon, the bakery would serve fresh *bolillos*, torpedo shaped rolls, crusty on the outside, soft and warm on the inside. To this you added some fresh goat cheese, some avocado—or as I did on many occasions—nothing at all. At the bakery, you used a large round aluminum platter, similar to a pizza pan, and a pair of metal tongs to choose from items on the shelves. The cashier would remove the items, put them in bags, and ring up your total. I would leave the bakery with three or four *bolillos*, two or three donuts, and perhaps something special like a thick slab of homemade bread smeared with melted butter and sprinkled with sugar. I don't think I ever spent more than one dollar per visit. Living the idle life as we did, anyone who returned from the bakery was obliged to share their loot with the other loafers in the courtyard. There was also a large *mercado*, or market, nearby which sold fresh fruits, vegetables, and cheeses. Restaurant vendors lined the perimeter of a large room while picnic tables occupied the main floor. Customers, elbow to elbow, talked and ate freshly prepared food. Each vendor had at least one specialty dish and a dedicated following of customers.

The other plentiful treat in La Paz were *palentas*: ice pops! These were not your typical over-processed, artificially flavored, hormone-injected, genetically modified American ice pops. *Palentas* were made from mashed fruit pulp and juice, frozen on a crude stick. There were dozens of flavors and colors stacked by their hue in cases, as if someone had frozen a rainbow and then cut little bricks of color from it. Sometimes during my recuperation, they were the only thing I could mange to eat. Flavors ranged from the ordinary to the exotic, and at about six cents a piece, I felt it was my duty to sample as many as possible.

My recovery took about eight days. Gradually, I began eating regular meals, finished the antibiotics, and generally was feeling pretty well. I decided that before leaving, I would investigate the free beaches north of town. Ten miles from La Paz, where the cape protrudes into the sea, a string of sandy beaches dip into the turquoise waters of the Sea of Cortez. I spent five days here with an American woman. Madeline, who I met during my convalescence at the Pensión California, was an artist from New England. She had come to Mexico to paint the green deserts. The colors in her canvases shimmered and swirled and set the desert on fire. Her paintings revealed the colors that our eye so often fails to detect. She brought the land to life with those simple tools of brush and pencil. She would wander off to paint while I scribbled in my notebook, vainly trying to wrestle beauty into words—as if such infinite and unbounded truths could be rendered like a grocery list or some civil communication. Clearly, there was nothing *civilian* about this landscape. We camped in solitude amidst wild sand dunes. We sauntered over the beach picking shells and counting pelicans. We swam and took long walks in the water, the sand under our feet rippled like tiny mountain ranges from the pulsing waves. By mid-afternoon, the wind would build from the north, relieving the heat and scattering sand and seed. At sunset, we climbed high into the rocky, cactus hills that surrounded our camp. Huddled together against the wind, looking out over the Sea of Cortez, we counted our fortune and considered our luck. We laid on the beach at night and watched the sky fill with an improbable number of stars. I realized that I was once again blessed with an extraordinary moment, a beautiful and gifted companion, and a deep draught of life which I tried my best to savor. For I knew, it would soon be over.

From my journal: "Feeling the heat! Sitting in a small cafe across the street from the Pensión California. Just ordered three *quesedillas* and a soda. Madeline has gone. She looked so sad in the back seat of that cab. She had to catch a flight out of San Diego in two days. I already miss her company. What a good camping partner she was. She even made me a little painting kit. My guts are back to normal again and the second part of my adventure is about to begin. Will send Madeline a long letter once I arrive on the mainland."

The next day, Dennis, a fellow idler from California, gave me a ride to the ferry terminal. Dennis and I had shared the doorway at the hotel many mornings and together had watched La Paz come to life. He had visited Madeline and me at the beach nearly every day. In town, the three of us went for ice creams and long walks together. In the short time I was in La Paz, I had made many good friends. But my mantra, "one more day," had been exhausted. That evening, leaning against the railing on the upper deck of the ferry, I said good-bye to Baja California and La Paz. As the engines churned under my feet and the salty air of the Sea of Cortez dampened my clothing, we slipped past the headlands where Madeline and I had just been camped. I watched the bright lights of the harbor fall astern, dwindle like dying embers, and finally disappear. *¡Adiós!*

> *"Distant sea, do you know your mystery?*
> *There, upon your shore,*
> *the smallest dream of man*
> *does not remain forgotten..."*
>
> —Emilio Prados from the poem, *Faithful Page.*

Chapter 8

"A permanent state of transition is man's most noble condition."

—Juan Ramón Jiménez

At the ferry terminal, I met a couple from London and within hours we were sleeping together. The ship finally tore itself from the dock at about 11 p.m. Though it was full with hundreds of passengers, few were in their seats. Women with babies and toddlers, teenagers, couples—everyone—staked out a few square feet, threw down a blanket, and tried to sleep during the 10-hour passage. The Brits and I found a small patch of empty floor space, filled it with our sleeping bags, traded traveling stories, and tried to sleep amidst crying babies and giggling teenagers. A trip to the rest room or the deck meant hop-scotching perilously between sleeping heads. At daybreak we took big cups of Néscafe from the snack bar to the deck and watched the sun rise over the distant blue mountains. The port town of Topolobampo came into view and soon we were boarding a shuttle bus to the city of Los Mochis. They were planning to take the bus to San Luis Potosí, about 24 hours south. I found a cheap hotel room downtown and the Brits stopped by to take showers before getting on their bus. I had to be in a cab at 5 a.m. heading for the railway station if I was going to board the Copper Canyon train for its 300-mile journey north into the Sierra Madre.

Los Mochis was an industrious city. It had none of the charms of La Paz or sleepy Baja villages. It was all business. It did have a bustling main street filled with sidewalk vendors offering food and clothing, boots and music tapes. I found a quiet park and sat for an hour or two on a shaded bench watching daily life unfold in this city of 250,000 people.

Without a watch, and without confidence in my arrangement for a wake-up call, I spent a miserable night. I woke up nearly every hour and wandered through the hallway and down the stairs to the desk to look at the clock. Finally, in the dark, a little before 5 a.m., I hit the streets of Los Mochis and walked a few blocks to where I was told there would be an early morning cab. The driver was slumped in the front seat, lost in his dreams. I tapped gently on the window, threw my pack in the trunk, and we were off. Even in my sleepy state, I felt the excitement building. I was about to board one of the world's most famous railways. The Chihuahua al Pacífico train climbs from sea level to 8,000 feet in about 300 miles, crossing the Continental Divide three times. It plunges through 86 tunnels and clatters over 37 bridges. The line itself took nearly one hundred years to complete. Construction was interrupted by revolutions and economics. But the biggest obstacle remained the impervious and stubborn geology of the Sierra Madre mountains. The rail bed was literally chiseled out of the granite. The numerous tunnels and bridges were not designed to provide a thrilling scenic ride for tourists, but to straddle a daunting, impenetrable landscape. The rail line had begun as a lofty dream to connect Topolobampo, Mexico's deepest port, and the rich farming regions of Chihuahua and the American Midwest. From Moon's *Northern Mexico Handbook's* detailed history of the railway's early challenges:

> . . . the train would stop anywhere along the line for passengers and it is said that 90 percent of the trains derailed at least once per journey. Passengers helped lever the cars back onto the tracks and stopped to chop wood along the steeper grades to fire up enough steam to get the train over the top.

Today, the train runs on diesel and derailings are rare (I think). There is one lingering connection with the past: Bandidos! Serious looking police and army personnel, wearing guns in plain view, continuously walk through the train. In the remote sections of the Sierras (where I'm going solo camping!), bandidos occasionally still hold up the train and its passengers. One story I heard occurred only a few years ago. A German tourist and his wife were on the train heading north. Bandidos boarded the train and commenced robbing the passengers. The German man began videotaping them! The thieves repeatedly told him to stop taping but he ignored them. He had, as the story goes, recently attended a re-enactment of some revolutionary skirmish and had mistaken this train robbery for more of the same. He kept taping and they kept telling him to stop. Finally, they shot him dead. I can't say whether this story is true, but it sure made the ride more interesting (for the rest of us at least).

"If an ass goes traveling, he'll not come home a horse."

—Thomas Fuller

From my journal: "After a day and night in Los Mochis I am finally on the Copper Canyon train! Leaving in a few minutes for the Sierra Madre. The car is clean with roomy seats and big windows. I have been thinking of this trip for a long time. This is one of those moments when you realize that your daydreaming has become reality. What is more exciting? A blurb in a book from somewhere long ago lingers in the back of my mind. It festers there, expanding, until eventually I find myself unexplainably sitting in a Mexican railway car about to begin a journey of a lifetime."

We climbed from sea level, through cacti and thorn brush, past the fertile plains through weedy clumps of mesquite and then finally into thick stands of piñon oaks, ponderosa pine, and Douglas fir. Sitting next to me was a Mexican man in his late 30s.

He was on his way to visit his family in Chihuahua. He has taken this ride many times and is obviously proud of the engineering feats of his countrymen and women. He knew little English but was interested in learning so we spent a lot of time trading words. He wrote his name for me in my notebook: Ramón Palomares Villalba. I wrote mine: Guillermo McLaughlin. Ramón knew his desert plants. The more I asked him about the plants that passed by our window, the more he told me. The presence of certain trees, he said, indicated that water was just below the surface. He showed me, on paper, where to dig and how deeply. He had spent many years herding cattle and crossing these arid landscapes with little food or water. He had me laughing at one story, embellished with lots of body language, when he and a companion were nearly dying of thirst, they snuck into a small ranch and began milking the cows and had to run away when they were discovered. The charm of the story was in his quick and exaggerated movements. I can still see his eyes darting left and right from behind his hands as he pantomimed the frantic milking.

A few hours into the trip a strange thing occurred. In the center of each rail car, was a small station from which the conductors sold sodas and bottled water. Snacks were offered by vendors who boarded the train during various stops. The conductors lifted a shelf revealing a griddle. After a few minutes, delicious aromas filled the air. The conductors had begun cooking peppers and vegetables. Stacks of warm tortillas appeared and it looked as if the feast would soon begin. Conductors from other cars now arrived. I surmised that they needed the extra help for dishing out the chow. What a great way to treat the passengers. Amtrak officials should get down here and learn something, I thought. Then, the conductors began eating. Well, it's only right they should eat first, after all, they're working. I waited for the announcement or other signs that we too would soon be enjoying this surprise supper. I watched anxiously for the conductors to finish eating. I realized that my last meal was the day before and I had not even had breakfast. No wonder I was hungry. Oh, and those aromas! Finally, for they seemed in no rush to finish their dinner, they began clearing away the utensils, scraping the griddle, and in a few puzzling minutes, dinner was over. I exchanged glances with another gringo passenger who was just as confused. I began rooting around in my day pack for a couple of ancient granola bars or squished raisins. Ramón had brought some home-made cheese and tortillas with him for the train ride which he generously shared with me. We sat there eating our cold snacks while the lingering smells of garlic and peppers slowly wafted past our noses and out the window.

Now we were heading into the mountains. My sense of excitement grew as pines replaced prickly pear and rugged granite hills began to reveal themselves in patches between dense hardwood forests. Suddenly, we were looking down into deep chasms. In some, freight cars lay smashed and on their sides. I would like to add that they were rusting remains of long-ago train wrecks, but they were not that old. The place to be was not in a seat but standing between cars with your head out the window. Each new tunnel and bridge added excitement. The bridges crossed trickling streams hundreds of feet below. The train slowed dramatically for its nervous traverse, precariously clattering over canyons or hugging the sides of steep mountain passes. It would repeat this 37 times. Some passengers would not look down, preferring to stare straight ahead waiting for the relief of the next tunnel.

Hours later we were nearing Tarahumara country. At one stop, a small village, there were families that had made their homes in abandoned railway cars. They peeked out at us from dark doorways. Women sat together in the dirt weaving baskets while a gaggle of girls and boys descended on the train, selling tamales, enchiladas, and other home-made snacks to passengers. The poverty, viewed from a comfortable train seat, was disturbing. As I traversed this country on foot, I would learn the consequences of that impoverishment. But here, my first look at the colorful blankets and dresses, the men in their wide, white sombreros, and the bright hope on the children's faces, told me only that I was entering another world, its vivid surface faithfully revealed in the crystalline sierra air.

The Tarahumara, or Rarámuri as they call themselves, have been written about extensively. They are known for their ability to run vast distances. They are resourceful and good-natured. They have developed innovative methods of agriculture and their existence in these wild mountains has been referred to as "Walden-like." As Carl Lumholtz wrote in his 1902 book, *Unknown Mexico*:

> The Tarahumare (sic) in his native condition is many times better off, morally, mentally, and economically, than his civilized brother; but the white man will not let him alone as long as he has anything worth taking away. Only those who by dear experience have learned to be cautious are able to maintain themselves independently; but such cases are becoming more and more rare. It is the same old story, in America, as in Africa and Asia, and everywhere. The simple-minded native is made the victim of the progressive white, who, by fair means or foul deprives him of his country.

Of course, many Tarahumara have been assimilated. Even hundreds of years ago, the missionaries influenced their religious ceremonies. Today tourists flock here every Easter to gawk at their elaborate religious festivities. The more resilient Tarahumara have pushed farther into the deep canyons and forests, deliberately avoiding contact with modern society. I did not come to the Sierra Madre to study the Tarahumara. I am no more interested in watching their religious ceremonies than I am in visiting the Methodist church up the street from where I live. But I confess that after having lately spent so much time in civilization, I needed to be among people who lived simple lives in harmony with higher laws. I needed to know if they still existed. From *The Old Gringo* by Carlos Fuentes:

> The mountains rose like worn, dark-skinned fists and the old man imagined the body of Mexico as a gigantic

corpse with bones of silver, eyes of gold, flesh of stone, and balls of copper. The mountains were the fists. He was going to pry them open, one after the other, hoping that sooner or later, like an ant scurrying along the furrowed palm, he would find what he was after.

There was another reason I came here. The Tarahumara are now threatened by something even more insidious than diabolical missionaries and do-gooders. Transnational paper and timber companies are removing the forests of the Sierra Madre. When they clearcut the forest, the land can no longer hold the rain. From a recent report authored by the Comision de Solidaridad y Defensa de los Derechos Humanos in Chihuahua and the Texas Center for Policy Studies in Austin entitled, *The Forest Industry in the Sierra Madre of Chihuahua: Social, Economic, and Ecological Impacts:*

> The Sierra Tarahumara and its forests are a vital link in the hydrological chain because they capture precipitation, hold and recycle nutrients in the soil, and form stable waterways that benefit enormous river basins. Shade provided by the forests is important for regulating temperature, sustaining the rain cycle, and providing habitat for unique species of flora. The water that originates in the Sierra feeds into five major river basins ... The loss of forest cover in the Sierra Tarahumara as a result of current logging practices has caused erosion, which reduces the filtration of rainwater into the aquifers, finally affecting the quantity and quality of water in rivers and streams.

The report emphasizes that endangering the water, endangers the Tarahumara and their traditions.

> The cultural survival of the region's indigenous people depends on their coexistence with the land, the forests, the springs, and the flora and fauna.

The Sierra Madre also contains the widest diversity of any forest on the continent. Again from the report:

> The Western Sierra Madre ecosystem combines transitions of extreme differences in altitude and climate to form the greatest biodiversity of the American continent... there are a large number of endemic species either considered extinct, near extinct, or endangered in the Sierra Madre.

But only six percent of the old-growth forest now remains standing. This is not some polite, academic debate that is occurring here. Like the land itself, feelings are raw and powerful. Resistance to commercial logging has resulted in the imprisonment of many forest activists, both *mestizo* and Tarahumaran. While rich tourists from Germany, Australia, England, South Africa, Canada, and the United States thumb wistfully through glossy travel brochures, a war is waging. This is not only a battle for the survival of a culture, but of an entire ecosystem. Tourism will not save them. Human rights workers here say that only the repeal of non-democratic global trade mechanisms like GATT and NAFTA will remove the economic pressures and return the management of these forests to the people who have inherited the first right of stewardship. But I could gather all I needed to know about logging abuses and ecological impacts from reports and scientific papers. What I couldn't learn from a distance was what it was like to simply be here. I wanted, or maybe needed, to be among these people, even for a short time. I promised myself that I would only do it on their terms. I would travel by foot and with few possessions. I would make myself available for contact, but they would have to be the ones to initiate it. And I'm glad they did.

The train stopped briefly at Divisadero, where from the safety of a rusty chain link fence you can look out over what is referred to as Copper Canyon country. Imagine the Grand Canyon but four times bigger and not one—but 20 different canyons. Imagine also that here there were no park rangers, no entrance fees, no 2-day waits for permits, and no $25-a-night campsites. This is a spectacular natural wonder without the turnstiles and toll gates of modern "resource management" dweebs and their bureaucracy. No need to control car traffic—there are few roads, none of them paved. No need to build campgrounds—not many are interested in "camping" without cell phones, beer-filled coolers, and SUVs. No need to charge admission—you will certainly earn the experience in your first 1,500 foot ascent out of the canyons. I could enter the canyons at any point. I could hike down a narrow trail, make camp along a river, and wander for days without seeing a town or village. This was not some cordoned-off museum wilderness, but a living, breathing—inviting—wilderness.

The next most striking difference between the Copper Canyon and the Grand Canyon is the color. Here, the layers of red Navajo sandstone are missing. Those glorious color displays at sunrise and sunset are not to be found on these green and gold mountains. And unlike the arid canyon bottom of the Grand Canyon, here, they are lush, alive with tropical flowers and butterflies, hummingbirds, fruits and figs. The rims are covered with the vibrant greens of pines and piñons.

Less than an hour later we arrived at the town of Creel. I said *adiós* to Ramón, swung my pack to the ground and was met by a horde of small children chanting: Margarita's? Margarita's? No, they weren't shilling cocktails, but volunteering as guides to take me the two blocks to that bit of backpacker's heaven known as Casa de Margarita's. A hostel-like hotel 8,000 feet high in the Sierra Madre mountains. Margarita's is a rambling, falling down kind of place that has been the victim of one awkward addition after another. There is a large kitchen and eating area where perhaps 30 people sit elbow to elbow at breakfast and dinner time. There are dorm rooms for the budget traveler and a few private rooms for the others. A narrow bunk in a crowded dormitory, hot showers, plus a home-made breakfast and dinner cost only $6 a night. Margarita's made the Pensión California seem extravagant by comparison. Meal times were whirling, chaotic feasts where travelers from all over the world exchanged stories and experiences, began friendships, and met new traveling partners. I would spend many an hour at that congenial board. I met a diversity of people from Himalayan mountain tour guides to Yukon dog-mushers, from Danish college kids to retirees from France. Margarita's was my home base while I stayed in the sierras. From here I would leave for camping trips to hot springs, lakes, and waterfalls. Between trips I would lounge around Creel, sit in the square, read books in the mission store, and have the best *huevos rancheros* (eggs with salsa) in Mexico, at Gaby's *Lonchería*. From Margarita's, I would also depart for a seven-hour nerve-wracking trip deep into the canyons to the tiny outpost of Batopilas where I would once again have a little trouble with the Mexican army.

Chapter 9

*"If there is to be any peace,
it will come through being, not having."*

—Henry Miller

I was yearning to get back outside, sleep in my tent, and explore the rugged hills surrounding the town of Creel. The next day I left Margarita's and followed the road out of town about five miles to an *ejido* where I could camp. An *ejido* is a form of communal land that has its roots in pre-Colombian indigenous cultures. For several decades after the Mexican Revolution, land was redistributed from the rich back to the poor (from whom it was stolen) forming the modern *ejido*. Much of Mexico's indigenous population live in *ejido* communities. Land ownership and control are central issues throughout Mexico, including the Zapatistas' current struggle in the Chiapas region.

A sleepy boy collected a fee of about $1.50 from me at a little booth and gave me a rough map of the area. I wanted to camp near Lake Arareko, but I was unsure if it was allowed. I decided to keep a low profile and camp high above the water in the surrounding hills. The lake itself was like a shimmering blue diamond in the midst of gnarly granite spires and thick green pine forests. Unlike eastern forests, there is virtually no undergrowth between the trees. What grew here instead was a long flowing grass, gold now, for the winter, but probably a luxuriant green with the coming of the spring rains. I found a level spot on a hill overlooking the lake, wedged between massive boulders. The light here was similar to that in the Sierra Nevada: clear and crisp.

From my journal: "The air is pure crystal tinged with pine. The clean light illuminates every blade of grass and patch of lichen as if a veil had been lifted from my eyes and I can only now see their real colors and patterns. Even the shadows are sharper: blacker than black!"

I made camp, fetched some water from the lake, and made a fresh pot of cowboy coffee. I found a boulder nicely sculpted to fit my back, kicked off my boots and tried to absorb the beauty around me. From where I sat, I could see horses milling about by the shore of the lake. Later that afternoon, I started exploring some of the many trails that incised the mountains. I saw a small *ranchero* and some young Tarahumaran girls in their brightly colored dresses and bandannas also gathering water from the lake. I went to bed early, still tired from the long train ride and the hectic socializing at Margarita's. The high elevation, crystalline air, and the lack of city street lights for hundreds of square miles, all conspired to fill every inch of the night sky with stars.

"If there is nothing new on the earth,
still the traveler always has a resource in the skies."

—Henry David Thoreau

I went to sleep that night listening to the frantic calls of coyotes. Hours later I awoke startled. Drums! At first I thought I was dreaming, unsure of what I had heard. I laid quietly in my bag, listening. Yes, it was drumming. There was one drummer somewhere in my vicinity. The other drum seemed to come from many miles away. They were drumming in turns. Talking? Here I was, alone in the Sierra Madre, snug in my sleeping bag and listening to perhaps the most ancient long distance communication on Earth. These were not some yuppies at a two hundred dollar a day "healing" session in Vermont suffering from a protracted case of ennui. These were real people whose everyday communication had achieved the ethereal subtlety of music. It is disconcerting to think that the same human genius behind those drums lurks as well behind people playing "Mary Had a Little Lamb" on their cell phones. I felt a bit guilty, as if I was eavesdropping on the party line. I found out later that the drumming was probably related to the upcoming religious ceremonies. The Tarahumara had begun traveling from all over canyon country and making preparations for the festivities. No one I spoke with was able to tell me the meaning of the drumming. For all that has been written about these people, there is much more that is unknown. Whether they were discussing who is bringing what to the party or just having fun, I hope I will never know for certain. The magic is in the mystery.

The next morning I was sitting outside my tent making coffee and oats when I noticed a small boy, dressed in jeans and a cowboy hat, staring at me from the top of a rise, about 100 feet away. I waved him over and offered him breakfast. From behind him came another surprise: about a dozen little goats. He was a goat boy! He sat on the ground with me and we shared coffee, a banana, and a few cookies. He told me he was 10 years old and it was his job to take care of the goats. He would stay all day with them, returning to his *ranchero* in the late afternoon. Our communication was difficult. Some Tarahumara children learn Spanish in school, and of course they are surrounded by it in the towns like Creel, where the *mestizo* population is much greater. Spanish was a second language for us both. He taught me a few words in Rarámuri and I taught him a few in English. But our serious conversing had to be conducted in Spanish. But unlike other Spanish speakers I had met so far, he had little ability to translate my bad Spanish, so we had plenty of good laughs at my expense. That first morning he stayed only about 10 minutes. He had, he told me, to follow the goats, which had kept going even after he stopped to investigate me. He returned the next day and we repeated the ritual with him standing at a distance waiting for my invitation. That bit of politeness and reserve would be repeated with each Tarahumaran I met. He was my first and I could think of no better ambassador than a shy, polite boy out with his goats. What more could I ask? Camped on a mountain less than 500 miles from El Paso, Texas, in the year 2000, I am still able to meet a boy tending his goats. A boy with no computer, no beeper, no cellphone. A boy who has not even heard of the internet. By the age of 12 he will be finished with school. By 16 he will perhaps be thinking about a wife and family. He'll live in these same mountains, his children will move the family's goats over the same paths he is walking today. He will coax corn and beans and squash from the impoverished soil (the goats are kept mainly for fertilizer, not for meat or milk). For his entire life he will pay no rent or mortgage, owe no taxes, own no car, contribute to no retirement plan, and in fact, the notion of retiring, if I could explain it, would be laughed at. His life and his work are inseparable. They are one solid thing, each dependent on the other. And though he won't be writing checks to the IRS, he will contribute to his community. He will help his neighbors prepare their soil, harvest their crops, and build log houses and granaries for those who need them. He will share what he has with the less fortunate and his parents will always have a place to live and food to eat. But what about Shakespeare? Will he never hear Mozart or the Beatles? Will he never ponder Nietzsche or read the plays of Tennessee Williams? All I can say is that without a doubt the people who dropped atomic bombs on Hiroshima and Nagasaki had heard plenty of Mozart and read reams of Shakespeare. The generals and politicians who authorized the use of depleted uranium bombs in Iraq and Kosovo have all had the benefit of a "modern education." The shareholders of the transnational logging companies who are destroying these forests, I'm sure, have gone to the best schools and have impressive libraries. I doubt any of them have as much "culture" as this young boy now sitting across from me in the dirt.

> *"How is it that little children are so intelligent*
> *and men are so stupid?*
> *It must be education that does it."*
>
> —Alexandre Dumas

Of course, not everyone has admired the primitive lifestyle of the Tarahumara. The following is from a report, quoted in the wonderful book, *Tarahumara: Where Night is the Day of the Moon*. The report was written by Father Juan Ysidro Fernández de Abee, S.J. from Mission Jesús Carichíc on July 8, 1744:

> The Indians live at great distances, separated from each other and scattered. They prefer to live in the ravines and canyons and in the cold, inhospitable mountains where they have their dwellings. Their native simplicity, barbarity, laziness and sloth incline them to this preference to being reduced to living a rational, civilized human life . . . From infancy they are brought up to be mountain vagabonds with no training in either morals or proper conduct. They are worse than beasts because the animals at least acknowledge their subjection to those who put them in cages and govern them.

And what did those "civilized" missionaries propose to do? Father Juan Ysidro Fernández de Abee has the answer:

> They should remove the Indians from their canyons and use armed force to make them live together in pueblos. They should burn their hovels and granaries in which they keep their corn. Eight or 10 soldiers ought to be stationed at this mission until the Indians learn to love their pueblo. If they flee from the pueblo after being settled there the soldiers ought to hunt them down and bring them back. In this way the will of Our Catholic Kings will be done and some useful purpose will be served by the sweat poured out by the padre missionaries for the salvation of the wretched Indians' souls.

On my return to Margarita's after about four days camped in the mountains, I passed an occupied cave dwelling. The cave was more of a rock shelter, an overhang which created a large space underneath protected from the elements on three sides and open in the front. The occupants, a small family, had also constructed a wall made of stones and sticks that extended part way across the front. It looked cozy, if a little on the dark side.

I dove once again into the pool of humanity at Margarita's. As usual, the joint was jumping with tourists from every country. What a treat after camping to have a home-cooked dinner and a hot shower. Sleep was a different matter. Three Norwegians had arrived during my absence and in true Nordic fashion sought to achieve a constant blood alcohol level of at least 50 percent. A giant bottle of cheap tequila or vodka was always at hand. These guys were like big overgrown puppies. They were happy to be in Mexico and they wanted you to be happy too. The tequila went round and round till just about everyone in the dorm room was either drunk or throwing up. They had a video camera and recorded people singing their national anthems. The international representation in the dorm rivaled any United Nation's get-together. Finally, the Norwegians were persuaded to occupy a small room off the main dorm. Still, the cigar and pot smoke, laughter, screaming, and most disturbing, brief periods of absolute silence, managed to slip under the door and yank me from my dreams.

I hung around Margarita's for a day or two before arranging a trip to the hot springs deep in the canyon of the Río Recohuata. Margarita's offered a day trip down and back. I decided to go down but not back. I thought it would be good to camp there a few days. I provisioned in town then piled into Margarita's van for the 30-minute trip to the canyon rim. Once off the main paved road, we bounced past a few remote Tarahumaran *ranchero*s. The canyon and the land surrounding it was also *ejido* land and we had to pay a small fee to enter. We came to a stop at the rim of Cañon Recohuata and looked out over a vista of canyons and forested plateaus that stretched for miles. No roads, no buildings, no power lines or telephone poles. Near the canyon was a small *ranchero* with a few rough-hewn log cabins and corrals. The hot springs lay at the bottom of the canyon, 1500 feet down a rugged winding trail. I tried to keep up with the day-trippers but the weight of my pack (once again I'm carrying all my guidebooks, dictionaries, camera equipment, winter clothes, and five days worth of food) seriously impeded my ability to negotiate the steep trail, especially on loose gravel slides and around hairpin turns. At one point, I had to stop. My knees felt as if they were about to buckle from the constant pounding of going downhill. While I rested my aching joints, I began wondering how I was going to make it back up. There was also the question of how to return to Margarita's. I would just have to trust my luck. *No problema!*

My first look at the hot springs dispelled the notion that I was insane for voluntarily stranding myself here. Hot water gushed from the side of the mountain, collected briefly behind a crude, concrete retaining wall, and then continued in long slender waterfalls to a sparkling pool in the canyon bottom. The pool was ideal for swimming. It measured 25 feet wide and twice as long. The steamy water mixed with the chilly waters of the Río Recohuata creating a pleasantly warm temperature. Small waterfalls plunged into the pool and provided perfect hot water showers to sit or stand under. I found a level spot near the upper reaches of the river, threw my pack down, and declared myself in paradise. Within minutes I was soaking in the soothing waters. Later, the day hikers were rounded up by a Tarahumaran guide for the long march back to the canyon rim. How glad I was not to have to leave so soon. I waved good-bye and watched as the last brightly colored daypack slipped around the bend. The pool in which seven or eight gringo tourists had been bobbing was now empty and the canyon was eerily quiet. Suddenly, I was alone— or so I thought.

I pitched my tent under the shade of a few junipers and began making—yes, a pot of cowboy coffee, when suddenly I heard someone say hello. I turned to find an anglo man about my age standing on the trail that led upriver. His name was Lee and he was a hobo. He and two other tramps were camped a little farther upriver. They were far enough away that we couldn't see or hear each other yet it was nice to have some company and talk with others who were also exploring the canyon. They showed me the location of the spring—pure, sweet mountain water dribbled from a fissure in solid rock and pooled into a granite bowl surrounded by a plush carpet of moss. They drank it straight, and so did I. (What? Bad water in Mexico? Ha! Don't believe it.) That evening they invited me over for a campfire. There was another man, Bruce, in his 40s, and Andrea, a beautiful young woman who was learning the hobo ropes from these two veterans. As we huddled around the fire, they recounted stories of train-hopping through Mexico and the US. They had come from California and were traveling exclusively—and illegally—on freight trains. They told me of narrow escapes from the Mexican police and the confusion of finding the right ride in crowded rail yards. They had taken the same Chihuahua al Pacífico train as I did, except they sat outside, clinging to a flat car at night, while rattling through cold mountains and over those same deep chasms. How thrilling it must have been to plunge through every one of those 86 tunnels, lying on your back in the open air. As we were talking, Bruce took out a harmonica and started playing softly. The campfire, the music, the talk of trains and old hobo legends, all melded together into a perfect harmony. Lee publishes a hobo-zine called *There's Something About a Train*, a sporadic, photo-copied collection of stories, poetry, and pictures about life on the rails. The following is an excerpt from a recent issue, a story titled, *On the Fly*, written by Mikal Jakubal:

> An eastbound approaches and we pack up quick! . . . Train slows up and rideable empty flatcars appear around the bend so we decide to have another try at it. Let's go! Ayr is on. I miss a couple cars, pack too heavy to run on the steep trackside gravel. Damn. Lee is on. Jeff, my "buddy," is on. Others are having a tougher time out of inexperience and caution—it's going too fast for them. Lacey is nearby and running. Grabs ladder but jumps too soon and she's thrown off balance. Her feet swing

scarily close to the wheels—closer than I think she realizes. She falls but gets up and tries again. Throw the pack on! She can't do it. I grab it and toss it on then toss my own pack own. Lacey runs along, holding on to the ladder at the end of the car. Keep running. Get your balance . . . Hop up! She's on. The bridge abutment comes up quick—gotta get on now or not at all! I move back toward the ladder, hand-over-hand along the flatcar's edge, while feet keep pace with the train. Reach the ladder . . . Grip tight. Check balance. And with one last big step I leave gravity and earthly concerns behind, nothing but wind underfoot . . .

They packed up and left early the next day. They wanted to camp farther downstream for their last night. I saw them again briefly the following day when they stopped to say good-bye on their way out of the canyon. It was the last I saw of them. ¡Adios, me amigos vagabundos!

Another visitor came by that day. He was about a foot high, the color of a golden retriever, shy, and of sad countenance. He wasn't interested in my caresses. His mind was on his belly. He took great interest in breakfast and watched me intently with those sad but hopeful eyes. From the first morsel he was mine, or rather, I was his. I called him Perroito, or little dog. He ate anything I gave him. Cold tortillas, hot oatmeal, and peanut butter all received his approval. Once it was made clear that meal time was over, he disappeared. At first, I thought this was cute. As the days wore on, I began to feel slighted. He was not holding up his part of the bargain. He would barely let me pet him, he refused to guard the camp or perform any other doggy duties for which he would have received my glowing admiration, deep respect, and extra chow. We could have taken walks together, played catch, or wrestled in the dirt. I had such high hopes. I wasn't asking for anything extraordinary. I didn't expect him to rescue me from icy waters, disarm *pistoleros*, or pull infants from burning houses. But he shared none of my enthusiasm. What good is having a dog around if he won't play with you? A shift in our relationship came about one day when he dragged my only pot into a ravine. Though I did not know the Spanish or Rarámuri word for "fetch," it didn't matter. He had no intention of returning the pot. I didn't need language, he knew what I meant. Later, as I cursed and scraped my way through sticker bushes to retrieve the wayward vessel, I decided to make a few changes. From now on I declared, you will eat off of rocks and I'm cutting your rations in half! All right, I was kidding about the rations, but I was serious about the rock part. The next day, in retaliation, he brought a buddy with him. This new dog looked similar except that he sported a thick leather collar through which bent and rusty nails had been pushed to give a spiked effect. Another dog soon appeared, also similar. None of them wanted to play or be petted. I was simply a gringo meal ticket and we all knew it. It seemed word was spreading fast among the canine canyon dwellers. Normally, I'd be happy to feed the little fellows, but since I was about 30 miles from the nearest grocery store and wasn't exactly loaded with extra supplies, I called everyone together for a meeting. I told them, with my own sad countenance, that the gravy train don't come by here no more. I was polite yet firm, resolute but sympathetic. Since they had all managed to keep from starving before my appearance in this canyon, I suggested that they revert to their old ways of making a living. I was only a flash in the pan, I explained, a temporary streak of good luck, predestined, as all good luck must, to vanish as suddenly as I came. Look around you, be thankful, I implored them, you're living in a remarkably beautiful place, free and unfettered. I went on for quite awhile even adding a few bars of *Born Free*, for dramatic effect, until finally they realized dinner would not be forthcoming. One by one they deserted camp. The next day a new group of tourists from Margarita's arrived at the hot springs. Accompanying the bathers were the three little *muchos* mooches, sitting on the rocks just out of petting reach, sporting their best starving-dog faces, begging bits of bologna sandwiches and cookies. And I wouldn't have traded one of them for a pack of well-coifed lap dogs.

From my journal: "Sitting in camp, contemplating the enormous vertical wall that forms the opposite side of this canyon. Near the top, jagged peaks and spires glow pink and green in the morning sun. Behind my left shoulder a tall sentinel rock abruptly juts 100 feet out of the trees and watches over the springs. Piñons and junipers cling precariously to the sides of the canyon while water seeps in trickles through solid rock and along clumps of verdant moss, relentlessly filling shallow teardrop shaped pools below. There is only five or six hours of direct sunlight here. The sun's arc crosses the narrow canyon at a sharp right angle. I am camped deep within a long gash in the Earth, cut and ground by the rocks and silt of the Río Recohuata."

The convergence of all these elements reminded me of a lovely passage from Thoreau's *A Week on the Concord and Merrimack Rivers*, perhaps the most exquisite book of travel ever written:

> The hardest material seemed to obey the same law with the most fluid, and so indeed in the long run it does. Trees were but rivers of sap and woody fibre, flowing from the atmosphere, and emptying into the earth by their trunks, as their roots flowed upward to the surface. And in the heavens there were rivers of stars, and milky ways, already beginning to gleam and ripple over our heads. There were rivers of rock on the surface of the earth, and rivers of ore in its bowels, and our thoughts flowed and circulated, and this portion of time was but the current hour.

Early one morning, a young boy stopped by. He was about 12 years old and wearing jeans, a flannel shirt, and the usual white cowboy-style hat. He also wore traditional Tarahumara sandals. The soles were fashioned from automobile tires and fastened with thin strips of leather tied elaborately above the ankles. Faustino lived in a small ranchero on the plateau above us. Like the other boy I had met, he tended his family's goats. He had been going to school three days a week but it seemed that he had now stopped. He told me he studied Spanish, Geography, and Mathematics. From the route he described, I estimated that he walked at least five miles in each direction to attend school. The first day I met him he was fetching water for the men working on the trail that led to the springs. He had several plastic soda bottles strung together so he could carry them over his shoulder. When we spoke it was in Spanish but in the days that followed, both he and I were often content to just sit together looking around. He laughed and said "no" when I asked him if he had a *novia*, or girlfriend. I asked him questions about the forests, the wildlife, and logging. I said that I had not seen many animals around. He told me that he had seen one wolf, heard a bear, but had not seen any big cats. He wrote some Rarámuri words for me in my notebook. He laughed again when I called myself a *chobochi*, which is the name, somewhat derogatory, that the Rarámuri have for *mestizos*, of which I apparently was now one. I don't think he had a word to distinguish a gringo from a *mestizo*. I felt like I had been promoted. I may have learned more from Faustino than any one I met here. He taught me how to sit quietly and listen and reminded me to savor small things. From *Tarahumara: Where Night is the Day of the Moon*, published in 1979:

> Our visits with Tarahumara suggested that they have great respect for themselves and for the rights of other individuals. They are shy and generally quiet, but ready with a smile or laugh. They are self-reliant in their mountain surroundings, able to take from the environment their most basic and essential foods and tools. They have invested heavily in one another: in the household, in the rancho or pueblo community, and in the circle of people on whom they can call for help and with whom they can share corn beer. Such investments work against the accumulation of material wealth, because they cannot prosper in the face of acquisitiveness. So a Tarahumara's wealth is primarily in himself and in the

numbers of family members and friends upon whom he can rely for help and companionship. To those of us who live in a world in which the primacy of the family and household has been in a state of siege, the sense of unity, warmth, and affection projected by a Tarahumara family—whether living in a cave or cabin—is astounding. It is also reassuring. Here in the mountains, at least, a very old-fashioned form of love has survived.

Looking through my notebook for some sage and witty scribblings I find only relentless notations on "soaking." My daily routine revolved around getting into and out of the hot springs. I would crawl out of my sleeping bag, make coffee, grab a book, and stumble to the pools where steam rose in wispy tufts into the cold morning air. Easing into the water my skin would tingle from the sudden heat. After perching my supplies atop the retaining wall, I slipped naked into the silky water, and floating, waited for the sun to climb the canyon wall, its first rays exploding like a star into a dark universe. Just minutes after the sun's appearance, the canyon was once again warm and I would climb out of the springs and shuffle back to camp for breakfast. I spent the early afternoons hiking the myriad trails connecting the hot springs with *rancheros* sprinkled throughout the canyons. Downstream the canyon widened, revealing broad sandy shores on either side. The river, its trickle recharged at the springs, flowed into wide, shallow pools and coursed over granite rocks, worn smooth as butter from eons of erosion. Discarded boulders and bent trees lined the shoreline, testaments to the river's rage in another season. Walking up a tributary stream, I found delicate orchids in bloom. They were nearly five inches long, white, with pink lips, and wildly protruding pistils and stamens. Like other epiphytic plants, they sprouted from crevices where branch met bole and a lonely seed had found a footing. The orchids' contrast with their rugged surroundings was startling. I couldn't walk more than 100 yards up this stream due to the jumble of boulders, some three times my height, yet here were these tender flowers proclaiming not only Nature's diversity, but an optimism unaffected—and even nurtured by—the raw, brutal elements. Each day I swam in the large pool of warm water where the springs emptied into the river. On days when tourists visited, I conducted my socializing. What an ideal compromise. I lived outside, swaddled in Nature's best, while civilization came to me. Humanity would stay two or three hours, have a swim, a little lunch, and then leave. Perfect. In the evenings, after dinner, I would once again head to springs. I watched the retreating sun flash its copper colors over the canyon walls. As the air chilled, I sank deeper into the warm water. Soon the first star appeared. One by one, the sky filled with its brilliant jewels. Miles from any town or village, deep within this narrow canyon, I was never more alive or ever less alone.

> *Who are you, oh mysterious star,*
> *so timid and sad among a thousand stars,*
> *that when gazing at your uncertain splendor*
> *I feel the beating of my heart disturbed?*
>
> *Perhaps Hope, with its golden dreams,*
> *caressed your pure youthful days,*
> *and your first light poured into the world*
> *glory and peace, and love, and happiness.*
>
> —José de Espronceda from *A una estrella* (To a Star).

One morning I discovered a woman doing her laundry in a rivulet of warm water near my camp. With her was a young girl about 10 years old. The girl, Maria-Louisa, had a bright smile and happy air about her. Her almond eyes and broad nose made me think of the Paleo-Indians who first settled here from the Asian continent 50,000 years ago. Her eyes were like windows on an ancient civilization—not dead and vanished, not merely scratched with charcoals on a cave wall, but alive—living, breathing, loving, crying eyes that transported me back to our common beginnings. Maria-Louisa holds not only our connection to the past but our link to the future. She is the seed, saved for a thousand generations, of our humanity. There are few indigenous communites left in the world and they are all in great danger. They are threatened from unbridled resource extraction and exploitation, from the by-products of a dominant industrial, over-consumptive civilization. Sadly, even Maria-Louisa's 10 year-old body may already contain a significant level of dioxin or mercury or lead. Hormone mimickers, from the pesticides and fertilizers used by the logging companies, may already be at work disrupting her ability to reproduce. It is happening to indigenous communites worldwide and in remote settlements a thousand miles from the nearest industrial center. We have released toxins into our world that are now infiltrating the genes and accumulating in the fatty tissues of every person and animal on Earth.

All of these cheerful thoughts went through my mind as I sat in the dirt sharing cookies with Maria-Louisa. Despite these problems, I realize I'm lucky to live in a time when I can still visit with her and her family in the solitude of this isolated canyon. Lucky, that we can share even these few minutes together despite the cultural gulf between us. I was straddling the cusp between a rich tradition and an impoverished future. Those eyes that stirred my imagination that morning may be missing from this canyon in a generation. Maria-Louisa let me take her picture. It may have been the most important photograph of my trip.

Like her brother Faustino, she seemed content to just sit and look at me. She watched me cook on my camp stove and write in my notebook. I gave her a tour of my tent and showed her my sleeping bag and other items I thought she might be curious about. Maria-Louisa wore a traditional long skirt and bandanna. She also wore a typical girl's department store shirt. She, like the other Tarahumara who live close to *mestizo* populations, are not purists. If something is useful they utilize it. It is this flexibility that has enabled them to survive the onslaughts of Spaniards, missionaries, miners, loggers, and now tourists. Anthropologists have long predicted the demise of their culture, yet the

Tarahumara have successfully adapted. I believe they will survive whatever western civilization throws at them. As our society moves further toward genetically engineered food, environments, and people, and as the distance between Nature and our daily lives grows ever-wider, I am hopeful that the Tarahumara will continue their delicate existence, like orchids among the rocks.

I enlisted Faustino's help in climbing out of the canyon. In addition to his fee, I gave him my tuna can candle given to me by the "wild man" back on Baja, my lucky quarter, and some nylon cord for tying up his water bottles. Following us all the way to the rim was Perroito! He had returned alone a few days before and I had resumed our previous arrangement. Also, I found that many of the day trippers discarded portions of their lunch in a garbage barrel near the trail to the springs. Each day, after the tourists left, I dumpster-dived for him, retrieving bruised bananas, bits of ham and cheese sandwiches, and other assorted, unidentified foods which he snapped up without pause. I also occasionally found a few choice nuggets, like bananas and apples, for myself. Perroito's friend, the one with the spiked collar, turned out to be Faustino's dog, and he also accompanied us. I think his name was Curly. Faustino and I had a good laugh about the homemade "spiked" collar. The third dog's whereabouts remained a mystery. We reached the top two heart-pounding hours later. Luckily, a van was waiting for a Swiss couple that had hiked to the springs (I learned later that they were on an around-the-world bicycle trip). I arranged for a ride back to town with the driver and just had to wait a few hours for the return of the hikers. I made photos, did some exploring, and finally found a spot in the shade and took a long nap under the pines. I also had a chance to sit quietly and absorb the dramatic landscape of these endless canyons and forested plateaus. Though I had just spent five days camping in the canyon, I felt as if I had not really seen it, that I had left it mostly unexplored. As if to confirm my suspicion, while we were waiting, the driver (after his nap) took up a rock, held it in his hand and picked a golden sliver.

"Mineral," he declared. Then pointing into the distance said, "Barranca del Cobre." Yes, I agreed. It really is the Copper Canyon.

Back at Margarita's, I threw my pack into a bunk, showered, and went for a hearty lunch of *huevos rancheros* at Gaby's Loncheria. Lunch at Gaby's was like eating in her kitchen, in fact, it was her kitchen. When the scene at Margarita's was too much, I would escape to the cozy atmosphere at Gaby's. It was a small place operated from the front room of her compact house. The entrance was up a concrete stair and through a heavy wooden door facing the main street. The first time I went there, I thought I had mistakenly walked into a private house. Standing at the counter between the tables and the stove, you could peer into her tiny bedroom off to the side. She always had pot of real coffee brewing despite the ominous jars of Néscafe strewn about. There were tables of odd sizes all covered in sticky plastic tablecloths. The walls were painted a thick yellow and adorned with fake flowers and amateur paintings. Gaby was in her early fifties— plump, cheerful, and a great cook. There was always at least one member of her family, or a friend, sitting with a snack, keeping her company while she cooked. Kids on their way home from school stopped in, as did young mothers with their babies. Old men read the papers over their afternoon sweet and coffee. After each excursion I stopped in to eat and tell Gaby about where I had been and the people I had met. I sat by the window and scribbled in my notebook, listening to the cadence of quiet conversations. In some small way, I felt that I was becoming part of this community. I came to know a man who kept horses and as I walked down the main road he would sometimes pass by, give me a broad smile and wave from atop his horse, and yell out, "¡Hola Guillermo!" Buenos dias, Norberto, I would reply and walk on. The sense of the familiar crept into my daily life in Creel. I was learning a little Rarámuri and my Spanish was rapidly improving. I spent time sitting in the square, patronized the local library, and read the newspapers. I knew what time of day to hit the bakery and which *tienda* had the freshest vegetables. My inculcation was complete when I began grumbling about all those damn tourists.

A few days of hot showers and socializing at Margarita's and I was ready to begin a journey to the remote, tropical village of Batopilas—6000 feet deep in the heart of Tarahumara country. Tiny Batopilas is the end of the road—a heart-in-your throat 50 miles of hairpin turns, narrow switch-backs, blind curves, and steep 3000 foot drops where the idea of guardrails has yet to take hold of the imagination-kind of road. And I hardly gave a thought to a young Canadian's warning about his friends that were roused from sleep at gun point while camped in scenic Batopilas.

Chapter 10

> *"Whoever has not felt the danger of our times palpitating under his hand, has not really penetrated to the vitals of destiny, he has merely pricked its surface."*
>
> —José Ortega y Gasset

The next morning, 14 people boarded an 11-passenger van for the grueling seven-hour ride to Batopilas. Scroungy backpacker types from Margarita's joined pairs of neatly dressed white-hairs from the fancy hotel in town. I remember one man in particular. He, like some of us, had apparently read about the roller-coaster aspect of the ride we were about to take and had insisted on sitting near the double-door in the middle, facilitating, in theory, a quick escape. Someone had beat him to the front passenger seat, an injustice for which he was visibly perturbed. He turned pale once we started down the most exciting parts of the road. His white knuckles formed a vise-grip around the door handle. My guess was that he was a hog farmer from Iowa and to him anything higher that a cow pie was considered steep. His apprehension, coupled with an elitist attitude, did not go unnoticed by us. We backpackers had been seated, our backpacks piled around us, in the distant nether regions in the back of the van. In this micro-Caste system, it was obvious that we were the most unlikely to escape should our overburdened vehicle suddenly leave the road for an unscheduled flight into the canyons. The talk soon turned to the physics of disaster. We loudly debated the odds of survival, agreeing that the lucky ones would be killed instantly. *A little shifting in his seat.* There was great speculation regarding which side the van might land on, or more accurately, come to rest on. Obviously, if it landed on the side with the double-door, there would be no getting out. *Grip tightens.* Of course, someone added, doors were unlikely to work after the impact of falling 3000 feet. Then another gleefully noted that the van would by then have turned into a raging fireball. *Turns and defiantly glares at us.*

And all the time we are plunging further down this narrow dirt road, inching around blind, hair-pin turns. The view was spectacular. There was nothing between us and the heart-stopping abyss. We paused a few times for pee breaks, leg stretching, and plenty of ooohing and ahhhing. From here we could see the famous Camino Real, a dirt path that is still used by the Tarahumara for travel into and out of the canyon. This is the deepest of all the canyons in the Sierra Madre's Copper Canyon country. Batopilas is a former silver mining town, brought to life by Alexander Shepherd, an American entrepreneur, at the end of the 19th century. He was the last Governor of Washington, DC-removed from office on corruption charges. Though a crook, his efforts to modernize DC succeeded in preventing the nation's capital from moving to St. Louis. In Batopilas, he built an extravagant *hacienda* and imported his broad consumerism and bulky opulence down the narrow Camino Real. Furnishings, mining equipment, and even a piano came down the mountain on the backs of the Tarahumara and their burros.

The following detail on Shepherd and his Batopilas mining operation comes from the Moon *Northern Mexico Handbook*:

> . . . and between 1880 and 1906 approximately 20 million ounces of silver were extracted from the company mines. At the 1893 Chicago World's Fair, silver ore from his mines took first place in the competition with a solid

silver mass of 380 pounds.... Shepherd's company cast the processed silver into bars weighing 30 kilograms each, then loaded them two per mule into the monthly bullion trains that transported at least 50 and often 100-200 silver bars on the backs of 30-100 mules to the Banco Minero in Chihuahua. Pancho Villa once stole $38,000 in silver bars from one of the company's mule trains...

And while all this history is interesting, it pales before the geological splendor now unfolding in front of us. We leave one steep-sided canyon, round a bend, and find another, even deeper. Golden slabs of rock tower above us and I'm reminded why this is called the Copper Canyon. Silver and gold may have lurked in rich veins below the surface, but the massive walls of igneous rock have weathered the miners' pick, repelled the entrepreneurs' greed, and supported the natives' dusty feet. We inch around yet another hair-pin turn, the rear wheel spins a rocky rubble into the canyon, and I realize that I am already rich, without ever having to stake a claim or bully an animal.

White-hair's condition worsened as the angle of our descent increased. At one point, a car coming too fast the opposite way (the event which we all dreaded!) tried to pass us on a turn. The other car was on the outside, and as the driver recklessly attempted to maneuver around us, his passenger-side front wheel went off the road. He came to a sudden, breathless stop. Everyone gasped. His tire now dangled above the void. No one moved. I thought White-hair was going to jump, if not out of his skin, at least out of the van. Our eyes were especially drawn to the car's passenger. He was sitting calmly, a little lower than the driver, glancing out his window into a drop which might have taken quite a few minutes for him to reach the bottom. Slowly, the car was able to back up and regain the road. We all cheered and the driver waved as he sped off, seemingly unrepentant despite his close encounter. To us, it was a rude reminder that this was for real. Farther down the road we hit a bump and a piece of the van fell off. The driver stopped, got out and looked around but found nothing. We all joined White-hair in a moment of silence, praying that the stray part was not a piece of the brakes.

At the end of our descent we crossed a rickety steel bridge over the rushing Rio Batopilas, and rumbled down the cobblestones of Batopilas' only street. What had been portrayed in guide books as a tropical paradise nestled deep in the canyon appeared at first glance to be a poverty-stricken, dilapidated, and charmless village. About seven hours after we had first began, we came to a stop near the town square. White-hair stumbled out of the van, shaking the cramp from his hand and mumbling something about hiring a helicopter for the return trip. I split a room with a young guy from Belgium at the modest Hotel Batopilas. Sebastian and I each paid $4 a night. Our room featured a splendid view across the street of the fanciest hotel in town, available only to guests who have plunked down thousands of dollars for a multi-day package deal. It was formerly the home of a wealthy Mexican family but has since fallen into the hands of an American tour operator. The Hotel Batopilas was economical and possessed a number of endearing charms and shortcomings. The lack of hot water and lumpy beds were to be expected. The phantom employees and scarcity of amenities kept the price down and we were grateful for any such deficiencies. But where was the toilet seat? Perhaps, when you live 6,000 feet in the bottom of a remote canyon, having an indoor toilet is considered high living; a toilet seat would be courting decadence. I wondered if the fancy hotel across the street had toilet seats and Sebastian and I briefly contemplated a late-night reconnaissance mission. We eventually resigned to accept character over comfort. But our naked toilet was an apt symbol for the growth of luxury tourism here. Once again from the report, *The Forest Industry in the Sierra Madre of Chihuahua: Social, Economic, and Ecological Impacts:*

> The Copper Canyon Tourism Project has been the State's grand project for the past two administrations . . . the

project has received strong support from the federal government, as well as resources channeled through federal institutions, private banks, and the Inter-American Development Bank (BID). Tourism, however, has generated serious problems for local inhabitants because the concept of tourism promoted by public institutions and the private sector—even though eco-tourism and adventure tourism is always mentioned—is based on five-star hotels. Under this concept, tourism requires a backdrop of folklore, land, water, and picturesque landscapes, putting pressure on and causing conflict among the local inhabitants who own the land. They may well be pushed aside in favor of private investors who plan to build huge hotels with toilets that use six gallons of water with every flush in a place where this vital liquid is scarce. Despite the possible harm to the indigenous community, no environmental impact study was undertaken prior to the launch of the tourism project, nor were studies conducted to determine how to transport water to the hotels.

Creel, the epicenter of all this tourism, has its own plumbing problems. From the same report:

> Zoning helped spur the real estate business around Creel. Now, its chaotic urban development has created numerous problems for the town's residents. Foremost on the list is the scarcity of water, a detail that government officials seem to have overlooked. Current tourism proposals for the Creel Ejido lack environmental impact studies for water consumption. Another problem is the city's handling of wastes. Currently, Creel channels raw sewage into the river, and the amount of solid municipal waste has outstripped the town's ability to deal with it. Furthermore, there is no way to adequately confine the garbage, nor are there any proposed projects to recycle it.

When I arrived in the Sierra Madre during winter of 2000, the Tarahumara were struggling through the fourth year of a severe drought. Crops had failed, emergency wells were being drilled, and the entire agricultural system, so dependent on natural water cycles and a healthy forest ecosystem, was in distress. Yet the tourists descended like locusts in slick chartered buses with blackout windows, cars, trains, and RVs. One morning, sitting in the square in Creel, the train pulled through town hauling dozens of RVs on flatbed cars. Gringos were shipping their motor homes to the US border while enjoying the scenery of the Copper Canyon rail line. Unfortunately, their 50-foot Winnebagos passed through some of the poorest and most desperate villages. The same people all this tourism was supposed to benefit could only watch the wealth go clicking and clacking past them. Tarahumaran women, displaying their woven baskets and cloth dolls, stared up from their dusty squats at the parade of plenty piercing the heart of their homeland.

In Creel, rich tourists stayed in expensive hotels and strolled the streets with an air of superiority. Perhaps they bought a trinket or two from Tarahumaran women and children on the street, remarking later over cocktails how sad the "Indians" look. But they would not sit in the dust with them. They would leave here without learning a single Rarámuri word or the name of one important plant or bird. The Tarahumara were merely a backdrop. A colorful, authentic movie set through which they, the stars, would parade, collecting snapshots and mementos. Luckily, their eyes were still filled with glossy brochure images and so the contemptuous stares were hardly noticed. The cultures clashed even more dramatically in Batopilas. We had taken one hell of a road to get here. And now that we were here, I realized that we knew nothing about these people and maybe even less about ourselves.

"The indigenous struggle in Mexico is a dream which not only is dreamed by the morning that will include

> *the color of the earth; also, and above all,*
> *it is a dream that struggles to hurry the awakening of*
> *that morning."*
>
> —Subcomandante Marcos,
> from a speech in Mexico City on March 12, 2001.

Sebastian, who was pining for his girlfriend in Costa Rica, rejoined the van the next morning for the return trip to Margarita's. He had decided to continue south through Mexico for a hastily arranged rendezvous. I was sitting on a bench in front of the hotel when the van left. I waved as they passed, and smiled when I saw old White-hair in the front seat looking unsettled. Now I would have to wait three days for the local bus to take me back to Creel. I went for breakfast in a small cafe off the main road. Like Gaby's, it was operated from the kitchen of a private home.

From my journal: "The owner's little girl is sitting at my table and playing with her pancake. Now she's singing to it. She won't look directly at me but she is acutely aware of my presence. We are in a small bright room with wooden doors and black iron gates that open on to the street. There are long tables surrounded by shiny aqua-green walls. Sounds of sweeping in the alley are mixing with the girl's singing and a rooster is crowing somewhere. A man just came in with a live chicken under his arm. I think he was trying to sell it. The woman told him to come back later."

The hotel's sunny courtyard contained chairs and tables, a trellis with thickly woven strands of red and purple bougainvillea. Prickly pears, flowers, and herbs in pots and coffee cans sat on the red-clay tile floor lining the perimeter. Batopilas did without electricity except for two hours in the morning and two hours in the evening. For those few evening hours, the town jumped to life. People turned off their flashlights and drifted out of the shadows. Vendors appeared with wagons, bright with garish lights, and sold fried snacks and sugary sweets. A street lamp on the square brought everyone together like moths while the basketball games continued without regard.

I began provisioning for my camping excursion into the canyon. While I was loading my pack, the hotel's owner asked me where I was going. I told her that I wanted to take the road out of town to the village of Satevó, about four miles away and do some camping for a few days. "Oh," she frowned. "*Muy peligroso.*" It was very dangerous she said because of the many drunks and guns. I figured it was just a clever ploy to keep my business.

Meanwhile, the Mexican Army had come to town. There were troop trucks, jeeps, and dozens of soldiers. Men clad in olive green T-shirts and cargo pants jogged in three's and four's through the square and down the crumbly streets. Special police also descended on us. They wore intimidating black uniforms and eyed everyone with suspicion, especially long-haired, backpacking gringo types. Batopilas' location at the end of the road and the beginning of deep canyon country meant it was the key connection point for shipping marijuana and cocaine north to Chihuahua and on to the US. It is widely accepted that these soldiers play an intricate part in the drug trade. "Sweeps" like the one I witnessed were thought to be mostly for show.

The next day I checked out of the hotel and began walking south toward Satevó. While crossing the square I was stopped by a tall, good-looking army officer. His name was also Guillermo. He was an army doctor stationed temporarily in Batopilas. He was eager to talk. His English was good and I sensed that he wanted an opportunity to practice. We spoke for nearly an hour while soldiers came and went through the square and troop trucks rattled by, providing a sinister subtext to our conversation. I recounted my bout with dysentery and he offered some medical advise. We never discussed the subject of drugs or arms or the reason for all the soldiers. Whenever I tried to bring it up he dismissed the presence of the soldiers as "routine." As we shook hands and said good-bye, he said in a confidential tone, "Don't forget Guillermo, you have a friend here." If that remark was meant to reassure me, it didn't. Did he think I was going to need a friend? I walked through the "occupation" trying to look innocent and repeating his name and rank over and over, trying to memorize it. But I couldn't get out of town that easily. Just as the road veered to the right, about to follow the river, I saw an Anglo man on a horse with several burros laden with packs and supplies. He was a gringo guide getting ready to take some wealthy tourists on a multi-day canyon trek. Grizzled and dusty, he looked like he had been born by the side of the trail, weaned on nopal juice. "Where ya heading?" I told him I was going to camp near Satevó. He frowned. "I don't know how safe that is." Really, a lot of trouble there? "Well, that's just it, you don't know if it's bad till somebody gets killed." He added that not too many people choose to stay overnight there. His skeptical "good-luck" leapt onto my growing pile of ominous warnings about this camping trip. All I wanted was to find a pleasant place to camp and have a look around. I thought this area would present good opportunities to meet or observe the more orthodox Tarahumarans, those who have put some distance between themselves and western development. Also, the tropical climate of the canyon was a nice change from the chilly weather in Creel. I left town on the dirt road heading toward Satevó feeling like I was walking back in time to the Old West. Unfortunately, I was a New East kind of guy and had left my six-shooter back at the condo.

> *I go along dreaming roads*
> *of the twilight, golden hills,*
> *green pines,*
> *dust-laden oaks! . . .*
> *Where can this road lead?*
> *I go along singing, a traveler*
> *along the trail . . .*
> *-Night is falling now-*
>
> —Antonio Machado from the poem,
> *I Go Along Dreaming Roads.*

The road left town level with the river then gradually rose

higher above it. When I estimated that I was about half-way to Satevó, or about two miles outside of Batopilas, I started looking for a riverbank campsite. By camping midway I hoped to minimize the danger from either town. I slid my pack down a steep embankment then followed it squatting on my heels. I found a sandy spot behind a massive boulder which hid my camp from the roadway. Only two cars had passed me on my hike but I felt safer in stealth mode. To preserve my low profile, I chose not to pitch the tent but to take my chances with the mosquitoes. Despite all the dire warnings, I spent a pleasant afternoon exploring the river. There were large, deep pools interspersed with wide sand bars and gravely beds that rose in long narrow strips just above the water. On the surrounding hillsides, a man was herding his goats along a web of thread-like trails winding up and down the steep hills. The goats would descend to the river, wander a short way, then head back up the rocky incline. They were accompanied by a black dog who followed them relentlessly up and down. At one point he crossed the river, saw me, and froze. I reached for my cookies in case he was a bad hombre. But he turned and made a beeline back to the opposite shore, swimming against the swift current part of the way.

Down river, I saw a man and a small girl fishing with nets. The two stood on either side of a small streamlet stretching their home-made lattice-work between the narrows, trapping the fish on their journey downstream to the Pacific. Upriver, two men were fishing with bows and arrows. They were poised motionless above the water on rocks jutting into deep pools, watching for the silvery glint beneath the surface. Gradually the sense of wariness deserted me, replaced by a feeling of well-being. I was witnessing, hopefully unobtrusively, a simple and ancient way of life. Fishing for sustenance, not sport.

Back at my sandy nook in the lee of the boulder, I was writing in my notebook when I noticed a young boy about nine years old walking up to me. I waved him over and offered him some cookies. His little fingers stretched as if made of rubber and gathered up quite a few. He noted my surprise and said that he was bringing some home for his nine siblings. He had a pail of river mussels pried from the river bed. He said he was out fishing with his father and sister. He had noticed me writing and told me proudly that he too, could write. Before he left he asked me, "*Dulce?*" Dulce means "sweet" and is the word children use for candy and other treats. No, I answered, I don't have any. He looked at me again, "*Dulce?*" No, I'm sorry, I repeated. Finally, he could stand it no longer and in his frustration, pointed at my hat, exclaiming, "*¡Dulce¡ ¡Dulce!*" I took off my hat and we both laughed. There, stuck in the band, was a lollipop Gaby had given me one day after lunch. I had placed it there for decoration. I handed him his prize, he thanked me and hurried off to his *ranchero*.

From my journal: "Thinking about Adriano and the lollipop. It's absence will lighten the load for tomorrow's hike. Just saw a great blue heron flying down river. It's now perched atop a hoodoo high above the opposite shore. A hawk is circling and a hummingbird with a reddish bill and iridescent green breast has just landed on a branch a few feet away. This has been the "place of hummingbirds." I have seen so many today. And I have never seen them sit still before. I don't think they do that in New Jersey. Maybe they are afraid of getting mugged."

Shortly before dusk, Adriano's father and sister stopped by my camp on their way home. I offered cookies and he showed me his mess of fish. About two dozen, each no more than six inches long, hung like gold and silver bars from a string. The father, friendly and cheerful, seemed satisfied with his day's work. The girl was shy, wore a traditional long colorful dress and bandanna and resembled her brother. He showed me a good spot to collect water and assured me that I would be safe camping there. They finished their cookies and we shook hands all around. Father and daughter left me alone on the river bank as darkness slipped into the canyon and the day of the night began with an eerie silence.

As evening descended I spread my sleeping bag over the soft sand, positioning myself behind the boulder and in front of a thick stand of thorn brush. With such a pleasant afternoon behind me, I now relaxed and looked forward to the new stars and sounds of my first night in the canyon. I was lying in my bag still awake when I heard a rumbling in the distance. I soon realized it was a truck coming from the direction of Batopilas. I could see the trace of its headlights cutting through the trees as it came near. My first thought was that I was so completely sheltered from sight, I had no reason for alarm. But as the truck drew closer I realized I was in trouble. It stopped about a quarter of a mile away. I listened for the sounds of soldiers crunching gravel. I strained to see if black silhouettes were advancing toward my hiding spot. But the truck began moving slowly again. As it came toward me, a cold white light ripped the dark curtain of cover. They were aiming a spotlight on the river. I panicked. I pulled myself, still in the sleeping bag, even closer to the boulder and gathered up my supplies. I grabbed my supper pot and spoon, fearing they would betray me. I threw every loose piece of equipment, including my pack, down into the sand. I froze as the truck rumbled toward me. I could hear voices now. The light crept up the riverbank, jumped to the other side, then bounced back again. The truck stopped on the road directly above me. They were no more than 50 feet away. I was certain I had been spotted. I heard the sounds of soldiers disembarking. The oval light turned the dark brush behind me to daylight. I dared not move. The light began probing farther upstream. The truck continued a little way, then stopped again. Finally, they rounded the bend and disappeared into the night.

    I felt confident that they weren't looking for me. But who were they looking for? Perhaps it was better to be found by the army. Clearly, I was in a lose-lose situation. I knew that if the army found me, they'd be asking questions for a week—if the other guys found me, they might not ask any questions at all. I made a mental note to avoid camping in the midst of drug wars in the future. *The Forest Industry . . .* report also sheds some light on the current "war on drugs" here and its effects on the Tarahumara:

> The cultivation of marijuana and opium poppy began to

spread to specific areas of the Sierra about twenty years ago. Some farmers began to cultivate marijuana and opium poppy in order to supplement their income. Now they have become major cash crops, and this has produced ominous social, economic, and political consequences for the region. Even though the cultivation of these plants is punishable by law, thousands of farmers who are disenfranchised from legal economic activities are willing to take the risk because it provides them with temporary and relatively well paid work. The cultivation of marijuana and poppy probably has ecological impacts as well, due to the chemical substances used in its cultivation and those used to eradicate the plants. No studies have yet been conducted on this topic, despite reported increases in certain types of cancer in the areas where these crops are grown. The official response to the cultivation and commercialization of these crops is the war on drugs. Promoted by the United States, the Mexican Government has used this campaign to militarize the Sierra Tarahumara and other parts of the Republic. This has given rise to numerous human rights violations in addition to the violation of constitutional guarantees of the inhabitants of the Sierra. There has also been a dramatic rise in drug consumption and in violence within the communities themselves.

I briefly thought about heading back to the hotel but realized that would be foolish. I also thought about scrambling to the road and surrendering but dismissed that idea as well. I had just about resolved that the worst was over when I once again heard the rumbling of a truck. Now the searchlight was reaching upriver and at one point, because of the angle at the bend in the road, it landed two feet from the bottom of my sleeping bag. But the truck rolled on. Somehow I even managed to steal some sleep. I bolted straight up in my bag several times during the night, half-awake, helplessly watching the intruding beam skip from bank to bank.

Morning broke clear and bright. I made oats and coffee and washed my face in a cool rill. I bid good-bye to my river camp and struggled up the same steep embankment I had merrily slid down the previous day. The morning air was crisp, the sun had not yet scaled the canyon walls. I turned my back on Batopilas and continued on the road to Satevó, glad to be moving once again. Glad to be alive.

The road wound downhill until it met the village of Satevó nestled amid a ring of green and surrounded by vermilion canyon walls glowing in the morning light. A swinging suspension bridge crossed high over the river and in the distance I could see the famed "lost cathedral" of Satevó. Visitors to Satevó come to see the old mission church though it was never either lost or a cathedral. I was less interested in the mission than in the people. If Batopilas is considered the end of the road, what about Satevó—four miles past the end of the road? Who were these people that lived so far from the civilization I know? I was about to find out.

I stopped at small, run-down house to ask a woman directions to the tienda in the village. She asked me what I wanted and I said something cool to drink. She disappeared into the house and emerged with a chilly bottle of soda for which she charged me 15 pesos. We sat on the back porch talking about the beauty of Satevó and its one hundred *mestizo* inhabitants. I told her that I had seen many army trucks the night before. She just smiled. Like the army doctor, she didn't want to talk about it with me. Children began dribbling into the yard and onto chairs all around me. It was Sunday and everyone was at home. Word spread fast: there was a gringo on the porch. The fact that I was dusty, unshaven, long-haired, and sporting a bandanna depicting Our Lady of Guadalupe, perhaps added to the mystery. The young boys took turns trying to hoist my pack. One small girl about six years old, very pretty, a Latina Natalie Wood—kept staring at me. She wouldn't say a word. She just stood there, clutching the pant leg of her older sister and staring. Another girl, about 17, tall and thin with fiery black eyes and long flowing hair the color of midnight, came out to the porch from the house. She was stunningly beautiful and I was about to suggest we go over to the old mission and get hitched. To possibly prevent an early death from lead poisoning, I asked her if she had a boyfriend. She told me she was too young for boys. I decided against the marriage, vowing instead, to return in a year or two with a proper proposal. Soon, the back porch was filled with about 10 kids. I took my dictionary and phrasebook from my pack and passed them around. We spent the next hour trading words and laughing at our gnarled pronunciations. The phrasebook had plenty of juicy bits to interest young teenagers. It was filled with slang and intimate words for lovers—dangerous, delicious words. They giggled, laughed, and teased each other. I've never seen kids have so much fun with a book before.

The young woman told me she attended school in Batopilas, walking the 8-mile round trip each day. There was an elementary school in Satevó housed in a small building with about 35 kids enrolled. They asked me where I was from. The idea that I had come all the way from New Jersey seemed to be more important, more unbelievable, than any adventure I could relate. Most of these kids had never been out of the canyon. They had no television, no movies, no malls. Sleepy Creel was their sole exposure to "city" living. Chihuahua, where even few of the adults had visited, was a world as far away and exotic as Hollywood, Moscow, or Hoboken. Though they possessed the beauty and simplicity that many in the world long for, indeed, get sick and die from the lack of, they also possessed a gripping poverty, partially the result of the extended drought. Cases of nutritional supplement were stacked six-feet high on that humble porch, provided by the government to ease the effects of malnutrition. The unbridled logging has caused erosion, reducing rainwater filtration and affecting the quantity and quality of the water in rivers, streams, and springs. As the last of the old ones fall to the loggers' blade and the capitalists' greed, abundant mountain water is replaced with cans of chemical supplements, and progress is declared throughout the land.

That afternoon I started back down the dusty road to Batopilas. I decided not to camp another night—I couldn't spare the sleep. I took my old room at the hotel and declared my camping trip a failure. I wanted out of Batopilas. I learned that the next bus would leave at the fresh morning hour of 5 a.m. I found myself again sorely missing one of those watches with the alarm buzzer. I strolled through Batopilas dodging soldiers during the two evening hours of electricity. I took a cold shower and went to bed early. Later, I awoke in a panic thinking I had missed the bus. I threw on my boots and pants and wandered unkempt and half-asleep down the street looking for a clock. Batopilas was cloaked in darkness. I stumbled over cobbles and imagined stooped figures lurking in the dark crevices between crumbling buildings. There was only one light and it came from the doorway of the police station. I walked up to the opening, the lamp light spilled down the stairs and into my face. Three uniformed men sitting around a desk looked up and stared at me, unsure of the apparition. Excuse me, I said, in my most polite Spanish. Could you tell me what time it is? I need to catch the bus to Creel. Puzzled. Laughter. They pointed to the clock behind the desk. It was 10:30! I had slept two hours; a little early for the bus. As I turned and walked back to the hotel I could hear them imitating me and laughing. I am always ready to do my part in boosting the morale of law enforcement.

At 4:30 a.m. I stumbled once again over cobbles to the square. I joined a few old men clutching paper sacks and coarsely tied parcels. I had arrived in a van which I though too big for the skinny road into the canyon. I was shocked when a full-sized school bus pulled into the square. Could this giant vehicle negotiate those hair-pin turns? Impossible. But I learned once again that anything is possible in Mexico. ¡No problema! The solution was accomplished with a two-stage maneuver. First, the bus would position itself across the roadway, back up to the edge of the cliff and then lunge forward around the turn taking advantage of every centimeter of roadway. The sensation of this huge bus rolling backward toward that crumbly edge was horrifying. I imagined how it would appear in the press. Just another rural bus in some developing country toppling over a cliff. Not exactly news. Maybe an inch on the bottom of 37B. Maybe not. There would be no panel of pink-faced men, slamming their fists on the table demanding answers, demanding to know why yet more poor people are dying needlessly. Adding to my terror was that I was deep in the back of the bus, in that overhanging part beyond the rear wheels. So while those bald and dry-rotting tires may have been on semi-solid ground, we in the back were suspended over the yawning abyss. And I am White-hair.

Seven hours after squeezing through Batopilas' narrow lanes we arrived in Creel. Never did its dust-filled streets, drifting wood smoke, and wild burros look so good to me. For the fourth time in six weeks I took a bunk at Margaritas, had lunch at Gaby's, and sat in the sunny square reading last week's news. Home.

At Margarita's I met a couple from Canada. Liz and Pete and I spent a week camping at the "place of eagles," near the foot of a lazy waterfall. We pitched our tents on a sandy spit in the middle of the river. Liz was an artist and she spent her days painting the water-sculpted rocks and pools at the bottom of the falls. One afternoon, she and a small Tarahumara girl named Maria, sat together for hours by the river drawing and playing with paints and colors. Liz gave the girl all the pictures they had made together. Later that afternoon I found them scattered among the rocks-discarded. We guessed at the reasons, reminded of how little we understood. After a week of camping together I said good-bye to Liz and Pete and watched as their train slipped away to the south.

It was now the end of March and the beginning of spring on the east coast. After three months of wandering, I decided to start the long journey home. I said good-bye to all the cooks and staff at Margarita's. I had come to know many of them and found solace in their quiet and earnest manner: Angelina, Chapina, Lupe, Lolita, Novelia, Libratta. I stopped to say good-bye to Gaby. I shook hands with Norberto. I lugged my pack to the cramped bus terminal in Creel and boarded a bus bound for Chihuahua. I watched the broken rows of wooden shacks and concrete buildings fall behind as the bus chugged toward the great city, toward steel and glass and treeless landscapes far from these Mother Mountains and the peaceful, complex people who had treated me so kindly. ¡Buenos suarte, me amigos!

> *"The river calmly flows,*
> *Through shining banks, through lonely glen,*
> *Where the owl shrieks, though ne'er the cheer of men*
> *Has stirred its mute repose,*
> *Still if you should walk there,*
> *you would go there again."*
>
> —Channing

Epilogue

> "*Do not plan long journeys because whatever you believe in, you have already seen. When a thing is everywhere, then the only way to find it is not to travel but to love.*"
>
> —St. Augustine.

After spending so much of my time in the wild, Chihuahua could not shed its grime fast enough to interest me. The next day I traveled north to the border, answered "no" to the official when asked if I had bought anything. The treasure I carried could not be declared on the usual forms. I took a room at the Gardner Hotel in El Paso. It was clean and bright, shared a bath down the hall, and even had a color television. I spent a day at the downtown branch of the El Paso library, unable to absorb what I needed. I bought a clean T-shirt for traveling. I purchased a ticket for the East Coast and once again hopped the dog. Three days on a bus will dull your senses, blend the landscape into a whirring blur of fast food chains, empty lots, and boarded storefronts. Desolate Texas. Stricken Alabama. Wealthy Virginia. Necklaces of street lamps and car lights streamed past; unrelenting novas interrupting a fitful sleep. Missing: the wind.

I spoke with a man in Texarcana. He told me he had just met his son for the first time while they were both in jail. "I have to get out that way again," he said, not meaning it. "Who knows how many kids I have. Everybody was screwing everybody else. It was the 70s."

As our bus threaded its way up the coast, I could clearly see the vague green blush in the trees which meant spring. Soon I would be home, camped for the summer between the Appalachian Trail and the Delaware River. I would swim in that old friend and find inspiration under the hemlocks; renew my spirit in the lumbering shuffle of a black bear and her clumsy pups.

And I am reminded of another bus ride. It was months before; we were streaking through the cold desert at night from Ensenada to San Ignacio. The winter sun had cast its last light on a landscape of russets and golds, ochre and sienna. In the silence of that tweedy desert the "Hi" guy had asked me where I was from. New Jersey, I said, braced for anything. He nodded, "¡*Ah, muy verde!*" Yes, I smiled. Very green. Very green.

Rarámuri girls Olivia (left) and Maria-Louisa in the Sierra Madre.

Woman in church doorway in Creel.

Rarámuri woman in the Sierra Madre.

Boy with hoop in Batopilas.

NORTH TO LABRADOR!

Cycling Atlantic Canada

*". . . But can't you hear the wild? It's calling you.
Let us probe the silent places,
let us seek what luck betide us:
There's a whisper on the night wind, there's a star
agleam to guide us,
And the wild is calling, calling . . . let us go."*

—Robert W. Service

Chapter 1

"Give me the storm and tempest of thought and action, rather than the dead calm of ignorance and faith."

—Robert Ingersoll

I wobbled down my brother's driveway in Wethersfield, Conn., on a dreary May morning and began clawing my way up the East Coast with a cold, wet wind in my teeth.

Of course, in planning this trip, I had expected blustering winds rising off the cold Atlantic along the southern shore of Nova Scotia and along the exposed cliffs of Prince Edward Island. But that first exhausting week of steep hills and constant cold cast a doubt on my ability to cycle thousands of kilometres around Atlantic Canada this summer. How could I possibly pedal to the wilds of Newfoundland and Labrador if suburban Connecticut was already killing me?

But the dream of cycling the northern-most edge of North America has been with me for many years. Not because Atlantic Canada is a foreign land, but precisely the opposite: it is, like Mexico, my native soil. The mountains that ripple through Nova Scotia and rise again in Newfoundland are the same mountains, the Appalachians, that I have been tramping around in since I was a boy. The same 600-million-year-old collision between North America and Europe that created that string of mountains from Alabama to Maine continues here, from Cape Breton's dramatic coastline, then dipping under the Cabot Strait, and emerging again as the serrated ridges of Newfoundland's Long Range mountains.

And I can't think of a better way to see Atlantic Canada than by bicycle. I'll be traveling 60-80 kilometres per day along highways and backroads. Self-sufficient, I'll be carrying all the essentials for camping each night: a tent, sleeping bag, cook stove, repair kit, food and water. I'll be toting those 20 kilograms of gear in a small trailer attached to the bike. Cycling will allow me to travel slowly, savour landscapes and observe small details. Details like the red and white sign in the window of a remote rural village along the south shore that read simply: "No."

At first, I thought the occupants had grown tired of giving directions for Peggy's Cove to wayward tourists. Later, I learned that the sign was a message for the local milkman. It is reassuring in this age of technology that there are still milkmen (milkpersons?) making their rounds in the countryside, relying on placards instead of cell phones. That simple sign has already come to represent to me a life indicative of Atlantic Canada's rural and remote nature.

> *"Rise free from care before the dawn,*
> *and seek adventures."*
>
> —Henry David Thoreau

At 9 p.m., eight days after leaving my brother's house in Connecticut, I boarded the Scotia Prince in Portland, Me., for Yarmouth. At 9 a.m. the following morning, I emerged from the ferry into a brilliant light and nearly a week of splendid weather. After a delicious night's sleep and a chorus of birdsong in the morning, I put all thoughts of soggy, crowded New England behind and headed east along the southern shore of Nova Scotia.

From my journal: "The light here is similar to the high sierras of California or Mexico. The air is clear and crisp. Pools of blue sky contrast with the luxuriously green pine and pale paper birches. Back home, the lilacs are in bloom but here the leaves of the maples have not yet unfurled. I am finally here!"

In the sleepy village of Birchtown, I met descendants of the original black Loyalists, now working to preserve their heritage and document their history. The black Loyalists were former slaves from the southern United States who had gained their freedom by fighting for the British during the War of 1776. After the war, they were promised land and provisions in Nova Scotia and New Brunswick. But the land they were allotted was a barren, rocky soil, unsuitable for farming. To acquire needed supplies for the winter months, many Loyalists became indentured, and slaves once again. Many decided, as free subjects of the British Empire, to return to West Africa. Descendants of those Loyalists can now be traced to the war-torn West African nation of Sierra Leone. Birchtown was once the largest community of free African-descended people outside of Africa, with a population of about 1500.

Kim Farmer, a descendant of the black Loyalists and a volunteer at the society's office, told me the story of a young pregnant black woman who was hung after having been accused of stealing a nightgown from a white woman's clothesline. Kim shook her head in disbelief and said, "Can you believe it? It happened right here in Birchtown." The black Loyalists were promised freedom, land and provisions. For their service to the Crown, most of them received nothing at all.

During my first week in Nova Scotia, I hopped on and off the 103 and the coastal roads, dipping down to waterfront towns like Barrington, Shelburne and Lunenburg, then back to the highway. Despite the looks I receive when I say so, I liked the 103. I liked the huge expanse of unbroken forest. Lakes and bogs, thick with snags, teeming with bird life, appear unexpectedly, too insignificant or inaccessible for a spot on the tourist's map. It is a boggy, wild land and I have come to love coasting silently through it. Riding from Yarmouth to Halifax on this first leg of the trip I am surprised at the diversity of landscapes. One night I am camped on a white crescent beach, the next in a grassy meadow or dense pine forest.

My initial trepidation about completing this trip has vanished. My legs have grown stronger and the hills don't seem as daunting. Already, kindness has met me at every crossroads, from Eddy the Elf in Bridgewater, who built Santaville, a Christmas village, in his backyard and who dedicates himself to helping traumatized children, to Al at the Bike Barn in Lunenburg, whose capable hands turned my squeaking, chattering bicycle once again into a smooth, efficient machine. To the young cyclists in Liverpool who spent a half hour giving me directions to a safe haven for the night, to the RCMP who stopped in the middle of the 103 to ask if everything was all right as I was taking a break; to the retired couple from Alberta who invited this bedraggled-looking vagabond into their fancy RV for a cup of hot coffee on a dismally damp morning.

It is only now that I see the immense task I have set for myself this summer. The challenge, I realize, won't be the pedaling, the hills, or even the wind. The toughest part will be squeezing this enormous landscape and the generous spirit of the people who inhabit it, into these too few pages of ink and paper.

I left Halifax under a solemn blanket of lead gray clouds, churned by the whip of a chill wind. I landed in Dartmouth and struggled across four-lane highways through a maze of donut shops, McJunkfood joints, gas stations and shopping malls. I eventually found the coastal road and began my trek along the ragged edge of Nova Scotia's Eastern Shore. But Halifax would not recede so easily. During my stay at the hostel on Barrington Street I had met three young men about to embark on a 30-day Atlantic crossing in a steel-hulled replica of a Chinese junk. The men, from California, England and Halifax, did not have an hour's open ocean sailing experience among them (though they were joining three experienced crew and a seasoned Captain for the voyage.) They had come to the hostel to launch a last night of shore-side revelry with friends.

Nothing in all of Halifax's harbour-side exhibits, museums or boardwalks spoke as loudly of its sea-faring heritage as the anxious faces of those three young men as they answered questions about their undertaking. The hostel kitchen crackled with energy, piqued with a hint of fear, at the prospect of straddling an entire ocean on a thin skin of steel. I thought of those men, bound for the Irish coast, as I followed Route 7, rising and falling on asphalt waves, while they put their trust in the invisible highways of wind and tides.

Another journey began from Halifax that week. Michael, a law student from Rome, explained over a few pints in the local pub, that when he was six years old, he noticed the town of Yellowknife on a map of Canada. He remembers telling his mother that someday he would see what a place named Yellowknife looked like. Now, years later, he was on his way to the Northern Territories just to visit Yellowknife. With all the glasses that were raised, and all the salutes shouted, "To Yellowknife," that night, I have no doubt that Yellowknife now has an Italian lawyer in its midst—at least for a while.

In Musquodoboit, while filling my water bottles in a pizza shop, a woman asked me where I was heading. "Cape Breton," I told her, and we both laughed at the ridiculous prospect of traveling so far on a bicycle. "Oh, I have a sister up there who runs a grocery." She told me her sister's name and the name of the town. "Don't worry," I said, "I've got it all up here," tapping my thick skull. "I'll give her the message." I walked out of the store and promptly forgot our entire conversation. Three days out of Halifax the weather worsened. I spent a long day in my tent as thunderstorms paraded overhead.

From my journal: "Socked in by a cold wind and heavy rain. Have set up camp in a picnic park near Marie Joseph. The weather is perfect—perfectly suited to this wild coastline. Outside my tent, lichen-splattered pines, draped in moss, march down to the sea's edge, halting abruptly before thick mats of rusty-orange sea grape and jumbled mounds of cobbles and shale, the rocky remnants of four ice ages." Even on that bleak day, as I sat looking out at the fog-shrouded bay, a harbour seal lazily swam by. In that silent moment, the rain and mist seemed as accommodating as the most gentle summer breeze. I was learning, at last, to befriend the weather.

> "This is the forest primeval. The murmuring pines
> and the hemlocks,
> Bearded with moss, and in garments green,
> indistinct in the twilight,
> ... Loud from its rocky caverns,
> the deep-voiced neighboring ocean Speaks,
> and in accents disconsolate answers the wail of the
> forest."
>
> —Henry Wadsworth Longfellow,
> from *Evangeline: A Tale of Acadie*

Six days after leaving Halifax, the sun returned and I arrived at the Mabou River Hostel where I had the best pizza and hot showers in Nova Scotia. I spent my time resting and watching bald eagles fish on the estuary. Though the trails in the Mabou Highlands are renowned, the only hiking I did was to the Red Shoe pub for a few draughts and the Rising Waters bakery for warm, fat loaves of porridge bread. After two days, I wrenched myself from that cheery respite and the pleasant company of a remarkable young woman from Holland. We have a tentative plan to meet again in Newfoundland and, though I know it is unlikely that we will, I could not wish for a better companion with whom to explore those mysterious mountains of Gros Morne.

On the Cabot Trail, four kilometers from Cheticamp at the base of French Mountain, my bicycle began to emit a groaning complaint, as if it sensed the impending pedal-mashing I was about to inflict upon it. On the side of the road, I discovered that I had a broken rear spoke—a potentially dangerous situation. My choices were limited. I could return to Cheticamp and attempt to fix it, most likely making it worse. Or, I could continue on and hope to find a bike shop along the Cabot Trail, a doubtful prospect. Since pedaling across Nova Scotia had given me legs like Popeye,

I wanted to put them to good use. I decided to climb French Mountain. I wove the broken spoke between some others and taped it in place to prevent further damage. I adjusted the surrounding spokes to reduce the wild wobbling, which was causing the wheel to rub against the brake pads, the source of the noise I had heard. I pedaled up French Mountain. I pedaled up MacKenzie Mountain. I pedaled up North Mountain, though barely faster than a walking pace. I zoomed down them all at 50 kph trying not to think of warped wheels and flying spokes.

But the highlands needed no drama from me. Did I say I knew these mountains? Maybe I do, in the way that we recognize the skeletal structure of something. But the true character and personality of a thing runs outward from there. The taiga forest, the snow banks in June, the moose and the whales, all conspired against my expectations of familiarity. I did feel at home in the Grand Anse Valley amid a green forest floor of maple saplings and Christmas ferns. But on the wind-beaten ridges, looking down at the Atlantic, I realized how little I know about mountains, or moose, or whales.

At the general store in North Cape I was given directions to the Sea Spray Cycle Centre in Smelt Brook where Dennis would repair my spoke, true my wheel and prod my imagination with his knowledge of the highlands in all its seasons. I nearly forgot, but at the last minute I asked the woman behind the counter if someone named Mavis worked there. "Yes," she said, a little surprised, "I'm Mavis."

"Mavis," I said smiling, "Your sister in Musquodoboit said to say hello!"

It is day 35 of my trip. I have pedaled almost 1500 kilometers since leaving Connecticut. I continue to be the victim of random acts of kindness each day. Now its off to the balmy breezes and palm-lined beaches of Newfoundland and Labrador!

Chapter 2

"It was a rock-hard land, and an ice-cold sea, and together they winnowed the human seed through generations of adversity until the survivors themselves partook of the primal strength of rock and ocean."

—Farley Mowatt, from *A Whale for the Killing*.

Early Sunday morning, preceded by its own throaty warnings, the ferry M/V Leif Ericson sliced through an opaque mist and landed its passengers, including a cargo of transfer trucks, cars, RVs, motorcycles—and one bicycle—on the black granite shores of the world's 16th largest island: Newfoundland!

The province, including mainland Labrador, is three times larger than Nova Scotia, New Brunswick, and PEI combined. Even traveling by car, the distances between towns are daunting. I had decided that of all the possibilities and directions of travel, I would pedal the western peninsula to Gros Morne National Park, a United Nations World Heritage Site, a distinction it shares with the pyramids of Egypt and the Great Barrier Reef of Australia. It's been said that Gros Morne is to geology what the Galapagos Islands are to biology. The reason: a 7 x 15 kilometer chunk of the Earth's mantle and ancient sea floor sits conspicuously in plain view: a rare window on the planet's early formation. The western peninsula is also home to the Long Range mountains, the dramatic, flat-topped extension of the Appalachian mountains.

Here also is the gateway to the southeast shore of Labrador—literally the end of the road in eastern North America.

I headed north on the Trans-Canada from the ferry terminal at Port aux Basque with a hefty supply of groceries. No one seemed able to tell me when I might find the next store. Corner Brook, the peninsula's largest town, was more than 300 kilometres away, a four-day ride that eventually took me eight days. This was the most desolate stretch of road I have yet encountered. I pedaled past innumerable ponds, rivers, lakes, and streams; past thick tangled strands of spruce and pine, tuckamore and muskeg. In the distance, the Long Range mountains began to appear, rising like great green velvet bulges on the horizon. The weather here is cooler, the wind sharper. It was not unusual to be rained out for an entire afternoon or morning. The hills are large and there are always too many. The wind blows at 35 kph from one direction or another every day. It has been a slow, steady grind northward.

I should have known better. When the old-timer at the café asked me about flat tires, I should have knocked wood, thrown salt over my shoulder, offered my thanks to Pneumaticus, the god of fully inflated tires. I should have been humble. But I waved away his question as if I was dismissing the possibility of ever having a flat tire. The penalty for my insouciance was as swift as it was inevitable. Barely three kms down the road my rear tire found an industrial-sized staple and began spitting out its every last molecule of air. Under a threatening sky, I removed the wheel. A gusty wind blew the bike over. It began to rain. It began to pour. It took three tries to finally patch the tube and still the best I could achieve was a slow leak. I now refuse to discuss tires, flats, or anything mechanical and instead, quickly change the subject.

On the fourth day from Port aux Basques I found an ideal campsite in a sandy cove nestled out of sight on a small pond. Nearby, spring water bubbled up into a deep pool. Someone had even built an outhouse in the woods. Mountains surrounded the pond on nearly every side. Paradise found! My only company for two days were a quartet of raucous crows and a few fish breaking the surface of the pond for meals. On Saturday, the locals rolled into Paradise. There were families in converted school buses, small campers, and trailers. Suddenly there was music: fiddle music; accordion music; Irish drinking songs and jigs. There were children splashing and screaming. Parents yelling. Snippets of shouted conversation echoed across the pond: "Who burnt the pork chops? Ok. That's it! We're going home! Whaaaa! You don't love me! No—I don't love your ass nor your Dad's! These pork chops aren't done. Who wants more crab?" By Sunday afternoon they were gone.

From my journal: "Quiet now. The crows have resumed their bickering. The last ghosts of mists are rising from the mountain. The wind has died, the black flies are back, and the pond is recovering its sheen. Tomorrow I leave for Gros Morne."

I spent my time in Gros Morne in the southern portion of the park, near the Tablelands, the geological formation largely responsible for the park's UNESCO designation. The Tablelands, lashed by wind, are barren, composed of peridotite rock on which nothing grows. But it is surrounded at its base by a palette of colors: the deep plum of the carnivorous pitcher plant; the violet and yellow of the blue flag; bright green lichens and yellow and purple wildflowers. And everywhere, the bleached white branches, stretching like bones across the rock, reminders of some distant season's struggle and death. I escaped the wind in a sheltered nook between boulders. Behind me rose the yellow ochre of the Earth's ancient mantle. In front, a green-cloaked mountain range. Lying below me mirroring the sky, was the miles-long Trout River Pond, an inland fjord long ago cut off from the sea by a rising land.

From my journal: "The serrated bevels of the Tableland's ridge tops are pocketed with snow. Rivulets of snowmelt are streaking the mountainsides with dark veins of icy water while water trickles from springs hidden in lush grottos. It is the end of June and the snow pack is still melting. The wind is blaring at 45 kph—swooping down between slabs of ancient seabed. I am totally alone though I have found moose, bear and coyote scat.

There is no sound but the wind cutting the rock and the occasional bird who sings a melancholy four-note song."

I am now camped in the village of Cow Head near Shallow Bay, a rare (for Newfoundland) white sand beach, fringed with dunes and grassy meadows filled with wildflowers. I have pitched my tent at the bottom of a grassy hollow behind a line of dunes, not far from the Bay of St. Lawrence. Though sheltered, the wind still sweeps in, rattles my tent, scatters my laundry and deposits its pinch of sand in my coffee. At night, I lie awake listening to the sound of moose munching grass just a few meters from my head. I have lingered here for a while, hoping to learn something of life in a small coastal fishing village. It has been years since the cod moratorium and Cow Head's population has fallen from nearly 1000 to less than 400. This village and the people who inhabit it are as endangered as the fish on which they once based their lives.

From my journal: "Day 53 of the trip. The idea of cycling to Labrador has thoroughly seduced me. Tomorrow, I head north again to St. Barbe and the ferry across the Strait of Belle Island to the desolate shores of Labrador. I am starting to think I may just make it."

> "From the top of a high rock I had a fine view of the
> most extensive and dreariest wilderness
> I have ever beheld.
> It chilled the heart to gaze on these barren lands
> of Labrador."
>
> —John James Audobon

Back in Connecticut, cold, tired and out of breath, I had stopped at a convenience store for coffee. The man behind the counter, large and pasty-looking, asked me the usual: "Where ya headin'?" I paused, then blurted out, "Labrador—if I'm lucky." He snorted and turned his back on me. He didn't like people messing with him. Labrador he knew, was a place you visited on the Nature channel. It was not a destination for wheezing, middle-aged hippies on bicycles.

I was thinking of that day when a voice came through the speakers from the bridge of the ferry M/S Apollo, announcing that we would soon be passing "whales in numbers" and a "large iceberg" off the starboard side. Fifty-four days and more than 3000 kilometers from Wethersfield, Conn., I arrived in Labrador a very lucky old hippie.

But before pedaling up the Great Northern Peninsula I first had to pull myself away from the village of Cow Head. I had arrived there for the annual lobster festival. Frankly, my only interest in lobsters is my wish that they may live long and happy lives. I was hoping for local music, home cooking, fresh veggies, and free camping. Sadly, the Cow Head annual lobster festival no longer exists. What remains is largely a marketing ploy on the part of the local restaurant/motel to sell over-priced lobster dinners to unsuspecting tourists. The one surviving remnant of its former festival glory is the ladies church supper. At this I was able to purchase a "salad plate" which consisted of potato salad, lettuce and tomato, cole slaw, and more potato salad. It was served with all the homemade bread and jams you could eat. I ate solemnly as giant lobsters, the color of sunburn, floated by on plates held by smiling, gray-haired church ladies. I tried to ignore the carnage and kept my head down grazing. But on the border of my paper placemat were the gruesome instructions for dismantling this mysterious creature. I ate my potato salad and read: "Open the body, crack it sideways Unhinge the back. Insert a fork into . . . ; the small claws are excellent, suck the meat out, etc. If those were the words to a rap song, it would be banned.

Cow Head's attraction for me was its people. I made many new friends there and felt at home almost immediately. Within an hour of my arrival, I was given generous time at the library's computer, names of people to interview, suggestions where to camp and told that the best water in town came from George Henry's well, its tap I would find on the side of his house. And no, George won't mind at all. Cow Head's location, sandwiched between the Long Range mountains and Shallow Bay on the Gulf of St. Lawrence, kept me surrounded by remarkable vistas, flowers, and wildlife. But like all the small coastal villages on this island, Cow Head is in danger of extinction. I spent most of my time talking with the local kids. None of them plan on returning here after university. Their predictions for Cow Head were the same: Ghost Town. Joan Payne, told me she recently watched a video of her Kindergarten graduation. "All of the boys said they were going to become fisherman," she said. "Now there's not one of them who says he can't wait to get out of here."

There is nothing to do because the cod are gone. The government limits the catch, limits the jobs. The cod fishery collapsed in 1992. The fisherman here blame the draggers, the large offshore commercial trawlers with nets kilometers-long that catch not just cod but everything else in their path.

The fisherman told me that they had warned the government that the cod were being over-fished. But the commercial draggers continued to come from all over the world (including Canada and the U.S.) taking their greedy harvest. Fisherman have now turned to lobster and shrimp, but lobster is unpredictable and there is an excess of shrimp, resulting in prohibitively low market prices. But what has now emerged as a profitable, dependable enterprise is a source of contention and deep division. Like many people, I had thought the killing of harp seals had been outlawed here. While it is illegal to kill baby harp seals (whitecoats), the government of Newfoundland now permits more than 275,000 juvenile and adult seals to be slaughtered each year. The seals are killed for their fur and meat. Newfoundland's dirty little secret is that fisherman are now making more money from killing seals than from fishing. Seals are eating too many cod, the fisherman insisted, despite any scientific proof. Others say killing seals is a tradition and a "right" they have inherited. The usual, tired criticism of opponents of the seal hunt is that they care more about seals than they do about the welfare of the people who live here.

This is not true. I care equally about both. Be assured, if

harp seals one day invade the land and begin splitting open the skulls of Newfoundlanders with "hakapiks," skinning them alive, eating their vital organs, and selling their genitals to the Asian aphrodisiac markets, I will be among the first to voice my outrage.

It will take me a long time for me to sort out the contradictions between these generous, good-natured people and the violence they condone.

The Labrador ferry actually lands in Blanc Sablon, Quebec. Labrador officially begins a few kilometres up the coast. The southeast coast is home to about a dozen small communities. At Red Bay, the paved road in North America comes to an end. I pedaled up the coast to the village of L'Anse Amour, romantic sounding but actually a mistranslation from Cove of Death, a more appropriate name considering all the wreckage strewn along the beach.

I camped at Point Amour just north of the lighthouse, 143 years old and the tallest in Atlantic Canada. I slept on a plush carpet of caribou moss and heather. I ate my dinner watching a 10,000 year-old iceberg drift into the cove. A large whale swam along the shore, rhythmically peeling back the water, blowing, and disappearing again. I thought about what the locals said, how the strait fills with ice in winter. The ferry stops running, polar bears come down on the pack ice and the people of this shore are alone for half the year.

After three days, a cold front blew in from the north bringing with it a weeping mist and a bitter wind. My time in Labrador was short but I won't soon forget the sense of peace and harmony I found camped on that head, high above the sea, surrounded by the wonders of an Arctic summer.

When I returned to St. Barbe, the wind was still pounding out of the S/SW. It had been blowing at 35 to 45 kph for nearly two weeks. I tried pedaling but could only make about seven or eight kph—on the flats! At that rate it would take nearly two weeks to backtrack the 700 kilometres to Port aux Basques.

I attempted a variety of methods: pedaling, hitchhiking, and even hopping the bus. But travel in Newfoundland is seldom predictable. The huge distances gobble up the best-made plans. Even the bus broke down—twice!

I have spent the last four days pedaling from North Sydney to Pictou. Now I'm dreaming of gently rolling country lanes, strawberry festivals and lazy days swimming in the warm waters of the Northumberland Strait.

Yes Marilla, I am dreaming of Prince Edward Island.

Chapter 3

*"I have perceived that to be with those I like is enough.
To be surrounded by beautiful, curious, breathing,
laughing flesh is enough"*

—Walt Whitman

I sat helpless for days on the shores of Pictou, held captive by 31 women as I watched my ferry, bound for Prince Edward Island, leave its berth each morning without me. I had become the happy victim of two distant and distinct cultures. Until now, if you had threatened to play the bagpipes, I would have run in the opposite direction, hands clasped firmly over my ears. But all that has changed. I have heard the Heatherbells! And I promise, I will never again yell at a piper, "Hey, let the cats outta that bag!"

Heatherbells is an all-girl band of 30 pipers and drummers based in Pictou. I saw them in concert on the waterfront there and for the first time understood the power and beauty of Scottish Highland pipes. They played traditional Celtic tunes orchestrated to distinctly highlight the drones and melody, the lonesome sound of a dreary Highland bog.

My friend from Holland finally arrived in Pictou after a series of cryptic messages passed between backpackers and cyclists, a flurry of emails and one frantic phone call. We had met in Halifax, reunited at the Mabou River Hostel and missed each other by just one day in Newfoundland. Now that she was here, I knew nothing would come between us. Well, almost nothing. We found a secluded campsite on a ribbon of pink sand stretched between the Northumberland Strait and a lush salt marsh filled with great blue herons, warblers and enough mosquitoes to turn our skin to bubble wrap. We went skinny-dipping under a blanket of stars and warmed ourselves before a snapping fire of bleached driftwood. We ate our supper of rice and tortillas and made plans for exploring PEI together. In the morning, she stumbled out of the tent, herself a victim of a foreign culture: a stomach flu. We eventually made it to a campground on PEI near the ferry terminal but the next day she was still sick. Suddenly, we were walking down the road, her pack lashed to my trailer and her thumb pointing toward Charlottetown. A pickup truck stopped, we hoisted her gear into the back, a quick good-bye, and she was gone. Her thin arm waving from the passenger window was the last I saw of her. Back on my bike, pedaling east as she sped west, I was once again alone.

> *"Only the wandering mists of the sea*
> *shall companion me;*
> *Only the wind in its quest shall come where I lie,*
> *Only the rain from the brooding sky with furtive footstep*
> *shall pass me by"*
>
> —L. M. Montgomery

The next day I headed north for the Rollo Bay Fiddle Festival, determined to drown my sorrow in a cacophony of Celtic fiddles, step dancing, and yes, bagpipes. Good god, I needed bagpipes! On the way up the coast I found bushels of new potatoes and buckets of fresh, ripe strawberries. How different from Newfoundland. I remember at one grocery in Labrador, they actually had green, red and yellow peppers. They were carefully wrapped in multiple layers of clear plastic and couched in soft cardboard cups. They could be yours for just a few small monthly payments: the Faberge eggs of Atlantic Canada. But now, on PEI, the sun was out, my shirt was off and summer was finally here. The festival was a hometown charm. There was not one corporate logo or commercial sign board. A solid community effort has been making this festival happen for the last 25 years. There was a simple home-made stage ringed with bare yellow light bulbs, food vendors, hot showers, and plenty of space for camping. A gaggle of kids step-danced in front of the stage as the performers— mostly their cousins, and uncles, sisters and moms—cranked out the tunes for friends and relatives till early in the morning. Two days later I left the festival and continued to trace the perimeter of the island, first north, then west. I camped beside the lighthouse at East Point and watched as sooty gray clouds blotted out the sunset. After dark, I was kept awake by a low humming sound. Eerie but familiar, I couldn't place it. I felt along the bottom of the tent floor. Had I camped over an electric wire? The humming gradually increased until I remembered where I had heard that sound before. It was three years ago deep in the mangrove jungles of the Everglades. The flashlight confirmed it. Clinging to my tent walls, like one giant, buzzing eating machine were thousands of hungry mosquitoes waiting to descend on me like a cheap suit. That night a 45 kph wind kicked in and brought with it a pelting rain, rolling thunder and lightning so brilliant I could see inside the tent as if it were daylight. As the lightning came nearer, I kept dashing outside, moving the bike and trailer farther and farther away from the tent. Continually battered by strong gusts of wind, high above the sea just a few meters from the edge of a red clay cliff, I wondered if my tent was about to become a boat, and I, the captain of a quickly sinking ship. Finding myself still alive in the morning, I had to wrangle the tent, now impersonating a kite, back into its bag. But for one errant stake that I had forgotten, the whole mess would have wound up in the water leaving me without a shelter, much to the delight of a million nearby drooling probisci.

It seems I can't go anywhere here without getting invited in for coffee or tea. "Hey Bill, come on in for breakfast!" It was the voice of a woman I had met earlier in the morning while packing up my rig. I was riding past her friend's house when she spotted me. Road Rule #1: Never, absolutely never, say "No" to free food. I found myself in Anna Holland's kitchen, sampling homemade strawberry jam and orange marmalade, dipping tea biscuits into warm maple syrup. Hummingbirds darted around the windows and antique roses as I listened to the history—not of PEI—but of the one hundred acres between the house where Anna was born and the house in which we were sitting. Debbie, the woman who had invited me in, assured me that Anna's teapot was always on for me as it was for her and that I was welcome back anytime. My only obligation that morning was to sign Anna's guest book and place my name among the dozens of other visitors from around the world who have been lucky enough to find this warm and generous board.

I have decided not to go to Cavendish, home of the Anne of Green Gables museum. I just don't feel the need to surround myself with frantic, bug-eyed tourists on their insatiable quest for over-priced memorabilia. And while it's easy to poke fun at the hype, it is reassuring to know that something as old-fashioned and low-tech as a book can still create traffic jams, propel people across continents, and maybe, even change the world.

I'm now at the Rendezvous-Rustico festival. My tent is pitched in a hay field by the bay, the French is flying in this old Acadian settlement and I'm looking forward to three days of fiddle music, pancake breakfasts, and a few more square-dancing lessons.

> *"Swing your partner Grand Change.*
> *Right hand to your partner.*
> *Promenade your partner. Promenade...*
> *Promenade and... Good Night!"*

It is mightier than the winds of Newfoundland's Great Northern Peninsula; more relentless than the Fundy tides. Its sting, sharper than that of the jellyfish of the Northumberland Strait. Its size, deceptively small-smaller even than a new Prince Edward Island red potato. It is the bane of cyclists, the subject of cruel jokes and the source of a thousand miseries: Oh, the dreaded saddle sore.

A single hair follicle gets slapped around, roughed up and rubbed the wrong way. Soon, a deep discontent sets in, festers, and grows until it finally becomes larger and more unbearable with each kilometer until at last: Revolution Down Below! The only cure—the complete surrender to that Robespiere of my nether-regions. I had to get off that bike. I left the Redez-vouz Rustico festival after three days of music, dancing and camping. Though I saw Rustico's own Lennie Gallant and PEI's Barachois, the highlight of the festival for me was a morning classical concert for cello, flute and guitar performed in a small church near the festival grounds. The performance featured local cellist and composer, Shirley Wright. I will never be able to think of PEI again without remembering the warm, liquid tone of her cello on that bright summer morning.

I stopped for a night in Charlottetown then pedaled west to the Confederation Bridge. Cyclists and pedestrians are prohibited from crossing on their own and must wait for a cramped shuttle van to taxi them across. No one seemed able to tell me why such a newly constructed bridge was not built to accommodate the self-propelled. The driver told me that one morning there were 18 cyclists waiting to board the six-passenger van. I'm not really surprised considering that PEI has no mass transit outside of Charlottetown; its only rail line has been ripped up and converted to a trail for recreational cycling and walking. Rails-to-trails seems a destructive trend designed to increase reliance on cars and treat bicycles as toys instead of clean, efficient transportation. More useful in PEI would be a light rail line, capable of carrying bicycles, wheel chairs, and baby strollers etc., and connected to towns by hiker/biker paths.

By the time I reached New Brunswick, my saddle sore had grown worse, making each hour on the bike more intolerable. I knew I had to stop riding for a few days. What I didn't know was that I would soon be living on the Devil's Half-Acre overlooking the Bay of Fundy. I arrived in Alma, a small town perched at the eastern end of Fundy National Park. While searching for a secluded campsite in the woods, I stopped at the hostel located in the park. With Robspiere demanding my surrender, I arranged to barter my labor for a bed. Now I could cook in a kitchen, shower every day and explore the Fundy shore.

The hostel is part of Hostelling International, a non-profit organization dedicated to fostering understanding among international travelers of all ages by providing clean, low-cost accommodations worldwide. The Fundy hostel is housed in several rustic buildings originally constructed in the 1950s for the New Brunswick School of Arts and Crafts. The cabin-like buildings once served as workshops for students of weaving, wood, leather and metal work. Its location on the Devil's Half-Acre, a deeply forested plateau overlooking the Bay of Fundy, is exquisitely secluded and peaceful despite the mysterious holes and caves reportedly forged by an outraged—and outsmarted—Satan. But the lure of this place is more than the luster of the original pine paneling, the cool sea breezes or the incredible view of Fundy. The real charm comes from the hostel's managers, Sue and Marlene. Newfoundlanders both, they have brought that province's generosity and warm good humor to this forest retreat. We are becoming good friends though they work me nearly to exhaustion each day. Adding to my suffering, I am constantly bombarded with "girl talk" and off-key singing (Sue's impersonation of Tammy Wynette singing "Stand By Your Man," complete with all the "moves" and a mop handle microphone is not to be missed!). Too often I serve as a convenient scapegoat for their sudden and uncontrollable outbreaks of male-bashing. And yes, I'd have it no other way.

Because Fundy National Park is an international destination, the hostel is visited by travelers from around the world. Last week we had a woman cycling alone from the Italian Alps, a couple from Holland and England, a young woman from Madagascar now living in Paris, a motorcyclist from New Hampshire, a young anarchist and her mother from upstate New York, and a family of five from Germany. But hostellers are not the only international visitors. Just a few kilometers away, at Mary's Point in the Shepody National Wildlife Area, 80,000 shore birds from the Arctic are currently resting and feeding on the mud flats in preparation for their 4000 kilometer migration to the north coast of South America. More than one million birds will stop here this season, making Mary's Point the site of one of the largest concentration of semipalmated sandpipers and plovers in North America.

At first glance the sight of these birds is under-whelming. They are small and gray and even 80,000 of them just doesn't look that impressive—until they fly. Perhaps disturbed by a fox or hawk, suddenly the beach explodes with wings as the birds rise meters from the sand in a broad, undulating ribbon of brown and gray. Driven by some mysterious, synchronous impulse, together they wheel and turn, exposing gleaming white bellies to the sun. Instantly, the sky fills with silver, mercurial jewels floating down to the beach like diamond confetti. Then this ribbon of birds ripples like a string of dominoes and suddenly swoops upward again, as light and effortless as a breath of wind. The undulations repeat again and again until the impulse subsides and the birds resume their innocuous posture in the sand and we curious onlookers simply sigh and try to catch our breath.

> *"If to live in this style is to be eccentric, it must be confessed that there is something good in eccentricity."*
>
> —Jules Verne, from *Around the World in 80 Days*

Phileas Fogg and Passepartout may have traveled the world in 80 days but it has taken me 99 days to see Atlantic Canada. I realize that the list of places I didn't visit is longer than those I did. But what a summer it has been! I have been challenged by the wind and the mountains, rewarded with beauty and kindness at every turn. I have met hundreds of interesting and friendly people, people who have momentarily put their lives on hold to offer assistance or share their stories with me. I have invaded many a kitchen, stolen whole afternoons and emptied more than my share of pots and platters. In Newfoundland, camped among weekenders at little Bonne Bay Pond, I was offered everything that hit the grill that weekend. I was invited into a converted school bus for tea and warmth on a damp chilly morning. Cold beer and Newfie music repeatedly found its way to my campsite. I was never excluded nor made to feel unwelcome. And though Atlantic Canada is renowned for its friendly people, I believe, there are friendly people everywhere. I'd like to think that a fisherman from Ecum Secum or a farmer from Souris could find the help they needed on 48th Street and 8th Avenue in New York City.

What impressed me most in Atlantic Canada was not what I found, but what I lost: my fear. I did not fear for my personal safety while camping alone in desolate woods or along the side of the road. I did not fear that my equipment would be stolen or vandalized. I did not fear that I would become the victim of an act of cruelty or malice. I did not fear retribution for things that others from the States may have done or said. Even when I was discussing controversial issues, like the seal hunt in Newfoundland, I was always treated with respect and courtesy. I can only hope that I have behaved as well. I can still hear the voice of one grizzled old fisherman in Newfoundland who had just given me directions to a campsite for the night.

"Will I be all right there?" I asked. He winked and cocked his head, "You'll be all right, b'ye. You've got no worries. You're in Newfoundland now, b'ye."

Well, the revolution seems to be over; Robespiere is retiring. Sue and Marlene keep reminding me that I am *not* Canadian and that I must—sooner or later—*Leave*! Yet I can't shake that feeling; the one you get when you think you have forgotten something at the start of a long trip. But whatever I've left behind in Atlantic Canada it is a small thing compared to the joy, the beauty, and the friendships that I am taking home with me.

> *"Twenty years from now you will be more disappointed by the things you didn't do than by the ones you did do. So throw off the bowlines, sail away from the safe harbor.*
> *Catch the trade winds in your sails. Explore. Dream. Discover."*
>
> —Mark Twain

Eddy the Elf in Bridgewater, Nova Scotia, in front of his *Santaville* workshop.

Made it! My bike and trailer on the Labrador coast beneath Atlantic Canada's tallest lighthouse.

Marlene and Sue at the Bay of Fundy Hostel.

ESCAPE TO THE EVERGLADES

"There are no other Everglades in the world. They are, they have always been, one of the unique regions of the Earth, remote, never wholly known."

—Marjorie Stoneman Douglas,
from her book, *The Everglades: River of Grass*

Chapter 1

"Hope and the future for me are not in lawns and cultivated fields, not in towns and cities, but in the impervious and quaking swamps."

—Henry David Thoreau

I came to South Florida to explore one of the world's most unique ecosystems. The Everglades: a fragile sub-tropical wilderness fighting for survival. An $8 billion restoration project, the largest of its kind ever attempted, is about to get underway.

The Everglades is home to hundreds of thousands of migrating birds. It is the only place in the world where both alligators and crocodiles coexist. The Everglades is also the only park in our hemisphere to hold three international ecological designations: International Biosphere Reserve, World Heritage Site, and Wetland of International Significance.

I came to see plants and animals found nowhere else in the world. I came to try to understand what life is like for the Miccosukee and Seminole Indians that linger at the edge of both a disappearing wilderness and a century that has brought the near death of their culture. I came to meet the farm workers who labor under a tropical sun in pesticide contaminated fields that threaten the health of both workers and 'Glades.

I came to set foot in the nearly one million acres of swamp in Big Cypress National Preserve. I came to discover the undersea world of coral reefs and tropical fishes in Biscayne National Park, the nation's largest underwater national park.

And yes, I came to escape yet another cold, gray New Jersey winter. I'm writing this introduction in the backyard of the Everglades International Hostel in Florida City. I'm sitting in a screened gazebo bordered by palm trees and palmettos. Exotic plants with long ruby-red seed clusters brush against the screens as hostellers play croquet in the grass while "El Capitan," a retired Mexican sea captain in his 70s, teaches Mark, our cook, how to throw Ninja stars. The temperature is in the 80s; I'm in shorts and sandals and a light breeze is blowing in off the ocean. I have fallen into a slow, tropical frame of mind. There are only five shopping days left until Christmas.

Less than a week ago, during my 11-day canoe trip through the 99-mile Wilderness Waterway in the remote backcountry of the Everglades, I was cold, wet, lost, accosted by alligators, and at the mercy of a raw and indifferent Nature unlike I have ever experienced. I think I have never been closer to death or to Nature's most intricate secrets.

> *"The true return to Nature is the definitive return to the elements—death."*
>
> —André Gide

The Wilderness Waterway extends 99 miles down the west side of the Everglades, from the Ten Thousand Islands region past Cape Sable on Florida Bay. The waterway trail passes through rivers, bays and narrow vegetation-choked creeks, winding through one of the largest remaining unbroken expanses of mangrove in the world. There is no fresh water, no ranger stations, no towns or settlements; no harbors, stores or phones. There are no second chances if I make a mistake. I will be totally alone, dependent on randomly spaced numbered markers and my ability to find my way with just chart and compass. I'll be camping on small clearings on the banks of the mangrove islands or on "chickees," raised wooden platforms designed to keep campers out of the jaws of alligators. I need to take 10 gallons of water (a gallon per day), enough food for at least 10 days plus my usual camping equipment (tent, sleeping bag, cook stove, mess kit, headlight etc.), extra paddles, and a good first-aid kit. The park also recommends bringing a weather radio, flares and a watch—three items I would later regret not having. This is the story of that canoe trip as well as some of the remarkable people and extraordinary places I have been lucky enough to experience while exploring this sub-tropical wilderness.

Day One: I leave the small fishing village of Chokoloskee and head across the bay toward the mouth of the Lopez River. From my chart it looks to be a simple five-mile run to the first campsite. I plan on an easy first day. But I make a critical mistake. I decide to wait until I can catch a ride on the outgoing tide, about 11:30 in the afternoon. Thinking myself pretty smart for traveling with the tide, I don't realize the afternoon wind has built into a 20-knot bluster, making paddling both difficult and dangerous. To combat the wind I used my kayak paddle. Canoes are inherently bad in strong winds because of their high profile. The wind tends to push you backwards even as you paddle with all your strength to go forward. Without that kayak paddle I am sure I would have had to turn back that first afternoon. My kayak would have been a better choice but is not big enough to carry all the food and water needed for this 10-day trip. Twice the wind completely turned me around so that I actually lost ground. Once I had to dart behind a small island, a lee shore, just to catch my breath and take a drink of water. In the days ahead, I would be forced to ignore the tide in favor of an early, predawn start, to avoid the wind whenever possible, especially in the big bays.

From my journal: "Made it to Lopez River camp. Only five miles—took more than four hours of the hardest paddling I have ever done. Got blown around twice. Went aground twice. Had to pole and push with paddle through mud flats. Tent and sleeping bag splattered with mud. Camp is infested with mosquitoes. Had to wear head net. Back is killing me."

> "That which does not kill me makes me stronger."
>
> —Nietzsche

That first day set a precedent that would last the length of the trip. Each day this place would throw something at me that required every bit of mental and physical resolve I could muster. But amid the brutality I would also find an enormous, unspeakable beauty. The Indians call it Pay-Hay-Okee: grassy waters. Nearly two million acres of water and grass, framed by an endless blue sky and dappled with a brilliant light. The edges of the mangrove islands are dotted by the statuesque figures of snowy egrets and dusky blue herons. The brilliant whites and subtle grays of these wading birds are one of nature's most clever camouflages. To the fish they hunt, these birds appear simply as clouds, softly mingled in the endless blue sky above. Camped alone on the Lopez River I heard what would become a nightly ritual of strange and sometimes startling sounds. As beautiful as the Everglades are during the day, it is at night when they truly come alive. Again, from my journal: "As night falls, I am surrounded by a chorus of unfamiliar sounds: chirping, splashing, moaning and whistling. Something is creeping along the outside bottom edge of my tent. High up in a tree is a weird buzzing, vibrating noise. Also, something like a rubber squeaky toy is making a fuss." The moment I put my foot ashore at the Lopez River camp, mosquitoes flew up from the ground like a rising fog. They attacked me with an unrelenting blood-sucking vengeance. I scrambled to put on my hat and attach the bug netting but I was too slow. Bugs got inside the netting, around my neck and into my shirt. Working hard to get my tent up, I think I swallowed more mosquitoes than I swatted. Luckily, I was forewarned to wear a long sleeve shirt and long pants despite the 80 degree heat and humidity. I had to repeatedly spray my clothes and exposed skin with insect repellent. I found that by sitting absolutely still, I could minimize the mosquito feed fest. I debated over every move—should I get up and get my stove—put away my water, etc. Every chore had to be weighed against the next onslaught of bugs. As soon as I moved anywhere around the campsite, they came out of hiding to attack me. And not just mosquitoes. No-see-ums were everywhere as were little biting flies. I was a walking dinner buffet for the Lopez River minutiae. I had forgotten to put on my new paddling gloves when I started out that afternoon; as a result, I already had blisters on two of my fingers, blisters I would now be unable to get rid of because of the constant friction each day. Soon, the bottom of the boat would be littered with wet band aids and gauze wrappers. Muggy, buggy, exhausted, and dripping with sweat and insecticide, I laid down in my tent that first night and thought, "Well, at least it can't get any worse than this." Ironically, looking back, that first day was, after all, the "easy day."

> "*The worst is not, so long as we can say,*
> "*This is the worst.*"
>
> —Shakespeare

Chapter 2

"To travel hopefully is a better thing than to arrive, and the true success is to labor."

—Robert Louis Stevenson

From my journal: "Day Two. Lopez River—early morning—in tent for sunrise—bugs seem bad. Will take a chance in a few minutes and see what happens. Tossed and turned all night, don't think I slept much. Still tired from yesterday. Many miles to go today."

The second day on the Wilderness Waterway required me to paddle up the Lopez River, across Sunday Bay, Oyster Bay, Huston Bay, Last Huston Bay and then finally, one and a half miles down the Chatham River to another riverside camp called The Watson Place. A total of about 12 miles. No problem. On paper it all looked easy enough. The bays, only a few inches wide on the chart, in reality, are miles wide and long. It was impossible to see across to the next marker. I would set a compass course and follow it, hoping to find the marker at the other end. Of course, a simple compass bearing cannot account for drift due to the wind and tides. I would spend many difficult hours back-tracking and searching for the little brown marker, usually hiding among the bright sun and shining mangrove leaves. The second day there were still some other boats in the area. I met two guys from Boston who gave me a beer and insisted on chatting for a long time. We sat there talking as the winds grew stronger until I finally begged off. I would see them later again in the day as they were heading home, merrily zipping along, oblivious to the wind that had me gasping for breath. An old fisherman gave me good directions around Crooked Creek, though it took me off the trail and caused me great anxiety: I could not find my next marker, Marker # 125. It was then I realized the seriousness of my situation. If I make a wrong turn, go down the wrong creek or channel, I could be hopelessly lost. Every mangrove shore and island looked exactly alike. There are no mountains, no valleys or ridge lines to mark your course. The old fisherman gave me only half the directions that day, assuming I knew which way to go. I didn't. A choice between bearing left and going straight ahead presented itself after about a half hour. Which way? Both directions seemed likely as I needed to go both North and West to get to Oyster Bay. I picked left. Luckily, that second day, I was not lost for long. When I finally saw old Marker #125 I yelled out, "Yes! Yes!" I was back on track—for the moment. By mid-afternoon I was not even half-way and the winds were building. I was heading west across the bays, the wind was directly out of the east. Huston Bay and Last Huston Bay are separated only by an island. The wind whipped straight through uninterrupted for three miles.

From a long journal entry at the end of the day: "5 p.m.—made it! 12 miles today. all went well until last few—crossing Huston and Last Huston—big wind and waves—slow going—very tired. Wasted too much time checking charts. Fisherman said charts were "exact" as I was about to say they stink! 'You have to get the rhythm for it,' he said.

While paddling through this wilderness I could not help but think of the first people that inhabited this place. The Seminoles and Miccosukee Indians were pursued first by the Spaniards and later by the U.S. government and Gen. Andrew Jackson. Here's a great account of Indian resistance from Marjorie Stoneman Douglas' book, *The Everglades: River of Grass*:

> Then there came that curious twang of a released bowstring, and in the next instant the thlock of an arrow reaching its mark. They stared at a man spinning and

clutching at his throat, with an arrow sticking through it, stared as he fell and flopped like a fish. Then they were all shouting together as the air thickened with hissing arrow shafts that found throats or joints or splintered and slashed like glass through chain mail to the vulnerable flesh. Spears came in fast and sure, spiking a man clean through before his blood could burst out, red as the flags, on the trampled sand. An arrow hissed and struck deep in a joint in his armor. So Ponce de Leon bled, and his blood was the same scarlet as the blood of all them spilled on that trampled whiteness underfoot. That was all he was ever to give Florida, besides her discovery and her name. She gave him his death for it.

The Indians known today as the Miccosukee and Seminole fought three bloody wars with the United States government. The longest war lasted seven years. A nation of more than 5,000 was killed, kidnapped, and relocated until only about 100 remained. They never surrendered; they never signed a peace treaty. These 100 resisters are the ancestors of today's tribal members.

> "Be as beneficent as the sun or the sea, but if your rights as a rational being are trenched on, die on the first inch of your territory."
>
> —Ralph Waldo Emerson

The resistance continues today, though the fight has moved from the mangroves to the courtroom, from arrows and spears to lawsuits and appeals. The Miccosukee just won another victory in a lawsuit against the U.S. Environmental Protection Agency. They enjoined a suit for stricter clean water standards than allowed under the recent Everglades Restoration Act. A casino on the Reservation gives them capital to hire some of the best lawyers. It is a strange world evoking modern legal warfare to protect the ancient resources of clean water and air.

Before starting on the Wilderness Waterway I visited the Miccosukee Reservation along the Tamiani Trail and spent an afternoon talking with a tribal elder. Buffalo Tiger is an elder and former Tribal Chairman. Back in the early 1960s when the United States government refused to recognize the Miccosukee as a separate tribal nation, Buffalo Tiger sought out international recognition. He traveled with a small delegation to Cuba. He met with Fidel Castro who gladly recognized the tribe and even offered them land in Cuba. The U.S. government was at last embarrassed into granting recognition to the Miccosukee. Today, Buffalo Tiger is concerned about what he calls the "fast life." He said the ever-spreading lights of Miami are slowly invading the sanctity of the Everglades, tempting tribal members with cars, drugs, and night clubs. He would like to see the tribe return to a more traditional, Earth-centered existence. We sit in his chickee along the Tamiani Trail. He is dressed in jeans but with a traditional Miccosukee shirt and vest. His face is a warm brown color, wrinkled but youthful. He doesn't smile much but has a kind, wise look as if his 76 years had not taken from him, but given.

"Going through the fast life is like going through darkness. I have seen some of the Indians handle a dollar pretty well. Others have not. The 'buck' makes you forget yourself. They're going to go places they've never been before, buying things. So we will have to wait and see," he says.

Buffalo Tiger said he thinks the present move away from Nature is detrimental to all people, not just his tribe.

"It's bigger than that. People should start listening when Indians speak. The dollar destroys everything. Our culture is dying away so fast. I don't see anyone living like they did 70 or 80 years ago. The fast life doesn't belong to us, it belongs to the white man."

Buffalo Tiger remains optimistic about saving the Everglades, a place to which his culture is inexorably tied. But he warns that we must not only save the Everglades, but restore our connection to the Earth.

"We are still hoping. We go to court, spend a lot of money,

talk loud. The people have to be together. Politicians don't see the Nature side of things. We forget, the doctors didn't make you. Everything will change. I am over 70 years old and have seen many things happen. We have to believe in all of Nature. I am like a tree. I bloom, flower, then the fruit drops back to the Earth, spreads more seed. I tell people that is who you are, particularly mammas. We all came from our Mother. We are supposed to stand up, grow and spread seed on the land where we are born," he tells me.

> "We do not see Nature with our eyes, but with our understanding and our hearts."
>
> —William Hazlitt

I finally make it to Watson's Place, my camp for the night on the Chatham River. Its namesake, Ed Watson, was a notorious backcountry homesteader who was reputed to have shot the infamous woman outlaw, Belle Starr, back in the Wild West. Locally, Watson became known as "The Barber," after shooting off half a man's moustache in a gun fight. In the fall of 1910, Watson was accused of murdering most of the help on his small backwater farm. When Watson came to town, a shotgun in one hand and a pistol at his hip, to answer accusations about the murders, it was suggested he surrender his guns. The following is from an account by historical columnist Stuart McIver:

> An argument followed and Watson pulled both the shotgun's triggers. The gun, loaded with wet shells, misfired. At that point, practically the whole crowd blazed away at Watson. So many bullets pierced his body that no one really knew who killed him. And no one tried very hard to find out.

There's not much left of Watson's place now, just the remains of water cistern and a small clearing where I set up my tent. The bugs here are as bad as at the Lopez River but I am getting used to them, sort of.

From my journal: "5 p.m. Plate Creek Bay chickee tomorrow should have less bugs. As soon as I move, they swarm all over me. Had dozens even in my tent. Saw osprey today. I'm learning that this place must be met on its own terms. 6 p.m.—sky is brilliant orange as sun is setting—fantastic sight—but can't get out of my tent to take pictures because of bugs! Too tired to write much more."

Tomorrow I paddle back up the Chatham River one and a half miles to rejoin the trail, then another 8.5 miles east to Plate Creek Bay where I'll camp on a chickee and begin the most remote and desolate section of the trail.

"There are days when solitude is a heady wine that intoxicates you with freedom, others when it is a bitter tonic, and still others when it is a poison that makes you beat your head against the wall."

—Colette

Chapter 3

"We wake from one dream into another dream."

—Ralph Waldo Emerson

Day three of my trip was probably the most pleasant, and thus, misled me into thinking that the rest of the voyage would be similar. I can remember thinking to myself, "Yes, I can do this. This place is not that different. It's going to be all right." Of course, as soon as that thought entered my mind, things were bound to change. But I made it to Plate Creek Bay chickee for the third night and was pleasantly surprised by the lack of bugs. Because chickees are located away from land and are open to breezes, the bugs are much less of a problem. There are other problems to take their place. I did not sleep well because of my fear that the canoe would come untied during the night. If that had happened, I would be stranded, without food or water (everything must be stored in the boat at night because of raccoons and other animals). I was up about every hour, checking the lines, listening for the creaking of boat against wood. Also, the movement of the tide constantly raised and lowered the boat so that it was always in danger of catching on the boards near the end of the platform. As I tried to sleep, I pictured one side of the boat gradually tilting up on the incoming tide until it capsized, spilling all my supplies. These are the thoughts, rational or not, that invaded my sleep. Sudden gusts of wind at night would bang the canoe against the dock and send me running out of the tent to see what had happened. By the third day, my blisters were worsening and the tropical sun, despite heavy applications of sun block, was starting to make itself known on my skin. My face and neck felt hot even at night. Each day I wore a heavy slathering of sun block, insecticide and antibacterial cream (for the blisters).

A few weeks before I started the Wilderness Waterway, I took my kayak out on Biscayne Bay, the nation's largest underwater park, for a nine-mile paddle to Elliot Key (keys are also known as islands). I spent three days on Elliot Key, the largest of the coastal barrier islands separating Biscayne Bay from the Atlantic Ocean. I paddled my kayak to the island in the morning after waiting out a line of passing thunderstorms. The surface of the water was calm and I could see through four or five feet of water to the bottom of the bay. Great expanses of sea grasses, corals and sponges dotted the sandy bay floor. Turquoise water, straight from a Caribbean travel brochure, spread out in front of me for miles. White sails in the distance appeared and disappeared along the horizon. This park is a combination of coastal wetlands, mangrove-forested islands, clear shallow water, coral reefs, and an enormous variety of fish, birds, and sea-dwelling creatures. More than 250 species of tropical fish swim among 60 varieties of coral reef. The kayak trip over to Elliot Key was nerve wracking. I was in totally new territory—salt water. My simple compass navigation seemed inadequate but did succeed in getting me here, though it was just a matter of heading due east and looking for the harbor. It was an eerie feeling heading out to an island I could not see. Storm clouds and morning fog obscured Elliot Key from view, yet I knew, due east, due east will get me there. But which way was the tide going? The wind was in my face and at a rough estimate of two miles an hour, it would take about three to four hours of paddling—hard paddling. Unlike paddling on the Delaware River, where I could stop on any shore if there was a problem, once I was out there, it was just me and my little cork of a boat. I checked the stress points and looked for water in the bottom. Everything seemed all right, yet the boat was open at the top; not the best design for bays and oceans. The wind picked up as the water deepened. Waves became choppy but not too severe, just a small, sober reminder of where in the world I was—among nearly 300 square miles of salt water, tropical islands, and coral reefs. Once visited by presidents and pirates, these mangrove thickets and shifting sands now hide buried treasure and the eroding remnants of man's attempt to colonize these wild islands. But the real treasures here are the dolphins, manatees, and uncountable numbers of sea birds and waders that congregate in and around the islands' mangrove jungles and sandy beaches. Uniquely, most of Biscayne National Park; lies beneath the water, inviting you below the surface, revealing its secrets only to those willing to explore Nature's hidden realm. Once I got used to the idea of being in this little boat, the ride became thrilling. Pelicans lumbered by barely a foot above the water. A spotted ray rippled past me just a few feet away. Double-crested cormorants, gulls, and terns sat on buoys and channel markers. They crossed the bay in minutes; my trip would require more than three hours of steady paddling. It was, however, a good paddling experience and gave me my first taste of slogging through a big, wind-swept bay. I set up camp near the harbor and spent my days paddling around the island, observing life along the coast. I drifted under the blazing sun, gazing down into the crystal clear waters. There were many plants and fish species I had never seen before. It was like floating atop a giant tropical aquarium. There were no other campers on Elliot Key (most likely due to the bugs—after sundown I had to be inside the tent unless there was a stiff breeze) and I rarely saw another boat. The bugs were so bad here that the park rangers, who had a station on the island and came in every night at dusk and left in the morning, would run past me dressed in full body mosquito suits—and still wouldn't stop to talk. They just waved and ran while I stood there swatting.

After three days I made a hasty retreat from the bugs and headed back to the mainland. It was on the return trip that I realized the extent of the peril the Park faces. On my left as I headed back toward the shore was Turkey Point, a large nuclear power plant sitting at the edge of the bay. On my right was what locals refer to as "Mount Trashmore," one of the largest landfills in the country, located in South Miami, and reportedly leaking leachate into the bay. The state and local government is trying to expand a small military airport into a new commercial airport a few miles away in Homestead, Fla. The expansion would bring nearly 250,000 flights a year over Biscayne and Everglades National Parks. Opponents insist that in addition to the flights, the outbuilding of roads, hotels, etc., will further threaten this already imperiled area. A federal judge recently ruled in favor of airport opponents, declaring that an extensive environmental impact assessment must be completed before any airport expansion can be completed. Proponents of the expansion, including the governor and his Cabinet, had tried to "fast-track" the development by skipping the environmental assessment.

> *"Not to know is bad; not to wish to know is worse."*
>
> —From a Nigerian proverb

To really know Biscayne National Park, I had to get to the bottom of the bay. I returned a few days later, this time via a tour boat, and went snorkeling. The dive captain on the trip, Nestor Morales, is the godchild of the late John Pennekamp, longtime editor of the Miami Herald and a vocal conservationist whose efforts resulted in the protection of many of South Florida's most valuable natural resources. It is a connection of which Nestor is obviously proud.

"I've tried living other places but I keep coming home. This was my backyard. When I skipped school they didn't look for me at the malls, they looked for me out here," says Nestor, a well-tanned man in his early 40s who has been diving this bay for more than 20 years. We are aboard the Reef Rover IV, heading east toward open ocean. He warns the passengers, a dozen tourists from Philadelphia to Israel, about what they might encounter while snorkeling. Moon jelly fish, pizza sized and grayish-purple.

They're only mildly toxic, he tells us. Then there are stinging cauliflower, which, because they eat moon jellies are also around, and finally, Portuguese man-of war, that sting with their tentacles. Stay away from them, he warns. Nestor calls us all to the bow of the ship and gives us his three commandments: "Don't touch, don't take, don't break." Remember, he says, "No contact is the best contact." And I can tell from his voice he means it. Nestor said he thought the reefs were still in good condition despite the assaults on them from outside pollution sources. He is firmly against the proposed airport expansion. As we're speaking about the proposed airport, a military jet flies over the bay, causing him to stop talking until the noise abates. I look at him for an answer.

"I don't mind that," he says. "That's the sound of freedom."

He tells me an occasional military jet is not so bad. They come over once or twice a day, but a 747 every three minutes would be intolerable. He also mentions the possibility for crashes and the additional roads and buildings that would destroy what's left of the nearby buffer zones.

"This is a non-renewable resource. If we lose it, it's gone forever."

After snorkeling we head back to the shore. I ride up above on the bridge with Captain Fred Mattson and Nestor. What a different view from the seat of my kayak just a few days earlier. Nestor looks out over the seemingly endless expanse of blue-green water, points toward the curving horizon with a blazing red sun heading south and says to me, "I'd say that's about as good as it gets."

> *"Beauty hath no true glass, except it be,*
> *In the sweet privacy of loving eyes."*
>
> —James Russell Lowell

From my journal: "Day Three, 4 p.m., Plate Creek Chickee. Made it! No bugs—set up tent and had dinner with hardly any interruptions. Canoe is tied to dock and I think the tide is going out. Saw another osprey. Bays, as expected, were very windy. The wind here is starting to let up a bit. Wind began this morning at about 9:00! Saw only two boats all day long. Very much alone out here. Getting more and more blisters on my hands. Clothes pretty dirty. Lemon drops melted in shirt front pocket—nice mess. At sunset tonight saw flock of 30 or 40 egrets flying right at the surface of the water then up and over mangrove island. Fish jumping all over the place. Tomorrow must do 13 miles—most yet. Something is quacking."

My fourth day on the Wilderness Waterway would bring a sea change, not only in wind and weather but in my mental and physical ability to deal with the ever-increasing solitude and adversity. I didn't know it then, but I would soon look back on that third night at Plate Creek Bay chickee as the most peaceful of all my nights on the trail.

Chapter 4

"Books on Nature seldom mention wind; they are written behind stoves."

—Aldo Leopold

From my journal: "Day Four. Stuck! 20 knot wind coming straight out of the east has stopped me cold. I am just four to five miles from tonight's camp at Rodgers River chickee. I tried to leave this protected channel but was turned back after only a few minutes. Back is hurting from the effort. Going to wait until later, maybe wind will die down this afternoon. I'll need to make up this time tonight."

Hiding in the protected waters of small channels, unable to get out because of suddenly high winds, I realized that my 13-mile goal for that day was going to be tougher than I had planned. I was at the mouth of a small bay just before Big Lostman's Bay. I needed to head due east for the next five miles, straight into the wind. My first attempt at crossing the bay brought me about 50 yards before I finally gave up and turned around. My back ached from the strain of simply trying to move the canoe forward. The wind was constantly pushing the boat to one side or the other, trying to turn me back. I returned to the protection of the little creek and waited. And waited. I waited until I couldn't stand it any longer, watching the tops of the mangroves as they blew in the wind. Sitting in the protected creek, everything was deceptively quiet. O.K. I'll try again.

This time I get a little farther but the unrelenting strain of paddling fast and hard tires me out too quickly. The wind has gotten even worse now. Gusts are skimming the tops of the waves, creating whitecaps. I stop paddling for forward gain and concentrate on keeping the nose of the boat straight into the wind. I don't want to lose the ground I worked so hard to gain. Again, I can't maintain the effort and fall back. I ride the wind and turn left into the little creek. It finally becomes obvious that I am not going anywhere for a while. The temperature is in the 80s, the sun is blaring hot and ironically, back in the creek, there is hardly a breeze to keep away the bugs. I sit there worrying about how I will make up the lost time. Even though it is warm here in the Everglades, it still gets dark at about 6 p.m. The wind doesn't die down until about 4 p.m., leaving me precious little light to find my way. I still have miles to go.

From my journal: "Going to pretend I'm on a picnic. Sit here—read and relax. Can't change the weather. I'll stay here tonight if I have to—better than injuring myself or capsizing. The weather will change—that is certain."

A few hours later the wind died down a little and I tried again. This time I managed to make it half-way across the bay and find shelter behind a small island. I stayed there another hour until the wind diminished. By then, it was getting dark. On the chart it looked like a fairly straight run to get to my night's camp. I had to cross Big Lostman's Bay, then south through Rodgers River Bay to my chickee. Unfortunately, the Wilderness Waterway in this area seems to have been rerouted. When I got into the middle of the bay, I noticed that there were two locations on my chart for Marker #38. "How can this be?" I wondered. Then, looking closely, I could see that the route had been erased and redrawn. I decided to go with the new route, thinking it would be the most accurate. I was wrong. I found all the markers until #38. Hours later, with the brilliant afterglow of sunset, I paddled down bay searching with my headlamp for marker #38. Marker #38 may exist, but I never found it. I tried to reconcile the shoreline with the chart but soon found I was stopping every five minutes, staring over and over again at the same spot, unable to distinguish one point of land from another. The farther down bay I went the more lost and disoriented I became. Finally, I decided to backtrack to marker # 39. From there I would be able to get a bearing and would at least know where I was. I still had not given up the idea of finding the chickee that night. It was now about 8 p.m.; darkness was setting in. At marker # 39, I took a compass bearing and decided to follow the old route. I could still see the line on the chart where someone had tried to erase it. As I paddled through the thickening darkness, I realized what a perilous turn this trip had taken. I had seen perhaps two boats all day and neither one had come close enough to help me if I needed it. I paddled slowly, scanning the horizon for any sign of a marker. Finally, my light reflected faintly back from the dark. I had found something, possibly a marker. But which one?

> *"Hope is a strange invention*
> *A Patent of the Heart.*
> *In unremitting action*
> *Yet never wearing out."*
>
> —Emily Dickinson

    I followed the glittering spark of light until it gradually became stronger. Markers are attached to square posts stuck deep into the bay. On the post are usually small, round reflectors. It was one of these reflectors my headlamp light had found. For a few minutes I thought I might still make it to the chickee, but that hope quickly faded. I paddled up to marker #37, tied my stern line firmly around the post and swore I would not move until I knew where I was. I looked on the chart. "This can't be. No, this can't be!" I yelled. Marker #37 was not on my chart!
    By now my stomach was tied in a knot so tightly my appetite had vanished and my hope of being found dissolved into the chilly night air. I forced down a few dates and took a long drink of water. The canoe may have been floating but my heart had

sunk. Then, I burst out laughing. After all, here I was, lost in the most perfect place: Big Lostman's Bay! I spent that night tied to marker #37. I put on my foul weather gear (rain jacket and pants), pushed a few things around to make room in the canoe, and contorted myself so that I could lay on the bottom with my feet pointing up into the stern under the seat and my head tucked under a thwart. I pulled the hood of my rain jacket tight around my face, attempted to ignore the cold, damp of the boat against my back, and tried to sleep. Laying there, looking up at the stars, I wondered how I had gotten myself into this mess. I slept little; every five minutes my eyes would pop open to make sure I was still attached to old #37. I no longer cared that #37 didn't exist. It was all I had to tell me where in the world I was and I wasn't going to lose it. I spent a cold, sleepless night in Big Lostman's Bay. Toward morning, an hour or two before first light, as a drizzling rain began to fall on my face, my thoughts turned to the hostel. How easy I had it there, I thought. Good food, nice breeze (back when the wind was my friend) and the security of knowing where I was going to be when I woke up. It all seemed so far away, so remote from my current soggy situation.

Every morning at the hostel, I could hear the school buses and cars filled with farm workers on their way to the fields. If I had little hope this morning, lost in the wilderness, I wondered how they felt, with hopelessness a daily companion. When Cesar Chavez died in his sleep on Earth Day, April 22, 1993, farm workers lost one of their most important leaders. He had told us that the American farm worker was the modern day equivalent of the coal miner's canary. His nonviolent methods of organizing and boycotting are needed now, in South Florida today, more than ever. I spent a lot of time walking the edges of the farm fields. On some days, my nostrils would burn from the pesticides and other chemicals in the air. Yet, the fields would be full of farm workers, wearing no masks, no gloves, no protection from the deadly chemicals. This is where many of our tomatoes, beans, and other vegetables come from during the winter. It is these huge fields, growing only one type of vegetable (monoculture), that are responsible for much of the Everglade's poor water quality and the poor health of farm workers and their children.

Farms in Florida are still using methyl bromide to kill bugs and weeds in tomato fields. The U.S. Environmental Protection Agency (EPA) has said that methyl bromide causes nausea, vomiting, shortness of breath, blurred vision, convulsions, coma, and neurological problems. It also destroys the Earth's protective ozone layer.

According to a report issued by the Pesticide Action Network, a non-profit pesticide watchdog group, the EPA estimated that 13.3 million pounds of methyl bromide were used on Florida crop lands between 1995 and 1996. Mostly on tomatoes. The EPA also found that most workers who suffered from methyl bromide exposure were unprotected due to inadequate enforcement of farm worker protection statues in Florida. Methyl bromide is known world-wide as the most dangerous pesticide on Earth. More than 160 nations have signed an international treaty requiring the phase-out of methyl bromide use by the year 2005. The U.S. Clean Air Act requires the U.S. to stop using methyl bromide by 2001. Growers here in Florida and California are attempting to delay the ban. The U.S. is the largest user of methyl bromide in the world.

"The rich would have to eat money, but luckily the poor provide food."

—from a Russian proverb

But I did see some signs of hope during my stay in South Florida. The farm workers who provide much of the East Coast with produce during the winter are making a little progress toward their fight against repression, illiteracy, and pesticide poisoning. I visited Centro Campesino (farm worker center) in the heart of South Florida's agricultural center where farm workers are being trained in construction trades and other skills. Jorge Garza is Director of the Adult Migrant Program. Under his direction, farm workers are learning how to build houses. The best part is that they are learning by building houses for other farm workers. Jorge knows the benefits of the program; he was one of the first workers trained more than 20 years ago. He sees construction jobs as a way out of the "killing fields" for many workers and their families.

"We got into farm work because that's what we know. The reason you don't move on from there is that's all we know," said Jorge. Jorge also told me that there are many doctors and lawyers from Mexico and other Latin American countries whose licenses are invalid here. Jorge said he has seen the harmful effects from the pesticides. Many of the children in the area, he tells me, have asthma and other illnesses.

"You can't hardly breathe in the morning. A lot of the kids in this area have asthma—three out of four nowadays," he says.

> *"The human being as a commodity is the disease of our age."*
>
> —Max Lerner

Most of the farm workers in South Florida are illegal aliens. I asked Jorge why the immigration people aren't rounding them up and deporting them. Jorge looks at me with a smile that acknowledges just how little I know about how things are done in South Florida.

"As soon as the season is over, they (immigration) come back," he tells me. Jorge said if these workers don't move on, immigration officials pick them up and deport them. They don't want them around once the vegetables are picked, he tells me.

> *"Slow rises worth by poverty depressed."*
>
> —Samuel Johnson, 1738

Jorge introduced me to a young woman, a former field worker who is now learning basic office skills and taking evening classes in English. She's working at the offices of Centro Campesino.

The moment I enter the office I can tell she is learning the ropes of working in an office; Noemi Delgado, 17, is playing Solitaire on her computer. We talk while she answers the phone and directs the flow of people coming and going in and around the office. Noemi tells me she prefers office work to field work.

"I didn't like it. Too much traveling," she says with a soft round voice and carefully spoken English. "The work doesn't pay enough. Lots of times I had to stay out of school to pick, to help the family."

Noemi tells me that many times her family would rent a trailer or shack from the company for which they were picking. The rent, she said, was so high that many families were forced to live together in the same house. Noemi said she was unable to finish school because her family would have to move before she could take her final exams.

"It would mess you up. You start here and then have to go school somewhere else. It gets confusing." Noemi said many of her friends drop out, turn to drugs and alcohol to escape their dim future in the fields. Jorge confirms this and tells me that the high school drop-out rate is a whopping 80 percent among the children of farm workers. Noemi is also a young single mother. I ask her about Elena, her two-year-old daughter. Would she like to see Elena work, like she did, in the fields, as a picker?

"No, I want her to have an education and grow up to be somebody," she tells me. I ask if she has a message for the people who buy the produce picked in the winter by her friends and her family. She smiles. She is shy and doesn't know what to say. But in her eyes I think I see the answer. She just wants a little hope. A little hope and respect.

"Si se puede." (Yes, it is possible.)

—Cesar Chavez

I passed the night safely, if not uncomfortably, tied to marker #37. At first light I tried to shake off the chill, ate some peanut butter and set a new compass course for marker #36. As the light of day spread across the horizon I found the next marker. And the next. I was back on track.

From my journal: "Pants hanging out to dry. Container of sun block opened inside pocket during the night. Quite a mess but now matches with shirt pocket with melted sour lemon drops. No sleep. Little food. Exhausted. Shaken confidence has me worried."

I decided to skip the Rodgers River chickee (about a 1.5 mile detour) and keep going to my next scheduled camp on the Broad River. There I hoped I would get a good night's sleep and recover from my ordeal. Wrong again.

Chapter 5

> "*It is suggested to me how unexplored still are the realms of nature, that what we know and have seen is always an insignificant portion. We may any day take a walk as strange as Dante's imaginary one to L'Inferno or Paradiso.*"
>
> —Henry David Thoreau

From my journal: "Day five. Now sitting on the dock at Broad River camp. Burning three mosquito coils at table. Just had coffee and oats. After 36 straight hours in the canoe, the ground feels like it is rolling. I am out of energy, out of everything. Hope to feel good tomorrow after a long and luxurious sleep."

I made it from the middle of Big Lostman's Bay, past Rodgers River chickee to the Broad River, about a 12-mile day. The lack of sleep the night before was starting to affect my ability to think clearly. I made it to Broad River camp just in time. But what I found there would cause me to lose yet another valuable night's sleep. It was on the Broad River that I first started to feel uneasy about being out of touch with my family. I began to worry about my daughter and my father. What if they needed me? What if something happens? There was no way anyone could get a hold of me. I had not spoken with another person for three days. I had seen only one boat go by in the last two days and I don't think they saw me. The National Park Service said they occasionally patrol the backcountry; during my 11 days on the Wilderness

Waterway I never saw anyone from the Park Service. I was starting to feel tired and uncertain about my ability to handle this trip. Lack of sleep, extreme physical exertion, and mental fatigue were beginning to affect me. The last thing I needed was to be accosted by a cranky alligator.

A few weeks before I started on the waterway trail, I spent some time in Big Cypress National Preserve, about 20 miles north of Everglades National Park. It was there that I first experienced just how tropical South Florida can be.

From my journal at Big Cypress: "As I feared, the trails are very wet and muddy, courtesy of Hurricane Mitch which dropped about 10 inches of water on Big Cypress the week before I arrived. Hunting season starts in five days so I need to get in and out right away. No time to wait for the water to recede."

I've hiked in the mountains of California, the deserts of Texas and Utah. I have hiked (and cursed) the knife-edged glacial rocks of the Appalachian Trail in Pennsylvania and New Jersey, but I have never hiked anything like Big Cypress Swamp. From the National Park Service brochure on the swamp:

> Hikers should be prepared for wet areas from ankle-deep to waist-deep in the rainy season.

A sign posted outside the visitor center explained that although it was November, it was still, technically, the rainy season. That would be my first of a few little miscalculations. The Big Cypress chewed me up and spat me out. I emerged from an eight-hour hike soaked, caked with mud, exhausted—and never happier. I was, I discovered, a swamp rat, a heretofore unsuspected full-fledged sweaty swamp stomper. My legs ached from churning through the water and mud. The sun cooked me in an 85 degree open air oven. The ever present threat of something eating me just made it all the more exciting. I made a 12-mile round trip journey with full pack (40-50 pounds) on a trail that I never really found through waist-high water, muck and grass. I had the best company: egrets, herons, ibises, limpkins, exotic insects, cypress trees, five flavors of poisonous snakes, and of course, alligators.

The plan was to spend the night alone in the swamp, but I never found a patch of ground clear enough or dry enough to pitch my tent. My eight hours spent there, in the middle of 2,400 square miles of solitude, filled me with joy and a sense of mystery unlike any I have experienced. About three or four miles in, I stopped to read my map and take a compass bearing. I had not seen a trail blaze or sign since the start of my hike. After a few minutes of head scratching, I put away the map and compass and tried to walk on. No good. I could not lift either foot out of the muck. While I had been standing there deciding which direction to go, Big Cypress made the decision for me. And the direction it chose for me was down. Suddenly, the reality of a swamp filled with alligators and poisonous snakes hit me. For several minutes I stood alone, in the middle of this million acres of swamp, realizing I was no longer at the top of the food chain. I could no longer hop into a car, call a cab, or get out quickly. It had taken me hours of hard hiking to reach this spot. It would take me hours more to get back. And now I was getting tired. My leg muscles ached from the constant work of treading water. And by the way, was I lost? I wasn't stuck too long before I finally "popped" the suction hold and moved on, but the experience left me a little more humble, a little more respectful of this place.

Also from the National Park Service brochure:

> Snakes are found almost anywhere in the preserve, so watch where you walk, sit, and reach.

Further down the "trail" I saw something slither past my leg. I froze and spotted a snake in the water stretched out among some cypress branches. The water had become muddy now with my walking (I would learn later that the use of swamp buggies disturbs the natural sediments; in parts of the swamp where buggies are not allowed, the water remains crystal clear, even when walking through it) and when the snake darted off, I could not see where it had gone. I walked slowly, making big swishes with a stick in front of me as I waded, up to my thighs, past the spot where the snake had gone. That was my second snake encounter of the hour.

Rationally, I know a snake is not going to attack me without provocation. I know also that alligators eat fish, birds, and turtles. But miles from help, waist-deep in water in which you cannot see to the bottom, can make even the most rational argument seem a little, well, hopeful. But I learned Big Cypress is not something to be feared, but treasured. To know this place, you must get in it, really in it. The risk is minimal; the reward was beyond all my expectations.

A few days after my hike, I visited with noted South Florida photographer Clyde Butcher. It was something Clyde said that day that caused me, weeks later, to lose a precious night's sleep at my camp on the Broad River. Butcher, 56, a big man with a Burl Ives beard, bright eyes and an broad grin, has been called the Ansel Adams of the Southeast, and is one of this country's most widely recognized landscape photographers. His photographs, exclusively black & white, are filled with the light and shimmer, the space and air of the Big Cypress. He and I talked while swamp stomping through a pristine section of Big Cypress behind his studio/gallery on the Tamiani Trail. I asked him about his stark black and white signature photos of Big Cypress.

"I'm not interested in photography," the most famous photographer in the southeast tells me. "I'm interested in the world around us. I do it for the love of the Earth. This is a living organism. This is a marriage of detail and texture." He is not just making pictures of Big Cypress but, "creating spaces for people to be in," said Clyde of the challenge of portraying this place on film.

Surrounding us as we speak are dwarf cypress, swamp apples, snowy egrets and herons searching for breakfast in the tannin colored water. Tree trunks are boldly splattered with white lichens, in some places so white, the cypress trees resemble the paper birches of the northeast forest. Gray-green clumps of Spanish moss hang delicately from the branches of the cypress, as if trying to compensate for the loss of leaves each fall. The scene, like the rest of Big Cypress, is subtropical. Cabbage palms, orchids, and the haunting sound of a wailing limpkin transport me to the jungles of Costa Rica, or Belize; all that's missing are the monkeys. Butcher, a real swamp rat, wades into the swamps, strands and sloughs of South Florida, hoping, through his art, to create an appreciation for this place, a place coveted by greedy developers, mismanaged by short-sighted National Park Service officials, and easily overlooked by the millions of people traveling through on their way to Everglades National Park. Butcher was recently inducted into Florida's Artist's Hall of Fame. He joins a small, select group of other artists, notables like Ernest Hemingway and Ray Charles. His photographs, taken with large format cameras, reveal his affection for this landscape; a landscape some dismiss as merely a swamp. As we talk, six or seven rare zebra butterflies congregate in the bushes. He points out orchids and fish that eat mosquito larvae. Clyde admits he doesn't know exactly what good his photographs have done but he knows that he must keep celebrating this place, keep raising awareness and above all, keep fighting. For the past few years, he and his wife Niki, also an artist, have spent a great deal of time and money fighting, unsuccessfully, a municipal waste incinerator, now operating on the outskirts of the swamp. Mercury poisoning in the Everglades is well documented, and according to the EPA, municipal waste incinerators are one of the largest producers of mercury. South Florida is ringed with incinerators. Clyde points out there are virtually no bugs back in the swamp, contrary to most people's perception of a swamp. Clyde defends the often maligned mosquito.

"Mosquitoes are the basis of the food chain. Without them, we would have nothing," he says.

Before we started on our walk through the swamp, Clyde handed me a walking stick. He tells me he uses his stick for nudging cottonmouths and alligators out of the way.

"Alligators won't bother you," I tell him (as if I knew what I was talking about). He tells me there is a gator living back here that gets nasty during mating season.

"He gets territorial. He doesn't like me in his area," Clyde tells me.

I had never thought about that but it's what I remember weeks later on the Broad River. The afternoon I arrived at the Broad River camp, I unloaded some of my equipment, had lunch, made a few notes and then went back to my canoe. And there he was.

> *"Sailin' down the river in an old canoe*
> *A bunch of bugs and an old tennis shoe*
> *Out of the river all ugly and green*
> *Came the biggest old alligator that I ever seen"*
>
> —from "Alligator" by the Grateful Dead

There was something about the way he looked at me. That icy stare; those eyes that seemed to follow me everywhere. He was about seven feet long from nose to tail. He had positioned himself right next to my canoe. His head, out of the water, was practically resting on my boat. His sides bulged and his short legs were bigger around than my arms. He was a killing, eating machine. And I was just another flabby tourist too stupid to stay home. I was screwed. I could not get back into my canoe. If I reached down from the dock into the boat, my head would be just inches from his. Warnings posted all over the backcountry say don't get closer than 15 feet. To retrieve my dinner, water and other supplies from the boat, I would be just 15 inches from his jaws. I know what alligators eat. They eat fish and turtles and birds. They don't attack full grown people. But I had guessed that this alligator had been ruined by people feeding him. He had lost his fear of humans. All the other gators I saw in the Everglades and Big Cypress slowly moved off at the sight of me. This one would not budge. The hungrier and thirstier I got, the more desperate I became to get rid of my uninvited camping partner. At one point, I stood on the dock (about a yard away) and started banging a stick and yelling.

He responded. Without moving, without altering his facial expression, without any noticeable change in his position, he started hissing. I had never before heard an alligator hiss. Deep down in my caveman genes I felt a cold terror that translated into mortal danger. I needed no biologist to explain, no alligator specialist to tell me that this was big trouble. I responded. I stopped banging the stick. I backed away off the dock and sat looking through the mangroves at his face nuzzled up to my canoe. It was then I remembered Clyde Butcher's observation about alligators and territory. Maybe I was in this guy's favorite spot. Maybe he was claiming his territory. And just maybe, there wasn't room for the both of us. I returned to the dock about an hour later to try to get some water and found him, unchanged, in the same spot. This time, as soon as I stepped onto the dock, he hissed at me, and just to remind me who was in charge, started snapping his jaws. That was it. Who needs food and water anyway? I found a long stick with a point on it that someone had used to poke a fire. I took the stick into the tent with me that night. I also took my life preserver, thinking that if he came after me, I could jam it into his mouth while I made a quick escape. I also slept with my pants and shirt on (there would be no sense surviving the alligator just to be bitten to death by mosquitoes). If I had not been so scared I would have had a good laugh at myself, lying there, fully dressed, with a big pointy stick and my life preserver, waiting, just waiting. I jumped at every noise; at every rustle in the bushes and at every splash in the river. My plan for a "long, luxurious sleep," disappeared into the white, cottony maw of that gator's jaws.

From my journal: "The thrills never stop. This alligator is big—six or seven feet long. Now I fear he will come into my tent. He is only 15 feet away. Keeps looking at me. This is silly, I know, but I just don't like the way he's hanging around. Can't get any water—thirsty!"

The next morning. From my journal: Day 6: Early morning:

"Still alive! Little sleep. I could hear him breathing on the shore. Slapping the water with his tail? Going to get into the boat, skip breakfast and get out of here."

> *"Creepy alligator comin' all around the bend*
> *Talking about the times when we was mutual friends . . .*
> *Oh no I've been there before,*
> *And I ain't gonna come around here any more."*
>
> —Grateful Dead

The next morning he was gone. I quickly packed up my tent, threw my junk into the canoe and paddled briskly down river. I kept looking back but saw no trace of him. As the knot in my stomach slowly unfurled, I managed to eat an apple, drink some water, and begin to think about the day ahead. I had to go about one mile downstream to find marker #24, the entrance to the Nightmare. The nautical charts warn that the Nightmare, (a small creek that cuts across McLaughlin Key connecting the Broad River with the Harney River) is extremely shallow. I must go through this three-mile stretch when the tide is high. If I miss the high tide, I could be stuck in the middle for more than six hours until the tide turns. Sleepless, hungry, and mentally fatigued, I thought to myself, "I wonder why they call it the Nightmare?"

Chapter 6

> "The life and death of the saw grass is only a moment of that flow in which time, the vastest river, carries us and all life forward."
>
> —Marjorie Stoneman Douglas

On day six I paddled down the Broad River about half a mile, turned left at marker #25, and started toward the Nightmare. At marker #24 I went left again. I arrived at the mouth of the Nightmare early in the morning to catch the rising tide. Nautical charts are marked "shallow" and warn that even canoes must travel here at high tide. As I paddled forward, the creek gradually narrowed until it was no wider than my canoe. I had about three miles to go until I came out the other side. Midway, I was supposed to find marker #23 and bear left. On the chart, it all looked fairly simple but once inside the Nightmare, nothing was simple, nothing was clear. The little creek slowly narrowed foot by foot until I was barely able to put my paddle in the water without hitting a mangrove. Soon I was enveloped by hanging mangrove roots and branches. The way in many places seemed impassable. Before too long I abandoned my paddle and had to pull my self through foot by foot while gripping roots and branches. A strong fetid odor of decomposition filled my nostrils. The surface of the water was covered with slime. The humidity was stifling. The temperature was once again in the 80s, but I left the breeze behind on the open waters. I was almost getting nostalgic for a wide, open bay and two foot waves. The mosquitoes were as thick as the air, thick as the mangrove vines and roots. I have never thought of myself as claustrophobic, but there, in the Nightmare, I felt trapped. The only thing I could be thankful for was that I was going the right way. Or was I? About one mile in I came to a junction. There was the possibility of going left or straight. Both routes looked equally impassable. I wondered, is this where I am supposed to turn? Is the marker (like #38) missing? Has someone taken it? I decided to go straight but was filled with doubts. At one point, I almost turned back to investigate the other route. There was no opportunity for lengthy deliberations. Each time I stopped, even for a moment, the bugs would swarm around me in a dense fog. Biting, biting—dozens all over my face and body. Alligators were an arm's length from me. After my experience with the gator at Broad River, I had little tolerance for feisty reptiles. I wanted out of there as quickly as possible.

From my journal: "So many bugs at one point that I just closed my eyes, held my breath and sprayed my face. Painful stinging as the repellent found its way into open bites. Alligators were everywhere. Too close. Couldn't stop to check chart."

The Nightmare was hell when I was sure of my direction; it became unbearable as thoughts of being lost now entered my mind. What if I was lost? No one would find me here for weeks. I could use all my food and water just going round in circles, heading down one small creek after another, never finding the end. About every 15 minutes the creek would open up into a wider, more open section and my heart would jump. The end! But time after time it would narrow again and I would be once more covered with bugs, branches ripping at my face and my paddle lying uselessly on the bottom of the canoe while I struggled hand over hand to pull myself out of the mangrove jungle. As the tide rose, the boat and I also rose, going higher and higher into the branches. The lack of air and light was getting to me. I felt trapped; unsure of where I was or even if I was going in the right direction. If I was lost, the tide would soon abandon me, leaving me stuck on the bottom, a captive dinner for mosquitoes and gators alike. I could not walk out because of the gators and I could not just sit there because of the mosquitoes and biting flies. The thought of being stuck in the Nightmare filled me with dread.

How simple it seemed, just a few weeks before, to speak about the Everglades in abstract terms. To merely list the unique animals and plants. To talk about the threats, like pollution and development. Now I was seeing a side of this place that would ground those discussions in a reality I had not suspected. To save bald eagles and panthers is relatively easy. They are attractive, glamorous species. But who will fight to save the mosquitoes and their habitat? Who cares about the Cape Sable seaside sparrow or the Key Largo wood rat? Who cares that the wading bird population in the Everglades has fallen by 93 percent, that pesticides and fertilizers from South Florida farms are destroying water quality and threatening the survival of both plants and animals? Who cares that the fish are poisoned with mercury? From a National Park Service publication:

> High levels of mercury are identified in all levels of the food chain, from the fish in the marsh through raccoons and alligators. The problem extends to the Florida panther, a species so endangered that its numbers may be less than 30 in the entire state . . . A panther with mercury levels that would be toxic to humans was found dead in Everglades National Park.

What the Park Service is trying to say, in their usual veiled bureaucratic lingo, is that the panther died of mercury poisoning. If mercury has accumulated in such high levels as to kill a large mammal, then we can safely assume it is also killing smaller, less resilient species as well, in other words, everything else on down the food chain. In 1947, with the publication of her book, *The Everglades: River of Grass,* Marjorie Stoneman Douglas sounded the alarm that the Everglades was in trouble. The message has been heard, some minor corrections were made, but the root problems, like farming with petroleum-based chemicals, overdevelopment, and the diversion of water for a burgeoning population, all remain.

The Everglades Forever Act of 1994 will appropriate nearly $8 billion of state and federal money to try to save this ecosystem. But already critics are finding flaws that will severely impact the ability of this legislation to affect the needed changes. The U.S. Army Corps of Engineers, who originally sliced up the Everglades water flow with canals and drainage ditches, is charged with undoing the damage. From an Oct. 19, 1998 New York Times editorial:

> One big question is whether the Florida Legislature and its patrons in agriculture and real estate development will go along (with the Everglades Forever Act). Thousand of acres—much of it coveted by developers and growers—must be acquired for water storage and purification . . . Jeb Bush (the newly-elected Governor) may not be as firmly wedded to Everglades restoration. Time and again, Congress has committed itself to undo its disastrous mistakes of 50 years ago, when it robbed South Florida of its historic water flow. It is duty bound to honor that commitment now.

Deadlines for the cleanup have already been pushed back from 1997 to 2006. Lawsuits are as thick as mosquitoes in the Nightmare. The Miccosukee have won their suit against the U.S. Environmental Protection Agency for tougher clean water standards and U.S. District Judge William Hoeveler last year admitted to "benign neglect" in his handling of the federal government's case against the state's agricultural interests.

Marjorie Stoneman Douglas may be the only one who ever had it right. She recognized that it was not just the Everglades that were in danger, but ecosystems everywhere. For what happens in South Florida is a test. Our willingness to change, to consume less and live lighter on the Earth, may be the only, long-term cure for this place and, indeed, the entire planet. From *The Everglades: River of Grass:*

> How far they will go with the great plan for the whole Everglades will depend entirely on the cooperation of the people of the Everglades and their willingness, at last, to do something intelligent for themselves. There is a balance in man also, one which has set against his greed and his inertia and his foolishness; his courage, his will, his ability slowly and painfully to learn, and to work together. Perhaps even in this last hour, in a new relation of usefulness and beauty, the vast magnificent, subtle and unique region of the Everglades may not be utterly lost.

So there are two Nightmares here: one a legal jungle revolving around special interests and politics; the other, a literal jungle in which I am determined not to be stuck.

After plowing on for more than two hours, I finally find marker #23. I have been on the right track and am halfway through. I could have kissed that marker. I eventually made it to the end of the Nightmare. Greatly relieved, I swore I would never return to that kind of situation. I would never allow myself to be trapped like that again. I checked my chart and saw that the trail continued to slice through McLaughlin Key until it hit the Harney River. My camp for the night would be on the Harney River chickee. I would find it just as I emerged from something called Broad Creek. I was in the clear, only a few miles to paddle and I would be sitting on the chickee, drinking coffee and watching the sunset. But then I noticed something. The line on my chart that marked Broad Creek was just as skinny and squiggly as the line that marked the Nightmare. "No, this can't be!" I screamed. But it was. It turned out that Broad Creek was exactly like the Nightmare, but longer! My heart sank as I saw the creek slowly narrow. "No fair. No fair!" I yelled. But yelling didn't help. Before I knew it I was back in the jungle. Back among swarms of bugs, fetid air, and humidity so high I could barely breathe. Hours later I emerged swearing I would never, ever, go through that again. I checked my chart for those thin squiggles. The only other lines that skinny were near the end of my trip at Tarpon Creek. The knot in my stomach tightened but I decided not to worry; I was still days away.

From my journal: "Harney River chickee, sundown: I never expected the Nightmare to be so bad. Hate to think about what would have happened if I got lost in there. Just finished dinner. Nice breeze, now dying down. Saw rainbow in the southern sky. All lines secured. Looking forward to my first good night's sleep in three days. Have not spoken a word to anyone in four days. Did not see even one boat today. Jungle sounds are starting. Have an easy 10-mile run tomorrow—I hope."

Chapter 7

"Let us spend one day as deliberately as Nature, and not be thrown off the track by every nutshell and mosquito's wing that falls on the rails."

—Henry David Thoreau

I completed the next leg of the trip from Harney River to Shark River with no major problems. It was a hard day of paddling but I was rewarded with a rich variety of wildlife encounters.

From my journal: "Day Seven: Shark River chickee: Started paddling at first light this morning, accompanied by porpoises returning to the sea. Some came close by and exhaled. Must have been at least a dozen. What a sight! Arrived here midday. Rode the tide up the Broad River then hit big winds on the Shark River. Stove is giving me trouble. Hope it holds out. I'm going to need all the nutrition I can get. Weather this morning was much improved but now clouds are thickening. Can't seem to shake a sense of impending disaster. Right now a nice breeze is keeping the swamp angels (mosquitoes) at bay and I am relaxing after a good workout of 10 miles. As if to shake me out of my doldrums, a yellow-crowned night heron just came stepping out of the tangle of mangrove roots behind the chickee, took a drink at the water's edge, hung out for about two minutes, then flew off up river. Across the river from me are about six white ibises sitting in a single tree."

That night a thunderstorm rolled in from the north. At first the wind came out of the south but then veered all the way around to the north. Luckily, I was camped at a chickee with a roof. I was thinking, "How nice to be so snug and dry," as the rain thundered down and lightning lit up the ink black darkness around me. But my clothes, sitting in a pile inside the tent, got soaked. Rain funneled down through a leak in the chickee roof and came down into one of the tent doors. It was only when I rolled over during the middle of the night that I realized I had a giant puddle in my tent. The thunder and wind were so loud that I never heard the water dripping into the tent. The following morning (day eight) I actually had a favorable wind for the first time since the start of the trip. It was now six days since I had seen another human being or spoken with anyone (other than myself). I had just approached marker #3 at the Shark River cutoff and was about to enter the northern part of Oyster Bay for a simple two-mile run. Suddenly in the distance I saw a paddle. Then two paddles. I could not believe my eyes. Was there really someone else out here? I felt like the shipwrecked sailor who finds a footprint on the beach. Two guys in fancy sea kayaks came alongside. I was so happy to see someone, especially fellow paddlers, that I forgot to take a new compass bearing. Usually, after finding a marker, I would set a new bearing and follow that line. As long as I didn't screw up (and the markers were where they were supposed to be) it was a good system for keeping myself on track. After about 15 minutes I said good-bye to the kayakers and started down bay. I was in a great mood. They had answered my questions about Tarpon Creek: it was wide! Tour boats even go through it, they told me. What a pleasure it was paddling with the wind at my back. I could hardly tell there was any wind. I must have also had the tide with me. I scooted along, quickly covering about two miles in just a few minutes. This was paddling! When I reached the point where the bay narrowed, I was surprised to find that my compass bearing took me straight into the shoreline. There were openings on either side of a large island. Which way was I supposed to go? I couldn't tell from my chart. It was then I realized I had forgotten to set a new course back at marker #3. Unsure of which way to go, I had only one choice: go back to marker #3 and reshoot the compass bearing. Now I had to slog into a head wind, against the tide. What took me just minutes before would now take close to an hour. But there was another problem. I could not find marker #3. I must have drifted either east or west while going down bay. I had to scour the northern shoreline, poking around every point of land, going farther and farther north, all the time fighting an increasingly strong headwind. The memory of my night in the bottom of the canoe in Big Lostman's Bay haunted me. I was not going to repeat that experience. As I became more and more panicked about being lost, my few options flashed across my mind. To try to find my way across the bay and through the passage would be foolish without first confirming my position. I could not go forward. And it seemed I couldn't go back. I suddenly realized I had made a tragic mistake before setting out on this trip. I had told my family and the folks at the hostel to wait until 14 days had passed before reporting me lost. I knew the trip would take anywhere from eight to ten days and I wanted the option of having a few days to relax and explore. That was before I knew what I was getting into. If I did get lost now, no one would even start looking for me for another seven days. I would not have enough water to survive. And how many days until they actually found me? I don't know how I did it. I think I recognized an unusual shape of mangrove tree limb. Dumb luck. I screamed. I whooped. I hollered. "Yes! Yes! Yes!," There it was—marker #3—nearly three exhausting hours later. I was found again. I reset my compass and flew back down the bay with a 20-knot breeze at my back. My goal for the night was a chickee on the Joe River. It would require some tricky navigation through Oyster Bay. After marker #2, I would no longer be on the Wilderness Waterway trail. There would be no more markers for two days, until I rejoined the trail at the entrance to Coot Bay. I wanted to take the Joe River to avoid the huge expanse of open water in Whitewater Bay. Whitewater Bay is about 15 miles long and five miles wide. After my experiences in the smaller bays, I had no stomach left for anything named Whitewater Bay. But could I successfully navigate through Oyster Bay to the Joe River?

After my stupid mistake this morning, I had little confidence. Dumb luck would once again come to my rescue. After passing marker #2 I found myself at the opening of Oyster Bay and broadside to that 20-knot wind, the most dangerous angle for a small canoe. I struggled to go just a half mile. My heart pounded and I quickly lost my breath. I decided the only thing I could do now was to seek shelter on a lee shore. I labored past one point of land and then another. Nothing. Nowhere to take shelter. I needed to get out of the wind and away from the waves. Every few minutes or so a huge wave would slap the boat and start it rocking and rolling, threatening to capsize me. Now, just two days away from Flamingo and the end of my journey, I was not going to lose it here. I was determined, once again, to survive whatever this wilderness threw at me. I finally found a small opening between two shores. I didn't care where it led or even if I had to tie up to a wet and buggy mangrove shoreline for the night. I had to get out of that wind.

> *"Why should we fear to be crushed by savage elements, we who are made up of the same elements?"*
>
> —Ralph Waldo Emerson

I paddled behind one point then around another. The wind was blocked. I paddled a little farther. Then, just as I rounded a small island, there appeared a sight I had not expected: Oyster Bay chickee! I knew the chickee was in the bay, but had no idea it was so close. It had not even occurred to me to try to find it, as any real navigation would have been impossible in those waves; I could not stop for even a second to check my chart or look at the compass. I went from near disaster to a snug harbor for the night, safely tucked away from wind and wave. Tomorrow I would worry about lost time and navigation. Tonight, I was safe.

> *"Fortune brings in some boats that are not steered."*
>
> —Shakespeare

Day Nine: From my journal: "3 p.m.—Made it! Successfully charted my way across Oyster Bay to Joe River. Finally found chickee and knew I would finish on schedule. Followed Joe River south and east to South Joe River chickee. Got confused many times but stuck to compass bearing. Flamingo should be a cinch to find. Today was beautiful. Clear skies and warm sun. Temperature was in the 80's again. Saw more porpoises this morning. Can't believe I am right on schedule again after all I've been through. I cannot wait to get out of here! In the distance crows are fighting with a hawk while two turkey vultures hang around. Just heard a barred owl. Porpoises swimming near chickee. Much time left now for relaxing. Stove worked long enough this morning to make coffee and oats. Now in good spirits but can't relax until Flamingo. Anything can still happen."

In the early part of this century, Flamingo was a ramshackle fishing outpost, home to moonshiners, fishermen, and smugglers. It was known as "The End of the World." After 10 days of utter solitude, wild weather, cranky alligators and blood-thirsting mosquitoes, Flamingo looked like to me not like the end of the world, but the beginning. My portal back to civilization.

I paddled through Tarpon Creek, down the Buttonwood Canal, docked my canoe at the marina and did what I had been dreaming about for the past five days: I called my family. I called the hostel: "I'm back. Can you come and get me?" How nice it was to say those words, to be standing on that dock with the trip behind me and a cold beer in my hand.

It will be a long time until I really know what happened out there. I know only two things for certain: First, I was lucky—real lucky. Second, the harsh reality of the Everglades: the salt water, sun, tides, waves, and mangrove islands, have given me a renewed appreciation (once again) for the quiet woods of New Jersey. Perhaps it is only by traveling that we ever really know where home is. In the end, I found I could not simply go to the Everglades, but had to let it come to me. This place demands patience, like the egrets and herons, ibises and limpkins that make their home here. I traveled slowly through the great expanses of water and sky like the alligators and crocodiles that have made these wide, sluggish waters their own. In return for my effort, the Everglades have shown me Nature in one of its most raw and brutal moods. It has also shown me Nature in one of its rarest and most spectacular forms. I have floated my little boat through one of the world's most unique places—one of the world's most critically endangered places. Regardless of my fears, my apprehension, my doubts; regardless of my relief at getting out of there, I would not trade the experience.

> *"It is difficult to conceive of a region*
> *uninhabited by man.*
> *We habitually presume his presence*
> *and influence everywhere.*
> *And yet we have not seen pure Nature, unless we have*
> *seen her thus vast, and drear, and inhuman . . .*
> *Nature was here something savage and awful,*
> *though beautiful."*
>
> —Henry David Thoreau, from *Katahdin*

And now, a few days after the completion of my trip, I miss the quiet solitude. I miss those early morning paddles at first light. I miss the porpoises, owls, eagles, and hawks. I miss that wide horizon of sea and sky. I miss the excitement and serendipity. And yes, incredibly, I even miss those damn alligators.

> *"What is hard to bear is sweet to remember."*
>
> —from a Portuguese proverb

Miccosukee elder and tribal leader Buffalo Tiger.

Chillin' at the Everglades Int'l. Hostel.

Photographer Clyde Butcher behind his studio in Big Cypress Swamp.

The author (center) with Edwin and Owhnn of the Everglades Int'l. Hostel.

AGAINST THE WIND

Cycling Across America

"*The soul of a journey is liberty, perfect liberty.*"

—William Hazlitt, from *On Going a Journey*

Chapter 1

> "They who dream by day are cognizant of many things which escape those who dream only by night."
>
> —Edgar Allen Poe

The idea for this trip was probably born during those initial few wobbly moments zooming down the sidewalk on my first two-wheeler. The bike was a Columbia. It was built like a tank and weighed about the same.

The equipment list was impressive: built-in headlight, electric horn, coaster brakes and a candy apple red paint job worthy of a '59 Harley. It was forged in an era before the advent of sting-rays, mountain bikes, BMXs, suspension forks, and titanium frames. That old Columbia was a low-tech dinosaur. But it was mine. My faithful, direct descendent of none other than Leonardo Da Vinci. Naturally, I was heartbroken after the accident.

The realization that I could actually travel on a bicycle—really get somewhere—sparked in me a sense of freedom and independence unmatched by any fossil fuel sucking contraption ever invented. The idea of a long distance journey on a bicycle would stay with me through the years.

> "Thou art to me a delicious torment."
>
> —Ralph Waldo Emerson

Then, last summer, I met a remarkable man. Albert LeBlanc was bicycling from Montreal to the Olympics in Atlanta, Ga. This would be his sixth Olympic event attended on bicycle. Watching him glide noiselessly down a smooth blue ribbon of county road one morning reawoke in me the dream of traveling by bicycle. Albert was in his 70's. His hale and hearty face glowed with the rosy blush of adventure. The seed was planted.

My plan is to travel from the East Coast, through the Plains states up into the Rockies then south through Utah and Arizona, and finally into Mexico for the winter. I'll be leaving from my father's house in Pennsylvania. I'll return in the spring.

Some of the destinations I'm especially looking forward to are Yellowstone and Grand Teton National Parks in Wyoming; Bryce, Arches, and Canyonlands National Parks in Utah, and the Grand Canyon National Park in Arizona.

I have been invited to pitch my tent on the Navajo Reservation in Northeastern Arizona. The Dineh, or traditional Navajo, are embroiled in a land dispute with the Peabody Coal Company. The matriarchal elders, the Grandmothers, want to tell their story. I'll be living on the Reservation and using an interpreter to listen to and record their stories about their land, their beliefs, and their vision for the future.

My food will be simple, lightweight, and nutritious. The usual will most likely be oatmeal for breakfast, peanut butter and noodles for lunch, and pasta for dinner. I hope to find plenty of fresh fruit and vegetables along the way. I'll be mixing up a batch of gorp (granola, oats, raisins, and peanuts) before I go. Another fast energy, easy to eat mix will be peanuts and raisins. I'll be able to eat this as I pedal.

Because I'll be passing through small towns along the way, I won't need to carry a lot of food until I reach the western states. Finding enough water may be a problem in some areas out west.

I hope to do a minimum of 50 miles per day, more if I can. The first week or two I will be taking it easy, stopping often and just getting accustomed to life in the saddle. I'll be camping every night so I need to take my tent, sleeping bag etc. The camping equipment plus a repair kit, water, and food will all go in a small lightweight trailer I'll be towing behind me.

I won't, however, be taking that old Columbia. I had it about a year when one summer day, I was leaning hard into a sharp left turn, looking over my shoulder for the guys that were chasing me, when I crashed into a car that was sitting at a red light. Upon impact, I was ejected from my faithful steed and went flying through the air smashing like a bug, face down, on the windshield of the stopped car. The woman driving the car, as I remember, was very excited. The bike was totaled.

The bike I'll be taking on this trip is a bit more advanced. My thanks to Scott and Kyle of Alpine Outdoors in Hackettstown, N.J., for donating a brand new GT bike. The equipment list is impressive: twenty-one speeds, lightweight steel frame, heavy duty brakes, odometer, aluminum wheels, and some of the best shifting components available. I have been hanging around their shop for the last few weeks, learning how to adjust derailleurs, install brakes, true wheels, and fix flats. With their support, plus what I have managed to learn, I feel well-prepared for most contingencies. They will be my back-up for tires, parts, repair advise, and moral support. In the store will be a map showing my current location, route, pictures, and postcards etc.

> *"What a pitiable thing it is that our civilization can do no better for us than to make us slaves to indoor life, so that we have to go and take artificial exercise in order to preserve our health."*
>
> —George Wharton James, 1908

But this trip is not just about bicycling. It is not just about visiting some of the most spectacular natural wonders on this continent. It is about freedom. The freedom to travel slowly, unencumbered by time and daily commitments. It will be about gliding down country lanes accompanied by bird song and wildflowers. It will be about knee-cap splitting climbs up endless hills. It will be about bad weather and good people. Freedom!

> *"Wherever a man goes, men will pursue him and paw him with their dirty institutions, and, if they can, constrain him to belong to their desperate oddfellow society."*
>
> —Henry David Thoreau

Of course, I will be going against the wind. I've read that the prevailing westerlies will keep me sloughing into a head wind most of the way. I will also be battling my internal wind. I have long suffered from asthma; it was especially bad this past winter. My hope is to be able to expand my lung capacity. I know there will be times when I won't be able to ride. Steep hills (the Rocky Mountains are just big hills, right?) and thin air may force me to walk up some of the climbs, but hopefully, I'll grow stronger with each mile.

A few days after the accident an insurance adjuster came by the house to look at my old Columbia. I doubt if he was as upset as I was at the sight of that crumpled beauty, but he did give my parents a check to buy a new bike, and they did. But it was never the same. There was just no replacing that bike. Until now.

> *"Afoot and light-hearted I take to the open road, Healthy, free, the world before me, the long brown path before me leading wherever I choose."*
>
> —Walt Whitman

Day One: From my journal: "Rode 21 miles today. Feel good. Very tired. Some doubts about the trip. Rain tomorrow."

The first day went smoothly. Starting out at my Dad's house in Harvey's Lake, Pa., I made camp a quarter of a mile behind a picnic area at Ricketts Glen State Park. The official campground sits on top of Red Rock Mountain, some 2,400 feet above my present location. The road is quite steep and, I decided, a little out of my range for the first day. The second day of the trip I spent sitting in my tent waiting for the rain to stop. Even though I had not gone far, my muscles were sore and I was in no rush to take down my tent in the rain, ride in the rain, then pitch my tent in the rain again. I decided to wait out the bad weather. If by the next day it was still raining, I would have to go. But the following day was bright, clear, and cool. I was off! Having coffee in a small cafe that morning, one of the customers, an older woman named Jane who lives on the mountain, told me about the time a Model T Ford came down Red Rock Mountain so fast that it lost control and ran right into her front porch.

"Them Model T's had lousy brakes. I'm still using a Model T brake rod for holding up my curtains. 'Bout all it was good for," she said. Jane said in the summer when tourists are camping on the mountain her whole house smells of burning brakes. "I'm going to put a big sign in front of my house, 'Pump Your Brakes!'"

On day three, I pedaled 42 miles, making camp high on the Allegheny Ridge. One of the few problems I encountered was with dogs. For some reason, dogs cannot resist a bicycle. I can't count how many times a barking, growling dog would jump out from behind a bush or garage and go charging after me with teeth flaring, ready to tear me to pieces. Fortunately, such vicious attacks would usually be quelled by someone at the other end of the dog's chain. Usually. I was cruising downhill at about 25 mph through a hamlet called Quigleyville when out from behind the house came that familiar roar and charge. The only thing missing this time was the chain. There are several methods employed by cyclists for repelling dogs. Some carry Mace or pepper spray, some carry electric devices that emit high-pitched sounds, others just ward off the beast with their tire pump. The method I chose was to get off the bike as quickly as possible and get the bike between me and the dog. Once you stop, the dog quickly loses interest. Talking nicely to the dog or firmly telling it "No!" or "Stay!" also helps. So when I was attacked in

Quigleyville, I jumped off the bike, put it between myself and the dog and said "No!" The dog apparently had not heard of this method. He charged over the lawn, racing into the road with a blood-thirsting delight. At the very last possible moment, the dog's owner appeared on the front porch and yelled, "Stay!" The dog quickly hunched its back, put its belly to the ground and slinked indignantly back toward the house. The dog's owner scowled at me; I had probably interrupted her favorite soap opera. "I'm fine, thanks," I yelled as she slammed the screen door and disappeared inside. The dog sat on the porch smirking at me as I walked my bike down the road and out of sight. Most of the conversations these first few days have gone something like this:

> Me: "Is it very far to Cheeseville from here?"
> Local: "No, not really, just a few miles."
> Me again: "How's the road, many hills?"
> Local again: "Oh no, it's mostly flat all the way out."

Of course, it usually turns out that the town in question is more like 10 grueling, gut-splitting uphill miles away. I've learned not to trust directions from anyone driving a car. What looks perfectly flat from inside a car is vastly different when viewed from over the handlebars. On day five, I learned the road I had planned to take was closed. The 40-mile detour would take me over Hyner Mountain, all 2,074 feet of it. The road out of town wound slowly uphill until I was pedaling just barely faster than walking. In one spot, I had to walk the bike because it was so steep. I started up the mountain at about noon; at 7:30 p.m. I pulled into a campground on the other side, just 20 miles away. I arrived tired and ravenously hungry. Muscles I didn't know I had were rudely introducing themselves. As I was getting ready to make another pasta and plastic cheese dinner, I met a couple from Kunkletown, Pennsylvania. Barb and Ken invited me to dinner. I feasted on veggie dogs, potato salad, baked beans, rolls, and macaroni salad. I ate at least three times more than usual. I had lost a bushing on my trailer and had to jury-rig it with an

Allen wrench and some duct tape. Ken, a mechanic, helped me fix the trailer so it was as good as new and I was on my way again. Ken and Barb ride motorcycles and are dreaming of another bike trip out West. I promised them a postcard from the Badlands of South Dakota.

Since starting my trip, I've traveled about 150 miles. The next five days will be spent paralleling the West Branch of the Susquehanna River through central Pennsylvania. I'll be riding on logging roads and camping in sections of Sproul State Forest, literally miles from any town or city. Once I'm done with the hills of the Alleghenies, my training will be complete. Then it's on to Ohio and westward—without a doubt.

Chapter 2

*"Life is either a daring adventure or nothing.
To keep our faces toward change and behave like free
spirits in the presence of fate is strength undefeatable."*

—Helen Keller

I came rolling down from the Allegheny Ridge to the great sweeping plains of Ohio. Finally, Pennsylvania's rippled ledges of bedrock gave way to the glaciated, fertile plains of the Midwest. There were however, a few more hills to climb as I entered the Cuyahoga River Valley. The Cuyahoga is the infamous "river of fire," that spontaneously combusted two decades ago and helped spawn legislation like the Clean Water Act and, indeed, an entire movement to clean, restore, and protect the nation's waterways. Though much has been done to help the Cuyahoga, it remains the victim of agricultural runoff and industrial waste from nearby Cleveland and Akron. The National Park Service visitor's guide to the valley offers this warning:

> Please be aware that the water quality in the Cuyahoga River varies and swimming is not advised . . . water sports (canoeing and kayaking) are not recommended.

On the afternoon I came to the Cuyahoga River Valley, I had been drenched by a passing thunderstorm. Seeking refuge and a place to dry out, I stopped at the visitor center where a kind ranger suggested a place to camp nearby. Camping is not allowed anywhere in the park; she would surely lose her job if anyone found out. She even visited me that evening, bringing a dinner of hummus, pita bread, organic strawberries and grapes, salad, and juice. Certainly, if rangers are going to range, they should all be so well-equipped. We sat and talked late into the night. I wanted to stop the trip right there. I never heard from her again, though I did send a short note thanking her. But in a strange twist of fate, on my way to the Everglades in the fall of 1998, I met two guys at a I-95 rest stop in Florida. They told me they were from Ohio and we talked about various places there. I mentioned my experience with that ranger and one of the guy's eyes lit up. It turned out that she was his girlfriend's best friend! He had heard about me passing through and her dinner delivery that evening. He told me that she had come back early the next morning to say good-bye but I had already gone. The two guys were on their way to Jamaica to help start an organic farm. He gave me his girlfriend's number so I could track down my mystery ranger but I never did.

Before I entered Ohio, I had to climb what turned out to be one of the worst hills of my trip so far. I crossed the Allegheny River thinking (hoping!) that I would soon experience a general leveling effect—the roller-coaster hills replaced by a more gentle terrain. I left the little town of Elmenton, Pa., crossed the river and suddenly found myself staring upwards at the steepest grade I had seen so far. The hill was at least a mile long, the grade about 20 percent, the shoulder about as wide as a pencil is long. Huge fuel and quarry trucks strained up the hill right alongside me, spewing diesel fumes and kicking up dust and debris. There is a road rule I've discovered: Whenever I am going slowly, struggling up a hill, sucking air deep into my lungs, that is the precise moment the smokiest, fume-spewing car or truck comes alongside. I suspect it is a law of nature and I harbor no hope of changing or eluding it. Another law I've discovered: The biggest hills come at the end of the day. The tougher the day, the bigger the hill. And so it was with this one. My map showed a campground less than a mile away. I decided to splurge. I normally just slip into the roadside woods at night to sleep. Campgrounds are a luxury I reserve for those occasions when I need a shower and a little rest. So far, my expenditures for camping have totaled $17, less than $1 a day. As I dragged myself into the Gaslight Campground, I knew my budget was in jeopardy; the manicured lawns, the swimming pool, the big travel trailers they all screamed out at me: This is going to be expensive! I had exactly $20 on me.

But the hill had done me in; I could ride no farther. The woman behind the desk, Sharon Sickler, told me the bad news: $20 for the night. I pleaded for a little grassy spot somewhere out back, behind the dumpster or in the swamp, I didn't care—I just wanted to sleep.

"Sorry," she said, "Our fee for a tent site is $20."

In a desperate attempt to avoid getting back on the bike, I offered to scrub the rest rooms in the morning in exchange for the fee. Her eyes lit up and the wheeling and dealing began. After a few minutes of hammering out the fine points, we were done.

"O.K.," she said, "Here's the deal. You give me $20 now and tomorrow, after you've finished—and if you've done a good job—I'll give you your $20 back."

I could do nothing but hand her my last $20 and hope that she was honest. The next morning found me merrily scrubbing toilets, showers and urinals. I got back my $20, politely declined an offer to stay another day and cut the grass (those toilets really sparkled!) and headed out rested and refreshed, less than a two-day ride from the Ohio border.

Beyond the Cuyahoga River Valley, Ohio gets flat—real flat. The architect of this table land was the retreating Wisconsonian Glacier. It leveled the northwest portion of the state and left behind rich glacial debris. The vegetation that grew here was mostly woodland. But today, the forest has been cut to provide access to the fertile deposits, or till, as this portion of the state is referred to as the "till plains." Ohio it seems, is an orphaned state. Not truly part of the sweeping Great Plains, no longer in possession of its vast woodlands; the cherry, sugar maple, hickory, the wildflower meadows and wildlife that inhabit those rare and special places, are all now gone. Ohio has traded its black bear for soybeans, its warblers for wheat. I would guess that there is more biological diversity in a square mile of northwest New Jersey than in 100 square miles of Ohio. The small farmer has also disappeared. "If you want to be in it, you have to be big," one farmer told me; big machinery, big acres, big debt. There are no picturesque farms here like on the East Coast. There are just thousands of acres of oats or wheat or beans. Huge combines dwarf the farmer; the land seems unreal, without variation. If the language of Nature is diversity, then Ohio has become a monosyllabic utterance, over and over, the same.

Friday, Day 14: I was pedaling my way westward on state route 303 in Ohio when I saw a simple sign propped up against a tree. It read: "I.W.L.A." in straight bold letters, and underneath, "Bluegrass," in script. The little arrow pointed south. I asked at a local garage what the sign meant. I thought perhaps it was a farm advertising seed. I also thought that I may have stumbled upon a bluegrass festival. The mechanics had no idea except that it might be a "bunch of weirdo environmentalists." I followed the sign for four miles (a long detour on a bike!) and found a bluegrass festival organized by the Izaac Walton League of America; (I.W.L.A.), a conservation group pledged to protecting habitat and wildlife (though they do promote hunting and fishing). Bill Ashbaugh, the local chapter president, let me stay for the weekend (for free!). He let me pitch my tent overlooking the Black River, high above the festival grounds. The local I.W.L.A. chapter has acquired 104 acres of woods, wetlands, and streams. They have built bat boxes, bluebird houses, and planted trees. But best of all, they have left the majority of the land alone. Izaac Walton members conduct stream testing workshops and regularly bring inner-city kids to the preserve to explore nature. The annual bluegrass festival, weekly bluegrass jams and other events help defray expenses. When I arrived the cornbread was in the oven, the beans were ready, and the music was about to start. I stayed for two days listening to music, talking, taking photos, and exploring the preserve. After hundreds of miles of soybeans, it was good to see woods and hear songbirds again. It was also good to be among people who care about their local ecology. Ashbaugh, who neither hunts or fishes, told me that the number of organic farms in Ohio has tripled in the last four years. He seems hopeful that Ohio can regain its rivers and rescue its soil from erosion, chemical contamination, and overuse. Members of the Izaac Walton League pledge to be "defenders of soil, air, woods, waters, and wildlife." And while they may not be the Greenpeace of the Midwest, I do know that today, without them, there would certainly be 104 more acres of soybeans in Ohio, and a lot fewer songbirds, wildflowers, and trees. The group, which has about 50,000 members nationwide, takes its name from the 17th century author of the fishing classic, *The Compleat Angler*.

It is Day 19 of the trip. My legs are getting stronger and my lungs are growing in their capacity. Only that part of my anatomy most intimate with the bike has voiced any complaints. The complaints have not been many, but they are hard to ignore. I'm averaging 50 miles a day. Yesterday I did 65 miles; the day before, 58 miles. A light tail wind and I feel as if I'm flying; a head or cross wind and each mile is a struggle. I crossed into Indiana yesterday and already have many stories of kindness to tell. There are more trees here and I am camped illegally by a reservoir outside the town of Huntington (the boyhood home of Dan Quayle). The forecast calls for rain; the wind is out of the west. Yet no matter how grueling the previous day, or how bleak the forecast, I have not yet had a morning where I could not wait to get back on the bike and ride west.

Chapter 3

"I expand and live in the warm day like corn and melons."

—Ralph Waldo Emerson

It has not rained since I left Ohio 11 days ago. Searing heat and stifling humidity have been my constant companions. By midday, the temperature screams into the high 90's; the humidity: 100 percent. Early evening brings the threat of thunderstorms and lightning, but the rain, the soft, cool, renewing rain, never comes.

"How beautiful the rain!
After dust and heat,
In the broad and fiery street,
In the narrow lane,
How beautiful is the rain!"

—Henry Wadsworth Longfellow,
from *Rain in Summer*

Each night I lie down exhausted, the day's sweat and grit clinging to my skin. The humidity has turned my tent into a sauna. Outside, beyond the thin nylon wall, blood-thirsting mosquitoes wait silently, imprisoning me. And to everyone in Ohio, Indiana, Illinois, and half of Iowa, and to everyone else who has yet to ask me, the answer is yes. Yes! Yes! Yes! It IS hot enough for me, thank you. Is it hot enough for you? I had just crossed into Indiana. It was late morning and I was taking a break, sitting against a fence post sipping tepid water, eating peanuts and watching the cars go by. Suddenly, a beat-up old Toyota charged across the highway against on-coming traffic and pulled up beside me. The driver, a scruffy guy in his late 20's, rolled down his window, looked at me for a second or two and finally asked, "Where ya heading?" This is it, I thought. This is where my little adventure ends. Shot to death by some crazy man while eating peanuts on Highway 1 in Who-Knows-Where, Indiana. "West," I said, trying to look bullet-proof. He nodded, then leaned way down and over to the passenger side floor, groping for something, something hidden. Just like in a movie; a short, violent movie. He re-emerged and I could see something in his hand. "Here," he said, tossing me an ice-cold bottle of water. "Have a safe trip."

I thought of him a week later. I was pedaling fast, trying to outrun a thunderstorm, when I saw, coming toward me, a Jeep full of kids. I heard laughter, saw an arm swing out, saw something in the air. Someone had launched an empty beer can at me. Luckily, it hit me in the chest, not in the face. The car (and the can) was moving at about 45 mph; the impact was startling. I managed to keep my balance and continue riding. For the next few miles, I nervously looked behind me every few minutes to see if they might return for another volley, the first one having been such a success. Two stories, two extremes. Fortunately, acts of kindness far outnumber those of stupidity. Like Bill the Pizza Man in Zanesville, Ind., who made me a special pizza and refused to take my money; like the park ranger in Van Buren Park in Ohio who let me stay for free; like the entire town of Monroeville, Ind., that allows cross-country cyclists to use their community center. Cyclists can sleep in the building, cook in the full kitchen, or, like I did, just take a hot shower and move on. Knock on the door of the little white house across the street and Mr. or Mrs. Meyers will open the building for you. After you've locked up and turned off the lights, go back and sign the guest register.

You'll add your name to the thousands of cyclists from around the world who have found a warm and generous welcome from this small town.

> *"Nothing has happened today except kindness."*
>
> —Gertrude Stein

I was sick of looking at mile after mile of corn. The farmers, when they were about, were encased in air-conditioned cabs atop huge tractors. Sometimes they waved. I rarely ever saw a farmer actually on the ground. At the end of the day, the tractors were left in the field, abandoned.

> *"And when that crop grew and was harvested,*
> *no man had crumbled a hot clod in his fingers*
> *and let the earth sift past his fingertips.*
> *No man had touched the seed, or lusted for the growth.*
> *Men ate what they had not raised,*
> *had no connection with the bread.*
> *The land bore under iron, and under iron gradually*
> *died; for it was not loved or hated, it had no prayers*
> *or curses."*
>
> —John Steinbeck, from *The Grapes of Wrath*

I turned north in Illinois. My map showed a small chain of green blotches. The green meant trees and streams and perhaps even lakes. Best of all, trees meant shade, cool air and soft brown earth to rest on. I stumbled upon a bike trail, a converted towpath from the Illinois & Michigan Canal. The trail runs about 60 miles from Joliet, Ill. to LaSalle, Ill. What a welcome respite from the baking pavement, exhaust fumes, corn rows, and flying cans. The trail followed the canal (dry at the moment due to construction), winding through a thousand-foot wide swath of trees and brush. Every few miles were clearings with picnic tables and campsites (free and legal!). The trail was an oasis for cyclists, walkers, and local wildlife. Early one morning, while pedaling at an easy pace, I saw a small coyote loping along just ahead of me. We traveled together for almost ten minutes. He looked back uneasily every so often to check on my position. When I tried to gain on him, he slipped into the woods and disappeared. Removed from the constant noise of the highway, gliding down that cool path, I saw deer and hawks; hundreds of white butterflies lined the trail in the late morning, bullfrogs sang in the evening. The whispered secrets of nature, so easily drowned by the noise of cars and highways, can be softly heard on a bicycle, traveling slowly on a smooth path through the woods. The I&M Canal was dug by the hands of Irish immigrants in the 1830s and 1840s. The canal connected the Great Lakes to the Illinois River, providing a shipping link between the East Coast and the Midwest. Mules trod the towpath pulling barges loaded with sugar, grain, and people. The railroads eventually replaced the canal. It closed in 1933. The entire canal is now a National Heritage Corridor, the first of its kind in the country. It contains more than 100 miles of protected parks, bike paths, and hiking trails. The corridor extends from Chicago to Peru/LaSalle, Ill.

> "Men travel faster now, but I do not know if they go to better things."
>
> —Willa Cather

The sign read:

REGAL IN APPOINTMENT
MAGNIFICENT IN CONCEPTION
OMNIPOTENT IN STRENGTH
THE CLEANEST, PUREST AND BEST!

No, it wasn't an advertisement for the latest Disney, sugar-coated, altered reality, mega-billion dollar, computer-enhanced multimedia propaganda cartoon.

It continued:

12 Acres of Canvas
1,000 Men and Horses
10,000 Seats—Three Rings—Four Trains!

The ad was for one of the "Great Wallace Shows," a traveling circus of the late 19th and 20th centuries. The placard was on display, along with photos, props, and other memorabilia at the International Circus Hall of Fame in Peru, Indiana. Some of my favorite exhibits were the portraits of Otto, Charles, Alf, John, and Al—the five Ringling Brothers. Bird Millman (1890-1940), billed as the world's premier female wire walker, was also represented. Millman went on to join the Ziegfield Follies in New York City in 1916 and was known as the "The Dainty Darling Queen of the Tightwire." The museum includes tributes to Emmett Kelley (1898-1979), creator of Weary Willie, and Tom Mix, whose real name was Thomas Edwin Mix. The Hall of Fame presents a show each day. Circus performers staying in Peru (pronounced pee-roo by some of the locals) between gigs supply the talent.

Bob-O-The Clown (Robert Hurley) told me the land around the Hall of Fame was once the wintering grounds for performers. More than 25 buildings on 2,500 acres housed performers, animals, and props during the coldest months of the year. About a dozen elephants drowned during the flood of 1913. "They're all buried right here, right where we are now," said Hurley, while looking out over the corn that has now invaded most of the land.

But things haven't changed that much. That afternoon, in the sweltering heat, a steam-powered calliope played in the background as kids, munching popcorn and eating cotton candy, got a small taste of the magic of live performance—the kind of magic Disney and Speilberg are still trying to recreate.

In Utica, Ind., on Day 25, my odometer read 1,000 miles. On Sunday, Day 29, I crossed the Mississippi River. I am finally west.

After crossing the river, I stopped under the few trees in a riverside park in Muscatine, Iowa, to rest, repair a slow leak, and relax. The Mississippi, for me, at least, remains more valuable as a symbol than an actual river. It is not much good for swimming and the U.S. Army Corps. of Engineers has shaped it to the human interpretation of what a river should be and do. Barge traffic and garbage scows have transformed the river into a watery interstate. The city of Muscatine was hot and lousy with traffic. The rudest drivers I have encountered so far were all within the city limits. I traveled away from that city, and that river, as fast as I could, holding thoughts of the cool air and clean waters of the Rocky Mountains as I pedaled westward.

"Good-bye, Good-bye
I bid you now, my friend;
And though 'tis hard to say the word,
To destiny I bend."

—Mark Twain on his good-bye to Hannibal
and the Mississippi

Chapter 4

*"The wind in the grain is the caress to the spouse,
it is the hand of peace stroking her hair."*

—St. Exupery, 1942

Red Rock Reservoir, Iowa: The park ranger came to my campsite warning me of the impending storm. "We had 90 mph winds here last week," he said. "Lost a whole bunch of trees and a sign."

He informed me the only safe place would be in the brick restroom near the park office. That evening, the temperature, which had been in the high 90's, crashed into the 50s, while the wind roared across the 35 miles of open water of Red Rock Reservoir. It slammed into my tent, defeated my little cook stove, and scattered my clothes and papers all over the campground.

The rain never came but the wind grew stronger and diminished only after several days. Riding into the wind is like riding with the brakes on. I now prefer hills to wind. At least with a hill you have the satisfaction of reaching the top; the ride down your well-earned reward. Riding into a head wind is similar to riding up a perpetual hill—there is no relief or reward.

Iowa had both hills and wind. My progress through this state was excruciatingly slow. Because of the wind, hills were twice as hard to conquer and I was cheated of the downhill ride. From my journal: "The weather in Iowa is not very good but there is certainly plenty of it. I can't wait to get out of here!"

Camping in Iowa was also a problem. I slept under bridges, in highway rest areas, and on the edges of farm fields. State parks were too few and far apart to be of much use. The trees have all been cut to make room for the corn. It's impossible to find shade in the middle of the day. Parks had few trees. On the highway, if I needed to stop, I looked for the pencil shadow of a utility pole or standing brush high enough for me to scoot under. I wondered, do we really need all this corn? Then I found out where most Iowa corn goes.

According to a statistician from the U.S. Department of Agriculture, Iowa has 13 million hogs. One million of these are kept for breeding, the other 12 million are slaughtered every year. Before they're butchered, those 12 million hogs eat an awful lot of corn. Many of these hogs are "produced" in giant factory farms. The hogs are born, raised, and slaughtered without ever seeing the light of day or experiencing life outside a steel cage. Hog farms have come under attack from many sides. Small farmers claim they can't compete with the large transnational corporate-owned farms which receive premium prices from packers and processors. Large processors are now buying up small farms, ensuring themselves a cheap and stable supply.

Some farms raise as many as 50,000 hogs at a time. The effluent from these hogs, the equivalent of the output of a small city, simply collects in waste ponds. Local ground water throughout the state has been seriously contaminated by this practice. Animal rights activists have consistently condemned the brutal and unsanitary treatment of these intelligent animals. Of course, hog farms are notorious for their stench. Driving past one in a car can be unpleasant; riding past one on a bicycle is nauseating. The hogs spend their day under flat, metal roofs, sweltering in the heat. Huge fans exhaust the sour air to the outside—to passing cars, bicycles, homes and towns.

I had run out of water somewhere in the middle of Iowa. I stopped at a quaint farmhouse which was surrounded by nothing but miles and miles of corn. No factories, no highways, no industry. Just corn. The man who answered the door said he woud gladly fill my water bottles. He brought out a couple of jugs of bottled water. "Just use your regular water," I told him. "Don't waste the bottled stuff on me." Sadly, he told me that his well water was contaminated from the pesticides, herbicides, and fertilizers used in growing all that corn. He was the statistican from the U.S.D.A.

A ranger at Prairie Rose State Park in Iowa told me that most of the campers had left the park in a hurry the previous weekend. The wind had shifted and brought the putrid odor of a local factory farm into the campground. She thought it was funny. Most of the campers, she said, were Iowa hog farmers.

I now join the legions of weight loss schemers and diet authors. Introducing:

BICYCLE BILL'S 45-DAY MIRACLE DIET:

- Eat all your favorite foods—as much and as often as you like and lose weight!
- No special foods to buy—no meetings to attend.
- It's guaranteed or your money back!

Here's how it works:

First, get a bicycle. Then, load it up with at least 50 pounds of camping equipment, clothes, and other necessities. Be sure to include a gallon of water, repair tools, extra tubes and tires, camera equipment, and a few books.

Next, start pedaling! If you live in the east—head west. If you live in the north—head south, etc. It really doesn't matter. Just pedal. (Note: A 50-mile per day minimum is recommended. Steep hills and head winds will improve your results.)

Now, start enjoying thick creamy sauces, rich desserts, giant portions. Eat until your sides are practically splitting. Go ahead! Enjoy hot fudge sundaes, cheesecake with chocolate-raspberry sauce, lasagna thick with cheese. Eat anything you want—as much as you want—*It's Guaranteed!*

At the end of 45 days (if you live) you will be thin and svelte. You will have actually lost weight while tripling your caloric intake. That's all there is to it. Happy Pedaling and Bon Appetit!

WARNING: Always consult a physician before starting any new diet plan; before starting this plan, consult a psychiatrist.

As my tolerance of Iowa and the Midwest diminished, my anticipation of Nebraska grew. I tried to enjoy the Midwest but I think, in the end, it was just something to get through, like a fever has to be endured until it breaks, before the recovery can begin.

The water was unfit for swimming in most of the rivers, lakes, and streams. I have not tasted sweet water since I left the Alleghenies. The landscape (cornscape) was boring. There were too few exceptions: the densely forested Cuyahoga River Valley, the Illinois & Michigan bike trail, and Red Rock Reservoir in Iowa.

Midwesterners seem to be subject to a word tax. They speak in slow, carefully chosen words, each one left to hang in the air until the next one arrives. If there is such a tax, I have spent a small fortune here.

The only exception seems to be in giving directions. Suddenly, the words pour forth.

> ME: "Excuse me, can you tell me how to get to Cornhusker Campground?"
>
> LOCAL: (scratching head, adjusting hat): "Well now, let's see . . . if you had been here last week I'd have told you to go down around Podunk, 'cause of the flood, you know . . . warshed the whole darn road right out. But you can go that way now I think. Wait, let me ask Merle, he lives down that way . . . Hey, Merle . . ."

Then more people are brought in, each with their own irrelevant data and obscure historical references, until a small din rises from the swelling crowd. Now I simply avoid asking directions. I've learned that it is far quicker to pedal the five or ten miles down the road and have a look for myself. I leave the frenzied crowd at the local Chat & Chew to fight it out among themselves.

When lost, I have to sneak a look at my map, fearful that someone will see me and ask: "Hey, where ya heading?" Always, the directions are delivered at about half the rate of the human pulse. As Great Plains poet Kathleen Norris observed in her book, *Dakota*:

> We also treasure our world-champion slow talkers, people who speak as if God has given them only so many words to use in a lifetime, and having said them, they will die.

I spent my last night in Iowa camped in the DeSoto National Wildlife Refuge. For a few dollars you can buy a license to kill deer, coyote, and waterfowl here. But a man, sleeping alone under the trees, is not tolerated. If caught, "violators are subject to a minimum fine of $50." I camped deep in the refuge, found juicy ripe blackberries and ate them while a family of coyotes sang and cried into the night.

I had heard gunshots all night long. In the morning, on the way out of the refuge, I noticed road signs stating that it is illegal to shoot a firearm from a moving car. Apparently, the wildlife fall victim to drive-by shootings from "hunters." As I dragged Leonardo and B.O.B. (my bike and trailer) through the underbrush and over several logs during my early morning escape from the refuge, I suddenly realized just what faithful partners in this adventure they have been.

Like most things (and people), the more reliable and dependable they are, the less we seem to notice them. Leonardo has taken me everywhere I asked and done so without complaint. I have ridden on dirt logging roads in the Allegheny Mountains, pushed and pulled it through thorny brush to evade rangers and farmers, pedaled 40 miles on dusty limestone bike trails, and even ridden through sand and water.

I have had only one flat on each so far. I try to give Leonardo a bath whenever possible, followed by a good chain cleaning and lube. Unfortunately, most nights I am usually too tired to attend to its needs. My promises go unfulfilled; Leonardo never complains.

Nearly 2,000 miles of gear-grinding and pedal-stomping, nights spent uncovered in the rain and days baking in the sun have not dissuaded this hardy pair from the journey. Every morning after breakfast, when camp is dismantled and packed, I get on Leonardo and head west. For me, after all these miles, it is still like flying. I can't speak for Leonardo.

Nebraska! Just the name evokes big sky, big land; a sweeping horizon on every side. On day 39, I crossed the Missouri River to the Great Plains. The landscape has changed. Corn has surrendered to cattle; white-faced Herefords and Black Angus dot rolling hills. My route has taken me through part of the famed Sand Hills region. Twenty thousand square miles of sand dunes stabilized by prairie grasses, yucca, and wildflowers.

The distant hills are covered in a velvety green moss. The sand shines through from blunt edges carved by the wind—the whole of it wrapped by a sky, bluest above you, then melting into lighter and lighter shades extending endlessly outward. Clouds with bottoms planed flat by the high winds hang in the distance as if sitting on glass shelves in the sky.

The Oglala Sioux, the Ute, Apache, Cheyenne, Pawnee, Comanche, Padouca, and the Dismal River Sioux have all made their home here. The buffalo hunters.

The pioneers, refugees from poverty and persecution in Ireland, Scandinavia, and Europe also made their home here. The buffalo slaughterers.

The Northwestern, the Burlington Northern, and Union Pacific once steamed through these hills. But the land and sky have swallowed them all. The scale is too large for mere human contrivances. Pedaling west into the sun, free from the glass and steel confinement of a car, I too, am swallowed up by this place.

Strings of small towns stretch out along my route. Some towns, like Wood Lake, have just 76 people, not including the dogs and cats. Most of the towns have little parks that permit camping. Some have showers; some are free, others ask for a small donation. The people in these towns seem to have grown accustomed to being dwarfed by the land and sky. They move about without spectacle or bravado. Small clusters and colonies of human activity—unrushed, subdued, and compressed by the great distances.

> *"In little towns, lives roll along so close to one another; loves and hates beat about, their wings almost touching."*
>
> —Willa Cather

Day 46: My odometer reads 1,903 miles. I am camped in a town park in Valentine, Neb., just nine miles from South Dakota. Tomorrow, I will ride north onto the Rosebud Reservation. I expect to be in the Badlands within three or four days. I plan to stop there for a few days to relax and catch up on my correspondence.

Last night, the evening sun, a golden globe, bowed down behind walls of pink and gray clouds. A mourning dove, a western meadowlark, and a red-winged blackbird joined in a chorus as swallows darted and dipped across the iridescent prairie. Later, the moon was bright against the southern horizon, shimmering down upon the Sand Hills and lakes, down upon the Platte, the Dismal, the Niobrara and Snake rivers. It shimmered down upon the bones and arrowheads, cattle and ranches. The sweet, spicy scent of sage filled the air and I fell softly to sleep, dreaming of the buffalo that once roamed where I now lay softly sleeping.

Chapter 5

"What I saw gave me the indescribable sense of mysterious elsewhere—a distant architecture, ethereal . . . an endless supernatural world more spiritual than Earth but created out of it."

—Frank Lloyd Wright on the Badlands, 1935

The Lakota called them Mako Sica: bad lands. Simple words best describe this place: hot, dry, large, silent. But the Badlands are complex. They are a book of knowledge encased in ancient soil, bound and held in place by billions of years of compaction and compression. They are the eroding remains of the bottom of an ancient, shallow sea.

Jagged spires and rounded buttes are striped with banded layers of cream and pink. Soft pastel colors contrast with the sharp, dark shadows of crevices and caves. This spectacle of light and dark, sharp and smooth, commands your eye and strikes a note of awe; seldom does Nature reveal itself so forthrightly, so plainly. It is this revelation, clear and bold, that makes the Badlands so inviting—yet so intimidating.

Before I arrived in the Badlands, I had to traverse another landscape, a landscape of poverty, despair, and isolation. A country within a country. My route took me through the Lakota Rosebud and Pine Ridge Reservations.

"Don't stop overnight," I was warned. "Don't ride at night," they told me. "The roads are full of drunk drivers."

What they really meant was the roads were full of drunk "Indians." One Lakota woman, a casino worker, told me her concerns for the people on the reservation. "It's like an inner city but without the city. We have all the problems: alcoholism, drugs . . . we're even starting to see AIDS now on the 'rez. It's like a Third World country here."

Pine Ridge is the second largest Reservation in the country. Lakota Holy Man, Black Elk, is buried on the Rosebud Reservation. Though the massacre at Wounded Knee and the 1970s uprisings and civil disobedience actions (dubbed Wounded Knee II) are generally forgotten by the rest of the country, there still exists a great deal of tension here. The Lakota themselves are divided between those wanting to return to traditional ways and those seeking to join the march of modern times.

There is also tension between local whites and the Lakota. It was the whites who warned me not to stop, not to camp on the Reservation. Though the Lakota own the land, the most productive parcels are leased to white ranchers. The Lakota are forced to receive government handouts and live in shabby government houses, clustered together on hillsides that reminded me of "colonias" or "poor towns" on the Mexican border. Meanwhile, affluent whites from all over the country make pilgrimages here to take part in Lakota spiritual ceremonies, for a fee of course.

An article in the Aug. 4 edition of *Indian Country Today* (billed as America's largest Indian newspaper) titled, *The Selling of the Sun Dance*, stated:

> The explosion of interest in Lakota spirituality has caused some Elders and community members to call a halt to what they believe is spiritual exploitation. On June 30, Chief Judge Patrick Lee of the Oglala Sioux tribe signed a permanent restraining order that would ban all non-Indians from participating in Sun Dances or other Lakota religious ceremonies upon Pine Ridge Reservation.

The restraining order has since been vacated, but it has sparked a heated controversy over religious freedoms on Reservations as granted in the Indian Civil Rights Act of 1968. There will be 43 Sun Dances held on Pine Ridge this summer, up from 38 last year. In one Sun Dance, 30 whites reportedly paid $5,000 each to participate. The money goes to the organizers, not the Reservation.

An entire sovereign nation is being held prisoner on its own soil. It is not the barbed wire that is choking the life from this land and its people, but the poverty, despair, and exploitation. As Lame Deer, a Lakota Wicasa Wakan (medicine man) writes in his book, *Lame Deer, Seeker of Visions*:

> We try to forget that even our fenced-in Reservations no longer belong to us. We have to lease them to white ranchers who fatten their cattle, and themselves, on our land. At Pine Ridge, less than one percent of the land is worked by Indians . . . There is nothing worthwhile for a man to do, nothing that would bring honor or make him feel good inside. There are only a handful of jobs for a few thousand people . . .

I pedaled 83 miles in 100-degree heat and arrived in the Badlands on Day 48 of my journey. Exhausted, I stayed in the park campground the first night. Early the next day, I searched for a backcountry camp that would offer solitude yet be close enough to a water source. Leaving the park road, I followed a dry wash back through a canyon until I reached a small, enclosed, bowl-like section. A semicircular wall called to me to camp by it. The wall blocked the view of my camp from the road and eliminated all sounds of cars.

Though only about a quarter-mile from the road, I was alone and invisible. Back country camps are supposed to be pitched at least a half-mile from a road or trail, but one ranger had told me that as long as I couldn't be seen, I would be fine. The canyon provided the perfect place for a base camp. I could relax here, explore, and make day trips throughout the park. I fetched water with the bike and trailer from the campground about two miles away.

I pitched my tent on a grassy patch above obvious drainages. The canyon's eastern wall provided shade until about 10 a.m., then I retreated to the opposite side of the western wall. As the sun rose to its highest point, there was no escaping it. Afternoons found me in the visitor center book store or lounging in a cool, shady juniper pine grove. By late afternoon, I was back at camp reading, cooking, or just gazing up at the spectacular walls rising above me, encircling me, in ancient rock and dirt. I reminded myself that I was sitting at the bottom of an ancient sea once rich with life, the remains now fossilized beneath layers of volcanic ash and shale. Bone fragments were everywhere.

The Badlands hold the country's largest deposits of fossils, from small invertebrates to the Hoplophoneus, an early relative of the saber-tooth cat. The world's largest remaining mixed-grass prairie surrounds the eroding buttes and spires. Once, a third of North America consisted of grassland prairies; now little is left. Too dry for trees and too wet for desert, grasses thrive here—more than 52 varieties, including bluestem and cordgrass, wild oats and wheatgrass. I wandered over endless acres of prairie with the scorched Badlands ringing the view in every direction. Some grasses felt soft, others stung like nettles.

Badlands weather was severe. Looking out over the prairie, I could see storms many miles away. Great sweeping clouds of blue-gray washed over the land, unleashing torrents of rain and hail. Walls of water, angled by the winds, crept over the horizon while I watched, bathed in sunlight, perhaps a hundred miles from the storm. Thick, vertical lightning struck the earth—and remained as if stuck in the ground. This was no flicker or flash, this was lightning! Thunder rolled across the prairie with nothing to stop it, nothing to absorb it, deflect it, until it echoed from canyon walls and bounced between buttes, vibrating under foot, finally absorbed by the Earth itself.

Prairie sunflowers, snow on the mountain, prairie clover, and prickly pear cactus grew around my camp. I found bobcat tracks deep in the canyon and each night cliff swallows left their mud nests high on the canyon walls and flew overhead. Small-footed myotis (bats) flew in circles around my little camp, flying within inches of my head as I watched them dart in and out of the canyon. Coyotes sang as the steep walls around me slowly crumbled, rocks and soil spilling softly down to the canyon floor like sand sifting through gentle fingers. For one full week, I heard not a single human sound—no voices, no radios, no cars—only footsteps lightly falling on the bottom of an ancient sea.

I had a little surprise on my last day in the Badlands. I was waiting for a replacement tent pole that was being shipped to me by the manufacturer of my tent (the pole had snapped in two, baking in the Badlands sun). It arrived at the park office late in the afternoon. I hurried back to my camp so I could pack up and leave in the cool of the early evening. I walked, with my bike, the quarter-mile back to my camp, turned the corner on my little wall and found—nothing! My trailer, my tent—all my equipment was gone. It looked as though I had never been there. I raced up nearby buttes looking over into adjoining canyons thinking that someone had played a joke on me, but there was nothing, no trace of my stuff.

"No!" I yelled. "This can't be!"

Until now, I had trusted people. I left my camp unattended, my bike unlocked. I felt betrayed. Who would do this and why take everything? My cook stove, my pots and pans . . . everything—my extra ATM card, my camera, all my pictures and notes. "No!," I yelled, my voice filling the canyon and bouncing back at me. I raced back to the park office to report the theft. My only hope was that a ranger had confiscated my camp for some reason. But I had not seen anyone and besides, a ranger, I thought, would have just left a note or a warning.

The guy at the desk nodded politely while I babbled on about my stuff, my heart pounding through my chest. "Let me check," he said calmly. He returned still nodding his head. "Yes, your camp has been confiscated. Wait outside the visitor center and someone will come by to explain."

A few minutes later Ranger John Donaldson appeared. "I

bet you're glad to see me, huh?" Glad? I could have kissed him. I could have run off to Mexico and married him. He said my camp had been confiscated because I was only a quarter-mile from the road, not the required half-mile. "You would've been OK," he said, "if a ranger hadn't led a nature hike down that canyon. He saw your camp and reported it."

"How about a note?' I asked. "Couldn't you have just left a note, or stopped by to tell me?"

Ranger Donaldson said that notes sometimes blow away. But not only did Ranger Donaldson have to pack up my camp in 90 degree heat, not only did he have to carry out the whole mess a quarter-mile to where his truck was parked, but he had to list every single item he confiscated. The list, which I plan on framing, includes such interesting items as: "one pair dirty socks; peanut butter—Jiffy; duct-tape, partial roll; space blanket-well used;" etc.

I thanked Ranger Donaldson for taking such good care of my stuff, repacked the trailer (he did it all wrong) and headed out of the Badlands thrilled to be lugging 55 pounds of gear and water up yet another knee-cap splitting hill. Leaving the park, I took the 30-mile loop road through the heart of the Badlands. The road climbed 1,000 feet onto the high prairie. The weather was cool, a storm was coming in but I rode on despite the threatening skies. As I neared the highest point the rain began. In just minutes I was soaked. The wind blew from every direction chilling me completely. A succession of storms moved through until at last the sun reappeared and a double rainbow lit the southern horizon. Two full arcs crossed the sky, each end clearly visible. I had never before seen both ends of a rainbow.

> "Once it chanced that I stood in the very abutment of a
> rainbow's arch, which filled the lower stratum of the
> atmosphere, tinging the grass and leaves around,
> and dazzling me as if I looked through colored crystal.
> It was a lake of rainbow light, in which,
> for a short while, I lived like a dolphin."
>
> —Henry David Thoreau

Warmed by the sun, I was back on the bike. Directly ahead of me I saw a giant wall of gray. "Wow, that's some nasty business," I said to myself. The next instant the wind was so strong I could hardly pedal. Hailstones the size of mothballs were rolling down the road coming from the wall which was now terrifyingly close. The wind stopped me cold. I jumped off the bike and threw it down into a gully off the roadway.

In an instant, the wall of hail was upon me. Alone on the high prairie, miles from any structure, I was totally exposed to the wind and the rain and the hail. I turned to run back to a small cliff I had noticed. When I looked to see if any cars were coming, I was amazed—the road had disappeared—swallowed up by the wall of gray. I ran as fast as I could and jumped down into the ravine, hugging the side of the cliff, tightly pressing my face against the mud and grass.

The hail shot from the sky stinging my head and hands, the wind slammed the hailstones in every direction. I was miserably cold and wet. I promised myself I would never be caught unprepared like this again. The worst of it was over in about 10 minutes, but the impression it made on me would last for days.

I finally left the Badlands and made for Rapid City, South Dakota. In Rapid City, I resupplied, adding a plastic tarp and an extra length of rope to my already heavy load. Now I can erect an emergency shelter anywhere using the rope, tent stakes, and my bike as a ridge pole.

I left Rapid City traveling on Interstate 90 heading to Buffalo, Wyoming. About half way to Buffalo I saw in the distance great walls of clouds rising from the horizon. In a moment, I realized they weren't clouds—they were mountains!

I checked my map. What I thought were clouds were actually the Big Horn Mountains. I checked again. Yes, I would have to pedal over them. I had completely overlooked these mountains. The route I decided to take was over the Powder River pass—9,666 feet high. Yikes!

It took me three days to climb up and over the Big Horns. My average speed on the way up was about 4 mph and about 30 mph on the way down. I stopped often to drink water and eat. Toward the top, the thin air made breathing difficult. My chest muscles ached from the work but my legs, surprisingly, felt fine. The Big Horn Mountains are surrounded by the Big Horn National Forest so camping was never a problem. I camped by fast-running, cold mountain streams and in dense stands of pine and spruce. My last night on the mountain, was spent at Meadowlark Lake. I laid on the beach and watched an incredible number of shooting stars shooting stars until late in the evening with three kids from the Midwest who were also camped here. We had such a good time together that we hung out for three days. Their only plan was to head west. They had little money and were going to go as far as they could on what they had.

The next day when I reached the summit, a long-haired bearded guy named Cooley Butler drove up behind me, parked his car and ran toward me with a bottle of spring water. "Congratulations, dude," he said. "You made it!" He drove off leaving me with the water as I shivered in the cold winds.

I stood at the summit for a long time looking out across at the jagged peaks that make up this mountain range. Rock and ice, pine forests; home to bighorn sheep, mule deer, pronghorns, coyotes, and bears. Lichens splattered the exposed billion year-old granite with golds and reds and greens. Small, fragile alpine plants clung to the thin soil as the wind whipped their tiny leaves and stems.

My only disappointment with the Big Horns was the constant sign of cattle. Everywhere were cow chips and fences. The cattle have trampled stream banks and vegetation and cut trails through the forests. Their incessant grazing has denuded hillsides of vegetation. They compact the soil, making it difficult for new plants to grow. At one camp, I had a difficult time finding enough room for my tent between the cow pies.

I flew down the mountains through Ten Sleep Canyon and camped for free in the town park in Basin, Wyo. The only other camper here is a tramp named Slider. He travels the country riding the rails. In his backpack he carries a tent, sleeping bag, etc. He cooks his meals in aluminum soda cans heated by railroad flares. Slider said he has been riding the rails for about six years. He's 44 and waiting in Basin for the Big Horn County Fair to begin next week. He's been promised a job, two week's work at the fair. I asked him about being a hobo.

"It's a way of life. I'm doing it 'cause I like it," he said. "I go where I want, work odd jobs, meeting new people, making new friends. We're like family out here. We take care of each other. We don't hurt nobody. We look for work and travel. Some towns like us tramps 'cause we work real hard. Not all of us are scandalous rip-off thieves; we're good people."

I asked him about the dangers of riding the rails.

"A lot of guys get chopped in two. Arms, feet, legs . . . ninety percent of the guys get hurt are drunk or doping it up." Slider said he is often ridiculed in towns he stops at. "Some folks treat you like dirt under their feet. Like scum." He said someday he'd like to get off the rails but it's hard to do. "People don't give you a break, they don't trust you once you're a tramp."

Tomorrow I leave for Cody, Wyo., at the foothills of the Rockies. I'll resupply in Cody for the climb up to Sylvan Pass (elevation 8,559) and the east gate of Yellowstone National Park. Tonight, I'll share a meal with Slider, drink coffee made in an old pot and listen to stories of life on the rails. In the distance, I can see clouds forming over the Big Horns—maybe rain tonight, certainly wind. Later, around midnight, the Burlington Northern will pass through town, its throaty whistle reminding us both of distant places, old friends, and future destinations.

Chapter 6

> "*To all wheelmen in search of a holiday amid the fairest and most wonderful of Nature's handiwork, I say, Take your pneumatic and see the Yellowstone Park awheel as I did.*"
>
> —Frank S. Lenz, 1892,
> first solo bicycle tourist in Yellowstone.

Forget Old Faithful. Forget the crowds, forget the tawdry trinket shops, road closings and traffic delays.

Forget the mile-long motor homes, drivers with their heads still in the city and their feet on the gas. Forget the tourists who won't get out of their cars. Forget all these things and you're left with 2.2 million acres of astounding beauty, rare and abundant wildlife, and the largest intact ecosystem in the lower 48 states.

Yellowstone is America's oldest national park and the first of its kind in the world. It is a World Heritage Site and an International Biosphere reserve and this summer is celebrating its 125th birthday.

Vice-President Al Gore was here a few days ago but I didn't see him. I was too busy soaking my old bones in a hot spring on the Firehole River. I bathed naked under a sheet of stars until the moon floated over the mountains, extinguishing the stars and illuminating great columns of steam escaping from fissures and fumeroles up and down the river, like a great sea-fog rolling up into the Rockies. Sorry Al.

Four million people visit this park every year. It is even more popular than Elvis (Graceland gets only 750,000 visitors a year). But just 100 yards off the pavement, down any trailhead, through a meadow or into a canyon, and you are alone. It is there, in the silence, that this place reveals its magic.

Hiking in Yellowstone is not just another walk in the park. In the northern Rockies, you are no longer at the top of the food chain. This is the home of *ursus horibilis*, the grizzly bear. It is also home to black bear, American bison (buffalo) moose, elk, bighorn sheep, and many other large mammals. A close encounter with a bull elk in rutting season could be fatal. A walk in these woods requires knowledge, respect, and the use of all your senses.

Lying down in a tent for the night in grizzly country can be unnerving; a clean camp is essential. Food, water bottles, scented toiletries (like toothpaste) and even the clothes worn while cooking and eating must be hung from a tree or stashed in a steel bear-proof container. There is a saying here: A leaf falls in the woods; the eagle sees it, the deer hears it, and the bear smells it.

And then there are the stories. The stories that come back to you uninvited during the night when the leaves rustle; when the wind speaks in whispers and something large, very large, shuffles past your tent just inches from your head.

Stories like the night (now referred to as "Night of the Bears") in Glacier National Park when two people, in different camps, were yanked out of their tents—and killed—by two different grizzlies. Reportedly, the campers had done everything right: no food in their tents, clean camp, etc. Three weeks ago, a woman trying to get a close-up photo of a bison was severely gored. Witnesses said she was so close that the bison inflicted the damage just by lifting his head. The woman suffered three broken ribs and a punctured lung.

I stopped to watch a bull elk and a few cows lazily grazing in a meadow. A woman pulled up, jumped out of her car, and ran toward the elk shouting to her son (who was holding the camera): "Quick honey, get up close to the big one!"

Just a few days ago in the Hayden Valley, a section of the park well known for its bison population, a group of people trying to get close to a herd of about 150 bison became trapped when a second herd moved in from behind. The frazzled tourists had to be escorted back out by armed rangers. They not only put themselves at risk, but endangered both rangers and bison.

But if the wildlife proves too much, you can always retreat to the 14 gift shops, nine hotels, seven gas stations, 11 general stores, or 31 eateries—all located inside the park. This is where most people seemed to be. It was a rare occasion to see someone on the trail. Rangers told me drive-through scenery is what people want. But giving it to them presents problems for the park, the wildlife, and the National Park Service, which is charged with the always conflicting goals of access and conservation.

There is an amusement park aspect to Yellowstone. Rangers told me that people will rush into a visitor's center (there are four of them in the park) gasping something like: "I've only got a few hours. What should I see?"

Well, there are more than 2 million acres of near-wilderness; 1,100 miles of trails; more geysers than anywhere else in the world including 10,000 mud pots, fumeroles, and hot springs. There are 110 waterfalls, some twice the height of Niagara, and a variety of vegetation ranging from near-desert to sub-alpine meadows. How much time did you say you had?

There is a 22-mile-long canyon carved to a depth of 1,000 feet by the Yellowstone River. There is North America's largest herd of bison, thriving wolf packs, rare white pelicans, the largest remaining population of trumpeter swans, not to mention lesser scaups, green-winged teals, osprey, bald eagles, picas, coyotes, and the ever-popular yellow-bellied marmot.

Overwhelmed, they head for the gift shop to buy a T-shirt, a few postcards, and maybe a video so they can "see the park" when they get back home. Then, it's off to the Grand Canyon!

I spent 10 days exploring just the southern half of the park. I made base camps and took trips on my bike with a small day pack. I explored the Yellowstone Canyon, several waterfalls, the Hayden Valley and many unnamed meadows, streams and hillsides. I found deep woods and wildflowers; saw eagles, elk, bison, and many others. I spent lazy evenings watching the sun go down over Yellowstone Lake, meandering among the beaches and coves along the 110-mile shoreline. It was here that I met scientists working to prevent the extinction of one of Yellowstone's most important species. Jack McIntyre heads a team of biologists trying to save the endangered Yellowstone cutthroat trout, a unique subspecies found only in this watershed. Lake trout, which prey on the cutthroat, were first discovered in the lake in 1944. Since they are not indigenous, park officials suspect foul play.

> *"Some circumstantial evidence is very strong, as when you find a trout in the milk."*
>
> —Henry David Thoreau,
> Journal entry, 11 Nov. 1850.

Lake trout may have been purposely introduced or could have been accidentally put into the lake as bait fish. Unfortunately, a mainstay of the lake trout's diet is the Yellowstone cutthroat trout. But it is not just the cutthroat that are affected. Like so often in Nature, the hand of man is like a pebble in the pond; singular actions, seemingly innocuous, cause repercussions far into the future. Many species depend upon the cutthroat for food. Bears, osprey, eagles and ravens all feed upon the cuttthroat when the fish leave the lake and venture up the region's streams and rivers to spawn. Conversely, lake trout spawn deep in sheltered sections of the lake, safe from predators.

Yet anglers can still fish for cutthroat trout in Yellowstone Lake. I asked McIntyre if this was counterproductive to their conservation effort. "Yes," he said. "There's good reason to make Yellowstone cutthroat catch and release only." McIntyre noted that even with catch and release, about eight percent of the fish die as a result of the stress and shock from getting hooked.

> *"We are the most dangerous species of life on the planet, and every other species, even the Earth itself, has cause to fear our power to exterminate. But we are also the only species which, when it chooses to do so, will go through great effort to save what it might destroy."*
>
> —Wallace Stegner

It is almost a decade since the great fire of 1988 in which a million acres were consumed. Everywhere, there is the contrast between dead, blackened tree trunks and the emerging green forest floor. Young lodgepole pines, growing as much as 10 inches a year, are shooting up all over, nestled from below by fireweed, paintbrush, and dozens of other wildflowers and green plants. The new pines are a shade of green more vibrant and fresh than any living thing I have ever seen.

And the forest lives on. Lodgepole pine cones need the heat of a fire to release their seeds. Right now in Yellowstone there is a rebirth happening on every mountainside and in every valley. On the trees that survived, the industrious pine bark beetle eats away at the soft tissue beneath the bark, eventually killing the tree. The dry, dead trunks will supply the fuel for the next fire, for the next re-seeding of the forest.

> *"All living creatures and all plants are a benefit to something."*
>
> —Okute

Now back to that opening quote. Be careful in Yellowstone! I suspect Frank Lenz only had to deal with a few horses and carriages and maybe a surly mountaineer or two. But today, the roads are narrow and winding; there are no shoulders and no signs cautioning motorists to yield to bicycles or pedestrians. Most motorists pay little heed to the posted 45 mph speed limit, which, given the road condition and the number of vehicles, is much too fast. One ranger told me at least one large mammal is killed every night in the park. Road kill inside a national park is not only unnecessary, it is disgraceful.

After leaving Yellowstone, Frank Lenz was brutally killed in some obscure country while attempting a solo, round-the-world bicycle tour. When I left Yellowstone, I spent three days camped on the edge of the Teton Wilderness. I soaked luxuriously in a hot spring on the Snake River surrounded by towering pines and sweeping, endlessly rolling meadows of wildflowers and grasses. I climbed Huckleberry Mountain (9,000-plus feet) and descended into a wilderness unbroken by any road or structure for hundreds of miles.

Grizzlies, wolves, mountain lions, elk and moose are the primary inhabitants here. I promised myself I would return and take a good long time to experience and savor one of the last remaining wild places in the lower 48 states.

Here, in the more than 20 million acres of the Greater Yellowstone Ecosystem, every hour of the day, each change of light brings new colors, shapes, and textures into focus. Every cloud, every flower, every whirling, buzzing, clicking insect plays its part like a section of the orchestra. But this symphony is Nature's own; it needs no conductor, no sheets of small black dots, no tickets or reservations. The parts are not merely played but lived. It is through the living that the music is made; only through the living can it be heard.

Perhaps that is why it feels so good to be out here, and here with the least amount of "things." I have only what I need to live: shelter, warm clothes, food and the necessities to prepare it, a few books, pencils and paper, and the most efficient method of human transportation: a bicycle. I have now come 3,000 miles with just these things. And the music never stops.

> "Touch the Earth, love the Earth, honor the Earth:
> her valleys, her hills and her seas; rest your spirit
> in her solitary places."
>
> —Henry Beston

Now, for the first time in nearly three months, I am no longer heading west, but south to Utah, Arizona, and Mexico.

Chapter 7

> "*Tell me, tell me, tell me, elm! Night! Night!*
> *Telmetale of stem or stone.*
> *Beside the rivering waters of hitherandthithering waters*
> *of. Night!*"
>
> —James Joyce

A string of fine days followed me on my descent from the high country of Yellowstone National Park and the Grand Tetons. My last morning camped above 7,000 feet found my tent walls stiff from a heavy frost. The forecast called for snow in the higher elevations; winter was creeping up on the Rockies.

I had raced across the country to reach the Rockies before the cold weather arrived. Now, heading south, I can travel at a more leisurely pace. I decided to take a week or two off and travel slowly, taking time to explore and relax.

I meandered through the Star Valley in Wyoming, cruised through the majestic Snake River Canyon and lingered in quaint towns like Auburn, Alpine, Thayne, and Smoot. I spent a few days camped on the Greys River deep inside the Bridger-Teton National Forest. The road out of Yellowstone, through the Tetons and into Jackson Hole, was thick with cars and RVs. The solitude of the forest, combined with the music of the river outside my tent, was a welcomed and much-needed respite.

> *"Riverbanks lined with green trees, fragrant grasses:*
> *A place not sacred? Where?"*
>
> —from a Zen saying

I finally left Wyoming and entered Idaho. I arrived at the town of Montpelier. One hundred and five years before I arrived here, George LeRoy Parker and two of his friends also rode into Montpelier. I headed for the grocery store and the post office. Parker and his friends stopped at the local saloon for a drink and then made an illegal withdrawal from the bank. Parker and his pals got away with about $16,000 in gold and silver.

A deputy sheriff gave chase to the bandits—not on his trusty horse—but on a hastily borrowed bicycle. The deputy lost the trail on the climb out of Montpelier canyon. One of the robbers, Billy Meeks, was eventually caught and brought to trial in the nearby town of Paris, Idaho. Meeks was just 14 years old at the time of the robbery. He eventually escaped from prison several times and was later pardoned in his old age. George LeRoy Parker was never apprehended for the Montpelier bank heist. He continued to elude the law until he was killed in Bolivia. Parker is best known by his adopted name of Butch Cassidy.

Back in Sundance, Wyoming, I saw the jail keys which kept Harry Longabaugh behind bars for 18 months for stealing a horse. I saw the court documents that convicted him as well as several photos of the young outlaw. He later joined up with Butch Cassidy and would be known forever after as The Sundance Kid.

Butch and Sundance, along with Kid Curry, Flat Nose George, and Harvey Logan, were known as the "Wild Bunch." The canyons of Utah, Wyoming, Colorado, and Arizona are littered with their famous hideouts and watering holes. From *The Outlaw Trail* by Charles Kelley:

> Butch Cassidy never approved of bloodshed and, so far as the record shows, never killed a man until his last stand, when he was outnumbered one hundred to one... All old-

timers interviewed for this biography, including officers who hunted him, were unanimous in saying: 'Butch Cassidy was one of the finest men I ever knew.'

Outside of Paris, Idaho, in the Cache National Forest, I stayed in a campground called Paris Springs. I was the only camper. The springs gush from a sheer rock cliff; the water is clear, cold and delicious. I feasted on that water. Above the spring, nestled among rock outcroppings, was an eagle's nest, vacant until next season.

Heading south from Paris, I discovered Bear Lake, often described as the "Caribbean of the Rockies." Limestone particles suspended in the water give the lake an arresting shade of turquoise. The lake, 20 miles long, was created by a volcano and straddles both Idaho and Utah. Bear Lake contains four species of fish found nowhere else in the world. A treasure of a different kind, the remaining loot from Butch Cassidy's Montpeleir bank job, is thought to be buried nearby.

After spending the day on the beach, I was peddling toward a campground on the eastern shore when I saw, from the top of a ridge, the head of a sea-monster stretching upward from between two weathered barns. The creature, hundreds of yards from the water's edge, was painted a slimy sea-green with crimson bloodshot eyes and two spiraling horns on either side of its head. And it was big!

I asked a farmer cutting thistle in a field if he knew anything about the creature. "Yes," he said. "It's mine." The farmer was Conrad Nebeker. The farm, Indian Creek Ranch, sits on 500 acres along the shore of Bear Lake. Nebeker told me about the legend of the Bear Lake monster. He thought perhaps it was started by the son of a landowner, Charles Rich, who had six wives and 52 children (this is Mormon country). A brochure on Bear Lake suggests that the Bear Lake monster and the Loch Ness monster may be one and the same; underground caves supposedly connect the two lakes. Sightings of the Bear Lake monster are remarkably similar to sightings of the Loch Ness. The Shoshone even had legends about a sea creature that lived in Bear Lake.

Nebeker's creature is constructed of steel and timber and covered in plastic, foam, and stucco. It has seven airtight compartments on each side. "It's as safe as the Titanic," Nebeker says, reminding me that the doomed luxury liner was similarly constructed. Conrad was hoping to launch the beast in about a week. He'll use a crane to lift it onto a trailer and then transport it to the boat ramp on the other side of the lake. The monster, as yet unnamed, is 62 feet long and 15.5 feet wide. Finally, I asked him why.

"People love nonsense," he replied. "And 'cause I do dumb things like that."

Conrad kindly offered to let me camp on the shore of the lake below the farm; even better, he showed me his garden. He told me to help myself—and I did. I picked two ears of sweet corn (and ate them raw), a pot of string beans, then visited his orchard for apples—and best of all—picked plump, purple raspberries for dessert, saving some for my morning oats.

Conrad is not only a farmer, not only a dragon maker, he is also a physician with a practice in Ogden, Utah. But more than any of these things, he is a warm and generous host who willingly shared the fruits of his garden and his friendship.

"Never laugh at live dragons."

—J.R.R. Tolkein

The next day, at the summit of Beaver Mountain (elevation 7,800 feet), I said good-bye to Paris Springs, Bear Lake, and the Snake River Canyon; two weeks of lazy beauty and vast expanses of unbroken forests had slipped past all too quickly.

Since crossing the Missouri River, I have been alternately intersecting and following parts of the Oregon Trail. Much has been written of the hardships of the pioneers who traversed this rugged country. My journey is luxurious compared to theirs. At the library in Logan, Utah, I found a rare collection of diaries and journals from some of those earlier travelers. Here are some samples with their original spelling and punctuation:

> From Virginia E.B. Reed to Mary C. Keyes, July 12, 1846:
>
>> ... the water was so hye we had to stay thare 4 days—in the mean time gramma died, she became spechless the day before she died. We buried her verry decent We made a nete coffin and buried her under a tree we had a stone and had her name cutonit and the date and yere verry nice, and at the head of the grave was a tree we cut some letters on it the young men soded it all ofer and put Flores on it We miss her verry much every time we come into the wagon we look at the bed for her.

From Daniel Toole to his brother, August 2, 1846:

> We arrived at this place on yesterday, which is situated in a beautiful plain on the Snake river, and is certainly a healthy place if there is one in the world.

But perhaps the most famous travelers through this country were the Donner Party. Loaded down with too many possessions (like dressers, beds and other domestic furnishings), they failed to cross the mountains in time and were caught in the first snow. Only seven of the original 15 survived. The grisly story of how they survived has fascinated people ever since. Here is an eyewitness account from a member of the rescue party:

> The picture of distress which was here presented was shocking indeed. Yet Patrick Briner and his wife seemed not in any degree to realize the extent of their peril, or that they were in peril at all. They were found sunning themselves and evincing no concern for the future. They had consumed the two children of Jacob Donner. Mrs. Graves body was lying there with almost all the flesh cut

away from her arms and limbs. Her breasts were cut off, and her heart and liver taken out, and all were being boiled in a pot on the fire.

And I get cranky when I run out of cookies. At the summit of Beaver Mountain, I met a Navajo man selling jewelry he and his family had made. He told me he travels here in the summer to sell jewelry to tourists and then returns to the Reservation in the fall. His two daughters had already left, telling him, "Hurry up and sell your jewelry, so you can come back home." I asked him if anyone hassles him for selling to tourists. "Yes," he said. "The ranger comes around and I have to take off. We come back when he's gone." He does this for the entire summer because there are no jobs, no means of earning a living on the Reservation.

His name was Steven Goodman. For some reason, it embarrassed me that he had such a "white" name, this man who was so distinctly Navajo. I didn't want to ask him about it. But later, while riding, I thought about the calm sound of his voice when he spoke of his children and how he missed them. I thought about how he looked me in the eye, unflinching. I thought about how his hands gently fingered the fragile strands of gems and silver; I remembered the pride he showed in his family's skill, and I thought, yes, it was all right. He was a good man.

"In peace there is nothing so becomes a man as modest stillness and humility."

—Shakespeare

Chapter 8

"Camerado, I give you my hand!
I give you my love more precious than money,
I give you myself before preaching or law;
Will you give me yourself? will you come travel
with me?
Shall we stick by each other as long as we live?"

—Walt Whitman

Two women and a Hispanic child thwarted my progress through Utah. The first and most troublesome of the trio was Delena, a cyclist and University of Utah student. I had shot through Logan canyon in a drenching rain and arrived in Logan cold, wet, and hungry. I was walking through town in my perpetual quest for pizza when I met her.

"Hey, I have a B.O.B. trailer too!" she said. She told me that she had also planned to do a cross-country trip this summer. She and three others were to pedal from Utah to Boston but a last minute quarrel canceled the trip. She went to Logan to finish school and start over: a new apartment, a new job, a new beginning.

We had lunch. We had dinner. We went to book stores and bike shops. Delena is a serious cyclist and owns about five bikes, including a hand-built Italian road bike. It is not unusual for her to ride more than 75 miles a day just for fun.

I parked old B.O.B. in her driveway and we rode together

through the streets of Logan. I cruised fast and silent in the middle of the night and early in the morning, free from the weight of my camping gear. This was a different kind of riding, the kind that first drew me to bicycles—flying on two wheels.

I stayed too long in Logan. Though I did have to wait for supplies and mail, I eagerly embraced any excuse to stay a little longer, just one more day, I kept telling myself, just one more day.

What a treat it was to cook meals on a stove in a kitchen. We made chili and cornbread, pasta and brownies. We ate ripe hunks of watermelon on the back porch. We camped in the canyon and took long naps under the sun in her yard. I took a bath every single day and used four of her pink plastic razors to scrape the beard off my face.

While she was at work, I spent mornings at the bagel shop splurging on dark coffee and "everything" bagels, reading the papers and writing in my journal. No mountains to climb, no wind to battle, no exhausting days dodging cars and RVs. It was much too pleasant.

> *"Allons! we must not stop here,*
> *However sweet these laid-up stores, however convenient*
> *this dwelling we cannot remain here . . .*
> *However welcome the hospitality that surrounds us we*
> *are permitted to receive it but a little while."*
>
> —Walt Whitman

I spent ten days in and around Logan. The dark cloud of leaving that had hung over us from the first finally settled, raining down its tears of loss on our last night together. My first night back on the road was strange, cold, and lonely. I thank Delena for opening not only her home to me but also her heart. I thank her for crossword puzzles, peanut butter and honey sandwiches; for renewing in me the thrill of riding fast and free. I thank her for the warmth, kindness, and companionship she shared without reservation or regret. But it was time to go.

> *"Henceforth I whisper no more, postpone no more,*
> *need nothing.*
> *Strong and content I travel the open road."*
>
> —Walt Whitman

The road from Logan, past Ogden and into Salt Lake City, was choked with fast food restaurants, motels, shopping malls, and flimsy-looking housing developments. Salt Lake City is getting ready to host the Winter Olympics in 2002. The main north-south route, Interstate 15, is undergoing a massive reconstruction in anticipation of the games. Officials predict traffic delays for the next four years. People are already going nuts.

I watched one woman jump out of her car and run up to the car in front of her and pound with her fist on the driver's window shouting all sorts of nasty things. This corridor between the Wasatch Mountains and the Great Salt Lake contains most of Utah's population. It is a miserable place to ride a bike.

It is as though Salt Lake City had spewed a filthy bile of vulgar commercialism down the valley. Yet a sideways glance to the east, rising above the video joints, fast fried chickens, auto parts, car washes, and "convenience stores" lurks the towering Wasatch Mountains, and in particular, Mount Timpanagos, soaring more than 10,000 feet above the neon and noise and the thick brown haze of the valley.

> *"We recognize defeated landscapes by the absence of*
> *pleasure from them."*
>
> —Wendell Berry

It was along this corridor that I ran into the second woman that would delay me: Linda—Hurricane Linda. She battered me with head winds and a bone-chilling rain every day for almost a week.

From my journal: Wednesday—Day 109—"Made only 20 miles today—big climbs plus head winds all day long—can't believe this is taking so long. Feels like winter."

It has rained in southern Utah every day for the last two months. Dwindling trade winds and a heat wave in the ocean, flood and drought, the largest measurable change in the Earth's atmospheric activity, by all signs, a visit from the "The Child" i.a/k/a El Nino. As I continue to make my way south, I have a feeling that this child and I are going to be seeing a lot more of each other in the next few months.

I finally left the Great Basin and entered the Colorado Plateau-high desert stretching across Utah, Arizona, and New Mexico. Late one afternoon, I stopped at a place called "Cafe" in the town of Loa. It was a cozy no-name joint where the locals sucked up coffee and passed the time. There were three paintings on the wall: Elvis, John Wayne, and a horse. Only the horse was not also a clock.

I asked the man behind the counter if I could still get breakfast. "Probably," was his answer. I waited for him to go find out. He waited. We waited. Finally, he said, "You want eggs?" "Sure," I agreed. He nodded and walked into the kitchen and started cooking.

I took a seat in a booth by the window; the counter was cluttered with cowboys. I could tell they were cowboys because they all wore cowboy hats and they all wore cowboy boots and they all wore cowboy shirts. They talked cowboy talk about killing elk and making fences. I tried not to listen. On their belts hung wire clippers and other tools I had at first mistaken for holstered guns.

I waited for my eggs looking past the blue checkered curtains, across Highway 24 between the Utah Highway Maintenance Building #331 and a 100-foot ponderosa pine—and there it was, about 50 miles distant, a red rock monolith glowing in the fading sunlight. Finally, I was about to enter Utah's red rock country.

First stop was Capital Reef National Park, a 100-mile long bulge in the Earth's crust. I spent my time in the orchards of the historic settlement of Fruita, located within the park's boundaries, where a Harvest Homecoming Festival was in progress. I listened to old-timey music and watched folk dances. I spent an afternoon lying in the orchard eating apples surrounded by the lush green valley floor and ripening fruit while gawking up at the smooth orange and pink cliffs rising above me on all sides. I promised myself I would return and explore the thousands of miles of trails and washes that wind through this park.

From Capital Reef I crossed the nation's newest National Monument: Escalante/Grand Staircase. This is 1.7 million acres of some of the most isolated and rugged terrain in the lower 48 states. I camped high on a plateau overlooking the Box-Death Hollow Wilderness area. From my camp I looked out over endless miles of pinnacles, buttes, mesas, and canyons; everything gloriously colored; deep reds and faint grays and oranges to the bright green and mysterious browns of the twisted pinyons and junipers. Vast walls of pink and cream granite stretched before me, slickrock bowls encased me like the soft palms of a gentle hand. Here, sunsets and sunrises are not mere mechanical movements but events to be attended: a good vantage point, an early rising, things to be considered as carefully as if attending a play or concert.

Unfortunately, because a National Monument lacks the degree of protection a National Park receives, Escalante/Grand Staircase is susceptible. Ranchers are allowed to graze their cattle here, Conoco is drilling for oil (thanks to Clinton and Gore) and locals are tearing up the fragile desert soil with ATVs, leaving trails of beer cans, shotgun shells, and fire pits in their wake. Hopefully, this unique and mysterious land will receive the protection it needs before it is too late. Once this place is lost, it will be lost forever.

My final stop is considered the most colorful national park in the world: Bryce Canyon. Not really a canyon but a series of 14 amphitheaters plunging a thousand feet down through layers of limestone and petrified sand. The Earth simply falls away at your feet exposing eroding spires and columns, sheer cliff walls glowing with brilliant shades of red and orange, glowing as if the light was coming from within, escaping from the Earth itself.

> *"I have loved the red rocks, the twisted trees, the red sand blowing in the wind, the slow, sunny clouds crossing the sky, the shafts of moonlight on my bed at night. I have seemed to be at one with the world."*
>
> —Everett Ruess, from *Vagabond for Beauty*

I had the sense, not only in Bryce but in all of Utah's red rock country, of having wandered into the workshop of a great sculptor; the artist nowhere in sight, perhaps napping in a corner, but no doubt close by. And even though the landscape stretches across millions of acres and thousands of miles, I know, one rock disturbed, one footprint in the fragile desert soil, will not go unnoticed. This is a solemn place. Even the usually gabby tourists stand at the rim of a canyon and speak to each other in hushed voices. We are like visitors to a holy temple, standing awkward and in awe long after the congregation has been dismissed. This is a raw, unfinished place. The tools of the sculptor: the wind, the rain, the silt-laden streams are everywhere and constantly at work. And in the midst of this red rock, limestone, and ancient sand are the vibrant greens and faded grays of pinyons and junipers; the majestic ponderosa pine. Ever optimistic, they shoot up beside the shadows of hoodoos and spires, emerge from cracks in rocks; lustily clutching each clump of soil, always reaching toward the rim, reaching to the sky itself.

> *"Trees are the Earth's endless effort to speak to the listening heaven."*
>
> —Rabindranath Tagore

Finally, a sad note. I recently learned that my outfitter, Alpine Outdoors, is going out of business. Sad news personally for Scott and Kyle but sadder still for the fate of alternative transportation in Northwest New Jersey.

The American Wheelman's Association's yearly survey reveals that fear of getting hit by a car is the number one reason people don't ride their bikes. There is perhaps no simpler, cheaper improvement that can be made than the painting of a white stripe down a road: a bike lane. How about car-free weekend mornings on Main Street?—families could ride together without fear. A rider on a bike equipped with a basket or trailer can shop for groceries, return a video, or pick up a prescription. An effective defense against mall sprawl? So while people waste more time in bigger and bigger traffic jams (getting sick from the stress), with more cars exhausting more emissions—more bike shops go out of business. But every time we don't use a car to drive around town, we save money, we save ourselves, and we save our Earth. Bikes are tools, not toys.

On Saturday, Day 119, in the town of Mount Carmel, Utah, just past the bridge over Muddy Creek, my odometer reads 4,000 miles. My next stop is the Navajo Reservation in northern Arizona. I have been invited to listen to the stories of the Grandmothers, the matriarchal leaders of the persecuted Dineh Nation (traditional Navajo). These peaceful sheepherders and weavers are being strong-armed off their communal lands to make way for the world's largest coal strip mine. They have been resisting for the past 22 years; now, the remaining Elders are dying and time is running out.

Chapter 9

"Injustice anywhere is injustice everywhere."

—Dr. Martin Luther King Jr.

In 1864, under the command of U.S. Army Col. Christopher "Kit" Carson, 8,000 Navajo were evicted from their homelands and marched more than 300 miles to an internment camp at Fort Sumner, New Mexico. Countless Elders and children died along the way; many more died from disease and starvation in custody. They remained at Fort Sumner for four years. Due to intense public outrage over living conditions, the remaining Navajo were finally returned to a small, restricted portion of their original land: the Reservation.

One hundred and ten years later, the Relocation Act of 1974 (Public Law 93-531) was passed, partitioning land that had been peacefully shared by both Hopi and Navajo for more than 100 years.

Suddenly, more than 10,000 Dineh, or traditional Navajo, found themselves on the wrong side of the fence. A bitter and protracted disagreement over what should be done with the Dineh has ensued for the past 23 years.

Many have already been relocated to "New Lands," an inadequately remediated U.S.Environmental Protection Agency (EPA) Superfund site. A building freeze has been in effect since 1974, prohibiting new construction or even repairs to existing homes, adding substantially to the misery of those remaining.

Fences have been erected through traditional grazing lands and the Dineh now need to apply for permits from the Hopi Tribe to cut wood, build a ceremonial hut, or graze their animals. This restriction is the equivalent of a U.S. citizen having to apply to the government of Canada for a permit to attend the church of their choice.

The U.S. Court of Appeals has set a deadline of March 31, 2000 to complete relocation of the Dineh. If the surviving Elders do not sign a restrictive, long-term lease with the Hopi Tribe, U.S. Federal Marshals will forcibly remove them from their ancestral lands.

The reason for the Relocation Act? Back in the middle of the "energy crisis" of the early 1970's, these simple sheepherders and weavers were found to be sitting on top of one of North America's richest deposits of coal.

This is Big Mountain, Owl Springs, Horse Look-Out, Cactus Valley. This is Black Mesa, home of the largest coal strip mine in the world. This is the home of the Peabody Western Coal Company's 100 square miles of smoldering open air stockpiles, towering mounds of overburden, and airborne coal dust so thick it kills crops. Here, in the heart of the desert, three million gallons of water a day are pumped from a sole-source aquifer to feed a 260 mile-long coal slurry. One billion gallons of water a year in a place where water is life, a place where Grandmother must haul her water by buckets. Coal slurry water can never again be used to grow corn, water orchards, or nourish sheep.

I came to hear the stories of the remaining Elders, the grandmothers or "the resisters" as they are called. Their case has now been brought before the United Nation's Commission on Human Rights. The Grandmothers are asking the world to listen to their story. They want only to be able to tend their sheep, practice their religion, and support their families.

The Elders I interviewed are illiterate. They cannot read or write English or Navajo and speak only Navajo. In many cases no English words exist for Navajo expressions or ideas. The words attributed here to the Grandmothers are as close as we were able to come to their original thoughts. My thanks to the guides and interpreters who helped me; translation was a difficult and time-consuming task.

To reach the Elders, we had to travel over dirt roads through rugged terrain, to some of this continent's most isolated places. Homesites are located 30, 40, even 50 miles from each other and from the nearest phone or store.

These families live without electricity, running water, or telephones. They have managed, like their ancestors, to wrench a meager living from the desert. It is a harsh life under the best conditions; under the threat of eviction and constant harassment, it has become unbearable.

And when the Federal Marshals come for them, when the Bureau of Indian Affairs (B.I.A.), the Hopi Rangers, and Navajo Nation police come, when even the bulldozers come, they will stay. This is their story.

My first day on Black Mesa we went to Horse Look-Out to visit Elder Rena Babbitt. Rena was dressed in a long, brightly colored skirt garnished with hand-made turquoise jewelry. Pictures of her grandchildren posed in football uniforms and in traditional dress hung side by side on her walls.

Rena, like all the Elders I visited, spoke in a soft lilting voice. She spoke slowly and carefully, pausing often. In the startling silence of the desert, this language, spoken so tenderly, is as gentle as the rustling sage, like sand skimming over rocks in the wind.

Rena made fry bread and placed a pot of coffee on the table. She explained why she has resisted the relocation.

"This is supposed to be our home. We are supposed to live in view of the four sacred mountains. The Creator told our ancestors that this is our home. Now we are being told to relocate to an unknown place which we are not familiar with."

Rena let me feel the lump on her palm. She pulled her finger backwards showing me how the Hopi Ranger had bent her finger all the way back when she tried to stop them from impounding some of her sheep. She realized later that day that her finger had been broken.

"Now I can only weave small rugs, not the big ones I used to make."

I asked her if she would ever leave her home.

"I'll probably stay here. It's the only place I know."

A look of quiet defiance swept over her weathered face. She looked up at me: "Probably will never give it up."

Livestock reductions, grazing fees, and health problems she attributes to the stress are taking a toll on her and her efforts to preserve a traditional way of life. "Here in the sacred mountains, the Thunder people, the Rain people, they make the rain come. Mother Earth and Father Sky work together here. Why should I pay a fee to someone who can't even make it rain?"

In the evenings I spent time with my interpreter's families. I slept in hogans and out in the sagebrush under the stars. During the weekend a coming of age or "First Lady" (kinadah in Navajo) ceremony was held for an 11 year-old girl.

Grandmother dug a pit in the ground about three feet across and a foot and a half deep. A fire was made in the pit and it burned for an entire day. Toward evening, the fire and coals were removed, the pit was swept, and lined with corn husks. Then, a large tub of cake batter was poured into the pit. The batter was covered with more corn husks and a fire was made on top. The fire burned until the next morning.

The girl had to stay awake all night. She was dressed in traditional clothes her mother made for her just for this ceremony. About 2 a.m., the medicine man arrived. I fell asleep that night with the light from the fire dancing on the walls of my tent and the chants and songs of the medicine man filling my ears. When I awoke the next morning, the fire was out, the cake was removed, and the medicine man was gone. Everyone ate a piece of the cake except the girl. According to their beliefs, if she were to eat a piece of her own cake she might become greedy later in life. Also, her teeth might fall out before she became old.

Katherine Smith lives in the house where she was born back in 1919. Chairs were offered and we sat outside while she spoke.

"This land belongs to the Sun and the Earth, the Tornado

and Hurricane. It is the land; that is the thing which cannot be replaced. People can be relocated, but the land, this is the land my ancestors are buried on. This is where our past is, where our future is."

I asked her if she was scared of what might happen to her. "No," she said without hesitation. "I'm old. I'm all by myself. I'm not sure what's going to happen. I'm going to sit in my house and let them bulldoze me."

On her wall is a photograph of one of her sheep eating a copy of the accommodation agreement.

"It's like I have been in prison for over 20 years and I don't know the reason why. Did I do something wrong? What crime have I committed?"

When we arrived at Mazzie Begay's homesite she was sitting on the ground with her spinning stick, stretching and spinning wool from her sheep, wool she will use to weave the rugs she sells to survive. After we had been talking a little while, she showed us a letter she had received from the B.I.A.

Mazzie cannot read English nor can anyone in her family. The letter was a five-day notice of impoundment for her horses. She had, the letter said, five days to move them from where they were grazing.

Mazzie, unable to understand the letter, panicked and sold some of her sheep. She knows the fees to get an animal back after it has been impounded are often more than the market value.

I asked her if she would leave this place if the harassment continued.

"No, I have no intention of leaving. The ancestors are still here and I was born right here. I still have my cradle board. We are used to this place and this is where I can make my livelihood. The land, the sheep, are all we have. It is the only thing we know."

Mazzie said the Hopi Rangers race their cars right by the front door of their house trying to intimidate them into signing the agreement. But Mazzie is determined to stay. "If they take all my animals I want them to take me too. Impound me! Since the way I make my living is being stolen you have to take me too. There would be nothing else to live for."

Zonnie Whitehair also received a letter. Zonnie was living in the Cactus Valley area of Black Mesa. Afraid the B.I.A. would take her sheep, she left her home and her husband and walked for two days with her herd-24 miles through the desert-to bring her sheep back to the Navajo side and her mother's original home, a house in severe disrepair and slated for the bulldozer by Peabody. The house is just one quarter of a mile from the mine.

We sat inside the crumbling structure with her daughter and two granddaughters that had come to visit over the weekend. Peabody is telling her that her mother's house must be torn down; they are going to dump the dirt from the new excavations here. Peabody has promised to build her a new house, a hogan, a building without running water or electricity. Zonnie said that she has not received anything in writing from Peabody. She is simply waiting, waiting while the walls around her fall to pieces.

"They told me this house will have to be torn down. But this place is the foundation of my family. I'm not sure of Peabody's promise of a house. I don't feel I want any part of it. I just need a place to live."

She explained that because of the forced reductions in livestock (she will be allowed to keep only eight sheep) she could not keep enough sheep to survive in Cactus Valley. Here, the blasting from the mine is causing her and her sheep a lot of stress.

"On windy days the sky gets so dark from the coal dust. My corn would not grow because of all the dust."

Her 18 year-old granddaughter, Shirlandra, explained what the land means to her.

"I would like to live here. This is where my grandmother's mother was born. This is the foundation of my family. Grandmother needs support from people. She lives in this house now. The roof leaks and the windows are broken. I don't know how she'll live here in the winter. Grandmother and Grandfather are not together now because of Peabody. They are eating food from cans and have no one to care of them. Her corn won't grow because of the dust. She has nowhere else to go. All she knows is herding sheep."

Shirlandra is a student at Northern Arizona University. She plans to study medicine and return here to help. She told me that these people, the Elders, need doctors who can speak Navajo and understand the old ways.

A lot of my time between visits was spent at Elder Glenna Begay's house in Owl Springs. It was here that I got to see sheep herding in action. A revelation to this vegetarian: sheepherders eat sheep! There was mutton stew, mutton soup, there were legs and heads and hearts and skins hanging from every hook and nail in the kitchen.

I managed to eat around the sheep. Luckily, coffee and fry bread, potatoes and eggs, were always on the table. I was told that I would be welcome in their home and at their table, and I was. I chopped wood for the fire, hauled water, washed dishes, and played with the kids. My presence was accepted with respect, a respect I hopefully returned in equal measure.

Life for the Grandmothers revolves around their sheep. They are mutually dependent on each other. And I learned that the extended family, perhaps 20 or 30 relatives, depend on the Grandmothers for food, for knowledge of traditions, and the sacred places like the hogans for practicing their "religion" (although there is no word in Navajo for religion). You cannot practice the Navajo way in an apartment in Hoboken; you need land to hold ceremonies, gather herbs, and raise sheep. Without land, there can be no freedom of religion.

Grandmother is the steward of the land and the family. She is the anchor, the foundation. The land, the sheep, the Grandmother—they are inseparable and indispensable to the traditional Navajo way.

From my journal: "It is Sunday night about 11 p.m. I'll be leaving the Reservation tomorrow. Tonight I'm sitting at the kitchen table in Glenna's house writing by the golden light of an old oil lamp. The soft music of Glenna's voice in the background is mingling with the desert wind at the window and the clinking of the ram's bell from the corral. I think it is the quiet music of this language I will miss most."

In a letter to the editor of the Navajo-Hopi Observer, Glenna wrote:

> I am a Dineh lady, and I am an Elder, and the land I live on is the same land my family has lived on for many generations, way back to the time when no one thought about who owned what.
>
> There weren't any fences back then. Yet no one seemed at all confused where they were supposed to be living. Now there's a big fence stretching all over the place and no one seems to know what's what anymore. When has there ever been a paper agreement between our people and the government that has turned out good for us? Never. So never is when I'll sign any more of their papers. We are Dineh. And whatever comes . . . that is who we must continue to be.

It is the land. The land which supports the sheep, the land which holds their dead, the land which furnishes the herbs for their physical and spiritual health, the land which is the fertile womb that holds the seeds of their future.

That is why there is no contract, no map maker's lines, no political maneuvering that can replace what they already know to be true. The coal, no matter how valuable at the moment, must remain where it belongs: far beneath the brown dusty feet of the Grandmothers.

Chapter 10

"We walk out to the brink of the canyon, and look down to the water below. I can do this now, but it has taken several years of mountain climbing to cool my nerves, so that I can sit, with my feet over the edge, and calmly look down a precipice 2,000 feet. And yet I cannot look on and see another do the same. I must either bid him come away, or turn my head."

—Major John Wesley Powell at the Grand Canyon

I ran amok in the Grand Canyon. I snuck in, littered, and camped illegally. I came here not to begin a life of crime, but to look for inspiration, for the answer to a question.

I had left the Navajo Reservation feeling unsettled. Suddenly my plan to spend the winter on the beaches of Mexico seemed frivolous. As I pedaled south through Arizona and the Colorado Plateau, I saw the weathered faces of the grandmothers where I should have seen mountains; where I should have heard the song of the western meadowlark and the raucous shout of the raven, I heard only the sweet ancient music of Navajo softly spoken. I promised myself I would not make a decision until I reached the canyon.

I arrived at the south rim of Grand Canyon National Park in the midst of a cold snap. By the second day, I was camping in an inch of snow and feeling a bit chilly. The temperature had plummeted into the teens during the night and rose only to the 20s during the day. I was wearing long johns (two tops), fleece sweater and pants, a big red wool hat, gloves, and double wool socks. I was still cold. My plan had been to stay ahead of the cold weather, but now, at 7,000 feet, time was running out. I decided to do the unthinkable: I got a job.

I applied for work with the park's main concession. They hired me as a busser at El Tovar, the premier white tablecloth joint in the park. My shift started at 5:45 a.m. and lasted until 4 p.m. I was lucky if I got a half-hour break during the day. I was making minimum wage but the company provided me with a room in a dormitory for which they deducted 40 cents an hour from my wages. My food was provided at cost at the company cafeteria. From my journal: "Day 140: Exhausted. Worked from 5:30 a.m. to after 4 p.m. today. Only 30 minute break, barely had time to eat something. The waste here is incredible. Too tired to write."

My busboy career lasted exactly three days. I think the contrast was too great. I went from a world of beauty to a world of shallow appearances. I missed sleeping outside. I missed songbirds in the morning; the smell of pine rising with the afternoon sun. I missed the silence, the aloneness of the woods. I missed the delight of heading down a new road each day.

> *"Who leaves the pine-tree, leaves his friend, unnerves his strength, invites his end."*
>
> —Ralph Waldo Emerson

My dormitory, Victor Hall, was known by park employees as "Victim Hall," due to the frequent thefts, muggings, and fist fights. It seemed most of the roomers were either dopers or drunks. I was warned not to leave my door unlocked even for a minute. Thankfully my roommate was sober and friendly.

To prepare for my shift at the restaurant, I went to bed by 8 p.m. But each night, sometime after midnight, I was awakened by the howls of drunks and dopers outside my window. They continued all night and into the early morning. Gone were the familiar night sounds: deer walking past my tent, the haunting hysterics of the coyote, the wind. No one complained for fear of reprisals; rooms were trashed, cars vandalized.

I called in on the fourth day, returned my monkey-suit uniform (bow-tie, tuxedo shirt, and pleated black pants) and was given 24 hours to vacate the dorm.

Now I can once again concentrate on the canyon, sleep in the quiet solitude of the forest, and wake with the birds instead of the burnouts. I spent two weeks living in and around the Grand Canyon. Because I was unable to carry a backpack and hiking boots on the bike, I did most of my exploring along the rim. I would wake early and have coffee sitting on the South Rim looking across the 11 miles to the North Rim. I watched the mules begin their descent, unenthusiastically bearing their burdens of tourists into the abyss.

From my journal: Day 143: "The South Rim: 7:30 a.m.: On my left, the moon, almost full, is floating high above the horizon. I'm sitting on a rock ledge 5,000 feet above the Colorado River, feet dangling into the canyon. A western bluebird, several ravens, and a cheerful nuthatch are keeping me in good company.

"The sun is working on the northwestern cliffs, coaxing the colors. To the east, much of the canyon is still covered in darkness. Distant green hills of velvet sage are rippled with the dark fingerlings of shadows.

"Like icebergs, the topmost layers of the rocky cathedrals are streaked with light, but the sulking masses below are obscured by darkness. Hulks of limestone and shale wait to be discovered, wait patiently to be brought into the light: delivered. The crisp October air offers no resistance to the clear, brilliant light pouring into the chasm. A daily rebirth at 7,000 feet.

"8:20 a.m.: To the west, colors are becoming more distinct. Bands of limestone and shale are now clearly visible, sharply differing from each other, bearing the truth of their age: precise degrees of separation two billion years in the making, each layer a million years apart; rock so old it makes dinosaurs look like newcomers.

"They are inextricably one: one mass, one hulking landscape boldly challenging my ability to comprehend the size and power of this Earth. Layer upon layer, color upon color, like some exquisite pastry. A lie! This place is rock, rock and light and water."

The plants and animals that live here have survived the often harsh, high desert climate. Some are familiar, the pinyons and junipers, the wild asters, Utah agave. Others, like the Kaibab squirrel (with a snow-white tail), the Grand Canyon pink rattlesnake (its color matching the red rock canyon walls), and the endangered sentry milk vetch are found nowhere else in the world.

My favorite critter here is the tassel-eared squirrel. Its long, vertical ears end in a frilly tassel. The tassel-eared squirrel would have a hard time in New Jersey; I am sure the other squirrels would give this frivolous looking rodent no peace.

While I was sitting on the rim a few days ago, I saw three bighorn sheep. They appeared to be a family unit: a ram, a female, and a yearling. The female came within just a few feet of me while the ram, with his massive curled horns, looked menacingly at me. I tried my best to look disinterested in his mate. They maneuvered on the steep slope with grace and agility, placing their hooves delicately in what looked to me the most unlikely places. Later that day, I saw two young sheep napping in the sun. They were surrounded by nearly vertical canyon walls, safe from predators and enjoying a view of the canyon that us two-leggeds can only dream of.

You cannot see the Colorado River from the South Rim. Far below the cathedrals and canyon walls, the Colorado River continues its work. In semiretirement for the moment due to the regulating effect of the Glen Canyon and Hoover dams, the river waits. Sediment is building up behind the dams just as it had built up behind the dams of volcanic debris millions of years ago. This I know: the river, in time, will win again.

The sculpting power of the river is incomprehensible. More than 500,000 tons of particles are suspended in the muddy water. In times of flood, this number has been estimated at 55 million tons a day. This debris is the equivalent of 11 million five-ton fully loaded dump trucks moving through the canyon at the rate of 125 per second.

Erosion above the rim is less dramatic. Lichens, combining with spores, colonize the ancient, exposed limestone. As the lichens grow they dissolve fine particles of the limestone. These particles collect in crevices and cracks. Seeds find their way to this "soil" and take hold. The roots of the developing plants slowly exploit other cracks and crevices until a single chip of rock falls to the river below; one tiny facet of a 300-mile-long razor-edged chisel.

The key to understanding the Grand Canyon, I learned, is erosion. Endless pressure applied endlessly. Small, seemingly insignificant forces, acting in concert over time, carving enormous changes in solid, immovable rock. And I think I have found the answer to my question.

I have decided not to go to Mexico. Instead, I'll return to New Jersey. I'll spend my time fund-raising and writing on behalf of the Dineh Grandmothers. Replacing my visions of tequila and white sand beaches will be stale coffee and snowstorms. Mexico can wait.

After 4,300 miles and nearly five months on the road it will be good to see my family and friends again. Five months of fighting head winds, five months of climbing endless mountains and eating bad food is enough for now. One hundred and forty five days of evading rangers and stealth camping in our national parks and forests is probably pushing my luck. Which brings me back to the beginning of this chapter. I didn't intentionally litter. A cap I had bought in the Badlands, my only souvenir of the entire trip, was ripped from my head and tossed into "the ditch" by a gusty south wind, the same wind that had plagued me all the way from Utah. I like to imagine that my hat landed in some hidden cave, perhaps in an Anasazi ruin far below the rim, only to be discovered a thousand years from now, completely confounding the anthropologists of the 31st century. As for my other crimes, I plead utterly and absolutely guilty.

I'll be camped in the Kaibab National Forest for another week until I can collect my pay for three days work and finalize a plan for my return. I should be back in northwest New Jersey; in time for the first snowfall. Now what could be better? Camped in virgin snow high above the Delaware River in the fresh, familiar woods of home.

Chapter 11

> *"And so the little freighter sat upon the sea, and, though Africa came closer day by day, the freighter never moved. She was old and weather-weary, and she had learned to let the world come round to her."*
>
> —Beryl Markham
> from *West With the Night*

It is Day 150 and I am sitting in a window seat on a Greyhound bus pulling out of Flagstaff, Arizona. The temperature is in the low 40s and there is snow on the San Francisco Peaks. Winter is coming. The trip is over and my thoughts turn to a warm June morning five months earlier.

I think of the people whose lives I intersected. I think of the kindness, the beauty, the wonder of traveling so far with so little. I think of the time spent: lazy and unrushed. I think about entire weeks spent wandering through the desert, over the Great Plains and in the deep forests of some of the last unspoiled wilderness in the world. I think of the solitude and the joy of good conversation after time spent alone. And finally, I think of returning home.

Below me, disassembled and packed in a box, is my bicycle and trailer. The odometer, now disconnected, reads 4,340.8 miles. The bus leaves the station and for the first time in five months I am traveling east. On the Navajo Reservation my guide introduced me to the Elders as someone who came from "where the Sun comes from." Despite my affection for Western landscapes, it is true, I am an Easterner at heart.

Before getting on the bus I say good-bye to a man and his six year-old son. They are southbound. They have been on the road for months looking for work. Father and son sleep in the same sleeping bag at night, all their possessions carried in an overstuffed backpack. He tells me no one wants to hire a man with a small child in his care. I wish him luck and get on the bus.

We cover in three days what had taken me five months. But this is a grueling three days, joyless travel compared to riding my bike. Crammed together with sneezing, coughing, screaming kids and adults I am almost getting nostalgic for a brisk head wind. What I get instead is a nasty cold, the first of my trip.

> "I'd rather go by bus. There is nothing nicer in the world than a bus."
>
> —Charles, Prince of Wales

Statistically, the trip was a dismal failure. I had wanted to make a dent in the list of places I felt I had to visit: the Badlands, Yellowstone, the Grand Tetons, the Grand Canyon. They were all places I had never seen. But despite my best efforts, the list has actually grown.

I want to go back to Yellowstone. I want to spend time in the northern section of the park. I want to spend an entire summer in the Greater Yellowstone Ecosystem. There, between Yellowstone and the Grand Tetons, is a section called the Teton Wilderness— unbroken wilderness stretching for more than one hundred miles. Immediately beyond that is one million acres of national forest. I want to go back, with a horse.

I want to return to that hot spring on the east shore of the Snake River. Sitting in that 10-foot pool of hot, soothing water you can look out over lush mountain meadows, thick ponderosa pine forests; to the south are the majestic snow-capped Grand Tetons. Close by are grizzlies, mountain lions, and elk. Three steps from the hot spring is the frigid waters of the Snake. I spent an entire day jumping from one to the other. It may be the most beautiful place I have ever seen.

In Utah, the 1.7 million acres of pristine high desert of the Escalante/Grand Staircase National Monument are calling me back. A person could wander for a lifetime through that place and never walk the same path twice. The Black Hills in South Dakota, the Bighorn Mountains in Wyoming, the thousands of miles of trails through the Grand Canyon and the Colorado Plateau, the Great Plains of South Dakota, they are all calling me back.

On the bus, the man sitting next to me is quiet. He doesn't speak much English but we communicate. At a rest stop in St. Louis he finally tells me his story. He is a Kurdish rebel. He fled Iraq after the revolution failed and has been wandering around the United States. He is on his way to a construction job in Pittsburgh.

He tells me he is in constant fear for his life, afraid of reprisals. He doesn't trust anyone. He misses his homeland, his family and friends. He can never go back. "The revolution is dead," he tells me.

I think how easy it is for me to go home: hop on a bus, my friends and family just a few days and hours away—no border guards, no barbed wire, no fear.

During the last five months I had met fellow travelers from Germany, Italy, England, France, Switzerland, Belgium, Australia, Japan, China and New Zealand. My journal is filled with names and places and bits of conversation, scraps of hastily scribbled addresses. There are notes like this one left on my tent from a German woman with who I was going to watch the sunrise over Yellowstone Lake:

> Dear Bill,
> In the morning it was very clouded, so I don't wake up you at 5:30. When you come to Germany, come and visit me.—Edith

By the time I awoke she was gone. My most treasured mementos though are the letters. I have thirteen beautiful letters from Mrs. Barber's second grade class in Mount Olive, N.J. The students asked all the right questions: "Are you having fun? Where are you now? Are you getting lots of exercise?" I have pictures drawn just for me from my young friends Willie and Andi. I have jokes and a yin-yang made from beads from my nephew Pat. No matter where I was, no matter how tired or discouraged, kind words from a reader, news from home or a simple hello from a friend could always make the hard miles a little easier.

"More than kisses, letters mingle souls."

—John Donne

A few seats ahead of me on the bus is a young man about 19 years old. He was released from prison yesterday. He had been jailed on drug charges and is now on parole for the next seven years. We were somewhere in Texas when he confided to me that he was not supposed to leave Arizona. On his first day of freedom he broke parole, bought a bus ticket, and was on his way to visit his ex-girlfriend in Chicago.

He had been awake for two days straight. The reading light above his seat had been on every night while the rest of the bus tried to sleep. He told me later he was slamming meth amphetamines. He had three syringes and a small supply of the drug in his duffel bag. He changed busses in St. Louis. I wished him luck.

I thought about his drugs and needles, the backpacks and suitcases, the hat boxes and duffels, all stuffed into dark compartments below us as the Greyhound rolled through the days and nights. I thought about this strange collection of people, baggage, and our portable lives.

It wasn't until then that I realized, finally, the incredibly huge chunk of freedom I had managed to grab in the last few months. Freedom was what this trip was about. And now, unlike my Iraqi friend, I had the freedom to return home. A freedom I now know to be even more precious than the freedom to leave.

> *"I should like well enough to spend the whole of my life in traveling abroad, if I could anywhere borrow another life to spend afterwards at home!"*
>
> —William Hazlitt
> from his essay, *On Going a Journey*;

Delena at our mountain camp in Utah.

Dineh elder Mazzie Begay with her spinning stick; Navajo Reservation.

Sign of the times on Big Mountain.

A DELAWARE JOURNEY

"Gradually the village murmur subsided, and we seemed to be embarked on the placid current of our dreams, floating from past to future as silently as one awakes to fresh morning or evening thoughts."

—Henry David Thoreau,
from *A Week on the Concord and Merrimack Rivers*

Chapter 1

> "*A man's life should be constantly as fresh as this river. It should be the same channel, but a new water every instant.*"
>
> —Henry David Thoreau,
> from *A Week on the Concord and Merrimack Rivers*

This river journey was the result of a longing whose origins began when I was boy dreaming on the banks of the Delaware river. Through the years, it has been a place of solace, a place of peace when my world was troubled. It was also a place I brought my daughter just as my parents had brought me. I don't believe there has been a summer in my life that I have not, on some humid August night, come here and wrapped myself in its cool waters. This trip was a celebration not only of this river but of life itself and the philosophy of living simply and in the moment. I started from the West Branch of the Delaware River, a few miles above Hancock, N.Y., where the Pocono and Catskill Mountains converge. The river officially begins here, at the confluence of the east and west branches.

Day one: I figured I'd be cold, wet, and miserable—I just didn't think it would all happen on the first day. A baptism by fire. More accurately, a baptism by lightning, thunder, and a driving, pelting rain. The shove-off was great. I actually fit all the equipment into the boat and was just starting to get the hang of maneuvering when the first thunderstorm moved in. I had been on the water about an hour before I was forced to shore under threat of severe lightning. I stood in a clump of bushes, put on my raincoat, and watched the kayak fill with water. In five minutes I was soaked to the bone. Four thunderstorms moved through in as many hours. Three days later I'm still wet. I made camp under "No Trespassing!" signs on the New York side, in a small grove of sugar maples, five or six of them gently bending their branches to the water. Clumps of debris in the branches told me where the high water had reached this spring, nearly eight feet above me. I pitched my tent in the unrelenting rain, climbed inside, and wringing out my clothes, wondered exactly why I was doing this. After dark, with the rain much lighter, I left the tent to move the boat farther up the bank in case the river should flood. The river bank was lit with thousands of fireflies sparkling like stars in a small, private universe. Back in my tent, I blew out the candle lantern, laid down and watched them glowing through the walls of the tent, dancing in little galaxies above me. I fell asleep that first night tired, wet, and cold but far from miserable. I drifted to sleep listening to the tapping of a slow steady rain above and the rushing waters of the Delaware right outside my door.

Paddling in the rain that first day I saw many great blue herons fishing on shore, beavers slapping their tails to announce themselves, and fish jumping at dusk to the chagrin of empty-handed fly fishermen on shore. I missed my mark the second day and had to paddle back upstream. I first tried to paddle up along the New York side but got beaten back by the current. I was taken sideways and spun around. I imagined the locals looking out of their windows, gathered on the sidewalks of the little town, all laughing at the idiot trying to paddle upstream. After I regained control I crossed the river to the Pennsylvania side. I lost ground and wound up much farther downstream, but the current on this side of the river was weaker. I finally landed within walking distance of the town. I was wet, exhausted, and more than a little concerned about my judgment. I decided to try to avoid paddling upstream in the future.

I was born and raised in Jersey City. My summers were split between camping trips on the Delaware River and hot summer days spent on the street playing handball and stick ball and hanging out on stoops. Those stoops and stairs and sidewalks, made of blue stone, came from quarries located not more than one mile from where I was now camped. I landed at the little village of Equinunk, Pa, on the second day. Less than 150 people live in this hamlet that hugs the shore of the river; in the two days I spent here, I probably met half of them. I pulled in behind a huge abandoned building, then walked through at least a hundred yards of grass and stinging nettles (in shorts, of course) to the main street in town. I was immediately befriended by two long time residents named Doc and Buzzy. Doc escorted me to the Red Barn restaurant (the only restaurant in town) and introduced me to Allison, the waitress, who pumped me full of hot coffee while I dried out.

"I love this river," she told me. "I was born on it and I'm gonna die in it." In it? I asked. "Yes," she said, "My husband and I are both going to be cremated and thrown into the water." I came to Equinunk to meet George Frosch, whose grandfather owned a blue stone quarry here. George, a tall man in his late 60's, owns Frisbee Island; at 65 acres, it's the second largest island on the Upper Delaware. He explained to me how the blue stone I played on as a boy in Jersey City made its way from the mountains to the city. The stone itself came from the Pennsylvania side of the river and had to travel down steep banks, almost vertical in some spots. It was blasted out of the mountain, cut into large blocks of two or three tons each and put onto wooden horse-drawn wagons. The horses had the unenviable task of walking in front of these loaded wagons down the steep hillsides. Roads were cut, by pick and shovel, into the mountains. Level spots were carved out at intervals so the horses could rest on the way up and slow down on the return trip. To slow the wagon's descent, a steel skidder was attached under the rear wheels of the wagon, this would keep the wagon from overrunning the horses. Usually. When the wagons arrived at the bottom, the slabs were put on a wooden scow and taken across the river to the mill and the railroad. The scow was attached to each shore with cables; the force of the river moved it from side to side. Once milled, the slabs were put on railroad cars. Before the railroad, they were taken on rafts down the river. Slabs of this smooth blue stone were sent to New York City, Philadelphia, Hoboken, and of course, to Jersey City, where I played handball on blue stone stoops and daydreamed about my next camping trip to the Delaware. Blue stone was finally replaced by reinforced concrete; the mill was closed in 1938. On my ridiculous (but successful!) paddle upstream on the Pennsylvania side, I noticed large rock caves and outcroppings. I had thought for a moment of camping in them if the storm arrived and I had not made shore in time. They looked like they would be good protection from the lightning. George told me the first white person born in this river valley was born in caves like those just a little farther upriver. In about 1780, a settler couple by the name of Parks were warned the Iroquois were on the way down river. Mrs. Parks was pregnant at the time. The Parks left their camp and found a small cave along the banks. Mrs. Parks gave birth to a baby girl in a cave upriver. Hannah Parks was the first white person born this far upriver.

On the morning of the third day, I was sitting in the Red Barn having breakfast and drying out, when I met a man who made my little adventure seem like a trip to the A&P. His name was Albert LeBlanc. Albert is from Maria, Quebec. In fact, Albert left Maria May 20 and is on his way to the Olympics in Atlanta. Albert is 72 years old. He is traveling alone on his bicycle. Albert told me this will be the ninth Olympics he's attended. He has bicycled around the world four times. He's bicycled to the games in Mexico, Munich, Los Angeles, Seoul, Moscow, Barcelona, and others, he said. He tries to get permission to sleep in garages and barns, saving his money for food. Everything he needs is on his bicycle. I asked him why. "I love to do this. To see the world, meeting people. It's freedom," he said. Albert told me he usually gets into the Olympics for free. "I am an ambassador for the old age and an example for youth," he said in a flowing French accent.

He didn't linger at the Red Barn like I did (more coffee and a toasted muffin). He ate a light breakfast, snapped a picture of his waitress, hopped on his bike, and was gone. I have no doubt that he will make it to Atlanta. I promised myself no more whining about the rain.

Before I left Equinunk and the Red Barn, Doc stopped by to say good-bye and show me his father's diary. "It has the history," he told me. The book was old and worn, the pages all yellowed and the ink and pencil marks had smeared in many places. Here are a few of the entries from Emmett Hathaway's diary:

- August 19, 1949: Florence passed away today 1:00 p.m. at Callicoon in coma. Ernest and I were with her. She was wonderfully brave. (His father's sister).

- Dec 13, 1949: Coyotes. Ran back across road above orchard.

- Jan. 1, 1949: New Year's Day Resolution by family: To be kinder and try to make each other happier. Prayer New Years Eve. Junior kneeled by Pa.

Next stop will be a little farther down river at Joe and Kathy Maloney's. Kathy is a volunteer eagle watcher and I hope to see some of the newly returned bald eagles. If it ever stops raining.

Chapter 2

"Be careful to sit in an elevating and inspiring place. There my thoughts were confined and trivial, and I hid myself from the gaze of travelers. Here they are expanded and elevated, and I am charmed by this beautiful river-reach."

—Henry David Thoreau

The thunderstorms that followed me, plagued me, and drenched me the first four days of the trip have gone. They have been replaced by clear skies and warm sunny days. The river, still high and flowing fast, now seems friendlier, more hospitable. I am finally dry.

I spent two nights on the river bank at Joe and Kathy Maloney's house about a mile and a half below Lordville, N.Y. I camped on a grassy landing a few feet from the river. On the opposite bank were tall hemlocks and mixed hardwoods. Kathy told me the hemlocks' large branches, hanging close to the water, are favorite perches for the eagles.

Growing behind my tent was a clump of quaking aspens, some willows and a distinguished old oak. Closest to the river, the quaking aspens played host to a small flock of cedar waxwings, which were constantly busy catching flies and other airborne critters. The marshy grasses and reeds along the bank attracted the usual sparrows and the ubiquitous red-winged blackbird.

I've been spoiled by the red-winged blackbird. Each

sundown, even in the worst weather, it has never failed to cheer me with its calls and trills. Its bright flash of red against a raven black shimmer of feathers always delights me. A common sight on the river, its charm is no less diminished by its abundance.

My field guide describes its call as follows:

> . . . a liquid gurgling: konk-la-ree or o-kay-la.

The Maloneys are New York City transplants. Joe is a professional photographer and builder and Kathy, formerly a director of an art gallery in Manhattan, now runs a small dried flower business from her home.

Kathy is also a volunteer eagle watcher with the Endangered Species Unit of the New York State Department of Conservation. I stopped here to learn more about bald eagles and their remarkable return to this river valley. I was told if I kept my eyes open I would see some. I had my doubts.

I had a little trouble finding the Maloney's. I'm learning that directions on a river are seldom precise. Joe told me if I could find his house I could camp there. "Let's see how good of an investigative reporter you are," he said.

The directions I had went something like this: About a mile and a half past the Lordville bridge. New York side. White house with a red roof, though you probably won't be able to see it from the river. If you go around the sharp curve, you've missed it.

I missed it. Luckily, I have acquired a talent for paddling upstream—paddling the wrong way regardless of how high the river or how swift the current. I hugged the shore and went back to a likely landing. I bushwhacked my way through knee high grasses and slipped and slid on the muddy bank like something out of a Three Stooges routine. Wrong house. I tried another and found it. If I missed the Maloney's it would have been a 12 mile race before dark to a campground.

On the afternoon of the second day at the Maloney's, we were standing in the kitchen talking about the Upper Delaware when

Kathy suddenly stopped what she was doing and said, "Did you hear that?" I hadn't heard anything. She grabbed her binoculars and off we went down to the river. Kathy had heard an eagle call. "There's one out there," she said, scouting the trees across the river. I looked into the thick mass of green and could see nothing. "There he is," she said, pointing across the river. Finally, I saw it. A mature adult with white head and tail. The tiny specks of white now glaringly apparent, I wondered how I could have missed it. "When the light is shining through those trees," Kathy said, "You can't see them at all."

We heard it call again and Kathy said there must be another one somewhere. "Keep your eyes open," she said, "If he's calling, I'm sure there's another." Kathy left to take her daughter to a ballet recital. I sat on shore with my binoculars watching the bird.

It is an auspicious occasion just to glimpse an eagle. You are indeed fortunate to get a chance to watch one for a few minutes. And you are damned lucky to sit on a riverbank an hour and a half from New York City, leisurely watching such a majestic creature. A creature that was almost poisoned out of existence by pesticides (DDT in particular) just a few years ago.

As an eagle watcher, Kathy hunts down nests and monitors the mating activities of the eagles year-round. She assists biologists in banding and measuring the birds. On the Upper Delaware, there is now a summer and winter eagle population. They are living here and breeding here, and their young are returning here. Eagles, because they are easily disturbed, need secluded areas like the woods along the Upper Delaware to thrive. Human activities can keep them from fishing and nesting.

Eagle watching can also be dangerous. Kathy told me about the time they had discovered two fledglings that had fallen out of the nest or perhaps had been blown out by a severe storm. One chick was dead. The other was barely alive; maggots had already started invading its body. All around the chicks were dead fish and small mammals. The parent eagles were trying to feed the chicks on the ground by flying over and dropping dead prey.

While the volunteers were there, one was almost hit by a squirrel bomb, headless and bloody.

Another time, Kathy said, they were watching a raccoon making his way up to an apparently unguarded nest of fledglings. Just as the raccoon got to the nest, a parent eagle swooped down, grabbed the would-be thief and soared with him high above, and suddenly, let go.

Kathy was right. After about 30 minutes another eagle landed in the hemlock, a few feet above the other. The eagles sat there for more than an hour before they decided to leave together. Damned lucky.

After leaving the Maloney's I was on my way to Callicoon, N.Y. and a commercial campground and canoe livery called the Upper Delaware Campground. About two miles from Callicoon I stopped on a gravel bar between two small islands to do a little swimming. Now that the sun was out again I wanted to get wet. I pulled out of the current which was running quite fast, made a soft landing in some tall grasses, barely scraping the bottom of the boat. Getting pretty good, I thought.

The water was deep, fast, and cool. I splashed around for about 20 minutes, dried off in the sun and prepared to leave. Back in the boat, I was attaching the spray skirt to the cockpit combing, making sure it was sealed correctly all around (the skirt attaches with Velcro and is designed to keep out any water that splashes on deck). I was busy concentrating on the skirt when I realized that the bow of the boat (I was pointed upstream, my usual direction) had drifted into the current and I was now being pulled out into the river—ready or not—and I was definitely not ready. My paddle was lying across the back of the boat with one end on shore. When the boat suddenly pulled into the current, the paddle slipped off and landed in the water. I lunged for it, nearly capsizing, but managed to grab a hold of it. I reached around behind me and pulled the paddle back on board. I banged both the nail on my middle finger and my thumb pretty good. But I was fortunate to be going down the river with a paddle, even though I was going sideways. About 100 yards down I finally managed to straighten out the boat. A mile later, I was pulling into Upper Delaware Campgrounds. Another lesson learned.

My only other ailments so far are a number of blisters on each foot from slogging around those first four days in wet sneakers. I can no longer wear my sneakers without socks and since I'm always either stepping into the water or stepping out of it, my socks are always wet and muddy. Like a true river rat, I only put on shoes when I'm in town.

Here's a story I heard from Al Kaufman, owner of the Upper Delaware Campground: Kate Smith had recorded a song called "When the Moon Comes Over the Mountain," written by Harry Woods. Woods, who lived along the river, also wrote, "I'm Looking Over a Four Leaf Clover." When the record sold one million copies, Kate Smith sang the song to Woods off the Callicoon bridge.

They say Harry Woods got plastered one night in a Callicoon Hotel on his way home his jeep went off the road. It would have careened down the bank and into the river had it not gotten hung up on a tree part of the way down. Harry, even though he was inebriated, sensed the imminent danger and sat very still in his jeep all night, afraid any movement would dislodge him. Supposedly, while sitting there sobering up, Harry watched the moon come up over the mountain. I've never heard the song although Al tried to sing it to me. I can honestly say I still have never heard the song.

The night before I left the Upper Delaware Campground, I had only one thing on my mind: Skinner's Falls. I decided not to make a decision until I got there which would be sometime Monday morning. Skinner's is the most notorious series of rapids on the Delaware. My fear was not for myself or the boat but for my little laptop computer and all the assorted electronic junk I'm carrying with me.

The falls invaded my dreams and kept me from getting a good night's sleep. Five guys from Queens drinking beer and raising hell in the campsite next to me didn't help either. Monday morning the clouds returned, the sky was grumbling once again. A bad omen, I was sure. I traveled about two hours in a light rain to the falls. On weekends in the summer this place is filled with whitewater thrill seekers. This drizzly gray Monday morning there was no one in sight. I stopped at a canoe livery and found a young guy who told me the falls weren't too bad right now. I told him about my fears of ruining my equipment. "It's up to you," he said. "The New York side is walkable, not too much brush in the way," he added, apparently sensing my anxiety. The falls were roaring in the background, like a dream.

O.K. I'm walking it. Why risk all this stuff. If my laptop goes, I'll have to write the rest of these reports long hand. If my modem hits the drink, I'll have to call in each story word by word. I rigged a line from bow to stern to control the boat as I walked through. I headed down the New York side but as I got closer, the falls didn't look too bad. Sure, the waves were big, but not that much bigger. I had already come through a few big ones. I must have learned something, I told myself. So I walked back. I took off my sneakers and untied the boat. Before getting in, I checked my guidebook.

Here are some excerpts from the book:

> A pass through Skinner's Falls requires every precaution. Heavily loaded canoes should be emptied of their gear. . . . Though the main passage is in the right center, even there high standing waves and submerged boulders can capsize the most experienced canoeists. The final ledge creates a potentially dangerous hydraulic in the middle and left of the river and must be carefully avoided.

And from the map notes:

> Boaters are urged to exercise extreme caution in attempting to traverse this area, particularly when the river is high (and the river was high from all the rain).

O.K., I'm walking again. I put my sneakers back on and

retied the line from bow to stern. I walked back down to the falls. But then I figured I was in a lose—lose situation. If I don't paddle I'll sound like I'm making excuses (laptop, modem etc.); if I go through and dump—and ruin my equipment—I'll look like a fool. O.K.—I'm paddling.

I walk the boat back to the eddy before the rapids, take off my sneakers and go. In a minute it was over. I hit a three-foot wave and saw the bow of the boat go completely underwater. It stayed under for what seemed like an awfully long time. The boat shuddered and slammed into another three-foot wave. A giant boulder appeared just below the surface. I backpaddled for a second and steered to the right. In a few moments I was out. I didn't take on a drop of water. Ha! I laugh at danger.

My next stop is the Yeman farm. A quiet, peaceful farm on the river 12 miles from where the Woodstock Festival had taken place. Barbara Yeman is going to show me her black maple tree. It is the biggest black maple tree in Pennsylvania and only 12 feet short of the tallest black maple in the country.

After conquering Skinner's Falls, I floated with the current in a drizzly rain for a long way down river. Suddenly, on shore, sitting on a large square rock, I saw a young bald eagle eating a fish. I sat as still as possible, raised my binoculars, and watched him eat.

Three crows sat on a fallen branch not more than a yard from him, cawing at him, begging and tormenting him during his breakfast. I floated past and just as I was directly in front of him, he flew off, leaving his fish for the crows. I couldn't have been more than 25 feet away. Lucky again.

I had a little trouble finding the Yeman farm. I eventually found it by walking down a country road about a half mile and knocking on doors. But if your idea of paradise is a 100 year old farmhouse on 12 acres, a weathered wood barn built in 1912, two pet goats named Frisbee and Peaches, chickens, warblers, a frog pond and an organic vegetable and herb garden—all with a view of the river blocked only by a four-story maple tree—then this is it.

I pitched my tent under that 150 year-old tree, made a cup of tea, and talked with Barbara about this special place. I asked her if she felt a sense of responsibility in the stewardship of this tree. "Yes," she said. "And it's home to an awful lot of things." There are orioles nesting in it, and ladybugs arrive in the fall to hibernate in the leaf litter on the south side of the tree, she said.

A few years ago she paid more than $1,000 to have the tree pruned. Last year, she enlisted all her friends and visitors to help to fertilize the tree. Since the roots are so far below the surface, she had to pound stakes into the ground, 12-to-18 inches deep then fill them with fertilizer. We figured she must have pounded over 800 holes. It took over a year to finish, she said.

The tree is remarkable. Its girth at waist height is 18 feet, 2 inches. It would take four or five people holding hands to surround it. It has the largest spread of any black maple in the country. A truly rare tree in the Northeast.

While Barbara and I were sitting there talking, a young bald eagle, still lacking the distinctive white head and tail, flew down river. We followed it with our binoculars (like most residents of the river valley, I now carry my binoculars everywhere, all the time). It may have been the same one I saw that morning upriver.

I would see two more eagles before I left Barbara's farm. I also saw at least two types of warblers, a deer with a young fawn still nursing, a bobolink, many great blue herons and many more species of birds I couldn't identify.

In the barn, Barbara has opened a nature center and children from the area come to visit and learn more about the local wildlife. Ed Wesley, a naturalist, has a unique collection of monarch butterfly larvae in the barn. Ed collects the larvae and cocoons, waits for the butterflies to emerge and then tags them so their migration can be traced. "Tagging butterflies?," I asked. Ed does it all the time. First he scrapes the scales off a section of the wing then a tiny tag gets bent over the outside forward edge of the wing. It has a number, the date the butterfly was tagged and a notice that says: "If found, please return to the University of Toronto." All on a tiny metal tag. I swear it's true.

Eagles are considered an umbrella species. If you protect their habitat, you protect an awful lot of everything else. Monarch butterflies return to Mexico, warblers to South America. From majestic bald eagles to fragile butterflies, this river valley is rich with a diversity of species. A richness made even more remarkable by its proximity to some of the most crowded, congested, and polluted areas in the country.

The forecast calls for rain for the next four days. In five days I have a date at Dingman's Ferry with one of the last remaining Lenape descendants who still speaks the Lenape language. In the meantime I plan to camp on Minisink Island and explore some of the Lenape caves and camps.

On a solemn note, there were two young men from New Jersey drowned here last weekend. They were swimming from the rocks on the north side of the Narrowsburg bridge. The pool of water looks calm but beneath the surface is a treacherous current, made worse by the high water condition of the river. One of the swimmers got into trouble; his friend attempted to help but was pulled down with the panicked swimmer. Despite its beauty and calm appearance, this river, like all of nature, demands respect. It can be as fierce as it can be benign. Perhaps the opposite of beauty is terror.

Chapter 3

"He who hears the rippling of rivers in these degenerate days will not utterly despair."

—Henry David Thoreau

I left Narrowsburg in a drizzly rain. I glided under the bridge and past the quiet pool of water where the two young men from New Jersey had drowned just a few days before. This was to be one of the hardest days I would have on the river.

My goal was to reach Barryville, N.Y. by the end of the day. To do this, I would have to traverse four Class Two rapids and numerous smaller ones. The rapids, No. 9 Railroad Bridge Rapids, Kunkeli Rapids, Masthope Rapids, Colang Rapids and finally Cedar Rapids, were all nerve-wracking but I managed to slip through them all without a problem.

From my journal: "Five rapids today. Exhausted. Everything is wet."

My map showed a commercial canoe livery and campground called Wild and Scenic River Tours just before the bridge at Barryville. When I finally arrived, after paddling more than 15 miles, wet (it was still raining) and exhausted, the campground was closed.

With no one in sight, I set up my tent. I decided it wouldn't be so bad if I were arrested. Jail would be warm and dry, I wouldn't have to cook and I could sleep late in the morning. Go ahead, arrest me. Please!

About 15 minutes after getting my tent set up, a woman suddenly appeared. She was walking toward me asking, "What are you doing here?" I said I was camping. "But the campground is closed, we don't open for the season until tomorrow."

There was no way I was packing up my tent and getting back into that boat. Besides being exhausted, directly beyond the bridge was Shohola Rapids, one of the worst, and I didn't want to attempt it late in the day in such a tired condition. The banks of the river, where not privately owned, were too steep to camp on.

After a few minutes of interrogation, the woman, Gertrude Robinson, agreed to let me stay. Her son owned the livery business and campground. A Brooklyn resident, she has been coming to the river since the late 1930's. She moved here permanently in 1969. Though I was tired, wet, and ready to fall over, we talked for more than two hours about this river and what it means to the people who live on it.

"I love this river," she said. "I've seen it wild. I've seen it calm and I've seen it come into my house."

Gertrude told me she had a special rock in the middle of the river where she sits. "My friend named it the Isle of Paradise. We take chairs out there and sit on it." We couldn't even see her rock now because of the high water condition.

"Yes, I'm very partial to this river. It's therapy. It helps the stress," she said. I asked Gertrude if she likes to travel. She said she had been to Europe once but she wasn't much for traveling. "I've never seen grass any greener than this," she said.

While we were talking, Gertrude had noticed my blistered feet. In the morning, behind my tent, I found a pair of sneakers with a note, written in pencil, tucked into one of the sneakers. It read:

> Mr. M: If these fit you are welcome to them. Have a safe journey.

The sun was with me for most of the next day. By evening however, the clouds had returned and rain threatened once again. I made it through Shohola Rapids and decided to make it a short day. I camped at the foot of Stairway Rapids on Pennsylvania Preserve lands.

I sort of slipped sideways down the last stair of Stairway Rapids but recovered. The rapids, like Skinner's Falls, consists of a series of bedrock ledges. You come shooting through with the current and then suddenly right in front of you is a drop of perhaps a foot or more, then over you go. The bow of the boat plunges down into the water and the waves cover the top of the boat. Going down sideways adds another dimension to the experience.

The shad were starting to appear everywhere now. Shad are anadromous fish, living their lives in the ocean and returning to the fresh water rivers of their birth to spawn. For many years the shad couldn't make it past Trenton and Philadelphia to reach the upper river; the water was so badly polluted some parts of the river contained no oxygen at all. The shad have returned to the river, but not in the numbers they were once found. I discovered a campsite in the woods with a sandy beach for the boat nearby. Wild roses, the first I've seen on the river, were growing on the banks bordering the little beach. On a walk through the woods, I surprised a red fox who scrambled out of the brush and into a ravine. I also heard a barred owl but could not find it.

Camping here was a welcome change from the private property on which I had been camping. This felt more wild; a taste of what was to come. That night I made a delicious cup of apple-mint tea from leaves Barbara Yeman had given me from her herb garden. Sitting by the river at sundown I saw a bald eagle and three red-tailed hawks. I took a bath in a small pool below the rock ledges, went to bed and slept like a baby.

Camped about 100 feet upriver from me were two guys on a four-day fishing expedition. They have been doing this for five years they said. Each year they spend time on a different section of the river. They had a good catch of small mouth bass which they were cleaning and readying for a big dinner on the last night, a tradition, they said.

I should mention here that fish and I have struck an agreement. They don't eat me and I don't eat them. They don't yank me out of my world and I don't yank them out of theirs—each of us content just to know the other is there. Enough said.

Like me, these guys were loaded down with equipment. They had swamped in a rapid just upstream the day before. In fact, they said they had gone through with the sides of the canoe six inches under water. The trick, they said, was not to let the boat roll. If it rolled, it was all over.

I asked them why this river. Fred Hallock from Wallkill, N.Y. told me, "It's a challenge. There's fish like—it's loaded with fish." Bill Yancey from Ringoes, N.J., agreed, "I love this river. Twenty years ago it was polluted. It's really been cleaned up," he said.

We all faced the Mongaup Wave the next day. They had decided to walk around. They had heard "the wave" was about four feet high. In a kayak, especially a heavily loaded one, a four foot wave is about two feet over your head. It was silly, we all agreed, to risk it. If they were walking, so was I.

Bad idea. I almost killed myself trying to walk around the rapids. I fell twice on the slippery rocks and where the Mongaup River enters the Delaware, the water was chest high and fast. I had to walk upriver before I could cross with the water at knee level. I would have been better going through in the boat. Someone later told me that you can avoid "the wave" by staying a little to the left. Next time.

My plan for the following day was to arrive in Milford, Pa., and resupply for the next leg of the trip (once inside the Delaware Water Gap National Recreation Area, there would be little chance to buy more food). I would then paddle a little farther to Minisink Island and camp for two days. I wanted to try to get a feel for what the Lenape Indians saw and smelled and heard here. Minisink was once inhabited by a great number of Lenape Indians.

But the rain gods were back and they had their own ideas for me. Heavy downpours, thunder and lighting, and a stiff head wind were apparently in their plans but not in mine. Because of the storm, I had to paddle over 20 miles that Saturday.

> *"I do not know much about gods;*
> *but I think that the river*
> *Is a strong brown god—sullen, untamed*
> *and intractable."*

—T.S. Elliot

Coming around the bend in the river just above Port Jervis, I saw the High Point monument. Home, I thought, at least for a short while. I was entering the section of the river I know best. It is mostly primitive. Camping is free, and can be done on both shores and on the islands. There are few if any rapids to worry about in this section. Instead, a new worry will be low water. The bottom of my boat is made of rubber. A hard grounding can rip it to shreds. I need to learn how to read the river for this new obstacle. I grounded in about six inches of water coming into Port Jervis. I should have seen it, but I didn't. On my left, in the deeper stuff, a flurry of little girls in their canoes (girl scouts?) zipped by giggling as I sat there stuck on the bottom.

I arrived in Milford late in the day, soaking wet. The storm clouds were regrouping and a heavy thunderstorm seemed imminent. I decided to make a run for Minisink Island, set up my camp and do my shopping the next day. Hopefully the sun would be back by then.

I don't know if I ever really got the full effect of Minisink. They say the big trees are gone. A Lenape wouldn't even recognize the place with these little 100-year-old trees. Much of Manhattan was built with the soaring white pine from these banks.

Saturday night, after the storm had passed, I was standing on the bank, watching the sun make a dim appearance before setting over the mountains in Pennsylvania, when down the river came 10 canoes bearing 22 boy scouts and their dads—all out for a father and son overnighter.

Within five minutes Troop 81 of East Stroudsburg was invading my island. I watched as they brought up bag after bag (all dripping wet) of equipment and set up a dozen tents, barbecue grills and bright, glaring lanterns.

This once quiet, peaceful island was now awash with activity: voices yelling and shouting, kids whining, dads wringing the water out of their shirts, cursing under their breaths, tossing away with disgust the mashed potato mix, made prematurely by the thunderstorms and swampings of the day.

These guys were wet and miserable. If a boat had pulled up and offered to take them home I don't think one dad or scout would have remained.

The contrast was shocking. Though I meet a lot of people on the river I spend most of my days and all of my nights alone. My campsites are dark except for a candle lantern in my tent for reading and a headlamp for finding my way on dark nights. I have a little cook stove and never make a fire. I spend the last hours of daylight usually in or on the river. I go to sleep when it gets dark. Very primal, very peaceful. Bird song, insects, and the wind in the trees are all I hear. Usually.

But they did manage to get a good fire going in spite of the wet wood. They gave me chocolate and we swapped stories about our stormy day on the river. Perhaps I came closer to the Lenape experience than I thought.

In the beginning, there was only water. Then the creator sent a great turtle which rose from the depths of the seas. And from the turtle's moss covered shell, a tree took root. And from that sapling's first bud, man was born; from the second shoot, came woman.

This is one of the Lenape's creation tales. There is another where life takes root from a bit of mud scooped up from the bottom of the sea by a muskrat. Thus the scene was set on the banks of the Delaware River for a deep and unresolvable clash of cultures. One culture firmly believing their existence was in and of the natural world, the other, believing it was their "divine" duty to dominate and conquer the land.

The Delaware River, known to the Lenape as Lenapewhihituck, meaning swift waters of the Lenape, was renamed by mid-17th century settlers for the English Lord De La Warr (who never even saw the river!). Within 100 years of the first white settlements, the Lenape would be gone. Turtle Island would be carved and cleared; the beaver, muskrat, deer, and eagle, all but gone. War, disease, and the loss of their lands would force the remaining Lenape west and north. The few surviving Lenape long ago settled in Oklahoma and Ontario. You can trace the migration of the Lenape westward by looking for towns with names like Munsee, which are derivatives of Lenape names.

The Lenape readily "sold" their lands to the settlers without truly understanding the concept of land ownership. To the Lenape, no one could really own land; no one could sell it. It was given, after all, by the Creator. They took what the settlers offered without fully realizing what they were trading away.

"This we know. The Earth does not belong to man; man belongs to the Earth."

—Chief Seattle

The white settlers took advantage of the Lenapes' naiveté, and in one instance known as the Walking Purchase, settlers overtly cheated and infuriated the Lenape. William Penn had signed a treaty for the sale of land, the dimensions to be determined by the distance a man could "go" in a day and a half. The Lenape presumed this distance to be about 25 miles. But after Penn died, one of his sons hired three professional walkers. The three athletes, accompanied by horses and well-provisioned, walked 65 miles, ultimately causing two of the runners to drop from exhaustion. The Lenape declared that they had been cheated. The next few decades were filled with atrocities committed by both whites and natives until the Lenape, substantially outnumbered, finally withdrew to the west and north. The runner who had gone the farthest during the Walking Purchase, Edward Marshall, was awarded cash and land for his efforts. But as often happens, deceit breeds despair. Marshall was eventually wounded by the Lenape; his wife was scalped and his daughter killed.

The Great Mother

> Not all those who pass
> In front of the Great Mother's chair
> Get past with just a stare.
> Some she looks at their hands
> To see what sort of savages they were.
>
> —Gary Snyder, from *Turtle Island*

Monday morning I met Chuck Zimnik and his son Chase below the Dingman's Ferry bridge. Chuck is one-half Lenape, lives along the river and is one of about a dozen Lenape who still speak the language. Chuck learned the language from his mother and is now teaching his son. Chuck told me the last full-blooded Lenape, Norma Thompson Dean, died in 1984. Translated, Lenape means "ordinary people."

Chuck brought with him a ceremonial rattle made from a gourd and decorated with gray and red squirrel fur, finch feathers, and skunk fur. Pebbles inside the gourd supplied the music.

The Lenape inhabited vast sections of this river. Their clans stretched from the Delaware Bay to upstate New York. Chuck said there are three distinct clans or tribes: the turtle, the wolf, and the turkey.

A young Lenape man seeking a wife would leave his village, traveling many miles to find a woman. Once he found a likely prospect, he would ask a close friend of her family to present, on his behalf, a gift or a meal. If the girl accepted, they would be married. Chuck said the average age of the boy was 16, the girl, 13. The couple would remain in the girl's village. It was in this way the gene pool was protected.

The Lenape lived in longhouses, constructed of wood and

bark. In winter, the houses would remain at a constant temperature of 70 degrees. Chuck said there was always a meal on the fire for visitors and special guests. Longhouses would last an average of 15 years without repair.

Chuck said the Lenape were not known for fancy decorations or intricate weavings like other tribes but Lenape women were "astounding cooks." Often meals would be given as gifts or presented as a special honor. Chuck seemed particularly proud of the role women played in Lenape society. White women, in the 1600-1700's were completely subservient. Lenape women sat on councils and had equal rights.

The number twelve was sacred to the Lenape. They held twelve things above all else. In addition to the creator, or Kishalamechkong, there was the Sun, Moon, Water, Wind, Fire, House, Corn, the four corners of the earth: east, west, north, and south and Mother Earth.

Chuck, Chase, and I painted my little boat with a Lenape name for good luck. We used red paint, the sacred color. Chuck told me that because Lenape men were usually painted with red paint, they were mistakenly called "red men." Lenape skin color was more of an olive color than red. William Penn even remarked that the Lenape, with their light color and gentle manners, reminded him of Europeans. Only their black hair revealed their heritage.

The name Chuck chose for my boat was "Kithane Maxkw," which means Big River Bear. "The spirit of the bear is determined; the bear always survives," he said. He didn't know it, but a bear was the first animal I had seen on my trip.

> *"The land, the Earth God gave to man for his home . . .*
> *should never be the possession of any man, corporation,*
> *or society . . . any more than the air or water."*
>
> —Abraham Lincoln

Chapter 4

"Never did we plan the morrow, for we had learned that in the wilderness some new and irresistible distraction is sure to turn up each day before breakfast. Like the river, we were free to wander."

—Aldo Leopold,
from a 1922 canoe trip in the Colorado River Delta

It has been an idyllic week. Though the last two days have been cloudy and rainy, the previous four days were warm and sunny. I spent this week cruising through the more than 35 miles of river in the Delaware Water Gap National Recreation Area.

Camping on islands and on wooded shores, swimming in deep pools and watching wildlife, this segment, so far, has come closest to what I had imagined the best of this trip would be. I've spent too many days doing nothing at all, yet I still need more time in this place; more time to explore the islands, more time to read in the morning sun, more time to learn the bird songs, the trees, the flowers and plants, and even the insects that inhabit this world of clear water and a thousand shades of green. When I leave here in a few days the river will change once again. Cities, power plants, and more rapids will follow. Camping will again be a problem. I almost wish I could stay here; forego the balance of the trip for another few weeks of quiet exploration.

It is ironic that the most primitive and tranquil stretch of this river was, in recent times, the scene of such ugly hostility. Today

I floated past Tock's Island, the infamous site of a proposed 160-foot dam that would have buried this river valley at the bottom of a 37 mile-long lake. The dam was proposed in the early 1960s to address the water demands of the growing downstream population. Estimates at the time claimed 22 million people would be thirsting for Delaware River water by the year 2000.

But people lived in this river valley. Families had farmed here for more than 100 years. The U.S. Army Corps of Engineers, the dam builders, used their power of eminent domain to move them, remove them and condemn buildings and land holdings. Some residents, intimidated by agents hired by the Corps, received only $50 per acre for their farms. The despair and disbelief grew so great, one resident even committed suicide.

The first battle was fought over Sunfish Pond, a glacial lake atop the Kittatinny Ridge overlooking the Water Gap. Plans to flood the mountain top and construct a reservoir with turbines prompted the first resistance to the Tocks Island Dam.

In his wonderful book, *Delaware Diary*, author Frank Dale, recounts the time in 1967 when U.S. Supreme Court Justice William O. Douglas hiked to Sunfish Pond. Douglas, 68 years old at the time, declared, "Sunfish Pond is a unique spot and deserves to be preserved." According to Dale, in an article Douglas wrote, which appeared in Playboy magazine, the opening sentence read: "The Army Corps of Engineers is public enemy number one!"

> There is a marker at the beginning of the trail to Sunfish Pond commemorating the efforts of Douglas and others who fought to save the little pond on top of the mountain. But Sunfish Pond was only the beginning. In 1980 the trail was named the 'Douglas Trail.'

I was fortunate to be able to spend time with Nancy Shukaitis, one of the leading anti-dam activists. Nancy is best remembered for her persistent and determined testimony in front of Congress. She is a local hero to many people in this river valley. Today she remains engaged in the fight to preserve the valley and this free-flowing river. She noted how tentative the federal protection here really is. In the year 2000, the Delaware River Basin Commission (DRBC), will once again review whether or not a dam is needed on the Delaware.

The DRBC is responsible for overseeing many issues on the river. Issues such as water allocations and usage are among their highest priorities. The commissioners are appointed by the four states along the Delaware: New Jersey, Pennsylvania, New York, and Delaware. The commissioners have no legislative authority.

Nancy is concerned about the number of approved uses for Delaware River water. "The problem is, in a severe drought, the uses that have been approved when there was no drought continue. If we allow more uses to come in, the river doesn't have the power. We need to learn to live within the rainfall," she said.

In his book about the Delaware River, *Natural Lives, Modern Times*, author Bruce Stutz talks about the commissioners who make up the DRBC and their political sensitivities immediately after dealing with a drought:

> Not that these commissioners don't know that houses, roads, and parking lots increase runoff while they reduce the amount of water able to sink down to recharge the vaults of natural underground storage, an estimated 2,000 billion gallons in the Delaware basin, which dwarfs the 300 billion gallons stored in reservoirs.
>
> Not that they don't know the runoff from new development is silt-laden and then becomes contaminated with pesticides and fertilizer, septic waste, the wash of oil and rock salt from new roads, the leachate from new landfills, the leaks from gas stations and dry cleaners. And not that they haven't ever acted to benefit the river. But by their nature as appointees of the governors of the states they represent, they tend to drift with the prevailing political flow.

Nancy said the Hudson River is the least-cost solution to New York City's growing demands for water. "Spend the money to clean up the Hudson and you'll not only have a source of water 20 times greater than the Delaware but you'll get a clean river in the bargain," she said.

The Tock's Island dam was eventually defeated, in part, because of the geology of the valley. Samples taken from Tock's Island revealed limestone and shale, an unstable and sometimes slushy substrate. The determined efforts of a small coalition brought to light many of the environmental and geological facts that would eventually doom the dam. Also, former proponents of the dam in the northern section became foes once they learned that their end of the reservoir would be mud flats and backwash at low water. "They forgot that the earth was round," said Nancy with a wry smile.

But the turmoil produced by the dam proposal has left in its wake this National Recreation Area free, for the most part, of dilapidated shacks hanging over the water's edge, faulty or non-existent septics, and over-development—threats still present on the Upper Delaware.

I asked Nancy if this protected stretch of river was even a small consolation for the loss of her family's farm and the years of upheaval and bitter fighting. Her answer surprised me, "My dad said he would have been glad to give up the farm—but he thought that to put such a valley under water was sacrilege." Farms and homes could have been preserved using a system of easements and land conservancies, she added.

After all this time, you can still see the pain in Nancy's eyes when she talks about those years and the people who were displaced. "Why did they have to treat them that way? she asks, "Why?"

The Tocks Island project was voted down in 1975 with Governor Shapp of Pennsylvania the only governor voting in favor of the dam. It was officially de-commissioned about four years ago. Nancy Shukaitis left me with a warning, "People have to remain on guard," she said.

> *"The supreme reality of our time is . . .
> the vulnerability of our planet."*
>
> —John F. Kennedy

Again from Dale's book:

> The dam might still have been built while these opposing forces gained momentum had it not been for a handful of women and men who loved Sunfish Pond and the free-flowing Delaware. The next time you canoe through Walpack Bend or the Water Gap, or hike on the Appalachian Trail past Sunfish Pond, think of them.

A merganser mystery: I have seen countless merganser moms and their ducklings on my travels down river. I've counted up to 17 little fuzzballs trailing behind diligent females. But I have yet to see one male merganser on this entire trip. Are male mergansers the deadbeat dads of the duck world? Where are they? Do they return to parts north once they have done their duckly duty? Do the males change their coloration to look like females? No one I've asked on the river seems to know.

As I was breaking camp one morning this week I was startled by a large man in hiking boots tramping through my campsite. He turned out to be a Field Botanist/Wetlands Specialist by the name of Bill Olson. He was hired by the National Park Service to look for threatened and endangered plant species along the river corridor.

Bill told me the NPS plans to construct a hiking trail on the Pennsylvania side from Milford down to the Water Gap. The trail would be about 35 miles long. It was his job, he explained, to check the proposed route for any unique plants or wetlands that could be harmed by the construction and use of the trail.

Bill carried a Global Positioning System (GPS) unit with him to record the position of any plants he found. The unit is about as big as a remote control for a television. The GPS works with two satellites in orbit around the earth. Switching on the system, it pinpoints his exact location within a 10-meter accuracy.

When he's done entering the locations, trail planners can map out the data and design the trail around sensitive areas and plant colonies. Bill told me the trail will be a low-impact path using existing trails and edges of farm fields where possible.

So far he's found an endangered sedge by the name of *carex typhina* which is related to the lily family. He also told me that areas closest to the river have the largest diversity of plants, as opposed to the more stable forest environment. "The river is dynamic," he said. "As the river changes, these areas need to be checked again and again."

I camped for a few days at Worthington State Park. I met with my family, made many new friends, and relaxed a bit. What a luxury it was to be able to leave my tent in the same spot for more than a day. Setting up camp, which usually involves lugging all my stuff up steep muddy banks, and breaking camp, which always involves lugging the same stuff back down steep muddy banks, has become a predictable part of every day.

But the excitement of finding a new campsite at the end of each day and the urge to get moving, to explore the next morning, usually cancel out any gripes I have with the procedure. Still, it was nice to stay put for a couple of days. Running water and hot showers added to the sense of extravagance.

I set up camp at the northernmost end of the park because I had to paddle two miles upstream on Friday to meet with Al Ambler, a biologist with the NPS, to discuss water quality in the river. This was the hardest upstream paddle to date and I didn't quite make it. Not on the water anyway.

About halfway to Smithfield Beach the current and a strong headwind got the best of me. Usually the wind is blowing upstream; in fact, I had counted on it. But once again the river reminded me that nothing is predictable, the river only *is*; it makes for neither a willing accomplice nor a vengeful enemy.

I ditched the boat on shore and decided to walk. I knew that

Route 209 ran parallel to the river. I figured I would just walk through the woods to the road. I took my red bandanna with me to tie to a tree when I left the woods so I could find the boat again (brilliant!).

I bushwhacked my way through the woods (in sandals) but came to a farm field instead of a road. I could hear the passing cars in the distance so I went on. I made a little rock cairn where I left the woods. A set of power lines crossed the fields so I followed them through more woods and out to the road. No need for the bandanna I thought (not so brilliant). I hitched a ride within minutes to Smithfield Beach. So far so good.

Al Ambler is a biologist with the National Park Service working inside the National Recreation Area. He is responsible for monitoring the water quality of the river and its tributaries. "This is a high quality water system," he said. Ambler explained that special protection regulations were put into place in 1992 to assure that there is "no measurable change" in the quality of the water.

The water is tested for several factors including temperature, nutrients, pH, suspended solids, conductivity and dissolved oxygen. Increases in any of these indicators would prompt an investigation.

Noting the number of farms along the river, I asked Al if run-off from agriculture was a problem. "We find very little agricultural run-off," he said. Farms, he added, are the traditional use in the valley and an excellent way to retain open space. There is a move within the NPS to encourage organic farming methods, he said, but there has not been a lot of interest among local farmers. Farmers' use of pesticides and fertilizers are strictly regulated, he said. In addition, large buffers are required between cultivated fields and the river (like the woods I had hiked through that morning).

Al said the biggest threat to the excellent water quality in the river is over-development in the surrounding areas. He said Pike and Monroe Counties in Pennsylvania are the fastest growing counties in the state. "With that going on around us, it provided the impetus for the (no measurable change) regulations."

Al gave me a ride back down the road. I wasn't really paying attention to how far we had gone. He had to turn around and go back until we found the power lines. After leaving Al I followed the power lines into a farm field but it was the wrong one. I had come through corn; this was something else. All the fields looked the same. It was impossible to tell where I had entered the road. Had I gone too far down or not far enough? I eventually found the right spot but it took more than an hour. My bandanna did come in handy—for wiping the panic-induced sweat off my forehead.

Justin Peas from Byram is 14 1/2 years old. I met him in Worthington State Park. He told me about hellgrammites and dobson flies. Hellgrammites are the larvae of the dobson fly. They are about 2 inches long, prehistoric looking, and prized by fisherman as live bait. I had never heard of them before but Justin filled me in.

"You find them under rocks in the current. It's got to be just the perfect mix of sand and soot and seaweed or else they won't like it," he said. "Hellgrammites look sort of like a crayfish but longer and they have two pinchers that really hurt—they can even draw blood," he added with an obvious delight in the danger. Justin had a bunch in his bait bucket. He told me he only takes a few at a time, "So they'll be here again next year." Justin said he loves the river and has been coming here since he was six years old. I asked him why. "It's so peaceful. There's lots of wildlife—deer and bald eagles. I woke up yesterday at 5:30 a.m. and saw deer walking through the mist. It was so cool."

Day 22: This evening, while sitting on the river bank, I heard something splashing. I thought someone had gone for a late day dip. I looked over to see a deer swimming across the river from one island to another. Behind that deer, another one entered the water. The light was fading and a gray mist spread from shore to shore, melding land and water into a single mystery. Golden fawns moving cautiously against a background of muted green were a pleasing end to a relaxed and lazy week. Now it's back to unknown territory and the ever-changing river.

Chapter 5

"A river is more than an amenity, it is a treasure."

—Supreme Court Justice Oliver Wendell Holmes

I left the Delaware Water Gap during a brief window in a series of violent thunderstorms. Each time I prepared to leave, another storm would roll in delaying me until late into the afternoon. I spent most of the time hanging around the National Park Service's Kittatinny Visitor's Center reading books and trying to keep dry. I finally left at about five p.m. Once again I was about to follow the river into new and unfamiliar territory.

I was also leaving the two protected segments of the river. The Upper Delaware, from Hancock, N.Y. to just north of Port Jervis, N.Y., is regulated by the Upper Delaware Council, which consists of representatives from the National Park Service, private landowners, municipalities, and local businesses. The middle segment is totally contained in the Delaware Water Gap Recreational Area, a part of the National Park system.

The Lower Delaware, from the Water Gap to tidewater, is now being studied for inclusion in the Wild and Scenic Rivers Act, the federal protection that is in place in the Upper and Middle segments. Areas where the river passes through heavy commercial zones like Easton and Trenton are excluded from the study. In addition, the Musconetcong River is also being studied for protection under the Wild and Scenic Rivers Act.

The sun broke through momentarily as I drifted with the river through the tight "S" curve of the Water Gap, tracing the route the river has followed for millions of years, carving through mountains with a slow but steady determination, day after day, year after year.

Interstate 80 runs parallel to the river, a noisy but telling prelude to the change the river was about to reveal. Eagles and canoes would soon be replaced by barking dogs and jet skis (the people who manufacture and sell these dirty, stinking, water and air polluting contraptions, hate it when journalists use the words, "jet skis," to describe these pieces of junk. Consequently, the term "jet ski," is used throughout this manuscript).

I've read that a jet ski in one afternoon pollutes as much as a modern car driving from coast to coast. I consider them a plague on our precious waterways.

I camped that night on a small island just past Columbia, N.J. where I met George and Scott Rogers. George and Scott are father and son and had just brought their teepee over to the island for an extended Fourth of July weekend celebration. They invited me to stay the night on their campsite.

They have been bringing the teepee to Washburn Island for four years. "Everybody recognizes it," said George, "Sometimes at night I put a lantern in it and it glows like a beacon." The teepee is about 25 feet high and can sleep eight people. It was a striking addition to the downstream end of the island. It was the reason I stopped there.

Fourth of July: I woke this morning with a queasy feeling in my stomach. I made coffee and oatmeal, my usual breakfast, and felt no better. As I prepared to break camp, I realized the source of my anxiety: Foul Rift.

Within five miles I would have to deal with what is probably the worst rapid on the Delaware. But just like I did with Skinner's Falls, I decided to wait until I saw it before making a decision whether to walk it or shoot it. Foul Rift is a little more than a mile downstream of Belvidere, N.J. and has a notorious reputation among local canoeists. I checked my river guide once again before shoving off:

> This is the most severe rapids on the Delaware and should be avoided by beginners.

And from the map notes:

> Foul Rift, a Class II rapid, deserves a special word of caution. It is one of the most hazardous sections of the river. None but the most experienced and best equipped boater should venture into this area. The only assurance of safe passage through this reach is to portage around the entire area or to lower the boat by line . . . and then continue the journey by water.

I pulled out into a fast moving riffle that led into a string of quiet pools, my stomach churning, as I tried to imagine just how bad Foul Rift could be, wishing the rest of the river could be as calm and worry-free as the little eddy I was now paddling through.

A change comes over the river as you approach even a small rapid. Many times, well before you can even see the tops of breaking waves and white water, you can hear it and feel it. Usually the noise is accompanied by a fresh moist breeze and you sense a gain in speed through the water. The waves become confused and you can feel the current and cross-currents pulling you in different directions. Paddling becomes more difficult; breaking waves slapping the boat easily toss you off-track.

Sitting in a kayak, you are very close to the surface of the water; a good view of the entire rapid, which is actually the river following a decline in elevation, is usually impossible. Not until you are right on it can you begin to see the entire layout of the rapid. But by then it is too late.

I've noticed that a change also comes over me when approaching a rapid. My breathing gets faster, my eyes seem to take in much more than usual and I can feel my muscles tightening. I think about what I will do if I swamp, quickly planning alternative routes through the exposed boulders. At the point I first hear the rapids, I fasten down the spray skirt, secure all the stuff on deck (usually a shirt and towel drying, extra paddles, sponge, sneakers, and sandals) and hope for the best.

Some rapids, like Skinner's Falls, are over quickly, almost before you know it. Others, like Stairway Rapids, are a series of descending ledges separated by high standing waves, and if you are having trouble (submerged boulders, going sideways, etc.), it can seem like forever. I've managed to hit rocks and boulders even on the smallest rapids, so I treat them all with caution and respect.

I would be saved at Foul Rift by Quakers. About an hour after leaving George and Scott, I ran into a group of canoeists from Camp Onus in Ottsville, Pa., a Quaker camp. They told me they were also going through Foul Rift that morning. A camper told me to speak to one of the counselors who was reportedly the expert on Foul Rift.

Jennie Josephson, 19, of Fairlawn, N.J., a six-time veteran of Foul Rift, saved my butt. Jennie explained to me the procedure for getting through with the least amount of trouble. I didn't really grasp what she was saying; it was difficult without actually seeing the rapids. Thankfully, Jennie invited me to pull over with the rest of the campers for a little talk on strategy. While we campers stood on shore, she told us about safety procedures and what to do if someone swamps. Best of all, Jennie drew a little map in the sand showing the safest way around and through Foul Rift.

Jennie's plan was to move to the left immediately after passing the island in the middle of the rapids. Sounded good to me. When we were leaving the shore she asked if I would like to get behind her canoe. I was not about to let her out of my sight. I felt much more relaxed about going through—until I looked at the river guide:

> The narrow channel to the right of the island is passable with few obstructions and is the safest route.

I looked over at Jennie, smiled and waved, then read on:

> The main channel left of the island is peppered with boulders and ledges... The safest passage remains near the Pennsylvania shore (the right side).

The right? Jennie had just told us to stay to the left. There's that queasy feeling in my stomach again. I had a serious decision to make; I could smell Foul Rift coming up fast. Do I trust a 19-year-old kid from Fairlawn, N.J. or a detailed river guide written by an experienced canoeist? I went with the kid. Six canoes plus one little kayak made it safely through the worst rapids on the Delaware without a hitch. No one swamped, no one fell in, and no one was hurt. Thanks Jennie!

I landed on a large island with a pleasant, sandy beach. But when I landed, I saw that many people had camped here before. There was even a camp with a few chairs around the fire pit. It looked as if someone might own the island. I was told most of the islands are private and campers are not welcome. I was too tired to go on but felt uneasy about pitching my tent until I was sure no one would be evicting me. I decided to have a look around to see if there was a house or someone in the area. I took the absence of "no trespassing" signs as a good omen. As I was looking around I saw dog tracks—a bad omen—then I heard voices. Rather than risk being shot as a trespasser I walked out into the river and around the next point in the island. I went about 200 feet when I saw two tents and a few people sitting around a camp in lounge chairs, reading and talking. I yelled "hello" as I started up onto the island and into their camp. The next thing I heard was something about "getting out the 38." It turned out to be a joke. The dog turned out to be about 100 years old and the two local couples that were camped here for the weekend told me the island was O.K. to camp on. They shared a beer with me and I went back to my camp, set up my tent, ate dinner, and went to sleep.

The Saturday after the Fourth of July I suddenly experienced a change in the river. Hundreds of tubers were heading down river from Tinicum Park in Pennsylvania bound for Point Pleasant. Along with the tubers were canoeists, jet skis, motor boats, and, late in the afternoon at the height of it all, two ultralight biplanes came zipping down-river barely 15 feet above everyone's head. On an island in the middle of the river was a giant sign announcing "The Hot Dog Man" with balloons in the air and another big sign for "Ice Cold Soda." I thought I took a wrong turn somewhere and wound up in Action Park or Disneyland. Did Interstate 80 flood? Are people now commuting by tube? What's happening here? Where did all the eagles go?

But people were enjoying the river. They were swimming and fishing and loafing in water that just a decade ago was seriously polluted. I was now closer to the major population centers of Trenton, Camden, and Philadelphia. This river supplies 10 percent of the country's population with drinking water, about 20 million people, from a watershed consisting of less than one percent of the land.

Protecting that watershed is the aim of the Wild and Scenic Rivers Act and the goal of the Delaware Riverkeeper Network, a group that promotes the conservation of the Delaware River, its tributaries, and the entire watershed.

I spoke with Mary Ellen Noble, a Riverkeeper, about her organization's role in preserving the river. She told me that the Riverkeeper Network's goal is to have groups of local people concerned and taking care of their local "home waters," streams that feed into the Delaware. How do you know where your home waters are? I asked. "When you hear it raining on your roof, get up and follow that rainwater. Chances are it will lead to a small stream. That stream is your 'home waters,'" she said. Mary Ellen said you can protect your home waters by taking personal responsibility for that stream. "Make sure the rain isn't rinsing anything bad off where you live," she said. She cited fertilizers, pesticides, and silt from construction as common, local threats to the watershed. The Riverkeeper Network has volunteers that periodically monitor stream health throughout the watershed.

A river is its streams. When you have clean streams, you have a clean river. "We want everybody to be a Riverkeeper," she said. Riverkeepers are an old European tradition, stemming from the time when large land owners would employ someone to ensure they had a good stock of fish. The equivalent of a groundskeeper for the river.

Mary Ellen gave the example of a metal fabricator located along the river which was discharging large amounts of a toxic chemical (TCE) into the river. Working with the manufacturer, they were able to eliminate the chemical from their discharge, the result of changing the process they used.

Another time people started calling their office with reports of "white rocks" on the bed of the river. The Riverkeepers followed it back to a paper mill that was using titanium dioxide, a whitening agent used in paper manufacturing. A one-time discharge had killed fish and colored the rocks with a white film.

Two new housing developments had been found to be causing the water in the river to turn green, the result of an algae bloom (algae flourish in nutrient rich waters, robbing other organisms of oxygen). The fertilizer from all the newly created lawns was washing into the river via local streams. The Riverkeeper Network enlisted the help of local Boy Scouts to distribute "door hangers" to educate the people in the developments about the adverse effect of the fertilizers they were using on the river. Because of the cooperation of the residents, the problem has since been cleared up.

"Maintaining the sponge" is how Mary Ellen describes the work of protecting the watershed. The solution to the growing demands for water, she said, "is not the diversions from one watershed to another, but the much cheaper route of prevention. Maintaining land so that it yields sufficient water. There's nothing radical about using what we have efficiently," she said.

> *"The care of rivers is not a question of rivers,*
> *but of the human heart."*
>
> —Tanaka Shozo

One advantage of this section of the river is that I can stop at little towns for coffee or a meal, replenish supplies and have a look around (I never could find a good loaf of rye bread). Though I was never sure how safe my stuff would be if I were gone for too long—or even five minutes—I decided to take a leap of faith that nothing would be stolen. And so far, nothing has.

I stopped in to see Fred Lewis, the last licensed commercial shad fisherman on the non-tidal Delaware. Fred told me this had been a bad year for catching shad because of the high water. He caught only 240. Last year, he caught 1,240. 1993 and 1994 were also bad years due to high water, he said. Fred said that in 1992, the best year, some 800,000 were counted by the Fish, Game and Wildlife Service.

The shad spawn in the upper reaches of the river and then make their way downstream by September or October, trying to escape the cold water. They are about 6 to 7 inches long at this point. Once at sea they head for the coasts of North Carolina, Florida and Georgia, he said. Males, or bucks, return to the river when they are about three years old. The females, or roes, come back at four years of age. They swim upstream at the rate of about 10 miles a day. On the trip downstream, they travel at about 10 miles per hour. They don't eat while they are in fresh water, and as a result, lose about half their body weight. About 15 percent of the shad make it back to the sea. Fred said that years ago more than 50 percent would return and live to spawn again. "That's the reason the size of the fish we catch is smaller," he said. Repeat spawners, because they are older, are usually larger fish. Fred blames pollution for the decreased rate of return spawners. Antiquated sewer systems in Camden and Philadelphia tend to overload sewage treatment plants during heavy thunderstorms, releasing raw sewage into the river, he said. But the water quality has improved. "Back in the 1950's, in hot weather, you couldn't stay on a boat it stunk so bad. It was like running down a sewer," he said. "Now, it's good here," he added. Fred, at 81, is content to let his grandson do the fishing. His family has fished this river since the late 1800s.

The next leg of the trip, past Trenton into tidewater and up Crosswicks Creek, will be the most challenging. I'll have to learn to use the tides to get into and out of the marshes. Drinking water and camping spots will be scarce. I'll be entering Hamilton Marsh, one of the last intact freshwater tidal marshes in the country. A sensitive area, quickly disappearing.

"I wonder why progress looks so much like destruction?"

—John Steinbeck

Chapter 6

*"You tides with ceaseless swell! you power
that does this work!
You unseen force, centripetal, centrifugal,
through space's spread,
Rapport of sun, moon, earth, and all the constellations,
What are the messages by you from distant stars to us?"*

—Walt Whitman

    I left Lambertville in the early morning hours, southbound for the fresh water tidal creeks and marshes below Trenton. Tides, cities, and industry downstream meant I would soon experience the most significant change in the river so far. Though I was curious to see the effects of these things on the river, I was also apprehensive about doing so in a 12-foot kayak. My plan was to arrive at Trenton in time to catch the outgoing tide. If I arrived while the tide was coming in, it would be difficult if not impossible, to make any progress downstream. The faithful current that had carried me all the way from Hancock, N.Y. would be lost in the ebb and flow of the Atlantic, the tidal influence reaching far up the Delaware. The tide begins to affect the river just below Trenton. There the river makes its last decline in elevation to sea level. Saltwater tides push freshwater forward, creating tidal marshes, a unique and important habitat for many species of plants and animals. Marshes and estuaries are valuable because they also cleanse and filter the water and help protect against coastal flooding. I bought the local paper, which listed the high and low tides for the day. According to the chart, the tide would be high at 12:23 p.m. As long as I arrived in Trenton after that, the tide would be ebbing, and I could ride the tide back out. At 8:01 p.m. the tide would be low, then the flood upstream would start again.

My destination was Bordentown, N.J. From there, I could enter Crosswicks Creek and meander through Hamilton Marsh, a 1,250 acre freshwater tidal marsh three miles below Trenton. I planned to spend a few days floating the tides in and out of the creek, going nowhere in particular, noting the various types of plants and animals.

> *"I loafe and invite my soul.*
> *I lean and loafe at my ease observing a spear*
> *of summer grass."*
>
> —Walt Whitman

But to get to Trenton I still had to go about 15 miles. I knew there were some rapids but I had avoided thinking about them. The easy hospitality of the Riverkeepers and the friendly bustle of Lambertville and New Hope had kept me pleasantly distracted.

I'd like to know why every time I open my river guide, I learn that I'm about to encounter "the most dangerous rapid on the Delaware." Didn't I already encounter that one, maybe three times now? I strongly suspect someone is sneaking into my camp at night and inserting pages into the guide. This time it's Wells Falls, only a half-mile below Lambertville. Once again, from the guide:

> Wells Falls is indeed the most severe rapid on the Delaware and is the only one measured above Class II . . .

The guide then goes on to describe a canoe accident that took place in 1981 resulting in the death of one of the canoeists. The map notes, as usual, provide no solace:

. . . the river falls swiftly for several hundred yards through an extensively rocky area that is quite dangerous and difficult to navigate. Boating in this area should be avoided either by disembarking at Lambertville or by lowering the boat down the rapids by rope.

The rapids are located just below a wing dam, a huge concrete "V" extending out into the middle of the river with about a 15 foot wide chute, or gap, in the center. The three wing dams on the Delaware were originally constructed to help enlarge existing eddies for commercial timber rafts and also supply water power for mills. The wing dam at Lambertville was constructed in 1812.

I paddled up to the left side of the dam and got out of the boat to have a look at the rapid to see if I could discover a safe route through. The dam is about six feet wide and makes a handy platform for surveying the rapids.

My only alternative to shooting the rapid was to lift the boat over the concrete wing and lower it into the eddy directly behind the dam. From there I could go down the left side where the current isn't as strong. It would still be dangerous; rocks and boulders were everywhere, "the rock garden," someone called it.

To lift the boat over I would have to empty it, then repack on the other side, a good hour delay; I had just loaded the boat ten minutes before when I left Lambertville. Out of laziness more than bravery, I decided I would go through the chute.

As I got back into the boat, a woman, apparently out for her morning walk, appeared on the dam. "Going through?," she asked. "Yes," I replied, "Just about to head out." "You better be careful, the water's low." I thought the water was high because of all the rain, but she told me when the water is really high it goes right over the concrete dam.

"Do you have a helmet?," she asked. A helmet? I told her I didn't and she shook her head. "A friend of mine died here a few years ago. Three of them were out fishing and got sucked in. My friend died; the other two were saved."

I asked her to standby, to call either the ambulance or the undertaker, depending on how I did. I paddled upstream a little to gain some maneuvering room, then went back down and through the chute. I cut sharply to the left, paddling like mad, and made it to the little eddy behind the dam. The waves were big, at least three feet, and the current was strong, trying to pull me to the right and into the main flow. I gave the woman the "thumb's up" and off she went, most likely as relieved as I was. All I had to do now was to stay to the left where the current wasn't as strong and negotiate my way through the "rock garden."

I was busy looking ahead for obstructions, but I should have looked up. Directly ahead of me was a tree with its branches hanging down over the water. This type of tree is commonly called a "strainer." It's called a strainer because your boat will go through, but you won't. I hit that tree hard, the current taking me right into it. I put up my hands to protect my head as best I could without losing my paddle. I made it through but my arms were badly scraped—my confidence equally bruised. Another rapid conquered; only two more to go.

The stretch of river between Lambertville and Trenton was surprisingly pleasant. I stopped at Washington's Crossing State Park in New Jersey and had lunch on a grassy strip overlooking the water. Directly across the river was the small island where the General hid the boats his army would use on Christmas morning.

I wondered if it really made any difference whether we won the revolution or not. Today, there doesn't seem to be much difference between the United States and England. They are after all, our closest ally. They have little crime committed with guns, they all seem to love the Royal Family, and they make their lawyers wear embarrassing wigs in court, which is maybe not a bad idea.

I passed through another wing dam at Scudder's Falls. It was a fast current through the chute but with no obstructions. The only rapids left were Trenton Falls. According to the guide they were dangerous, especially during low tide.

At about 2 p.m. Trenton came into view. I burst out laughing at the sight of the buildings and highways now starting to appear on my left. The steady hum of traffic had crept up on me and was now added to the chorus of river sounds. Bird song and the trickle of water past the bow were temporarily left behind while the roar and clatter of trucks and cars took over.

The impact of how far I had traveled seemed to hit me all at once. Images of the Upper Delaware, complete with bald eagles, desolate shore lines and sparkling clear water flooded my mind. Was this the same river?

The rapids at Trenton were hazardous not only because of the rocks and swift water but also because I found the presence of highways, now on both sides, extremely disconcerting. I also had to pass under three bridges, including the "Trenton Makes, the World Takes" bridge. In all the previous rapids I had encountered, I knew that if the very worst were to occur, I could always swim or limp to shore, grab hold of a tree and recover (or die quietly). Here it was different.

The river was bordered on both sides by multi-lane highways with a steep concrete embankment on the New Jersey side. If I were to lose it here, there would be nowhere to go. I imagined myself standing on the shoulder of Interstate 95, broken paddle in hand, life preserver ripped to shreds, bleeding profusely—broken thumb extended, waiting for a ride: "Excuse me, I just happened to be kayaking through town and I was wondering if . . . etc." I was determined to make it through Trenton with no unscheduled stops.

There would be no more rapids. The river had passed from bedrock and glacial rubble making its final descent into the sand and clay of the tidal estuary. From here, the river flows another 130 miles to the Delaware Bay and finally, to the Atlantic Ocean.

> *"Here the earth is fluid to my thought, the sky is reflected from beneath, and around yonder cape is the highway to other continents."*
>
> —Henry David Thoreau

I made it safely to tidewater just below Trenton and found the tide, as I had hoped, heading back toward the ocean. A fresh downstream breeze working in concert with the tide had me moving at a good speed. I paddled only to correct my course. The river here widened considerably and the waves resembled those you might find in a bay.

Large powerboats, water skiers, and jet skis were soon buzzing around me, adding to the size of the waves. I hugged the shoreline and exaggerated my paddling strokes to help the speed demons see me. I had only three miles to go.

I found the entrance to Crosswick's Creek easily, passing by Duck Island on the way in. Duck Island, on the edge of Hamilton Marsh, is home to a coal burning power plant, a sewage treatment plant, and is the proposed site for a Mercer County incinerator.

Meanwhile, the marsh has been sliced by newly constructed Interstate 295, allowing motorists to skirt Trenton, saving time on their daily commutes. The highway was built over the marsh on stilts, but its effect is no less apparent.

A canoeist coming down the Crosswicks told me of a good camping spot 15 minutes up the creek. I found it with no problem. It was a grassy area about two feet above water at high tide. There was a little fire ring and good clearing for my tent. On my way up the creek I spotted an osprey perched on a snag eating a fish. We silently watched each other until he was out of sight around a bend. He was to be my only constant companion for the next three days; I would see him each morning and evening.

Though I could still hear the traffic on Interstate 295, the noise was now just a dull hum. Once again, the song of the red-winged blackbird returned to welcome me home.

The next day I met with Vernon Applegate, a long time resident of Crosswick Village, a small village located three miles up the creek. Vernon brought along Malcolm Knowles, a local historian. The three of us spent the day touring some of the significant historical sites in the area.

We visited a Catholic seminary which was formerly the estate of Joseph Bonaparte, the brother of Napoleon. It seems Joseph, exiled from France, came to New Jersey. Living in exile didn't appear to be too harsh. The estate was beautiful and Joseph even had a girlfriend in Trenton. We also visited the first public school built in New Jersey. The school was started by Clara Barton, founder of the American Red Cross.

Malcolm was a Quaker (better to say member of the Society of Friends I learned, though they take little offense) and gave us an interesting tour of a Friends meeting house. The red brick house has been used continuously since the 1600's. A cannonball, stuck into the side of the building, attests to its Revolutionary war days. The same Hessian soldiers that Washington would later surprise and defeat in Trenton had spent part of the winter here. Gun barrel circles on the floor and bayonet marks etched into the benches can still be found just as the day they were made.

We also stopped to look at an old farmhouse that was used in the Underground Railroad. Escaped slaves would arrive here from the river and also by road, hidden in hay carts. They would find a safe haven in this house until they could be moved farther north. Though a northern state, New Jersey was not a safe refuge for slaves. It was the last state to abolish slavery; the South was a good customer for its industrial products; farms benefited from the economic advantages of slavery's forced labor.

"If slavery is not wrong, nothing is wrong."

—Abraham Lincoln

The village of Crosswicks, just eight miles from Trenton, remains much as it did 200 years ago. Hamilton Marsh and Crosswicks Creek have not fared as well, though water quality has improved and eagles and osprey are reportedly making a comeback. I had drunk the water of the Delaware River during the entire trip, using a filter which eliminates bacteria, chemical compounds, and pesticides. But the water in the marsh I not only didn't drink, I didn't feel safe even stepping into (I usually have a few open blisters and cuts on my feet and legs).

I met three teenagers from Bordentown at the local boat access one evening. Together, we watched the sun go down over the river (except for when it is eclipsed by the highway). They told me they were attempting to get a community center for teens, a place for them to go and hang out. They used to come here, to the beach. But now, with the interstate looming overhead, a chemical plant across the river (recently accused of illegal discharges) and a sewer treatment plant upriver, city officials have closed the beach to swimming. The municipal waste incinerator, if it comes, will be the finishing touch.

While we were talking, dozens of power boats and jet skis launched from the boat ramp, exhausting fumes over the entire beach area, forcing us to move as we talked.

"It's a real shame. They built it (the highway) just so they could get to Bordentown quicker. They cut down all the trees, killed the deer, all the animals," said 12-year-old Caitlin Martin.

"Ever since the factory started dumping stuff, they don't want you swimming here," added 15-year-old Matt Vannozzi. "There used to be an egret living out there, but he hasn't come back, that was two years ago." A fisherman also told me that bald eagles had been active close to the beach, but have not been seen since construction started on the highway.

"This was the most scenic place. All the kids used to come down here, swim, and hang out. Now they stay in town, they make noise and get into trouble—there's nothing to do," said Alesha Vega, also 15.

Alesha, who lives within blocks of the river, also complained about the smell of the water, "We were swimming in my pool and it was bad. It made you want to pass out." There is a petition circulating in Bordentown to restrict the operations of a factory on the Pennsylvania side which is reportedly also contributing to the stench.

The kids have written letters to their Mayor, Assemblyman

and a local judge. So far, only the judge has offered any support. The Mayor and Assemblyman have not responded. Caitlin summed it up, "We just need a place to go to get off the streets."

> "If a man walk in the woods for love of them half of each day, he is in danger of being regarded as a loafer; but if he spends his whole day as a speculator, shearing off those woods and making the earth bald before her time, he is esteemed an industrious and enterprising citizen."
>
> —Henry David Thoreau

I spent the remaining days of my journey meandering through and around Crosswicks Creek and the Hamilton Marsh. I would take the flood tide in, drifting, floating, wherever the tide took me. I would float out again hours later, back to my base camp to record what I had found. My binoculars and field guides at hand, I tried to identify as many plants and critters as I could. I've learned on this trip that serious bird watching is best done by ear. I heard so many birds but could not see them. One bird woke me each morning. Its call sounded to me like : "Ready to, ready to, get ready to."

Pickerelweed was in bloom all along the marsh. Six inch spikes of violet-blue flowers rising from smooth green stalks delineated the shoreline. My field guide tells me that the seeds are good to eat; the young leaf stalks can be cooked as greens. Buttery colored flowers from yellow pond lilies dotted the endless green carpeting where they flourished. Buttonbushes growing on the banks added round globes of white cottony flowers to the predominantly green thickets of grasses and sedges. Most surprising to me was the presence of wild roses, although here I think that they may be more accurately referred to as the swamp rose (*R. palustris*). The scent was strong and sweet and the cluster of bushes around sandy beaches and open areas made for inviting landings. Each morning and evening, swallows would make their rounds, lightly dipping and arching over the water in search of food.

I spent two days wandering through the marsh, peaceful and serene—until Hurricane Bertha came to visit.

My campsite was two feet above flood tide; safe, I thought. But I was surrounded on three sides by water: Crosswicks Creek in front, a feeder creek to my left, and a marshy area to my right. The land in back of my campsite led away toward town. I would just move back from the edge if the water should rise that high, I thought, though I was sure it wouldn't. Of course, it did.

After raining all night and most of the next day, by afternoon the water was within six inches of the bank. Now the tide was coming in, pushing the water back into the marsh. I had no way of knowing how long until ebb tide. I started packing. When I went looking behind me for a good campsite I discovered that the marsh had already flooded and was making its way toward me. The little feeder creek on my left was gushing. It literally woke me the night before, like a freight train coming through the woods. The previous day it had been a pleasant trickle of a stream.

I placed a stick in the muck to track the rate of the rising water. I figured it might rise an inch per hour. I had six inches or six hours, I thought. In about 20 minutes the stick was covered. I was outta there!

I had seen a sandy beach a few minutes upstream with a level landing about five times higher than where I was; I decided that was where I would move. As I was loading the boat, which was now two feet from my tent, three shots rang out, seemingly over my head. BaChing! BaChing! BaChing! I froze. The thing I had feared most on this trip was not animals, insects, rapids, or weather—it was people.

Shots rang out again. This time I could discern that they were coming from a little farther upstream; in fact, I guessed they were coming from the very landing I was about to head for. And the water was rising. I hunkered down behind a tree to wait. I thought of calling out to let them know someone was here, but I hesitated. Whoever it was, they weren't hunting, they were shooting across the creek into the marshes. Shooting for fun. If they were to shoot something, like a duck, they couldn't retrieve it. They were shooting for the sake of shooting. Target practice. Were they drinking? If I paddled around the bend would they see me in time? I stayed put and watched the water rise, more eager to take my chances with a rising tide than with an armed person.

I cringed each time a shot went off; the contrast to my peaceful time here was violently startling. After the shots stopped I finished loading the boat and headed for the landing. The water was an inch from the bank, the bottom of my tent, before I struck it, was awash in the soupy ground.

I sang as I paddled to give the shooters some notice but they were gone. At the landing I found empty shells marked "Winchester 12-gauge." They were warm and smelled of gunpowder. There were dozens of spent cartridges lying around. I picked them up and piled them in the fire ring. What's worse than a slob with a gun?

Bertha departed and left me with a magnificent sunset of reds and blues and purples. A brisk wind came from the west as if special ordered to dry my tent and sleeping bag. I made a small fire on the beach to celebrate my last night on the river. I sang songs and danced on the sand, naked under the stars, and no one, not the red-winged blackbird, not the osprey, not even the swamp roses, seemed to notice.

> *"Now I see the secret of the making of the best persons.*
> *It is to grow in the open air and eat*
> *and sleep with the earth."*
>
> —Walt Whitman

Postscript

During the 34 days I spent on the river, I had been searching for something, something I was sure existed but couldn't define. During my first week I remember telling an old-timer who had lived along the river all his life about my trip. "One thing is for sure," I told him with a certain cockiness. "When I'm done, I'll know this river." He looked at me with an amused smile. "No," he said. "You'll know the river—in this season." He was right of course. Winter ice storms, spring freshets, and the explosion of color in autumn all change the character and temperament of the river. Even in summer, a hard rain can change it from benign to deadly in a matter of hours. It is probably not possible to ever know this river in its entirety. That is how it should be; some secrets should never be told.

The river threads its way through mountains, through ridges, towns, and even people. I was looking for a seam, for the common thread I could trace from one segment to another, from one town to another, from one person to another. Instead, I found a collage of people and places, their differences subtle but distinct. Maybe I was looking too hard. Something a young woman in Lambertville said to me seemed to make sense. "You know you are someplace special when you are in this river valley."

The river valley is alive with eagles and osprey, wildflowers and pure clear mountain streams. But kindness also flourishes here. I cannot count the times strangers helped me. So many people stopped to share a story, give advice, or just offer a kind word or a cold beer. Rather than attempt to list all the people who helped me, let me tell you something that happened on the last day of my trip that illustrates the many kindnesses I've received.

While I was waiting for photographer Anna Murphey to pick me up from Bordentown, a woman walking her dog stopped to talk. We spoke for about a half-hour. We talked about the river, the proposed incinerator, water quality, her kids, her dog Fudgey, Bordentown, and the state of the world. It was a nice chat. About 15 minutes later she was back. She handed me a brown paper bag and a plastic pitcher of ice water. Inside the bag were two paper cups, wet soapy paper towels, an apple, half a banana, and a toasted corn muffin with jelly—still warm. "This is Bordentown water," she said proudly. "It's great. Have a safe trip back." I had to practically throw myself in front of her car so that I could thank her properly and get her name. Thanks, Donna.

So the next time someone complains to me about "people," I'll have a few examples to give them. And all those examples will have something in common, a thread, a shimmering ribbon of extraordinary beauty. The river, you see, will be in each of them.

Around-the-world cyclist Albert LeBlanc on his way to the summer Olympics in Atlanta, Georgia.

Doc at the Red Barn; Equinunk, NY.

*"I think over again my small adventures: my fears,
Those small ones that seemed so big:
For all the vital things
I had to get and to reach,
And yet there is only one great thing,
The only thing;
To live to see the great day that dawns
And the light that fills the world."*

—from an old Inuit song

BVG